"Sweetheart, you make twenty-five cents for a thirty-minute piano lesson. . . .

"Right now, I'm making that in five minutes. You tell me why you won't pay a kid to mow your lawn anymore, and that upright is yours. Just tell me why. Do you need money?"

For a minute, he thought she might wallop him.

"My aunt left me financially sound, Mr. Brody, so I most certainly do not need any charity from you." She took a step toward him to reach for the doorknob, and he could smell the faint scent of some kind of floral perfume on her skin. "Now, if you're finished—"

"No, I'm not."

Before she could protest, he kissed her on the lips. Nothing lingering, nothing deep. Just long enough to make him realize a quick kiss wasn't going to satisfy him. Just long enough for him to change his mind and give her something lingering and deep. The texture of her hair was erotic, making him kiss her harder. Making him want to . . . damn.

"Christ," he muttered, and shook his head, needing to clear his thoughts.

"Mr. Brody," she gasped, her bosom rising and falling. "Mr. Brody . . . Well . . . I . . . I like that."

"I was hoping you would." He turned and opened the door to let himself out. "I was hoping I wouldn't."

Books by Stef Ann Holm

Harmony
Forget Me Not
Portraits
Crossings
Weeping Angel
Snowbird
King of the Pirates
Liberty Rose
Seasons of Gold

Published by POCKET BOOKS

WEEPING ANGEL

STEF ANN HOLM

POCKET BOOKS

New York London Toronto Sydney Tokyo Singapore

An *Original* Publication of POCKET BOOKS

A Pocket Star Book published by
POCKET BOOKS, a division of Simon & Schuster Inc.
1230 Avenue of the Americas, New York, NY 10020

ISBN: 0-671-02594-5

First Pocket Books paperback printing June 1995

10 9 8 7 6 5 4 3

POCKET STAR BOOKS and colophon are registered
trademarks of Simon & Schuster Inc.

Cover art by John Stephens

Printed in the U.S.A.

For my husband, Barry, who got the chicken pox nine days after his fortieth birthday. Your cussing and itching were pure plot inspiration at a time when I really needed some!

And to four great pals—Jill Barnett, Patricia Gaffney, Arnette Lamb, and Sue Rich—whose talent to write excellent humor makes me crack up out loud. I'm hoping you'll appreciate my borrowing your names for the "girls." It was just too tempting an idea to pass up.

Chapter

1

❦

**June 1897
Weeping Angel**

*E*very female out of diapers thought Frank Brody handsomer than a new catalog bonnet, and Miss Amelia Marshall was no exception.

The upstanding ladies in the small Idaho town didn't know Amelia harbored a secret attraction to him. What they did know was that the odds of Miss Marshall ever associating with a man who served alcoholic refreshments were nonexistent. After all, it was because of a saloon her chance for a beau and romance had been snatched away.

Since Miss Marshall's embarrassing incident, she'd turned rigid as a washboard. The ladies said Amelia had enough starch in her little finger to stiffen every shirtwaist west of the Mississippi. They also said Miss Marshall's temperature never went above ninety-eight point three. Except on those days when yard thermometers bubbled over the ninety-nine degree mark.

But while waiting for the 3:00 P.M. Weeping Angel Short Line to arrive on a cooker of a Wednesday,

Amelia felt herself wilting. She looked out the corner of her eye to view the other occupant at the far end of the train platform. Amelia knew who he was. That tapper of strong waters from the Moon Rock Saloon —none other than the owner himself, Frank Brody.

A heat ripple undulated in front of Amelia, practically scorching her skirt. If Mr. Brody had been any kind of gentleman, he would have offered to switch places and allow her the luxury of standing where the limbs of a giant oak shaded the platform. But he obviously wasn't a gentleman.

And she wouldn't consider moving closer to him. He might try something objectionable—like talking to her.

Mr. Brody stood next to the ticketing window, one knee bent and his foot on the wall, eating a peach. From Amelia's vantage point, he looked as cool as peppermint candy. The instant she thought about his comfort in the shade, dewy perspiration had the audacity to trickle in a slow, itchy line between her breasts. Her bolero-style jacket, lined with silk taffeta and trimmed with lilac crocheted buttons, suddenly seemed two sizes too small. She longed to blot the moisture dampening her skin but dared not, for fear of drawing attention to herself. Instead, she turned her head a wee smidgen for a better look at the man who'd thrown her lady friends into a dither.

Beneath his straw panama hat, he had hair the same jet black as the ink Mr. Spivey used to print the *Weeping Angel Gazette*. His profile came across strong. And if she were to be objective, his mouth seemed kindly. By leaving his coat behind, he'd gone against the social standards. Both a white shirt with the collar softly turned down and a scarlet silk vest with a trail of gold buttons he'd neglected to fasten made him appear casual and unconcerned over his appearance. His black linen trousers were pleated at the waist and tucked into knee-high boots of a matching color.

He brought the peach to his lips and sucked its juice. Amelia's stomach jumped like popcorn on a hot skillet. Straightening her spine, she quickly removed her gaze from his person and stared dead ahead at the empty train tracks. She remained that way for all of ten seconds before her gaze wandered toward him again.

The way he ate bordered on indecent. After every bite, he licked peach juice from his full lower lip, catching it before it ran down his clean-shaved chin. Amelia felt the pulse beating in her throat and absently brought one hand to her high collar as she studied him. He sank white teeth into the fruit, chewed, then looked right at her. A knowing smile slowly curved his firm mouth.

Gasping, Amelia abruptly turned her head and feigned interest in seeking the train through the aspens. Her heart thudded noisily, and surely her cheeks were the same bright color as his vest. He'd caught her staring and they both knew it. From now on, she would ignore him.

Summer heat carried the wonderful sweet smell of ripe peach, and the scent kept reminding her he was there. She tried to view him from the corner of her eye but was struck with such a fierce headache that she instantly shifted her gaze forward.

Agonizing minutes ticked by. Her hairline became damp, and she felt her smart, brown velvet hat drooping. If she hadn't been so caught up in meeting the train on time, she wouldn't have forgotten her parasol—the kind of blunder she never committed. And an unnecessary impropriety, what with the Short Line so late; she needn't have rushed at all. Without her crook-handled umbrella, her skirt of lightning-blue serge bound with velvet felt like a bearskin rug.

She shaded her gaze with a gloved hand and stretched herself up on the toes of her laced kid shoes. *Where was the train?*

A sweltering wave of nectar-scented air slapped Amelia's cheeks. Resuming her usual posture, under the guise of reading the thermometer on the side of the yellow-and-brown depot, she discreetly permitted her gaze to roam in Frank Brody's general direction. He wasn't looking at her anymore, and she let out a silent sigh of relief but did not readily turn away. She watched as he held on to the pit, drawing the last bit of yellow flesh into his mouth before tossing the stone over the railroad tracks into the dirt. While he thoughtfully gazed at his masculine hands, she felt a queer sense of justice. He'd gummed up her insides— let him have sticky fingers. Now he'd do something repulsive like wipe his hands down the sides of his pants legs. That would put an end to her preoccupation with him.

But to Amelia's utter chagrin, Mr. Brody strode casually to the nearest horse trough, dipped his hands inside, and swished them around a bit. Lifting his arms, he snapped the water off his fingers with abrupt flicks. He went so far as to remove his straw hat, tucking the brim between his knees while he scooped handfuls of water onto his face, before combing hair away from his forehead with wet fingers and replacing his panama.

She'd nearly convinced herself his crude method was repugnant by thinking of all the green algae clinging to the sides of the trough and dead insects floating on the surface—not to mention the animal slobber. But then she remembered Ed Vining came by every Wednesday with his water wagon to drain, clean, and refill the metal tubs.

Suddenly Amelia's spine lost its tautness. She imagined that cool, invigorating water and caught herself in a deflated slouch. She would have given anything to push the tight leg-of-mutton sleeves up to her elbows and plunge her hands into the water, too.

The wire forms clamped over her bosom began to pull the air from her lungs, while the canvas and whalebone lashed around her waist squeezed her ribs in a crushing grip. The steel bustle protruding behind her became a sinking weight, and her knees started to buckle. Had the Weeping Angel Short Line not taken that moment to blare its steam whistle, Amelia would have collapsed.

Frank didn't move a muscle as a tuft of white billowed from above the treetops and the chugging locomotive came into view from around the bend. The No. 1 was a massive black machine, panting in labored puffs and belching a wide plume of gray smoke from its funnel stack. One boxcar and one combination mail-passenger-baggage car were sandwiched in between the 4-4-0 engine and the red caboose. In a drawn-out sigh, the beast screeched into the depot with a final wheeze as the hand brakes snuffed the drive in the pistons.

Frank waited in the sluggish shade as both Grenville Parks and Herbert Fisk, the ticket agent and porter, scuttled out of the depot house to greet the No. 1.

Crossing his arms over his chest, Frank propped his leg up on a flatbed luggage dolly. It was a damn hot day to be exerting himself, but he figured in the next few minutes he would be. As soon as he got his delivery loaded up, he was going to head back to the Moon Rock, shoot some seltzer in a glass of ice, and let Pap worry about getting the eight-hundred-pound crate through the door.

Lew Furlong, the chief engineer—and only engineer for the Weeping Angel Short Line—leaned out the No. 1's cab window and sneezed with gusto. His short-billed hat flew from his head onto the oiled gravel. "Sorry we're late, Grenville. Had us some trouble—deer carcass on the tracks. Saw it hooves-up when we came to the Thorn Creek grade. Some blame fools out of Cottonwood must have put the remains there as a prank—there were ladies' garters on his antlers." Lew tugged a large bandanna out of his overall pocket and noisily blew his nose. "Hardy and I had to stop to yank the buck off." Stuffing the wadded bandanna back into his bib, Lew sneezed again. "Else I would have had to clean the fur and bones off the cow catcher."

"But, Lew, that's what the cow catcher is for," the brakeman, Hardy, grumbled as he stepped out of the caboose. "To fling the cows—or deer—out of our way."

"Bah." Lew hopped down from the engine and bent to pick up his hat. Replacing it on his wind-ruffled hair, he sniffed off a sneeze. "Good afternoon, Miss Marshall."

"Mr. Furlong," she greeted in a prim tone. "May I suggest a nasal wash of salt tonic for your hay fever?"

"You may, but I'm not apt to stick anything up my nose except my handkerchief."

Frank choked on a laugh and gave Miss Marshall a speculative glance. Looking as though she was about to expire, she didn't yield her spot in the blazing sunlight. He wondered why she'd chosen to wither like a daisy when she could have shared the shade with him. Her austere face appeared rather flushed. He'd been trying to decide whether the heat put the bloom on her cheeks, or if it had been his confronting stare. He rather liked to believe he'd been the culprit. He'd caught her sneaking haughty peeks at him. He might have been inclined to return the perusal if she'd been something to kindle his interest. But his tastes ran toward warm women, and despite the heat curls rising from the platform, she looked as stiff as the dead deer Furlong had almost run into.

The unnaturally straight way she stood reminded him of the stodgy nuns at St. John's Catholic Orphanage for Boys. Put her in a crow black dress, toss a veil over her head, and wrap a wimple up to her chin, and she could have passed for one of the sisters. Sister Mary Prim.

He'd seen her walking across Divine Street on several occasions, and once she'd passed by the Moon Rock when he was opening up. But she moved on swiftly, her eyes forward and without acknowledging him. He'd only been in Weeping Angel three months, and trying to refurbish Charley Revis's run-down shebang into a decent thirst parlor hadn't left him with quality socializing time. Not that he would have socialized with the likes of Miss Marshall. He liked encounters to be with ladies willing to keep their hair spread out on his goose down pillow for a few hours.

The only liberal-thinking takers thus far had been Arabella Duchard, an actress from the traveling Shakespearean performers who had stayed a week in May, and Emmaline Shelby, the not-as-virtuous-as-the-town-thought laundress who saw to his shirts as well as ironing some steam into his pants. Each woman had shared his company, but not his bed. He and Arabella had gotten amorous under the stars, and Emmaline wasn't willing to risk her character by going to his room in back of the Moon Rock. Their brief liaisons were conducted on the flipped-down strainer lid of her granite laundry tub. Just once he'd like to do it with Emmaline without standing up and getting his boots splashed with soapy water.

Disadvantages aside, the idea of dirtying up some clean clothes so he could take them over to Emmaline aroused his imagination. She had long legs, and he liked that in a woman. Lazing his forearm on his knee, Frank watched as Fisk yanked the handle on the boxcar door and slid the cumbersome panel on its runners.

"Any incoming passengers?" Grenville Parks asked while arranging the knot in his neck scarf.

"Nope," Lew replied, rubbing his watery eyes. "Any outgoing?"

"No."

"Got a crate this time, though," Hardy commented as he unloaded a dozen milk cans into a nearby dairy cart. The hollow ring of metal mixed with his words. "All the way from Boston, Massachusetts."

"Big deal," Grenville said, then flopped down on a wooden bench.

"Yep, it's big, all right." Hardy stepped inside the car and rummaged around. "Haven't seen a crate this size since we brung up that Acme Royal Range for Mrs. Beamguard. Herbert, I need a hand with this."

"If it's as whopping as you say," Fisk said as he poked his head inside the dark opening, "you're going to need more than my hand."

"Get the luggage cart and we'll load it up on that."

"Yup." Fisk turned around and headed toward Frank.

Straightening, Frank put his foot down.

"How do, Mr. Brody." Fisk grabbed the T-handle on the dolly and started pulling. "You waiting for something?"

"I wouldn't be standing here if I wasn't."

Hardy tried to shove the crate, but it wouldn't budge. "Lew, get on in here. And bring Grenville with you."

Frank watched as the four men shoved, grunted, strained, and sneezed to push the crate toward the edge of the boxcar floor.

"Oh, do be careful!"

The slightly throaty voice caused Frank to turn his head in Miss Marshall's direction. An expression of distress overtook her features as she clasped her dainty hands in a worried knot at her waist.

"They're all right," Frank drawled. "They've had

enough practice lifting my liquor crates to know when to be careful."

She eyed him with reservation, a suspicious line at the corners of her mouth. Making no further comment, she merely stared at him as if he had egg on his face.

He stared right back.

She wasn't really a bad-looking woman. In fact, he could admit in all truth, she was rather pretty. Ivory-skinned with nice cheekbones heightened by an agitated hue of rose, brown eyes reminding him of the Circassian walnut bar in the El Dorado, and lips that could have been tempting if they weren't expressing so much disdain.

She made a noise from her throat sounding like *humph* before whipping her gaze back to the boxcar where Fisk's and Lew's sorry behinds were wiggling like hootchy-kootchy girls as they shimmied the crate onto the dolly.

Frank didn't much care for women who made disapproving noises in the backs of their throats. Her *humph* leaned toward the croak of a frog. Could be she used too much of that nasal wash she'd suggested to the engineer.

"It ain't moving much," Grenville panted, leaning against the five-foot-high wooden crate.

Walking toward the freight car door, Frank braced his hands on the floor and jumped inside. "Slide over, Fisk, and give me some room."

Huffing, the porter readily obliged.

Frank flexed his knees, expanded his lungs with several deep breaths, then positioned himself behind the box. "On the count of three, everybody shove the crate forward. One. Two. Three."

The crate protested and groaned, but once it got started, it took off like a cat with its tail cut.

"Hold it!" Frank ordered in a rush. "Hold it!"

The five men bolted in front of the mammoth

receptacle just in time to steer its foundation snugly on to the dolly.

Frank's thigh muscles burned, and he could feel the blood rapidly pumping through his body. Leaning on the backside of the crate, he wondered how many free beers it would take to bribe Lew, Hardy, Fisk, and Parks to give Pap a hand at the Moon Rock.

Lew swabbed his brow with his handkerchief, then squinted to read the bold inscription burned into the side of the wood. "Rogers and Company, Piano Manufactory. Boston, Massachusetts. Don't say who it's for. Just says Weeping Angel."

"That's quite all right, Mr. Parks." Miss Marshall sauntered forward, every curve of her body steadfast. "I sent away for the piano."

Frank swung around. "Hold on, sister. I didn't work up a sweat just to have you take the goods."

She blinked once, her eyes shimmering with dislike for him. He hadn't done anything to her to deserve her snub. "I beg your pardon?" she said in a tone lacking sincerity.

He didn't miss the cool challenge in her voice. "A woman's never begged for my pardon before. Begged for a few other things."

Aghast, her brows shot up. "Well!"

"Well yourself," he said, feeling the sun pour over him like hot buttered rum. "I ordered this piano three months ago."

"So did I."

"Fisk," Frank shot over his shoulder, "is there another crate on this train from Rogers and Company?"

"I dunno." The porter shrugged. "Is there, Hardy?"

"No."

Frank gave her a polite smile with enough forced charm to set his teeth on edge. "Then that settles it. This piano is mine."

She stiffened her spine to a ramrod, her brown eyes flashing a warning. "You're sadly mistaken, Mr. Who-ever-you-are."

"Brody. Frank Brody. Owner of the Moon Rock Saloon. And owner of this upright piano."

"You may own that whiskey mill, but you don't own this piano. I do. I am a piano teacher and I—"

"Weeping Angel doesn't have a piano teacher."

"They do as soon as I get *my* piano into *my* parlor."

Frank didn't like being burned at the stake by a woman he could easily picture with a rosary swaying in her hand. "Put your ruler away, sister. I'm not one of your pupils."

Her mouth dropped open.

Grenville came forward. "I do believe this is an official matter for the ticket agent to handle. Might I suggest we bring this discussion inside and find a solution to the problem in the depot where it's cooler?"

Frank was already walking.

The station house remained cooler, but not by much. Frank gave the large clock mounted on the wall enough of a glance to note the hour. 3:48 P.M. He had twelve minutes to get the piano to the Moon Rock in order to open on time.

He'd put his all into fixing up the saloon, sparing no expense on the decor to revive the western showplace of the sixties and seventies. The upright piano was his mail-order ace in the hole.

Lloyd Fairplay who owned the Palace four doors down and around the corner from the Moon Rock, had music—a discarded church organ. The instrument wasn't in the best shape, but music was music. When Lloyd's feet pumped the rubber-cloth bellows, passable notes burped up the done-for reeds. And depending on how many drinks a customer had, they could make out the songs and sing right along.

Lloyd's organ was orchestrating Frank's business down to virtual stragglers, basically just those who passed through Weeping Angel and didn't realize the Moon Rock's menu was minus musical entertainment until after they'd plunked down their two bits.

Without a piano, the Moon Rock Saloon would continue to play second fiddle to the Palace. Dammit, he needed a New American upright. He'd paid for one. He owned one. And woman or not, he aimed to fight her strings and keys for the crate.

Sliding a taxidermic hoot owl out of his way, Frank put his hands on the hardwood counter and drummed out his irritation. Miss Marshall came inside and stood a healthy six feet away from him.

Grenville slipped through a double-hinged door the same height as the counter. He made a big to-do about putting on a pair of half glasses with tarnished wire frames before fitting a green-billed visor on his head. His expression took on a professional air as he lifted his gaze. "Now then, do either of you wish to file a complaint with the Union Pacific for lost or damaged goods?"

"Cut the bullshit, Parks," Frank returned, slamming both his hands down on the counter.

"Mr. Brody!" she exclaimed. "May I remind you, you are in the company of a lady."

He might have taken a moment to remember his manners if she hadn't been looking at him as if he were something she needed to scrape off the bottom of her shoe. "May I remind you to loosen your corset—you're laced too tight."

"Well!"

"Well yourself." Frank turned his glare on Grenville. "Parks, I ordered a New American upright parlor piano from Rogers Pianos in Boston. I paid one hundred and fifty-nine dollars for it—not to mention the goddamn shipping."

"Excuse me, Mr. Brody," she disputed as if she had

him over a barrel, "but why would you order a *parlor* piano?"

"Because I have a *drinking parlor*. And a man's thirst isn't at its prime unless he can drink his liquor while he's listening to a piano player belt out obscene songs."

Her lips parted in surprise.

Grenville shook his head. "Well, I can't release the piano until someone can prove ownership. Does either one of you have a bill of sale?"

"Certainly." She set her black-tasseled pocketbook on the counter, opened it, and produced the proper document.

"I didn't plan on having any trouble," Frank said, irked she would come so prepared. "I don't have mine with me."

"Ah ha!" she blurted.

"Sister, nobody your age should ever say *'Ah ha!'* You just put ten years on yourself." Frank ignored her offended gasp and yanked his hat off. "Parks, trust me when I say I have the bill of sale. It's at the Moon Rock. Where I should be." He swiped his hair out of his eyes before putting the panama back on. "I'll concede, by some damn coincidence, both myself and the lady here have ordered the same piano from the same manufacturer. There's apparently been a mix-up at the company, and they've only sent us one upright."

"But only one of you has shown proof of sale," Grenville said. "If you can't produce your receipt, Mr. Brody, I have to give the piano to Miss Marshall."

"I've got it at the Moon Rock," Frank repeated. "I'll show you the receipt after the piano is at my saloon."

"No, that won't do. Even if you do have a proof of sale, there'd still be only one piano and two receipts. Nothing like this is in the Union Pacific manual," Grenville mumbled. "If we had a telegraph in town—which we don't—this matter could be cleared up right away. But because this will have to be handled through the Wells Fargo, I can't legally let either one of you take it."

Miss Marshall gazed at Frank. "You're right, there's obviously been a dreadful mistake made at the factory. One that will take weeks, perhaps a month, to figure out. Time I don't have to sit and wait. If you would be so kind as to give me this piano while—"

"Look," Frank said in what he felt was an indulgent tone, "I don't begrudge you your hobby—"

"Hobby!" she cried as if he'd paid her a paramount insult.

"If you want a piano as an ornament in your parlor for some kids to dabble on, that's fine with me. In fact, I think lessons would be a good thing."

"Well, thank you so much," she snapped.

"I don't think you meant that."

"And I don't think you meant what you said. You were maligning my intentions."

"I wasn't. I was trying to make a comparison here. Which is my point—there is no comparison. I *need* this piano, Miss Marshall. If I don't get *this* piano, my business is going to be busted. So, you're going to have to do your teaching on another piano when one arrives."

She boldly met his eyes. "I can't."

"Why not? One good reason."

Flushing, she grew very distraught; her fingers twisted the fringy stuff on her purse. For a moment, he thought she might cry. Wrong choice on her part. Hell, he could squeeze out some tears, too, if he thought of something to rip his gut. *If* he was so inclined to turn on the waterworks. Which he was not. Men didn't cry. And smart women didn't either. A fatal mistake because this man never surrendered to theatrics.

Frank rested his hip against the counter. "Are you having trouble thinking up a good reason, Miss Marshall?"

She showed no signs of relenting. "I don't need any reasons, Mr. Brody. I paid for the piano and the piano is mine."

Feeling every muscle in his body grow taut, Frank nodded and turned to the ticket agent. "Parks, I've been about as pleasant as I can, this being a hot day and all." He pressed his palms on the countertop and leaned toward Grenville until they were nose to nose. Frank kept his tone level and low. "Just so we're clear on this. I want my piano. And I'm going to have my piano. Not in a few weeks or a month. Now. Right now. As of"—Frank shifted his gaze to the clock and back—"four-oh-three, it's mine. I think we're clear on this, Parks. I know I am."

Grenville's eyes bulged, making them appear twice their size through the short lenses of his glasses. "B-But I've explained you can't take immediate possession."

Frank backed away and shrugged his shoulders in mock resignation. "Hell, then I'm just going to steal it."

"You can't let him!" Miss Marshall implored the ticket agent. Twirling toward Frank, her fancy skirts swished around trim ankles and sounded like a high wind in tall grass.

He tipped his head with a challenge. "Step outside and watch me."

"You couldn't possibly roll the crate over the boardwalk yourself!"

"I have thirsty men to help."

"They won't help you unless I tell them they can," Grenville warned. "It's like I said. We're going to have to go through the Wells Fargo office. Until that time, I have to keep the piano here."

"I'll be damned if I'm going to let a perfectly good piano sit in a train depot," Frank ground out. "It's either coming with me, or I'm setting up my bar here. What's it going to be, Parks?"

"That's not at all acceptable to me," Miss Marshall broke in.

Frank kept after the ticket agent. "What's it going to be, Parks?"

Grenville ruffled the tidy edges of the Union Pacific manual. "My official ruling as a representative of the railroad is to organize an emergency town meeting to decide what to do. We've got ourselves a monumental problem."

The only monumental problem Frank could see was standing in front of him with a hat of garden foliage and duck wings on her head.

Chapter

2

⚜

*I*nside the Christ Redeemer church, the flock of Weeping Angel gathered to decide the residence of the New American upright parlor piano. Paddle ceiling fans stirred the warm air under the guidance of five boys who'd been elected to pull the cords up and down.

As the congregation took their seats on the polished mahogany pews, there was murmured reflection as gazes lifted to the gesso—plaster- and paint-coated—winged angel, classically posed and based on the statue of Artemis at Versailles. She'd been put up with twenty lengths of clear fishing line, and only on those Sunday mornings when the dawn's early light beamed through the stained-glass windows could a person see the strings holding her. After nine o'clock she seemed to be suspended by the will of God.

The angel meant a lot to the residents of Weeping Angel—they'd named their town after her. It had come about the day after a spring shower passed over the town, and Reverend Thorpe went to inspect his newly constructed church. He found the angel with what looked to be tears streaming down her face. He'd fled the hallowed hall, screaming that the Lord had given him a sign. Not fifteen minutes later, the whole of the town gathered in the church to behold the miracle. But it wasn't until after everyone was huddled with awe around the weeping angel, that Oscar Beamguard had the bad grace to point out the steady drip coming from a leak in the roof and landing on the angel's head to run down her cheeks.

There'd been a moment's hushed quiet before the folks still proclaimed the event as a miracle. After all, God had made the rain, and even though the roof was at fault, the leak had as much power as the angel crying herself. They decided then and there they must name the town Weeping Angel in honor of the divine omen.

Retelling the story of how it had all come about was considered a privilege. The citizens took pride in relating the story, careful to keep the recounting accurate. A person couldn't stretch the truth about the Lord's work and not worry about penitence.

Not giving a minute's thought to how the town was named, Amelia sat in the first row pew, along with Narcissa Dodge, Grenville Parks, Herbert Fisk, Lew Furlong, Hardy, and Mr. Frank Brody. She had more pressing things on her mind than the blessed angel.

Namely, gaining possession of the New American upright parlor piano.

Why couldn't Mr. Brody let her have this piano and wait for a new one to arrive for his saloon? What was more important—nurturing the minds of the children or contributing to the delinquency of the town's men?

Amelia leaned forward ever so slightly to regard Mr. Brody with a wary gaze. He sat on the end, next to Hardy, and had the poor taste to appear comfortable

—this being his first time in the church. Resting his arm on the pew's back, he'd propped one foot on his knee; his hat dangled from the toe of his boot. He'd seated himself as indolently as he'd eaten his peach, but the expression marking his profile gave him away. He was mad enough to eat hornets. She refrained from taking in his appearance further, mad herself, and more than a little offended because he'd called her sister in that tone. Why, everyone in town knew her family came from Methodists.

She resumed her position with a straight back. She *needed* to have *this* piano or she wouldn't last through the winter. She had withdrawn most of the money from her savings account—one hundred and fifty-nine dollars—and put it toward the piano. Of course she still had her aunt Clara's nest egg hidden in the broken-handled coffee mill on the top shelf of her pantry. But it was fast becoming too small for even a hummingbird to sit on.

If only she hadn't spent two hundred dollars on the Legacy Collection—the complete Bible spelled out in twenty-five marble-edged Italian leather volumes for easy reading.

Amelia hated to think about Jonas Pray, the book and Bible salesman from California. He'd been the handsomest man she'd ever seen. Like fine honey, he'd been golden, smooth and sweet with words. What a naïve fool she'd been.

She'd been raised to believe young ladies only acquainted themselves with respectable men while they waited for a marriage proposal. What more earnest occupation than a Bible salesman? She'd learned the hard way that a man's calling card wasn't enough to spell out his character.

After her public humiliation, she'd immersed herself in the upkeep of her home and the tending of her yards because she'd also been taught that the greatest cause of misery and wretchedness in social life was idleness.

Her aunt had instructed her on the laws of physiology and hygiene. Her mother had cultivated in her a spirit of independence. Yet with all this knowledge at her disposal, Amelia had only been trained to be a wife, not how to transact business and be a financier. So it was with horror that she reacted to the news from Mr. Hartshorn, the manager of the bank, that her account was on the verge of collapse.

It was the second most humiliating day of Amelia's life.

After great consideration for her predicament, the only dignified way she could think to salvage herself from poverty was to teach piano lessons.

She had eight confirmed pupils—all girls. At twenty-five cents a lesson, and lessons being held once a week, she would be supplementing her diminutive savings with two dollars every seven days. She could have had an extra two dollars and fifty cents and would have had ten more pupils—boys—if she'd been able to convince their mothers the importance of musical awareness for a son as well as a daughter. But she'd exhausted her speech on the matter and had had to settle for the eight girls.

Eight girls she wouldn't have if she didn't get her piano.

The town's mayor, Cincinatus Dodge, took up the pulpit to direct the meeting. He'd gone beyond the prime of his life, the spark of his youth starting to fizzle out. But he was still a man of much character and had aspirations of becoming a renowned orator. He'd been trying to recite the whole of the Declaration of Independence since last Fourth of July whenever he had the authority to hold the town captive. But he hadn't gotten past "all men are created equal" before someone interrupted his recitation. Because he'd memorized the document from the order in which it had been written, he'd have to start over to gain his momentum back. And by then, his audience had grown wise to him.

"Come to order, citizens," he called in a clear voice freshly sprayed with saline water from his atomizer. The church full of people didn't readily cease their steady whispers. "It has come to my attention—quiet, please—we have a monumental problem."

There were numerous nods of men's heads and women conspiring in hushed tones behind their gloved hands.

"Now then—quiet, please. Quiet, please!"

The room instantly fell silent as a graveyard.

Mayor Dodge's brows rose a fraction as all eyes focused on him. He kept his appearance neat and tidy—as would a mayor in his late fifties. The part in his pomade-oiled silvery hair was so deep and exact, Moses couldn't have done a better job with his staff. His tailor-made clothes were respectable and fit him well. He glanced at his wife, Narcissa, who sat at Amelia's left. She gave him a frown and discreetly shook her head no. He placed his right hand into the fold of his jacket and took on a Jeffersonian pose. "When in the course of human events, it becomes necessary for one people to dissolve the political bands which have connected them with another, and to assume among the powers of the earth, the separate and equal station to which the laws of nature and of nature's God entitle them—"

"What about my entitlement to the piano?" Frank broke in, his voice heavy with impatience.

"—entitle them to a piano . . . to a piano?" Mayor Dodge crinkled his nose. "Horse feathers! That's not right!"

Frank stood, panama in hand, and headed toward the pulpit. "Slide over, Dodge, I don't have time for high jinks."

"But I always oversee the town meetings!" the mayor blustered, refusing to move.

"Come over to the Moon Rock after this is settled and oversee me making you a gin cocktail—on the house."

"Mr. Brody, you may have the podium."

"I had a feeling you'd see things my way." Frank turned to the crowd to deal with the problem himself, galling Amelia. "Grenville Parks here, our ticket agent for the Short Line, seems to think this meeting is necessary in order for me to take ownership of a piano I bought."

"That *I* bought," Amelia amended.

"All right," Frank said, looking pointedly at her. "The piano we *both* bought, but had the damn luck—"

A rush of feminine gasps befell the congregation upon his slip of the tongue in the Lord's house.

Frank frowned, his gaze growing dark as if he didn't put merit in the eternal consequences of swearing in a church. But at least he had the decency to rephrase, "Had the bad luck of having only one piano delivered."

"I can vouch for the one crate," Herbert Fisk, the porter, added.

"Me, too," said Hardy. "Heard the chords strike when we put her on the dolly."

Lew Furlong sneezed, then blew his nose so loudly the boys pulling the fans broke into peals of laughter over the honking sound. Rubbing his watery eyes, he sniffed. "I helped get the one and only crate off my train."

Grenville scratched the back of his head. "That still doesn't change the fact only Miss Marshall has shown documentation for the piano."

Amelia sat straighter than ever before. That was right! Frank Brody hadn't produced his receipt. Quick as a whip, she dug into her purse and retrieved the voucher. "Here is my proof of sale," she said, holding it between her gloved forefinger and thumb, going so far as to wave the paper a tad for emphasis. "See?"

"Don't start moving furniture yet," Frank advised, looking at her with a bland smile. He slipped his hand into his trousers pocket and withdrew a folded piece of paper. "My receipt. Who wants it?"

"I'll take it," Mayor Dodge said, and relieved Frank of the sales slip. After scanning the paper, he nodded. "It says Mr. Brody did indeed buy the piano."

"Not the piano," Amelia corrected. "*A* piano. His piano might not be this piano."

A murmur of agreement rose from the mothers of Amelia's students, and she felt a moment's triumph. The men thoughtfully put their fingers on their chins, as if thinking of a plan to contradict her observation and douse her supporters. After all, they had everything to lose if the piano went to her.

Mayor Dodge's seasoned face became somber. His mouth dipped into a frown and he drew his light brows together in thought. Then, without preamble, his eyes twinkled with purpose. "I know what to do! Compare the dates on the receipts. If the date on Mr. Brody's is prior to the date on Miss Marshall's, the piano will go to the Moon Rock. But if the date on Miss Marshall's receipt is before Mr. Brody's, she will take the piano."

"I would have gotten to that," Grenville grumbled. He took Amelia's bill of sale. "But Mr. Brody didn't have his receipt on him, so I couldn't."

The ticket agent approached the pulpit and handed the mayor her slip. Fisk resumed his seat and folded his arms across his chest to brood.

Amelia waited with her heart in her throat while Mayor Dodge compared the two pieces of paper. She hoped her strained smile hid her anxiousness. No one knew what dire straits she was falling into. She'd die of shame if they did. She'd pretended not to be concerned by her bank balance in front of Mr. Hartshorn and had implied to him she had funds elsewhere.

"Same dates," the mayor muttered. "Must be why there was a mix-up."

Thank goodness. She hadn't lost the piano. But neither had she won it.

"I think Fra—" Emmaline Shelby cut her sugary voice short to amend, "That is—Mr. Brody," she cooed, "should have the piano."

Amelia caught Frank's wink at the laundress. She craned her neck to see what kind of reaction the audacious gesture had on Emmaline. Emmaline blushed, her cheeks turning the same shade as the number-three red dye she used to color linen ticking—a startling contrast to her alabaster skin and raven curls. Amelia was instantly reminded of a riddle young Daniel Beamguard had asked her: What's black and white and read all over? If she'd known in advance how profusely the laundress could blush, Amelia would have answered: Emmaline Shelby.

Emmaline tilted her head, suddenly overtaken with the need to fan her rosy face.

Narrowing her eyes, Amelia faced forward again, not at all liking the way her insides felt like saltwater taffy—pulling her in all directions, and having no tangible explanation as to why.

"Thank you, Miss Shelby." Frank smiled. "I appreciate your vote." He leaned into the pulpit, resting his elbow on the sheets of Reverend Thorpe's sermon. "How about a few more votes? Gentlemen, Pap will play the best tunes you'll ever hear."

"I protest!" Amelia rose as gracefully as she could from the pew, clutching her purse by the snap frame. "This isn't a political rally. He can't drum up votes with coercion and promises!"

"Why not?" Mayor Dodge replied. "The president does."

"I think we should bring the matter to a vote," Emmaline said, and Amelia had to keep herself from glaring at her.

"I don't think that's necessary," Amelia replied. "Aren't you all forgetting Weeping Angel already has drinking music in Lloyd's Palace?"

Ed Vining voiced his opinion, "I wouldn't call the asthmatic wheeze of that clunker church organ drinking music. Those pipes were condemned before Reverend Thorpe bought them to use until we could afford this new Cathedral Chapel organ here."

"But the old one still works," Amelia hastened to add.

"Oh, it works," Ed whined. "But frankly, every time I hear Lloyd playing it, I'm thinking I ain't ought to be drinking on account of the godly notes being bellowed out of that organ. It don't matter Lloyd is playing 'Oh! Susanna.' It still sounds like 'Onward Christian Soldiers' to me."

"You never told me that," Lloyd burst in without amusement.

"I didn't want to offend you, Lloyd. You serve nickel beer."

"That's right," Lloyd said crossly. "You won't find Brody serving nickel beer. He charges a dime a glass."

"You come over to the Moon Rock, Lloyd," Frank suggested, "and I'll give you a free glass."

"Well, I like that," Amelia declared sarcastically. "This meeting wasn't called to debate the price of beer. We're supposed to be deciding where the piano should go."

"I say it should go to the Moon Rock," Ed remarked. "It's just what that place needs, it being so fancy, and all."

"And the vote is the only fair way," the mayor concurred, "until you both can get an answer from

Boston as to whose piano this actually is. And then, they'll ship out a second one."

"In the meantime," Grenville piped in, "the crate can't sit on the Union Pacific's dolly, so we best decide where it goes."

Mayor Dodge agreed. "Then let's call a vote right now."

Amelia panicked. The situation wouldn't have been so severe if the *un*married Frank Brody had been *un*attractive. The problem was, he was too disarmingly handsome for the ladies in town to take a deserved dislike to. They'd forced Charley Revis out of business, and the only reason they tolerated Lloyd's Palace was because the rickety building with its washed-up singer was so sorry, it posed no threat to their delicate senses. Besides, the bar had been there since Weeping Angel's founding, and it was somewhat of a monument with its broken shutters and crooked front doors.

Though no respectable woman had ever set foot inside the false-fronted Moon Rock Saloon with its rumored diamond-dust mirrors, thirty-foot golden walnut bar, crystal glasses, scarlet carpet, and brass fixtures, Amelia suspected they were dying to. Mr. Brody's showplace was the topic of the day, and she feared anything to help him add luster to his saloon would be at her expense. Allowing all these infatuated ladies the vote could sway the result in his favor. But by the same token, the men had been interested in the Moon Rock since its opening and they would surely vote for the piano to go there so they wouldn't have to hear the Palace's secondhand music. "Wait!" she rushed. "I propose only the married couples vote, that way we know the ratio of men and women are equal." At least she would have a fifty percent chance of winning. Perhaps even greater because eight of the wives had daughters signed up for lessons. Certainly they didn't want their girls inside a drinking parlor practicing their scales, and would whisper their objective views to their spouses before the vote.

"That does seem the democratic way," the mayor remarked in a resonant voice filled with authority. "Do you have any objections, Mr. Brody?"

Frank shrugged. "None I can speak in a church, so I guess this is the way it has to be." His gaze landed intimately on Amelia and inexplicably put her at odds. Then he moved on to give the whole of the room—the ladies in particular—a lazy smile. His full curving mouth oozed so much masculinity, Amelia felt gooseflesh rise as if it were the dead of winter.

"All right, everyone who can vote, get themselves a scrap of paper," Mayor Dodge stated while walking toward his wife to procure a torn-off piece of her grocery list to cast his vote on.

"Are you sure you know what you're doing?" Narcissa asked her husband.

The mayor cast a glance at Amelia. "Yes, dear. This is the only fair way."

Amelia nodded in reluctant agreement, hoping her dearest friend and her husband would be of some help in swaying the decision in her favor.

As everyone thought on their vote, Frank began to whistle "The Yellow Rose of Texas." His musical pitch was perfect; and she admitted to herself with reluctance, he had an ear for music—even though he harmonized a common melody.

Catching her staring at him, he winked, making no bones about the fact that the sparkle in his eye was meant for her.

Amelia's mouth dropped open. Aghast, she suddenly knew exactly what he was up to. Whetting the men's appetites with a tuneful reminder of what they'd be hearing if they voted for him to take the piano.

She tried to disguise her annoyance in front of the others, wishing she knew how to whistle, too. Since she didn't, she began to hum Beethoven's Fifth Symphony in as loud a voice as she dared. She'd barely gotten into the twelfth bar when a hand touched her shoulder from behind.

"Are you all right, dear?" Esther Parks whispered.

Amelia immediately ceased her humming and turned her chin a notch. "I'm fine."

Grenville cocked his head around and said, "Miss Marshall has phlegm in her throat, Esther. Leave her alone."

Amelia wanted to slither from her seat.

The ushers from the prior Sunday's service took the ballots. Mayor Dodge collected them, and after tallying the votes, he prepared to read the outcome.

"My fellow citizens, silence please."

The room quieted posthaste, and Mayor Dodge quirked his brow at Narcissa, who shook her head at him again. "When in the course of . . ." Catching Amelia's anxious gaze, he sobered. ". . . piano disputes, it becomes necessary to take a vote, which we have done. Now, allow me to report the results."

Amelia tensely awaited the verdict. Closing her eyes and clutching her purse tightly, she held her breath until her lungs burned.

"By a margin of twenty-nine to twenty-one in favor of, the New American upright parlor piano will be going to the Moon Rock Saloon."

Amelia's heart sank. Exhaling, she opened her eyes, only to find Frank Brody's gaze fastened on her. She wouldn't show him her defeat. She could take the loss graciously. Facing him, stare for stare, she held her chin high.

His clear, observant eyes chipped at her composure. Could he tell she was desperately holding back tears? Determined not to reveal her disappointment, she kept all expression from her face. But her blood pounded at her temples, and she couldn't stop the heat from stealing into her cheeks.

She thought she saw a sign of empathy in his gaze. How could he identify with her? He'd won the piano. She hadn't. What made the loss hurt all the more was, he'd been the outsider in town, and she'd been here for six years. Apparently loyalty didn't count when the issue at hand involved glasses of beer.

Amelia couldn't bear Mr. Brody's false sympathy, so she broke away from his gaze to look around her. The men patted themselves on the backs and the women, who she thought were her friends, were glancing at one another with suspicious guilt in their expressions. Only Narcissa put her hand on Amelia's forearm for comfort.

Folding her hands in her lap, Amelia dropped her chin and waited for the meeting to be finished. The strain was wearing her down. She was afraid she'd disgrace herself by crying.

"Hey, Dodge, come here a minute."

Amelia looked up to see Frank conferring with the mayor at the pulpit. Mayor Dodge's brows rose, and he nodded with a wide smile. "Splendid idea, Mr. Brody. I'll let you make the announcement."

Frank took his straw hat from the lectern and let the band hang on the crook of his finger. "I appreciate the vote coming my way, but I think it needs to be said—Miss Marshall is out a piano until another one can be shipped." Their eyes met and, half in anticipation and half in dread, she waited for him to continue. "I'd like to offer her use of the upright at the Moon Rock. During my closed hours, she can teach the kids at the saloon."

She stared at him in astonishment, too surprised to move. His generosity caught her off guard, and she couldn't help but wonder what his ulterior motive was for making the offer. Unfortunately, he'd put her on the spot in front of everyone, and she couldn't exactly cross-examine him. Far worse than the damage done to her pride was the simple truth: She couldn't afford to refuse his charity.

"You're being very gracious, Mr. Brody. I"—she had to swallow the lump in her throat—"I accept."

"There now," Mayor Dodge declared. "Everything turned out just fine. The excitement is over, folks. The special town meeting is adjourned. Miss Marshall, in the meantime, I'm sure you'll be taking up the matter over at the Wells Fargo office. And Mr. Brody, I'll be seeing you shortly." Licking his lips, Mayor Dodge left the pulpit to join his wife.

Amelia stood, said her good-byes to Narcissa, then filed out of the church with the crowd. Esther Parks met her.

"Amelia, dear, I'm afraid I was too hasty when I said my Elroy wouldn't be taking lessons. I've changed my mind."

Amelia looked at her with surprise, remembering how adamant Mrs. Parks had been. She didn't have a chance to reply when Mrs. Dorothea Beamguard drew up next to them. "I've changed my mind, too, my dear. You can expect to see Daniel."

"That goes for Jakey," Mrs. Luella Spivey added.

Mrs. Viola Reed chimed in, "Oh, yes. Do count on my Walter and Warren to be there."

The twins? Amelia had never seen them with clean fingernails or the bibs on their overalls fastened. Imagining the rambunctious red-haired duo at a piano whacking on the ivory keys frightened her.

Other women approached as she passed the baptismal font. Students were popping up like spring daffodils.

By the time she reached the narthex, she'd added ten new pupils. Every boy's mother who'd turned her down before had a sudden change of heart. They were being so nice, even though some of her lady friends had obviously voted against her. Amelia knew from attending the Thursday Afternoon Fine Ladies Society canasta games, these women did nothing without gain. If Frank Brody had been anything but a novelty, they would have snubbed him and his stale saloon.

The closeness of people, the stares, and the heat were all overwhelming Amelia, and she sidestepped her way out of the flowing crowd to rest by the coatracks and cold radiator to catch her breath. She pretended to be engrossed with the visitor's register sitting on a small pedestal. Rigidly holding her tears in check, she would not cry.

Amelia felt a light touch on the small of her back, felt the presence of someone standing so close behind her a book of sheet music couldn't fit between them. The air suddenly smelled faintly of tobacco and . . . peach. She rapidly blinked the moisture from her eyes as he spoke. "I know you wanted the vote to go the other way." Frank's voice held a quiet note of apology she found odd. Even though he'd made a gesture of compromise, surely he'd done so to look considerate in front of the others.

She didn't dare turn around and face him. She couldn't. Not without dying.

"I meant what I said. You can use the piano. I'm open from four in the afternoon until two in the morning. I thought we could divide the time into twelve-hour shifts."

Amelia stared at a child's knitted blue muffler left over from winter on the shelf above the coat hooks. She fought hard not to tremble and let him see her so emotional. All she could do was nod. She didn't have a choice.

He continued in a low tone. "You can have access to the piano from four in the morning to four in the afternoon. Mostly I'm in bed until noon, but don't worry about waking me with the noise. I sleep like the dead."

Pressing a key into the palm of her hand, he closed her fingers around the warm metal. The mere touch of his hand against the thin cotton of her gloves sent a shiver through her. "This unlocks the front door."

She mutely nodded again, wishing she didn't have to know the details of his sleeping habits.

Then he left, and she almost stumbled backward from the power his close proximity had on her. The world spun and careened, seemingly taking her with it on its axis and making her dizzy. A man hadn't touched her in such a fashion since . . . Jonas Pray.

Amelia stayed in the church long minutes after everyone else had left. She didn't want anybody to see her when she walked home.

The burning imprint of the key in her palm reminded her of Frank Brody and the implications of its intimate meaning. The key symbolized a connection between the two of them in a secret, wicked sort of way.

She'd sworn never to have anything to do with a saloon after Jonas ran off with Silver Starlight, and now she clutched the key to one.

Being voted down had been bad; having four of her own gender go against her had been worse. How could they have done such a thing to her? They knew how she felt. They knew about . . . about what happened . . .

Fresh tears brimmed her eyes and she fought them.

Passing her fingertips under her lower lashes to make sure her face powder hadn't smudged, Amelia turned on her heels to leave.

The light of day blinded her as she hurried across Divine Street, thankful no one had milled around to speak with her. And even more thankful Mr. Brody wasn't anywhere in sight.

She heard a *thumpity-thumpity* coming from down the block. When she glanced in the direction of the noise, she saw the big crate with the New American upright parlor piano being rolled inside the Moon Rock Saloon's double front doors.

Her chest ached anew, and Amelia wanted nothing more than to go home, strip out of her clothes, slide to the bottom of her bathtub, and pull the cool water over her head to hide.

Chapter

3

By two-thirty in the morning, the candle-melting heat cooled to a temperature that would have kept a puddle of wax only lukewarm. The seductive breath of garden roses consorted with the scents of freshly watered vegetable gardens and lawns. The combinations milling through the air roamed sluggishly under and over the paneled, frosted cut glass doors of the Moon Rock Saloon.

Frank lounged in a chair, his boot heels caught on a round table's edge while he enjoyed a beer mug of 5-Star Hennessy cognac. Forgoing the handle, he slipped his hand around the fluted glass to warm the liquor with his right palm. Far from drinking fashion, he rebuffed the idea of a snifter; they were too ostentatious and too large. Their wide mouths allowed the bouquet to evaporate into the air, rather than his mouth. Savoring the taste, he indulged in his favorite drink. The mellow brandy capped off his long night as he listened to Pap O'Cleary romp through "Buffalo Gals" for the dozenth time.

"Can't you play anything else?" Frank asked between leisurely sips, growing tired of the song's square-dance tempo.

Pap didn't miss a beat while shaking his derby-covered head. "Got this one under my skin," he replied in tune to the music. "Under my skin . . . under my skin."

Frowning, Frank struck a match with his thumbnail and lit a cheroot. He brought the thin cigar to his lips, then inhaled. Exhaling a slow ribbon of white smoke as he spoke, he suggested, "Play 'Sweet Betsy from Pike' or 'Down Went McGinty.' Better yet, 'A Hot Time in the Old Town.' We did a damn hot business tonight."

"Best since we opened," Pap agreed above the virgin-sounding chords he ravished from the New American upright parlor piano. "Oh, buffalo gals, won't you come out tonight and dance," he sang in a deep-pitched voice, "by the light of the moon?" He abruptly stopped his jaunty playing and swiveled on the hardwood stool to face Frank. Meshing his fingers together and extending his arms, he cracked his joints. "Feels good to get the kinks out."

"Feels good just sitting here."

"You always say that at closing time." Pap stood to shuffle through his repertoire of sheet music on top of the piano. He wasn't a tall man, but he was solid as a brick. Beneath his Danbury black derby, he was bald as a baby's bottom, but made up for nature's premature deficit by sporting a whopping red mustache.

"I always mean it." Frank took a pull on his square-tipped cigar. "The best part of the night is smelling what everybody else has done with their day. That fragrance of roses belongs to Narcissa Dodge. She pruned the bushes at sundown when that elm of hers shaded her planting beds. And the whiff of grass is coming from Doc White's yard. He just mowed his lawn this afternoon. Watered it right after supper." Frank tapped the ash off his cigar onto the floor.

"Jakey Spivey washed his yellow hound today. General Custer trotted by the saloon a couple hours ago, leaving the scent of Ivory soap, fresh dirt, and dog behind him. If you breathe in deep, you can still smell it."

"I have no interest in sniffing after a dog who's half clean." Selecting a folio, Pap pushed the brim of his hat up his forehead. "Besides, I don't smell anything but your cigar and Rupert Teats's livery."

Frank let the last of his Hennessy slide down his throat, then licked his lips with a satisfied swallow. "That's because you don't know how to smell life, Pap."

"I can smell food and I can smell women—and not necessarily in that order."

Frank laughed as he felt along his jaw for the heavy stubble roughing up his chin.

A June bug bounced off the crystal chandelier above Frank. The hot, cut glass globe glowing from kerosene light burned the insect's wings, and the bug plummeted to Frank's beer mug with a plop. "Damn good thing my glass was empty," he said to the dead beetle, and dumped the brown spot onto the sawdust-covered floor with a drop or two of cognac.

"Play me something unrefined if you won't play 'Hot Time,'" Frank persisted.

Pap gave his elbows a bone pop to stay limber. "I'll play you 'Hot Time.'" He set the sheet on the music desk and began with the chorus.

Frank closed his eyes and let the song dance through his mind. He pictured sunsets in the Mexican desert —an almost endless pancake of land barren as a ninety-year-old woman—where the only shadows on the ground came from his horse and himself. He waited for an arid breeze to mantle his face with dust, but the dry wind never came. And never would again. Gone were the days of rambling and a panorama sprawling as far as his gaze could see. He'd traded in empty prospects and an empty life and decided to travel a road of stability instead.

Though the shoe of proprietorship didn't quite fit him yet, he hoped time would soften the leather and his sole would adapt to the size of small-town life. Hell, he had no place else to go. This was it for him. The final watering hole in a long line of thirsty ventures as a jack-of-all-trades. He'd mined silver on the Comstock, laid track for the Southern Pacific, ridden shotgun on the Overland Stage, ran a trading post in Nogales, and his last occupation—bardogging at the El Dorado in Frisco.

It was there he'd met Charley Revis and bought this building from him sight unseen. Old Charley had said he'd tried to make a go of things in Weeping Angel a couple of years ago, but fortune hadn't been on his side. He'd had a string of bad luck, most notably run-ins with the crones who didn't abide a second saloon in town. He'd been in business just shy of a month when his cash box disappeared the same day his hurdy-gurdy dancer ran off. After that, Charley had called it quits, boarded up the place, and went to San Francisco.

The night Frank met Charley, Charley had ordered a round of drinks for everyone in the El Dorado to celebrate his newfound wealth in the stock market. They got to talking, and Charley's description of Weeping Angel had appealed to Frank. There was a crystal-clear lake with trout for the taking, the seasons were pretty to watch, and a man need only bother to keep a dog at his side instead of a gun. Frank had been looking for just such a town to hang his hat up. The challenge of turning the shebang into a glory house had cinched the deal for Frank, and he and Pap had ridden out of Frisco by the weekend.

Frank felt the whir of June bugs as they flitted

through his saloon and opened his eyes to the false light. He viewed the Moon Rock as if he were seeing it for the first time.

A fine diamond-dust mirror ran the length of his thirty-foot, golden walnut bar. His back bar—or altar as the bartenders called it in the El Dorado—had shelves for pyramids of brightly labeled liquor bottles and the knickknacks forming his saloon's "museum." He displayed a cracked in half geode—two pieces of split rock with pale lavender prisms of quartz inside —on the mantel. And to anyone who asked, he swore the rock fell out of the sky from the moon and hit him on the arm; he had the scar to prove it. He supplied towels at the edge of the counter so his customers could wipe the foam from their mustaches or beards. He offered men drinks out of crystal glasses. He'd scattered scarlet runners of carpet throughout the joint to add a touch of elegance, and he gave the patrons fancy brass cuspidors to spit in.

Coming from his rebellious, empty-pocket beginnings, Frank had done well for himself. He should have been happy and downright content. He'd be turning thirty in less than two months, and he could celebrate in the Moon Rock—the closest thing to a home he'd ever had. He seemed to have been taking his life in recently, trying to make it add up to something, but he was coming up with a zero.

Finishing "Hot Time in the Old Town" in a crescendo of finale chords, Pap chuckled. "Goes to show I can still twiddle the ivories and make 'em cry. What do you want next?"

"Girls."

Tilting his head, Pap snorted, "Girls? You've got every female in this sleepy-eyed town tripping over you."

"I don't mean the batting-eyelash and wave-of-the-handkerchief women. Their giggles and blushes wear on my nerves. I'm talking *girls*—as in decadent, white-fleshed girls who can run around the place showing off real skin so pearly it would put an oyster's work to shame. The kind of girls who sing and dance and make a man feel like a man even if he's short on guts and not strong on brains. You know what I mean—dancing girls."

"Yeah, I know what you mean. Do-si-do girls. Girls who charge for a look, a feel, and a do." Pap shrugged. "Town ladies won't go for dancing girls."

"What about Iza Ogilvie down at the Palace? She sings and dances."

The drone of crickets chirped with Pap's laughter. "Iza Ogilvie is a dried-up British flower whose skin isn't pearly. I'd say her flesh is more along the lines of a lizard's belly, and so stretched out, it hangs off her like a dress that's too big. Oh, she can sing passable, but when I fantasize about a woman, I surely don't fantasize about a washed-out, middle-aged crumpet named Iza." Pap stood and put his music away. "Now, I did hear tell, this place used to have a fine looker named Silver Starlight when Charley was here."

"Yeah, Charley mentioned she was his dancing girl. Stole his cash and ran off."

Pap nodded. "And took a Bible salesman with her. Caused quite a scandal, too."

"I'm disappointed in you, Pap. You've been hunting down gossip like that gaggle of matrons who honk in the churchyard after Sunday services."

"A man's got to learn all there is to know about a woman before he makes his move in the flock."

Frank narrowed his eyes skeptically. "Who are you fixing to make a move on?"

"I've had my eyes on someone." Pap unfolded the fall board on the piano keys to keep the dust off them. "In fact, she's part of the disgrace with the book and Bible salesman."

"How so? Silver Starlight ran off," Frank noted, not

particularly getting caught up in the hearsay, but went along for lack of anything else to talk about.

"She did. With the salesman—Jonas Pray." Pap began to take down the fly traps one by one from the broad-beam rafters. He lifted the conical covers from wire cylinders and dumped the flies onto the floor. "It was the salesman who left Miss Marshall high and dry."

The woman's name made Frank frown. He'd been trying to forget about her all evening, but that forlorn look of hers had periodically popped into his mind—predominantly when he'd been appreciating the songs Pap heralded from the upright. "What does she have to do with any of this?" Frank asked, not certain he wanted to know.

"She was set on marrying Pray until he ran off."

Frank took a moment to absorb what Pap was telling him. He didn't like it. He didn't want to feel any sorrier for her than he already did. Having sentimental feelings for a woman was bad news, and he made it a practice to write himself out of the headline. Then Pap's meaning dawned on Frank, and he snapped his head toward his friend. "You're fixing to go after the piano teacher?"

"That fanciful notion has crossed my mind more than once, so I've decided to act on it."

"No shit?" Frank smoked his cheroot a minute. "Damn," he muttered and lifted his brows. "Well . . . damn. I'm not anyone to stand in your way, Pap, but I've seen warmer women in this town. When Miss Marshall walks, I can hear the ice cracking off her skirts."

"I've never noticed." Pap removed the last fly trap and broke into a leisurely smile. "But I have noticed how pretty she is. Haven't you?"

"No," Frank replied too quickly. But he had noticed—less than twenty-four hours ago. He'd thought she dressed like a mail-order catalog on foot, but with nice features to go with the rigid trimming.

A sappy expression lit Pap's face. "Her hair is shiny brown. Kinda matches the color of Cobb Weatherwax's mule. She has velvety skin with no freckles. Probably uses store-bought toilet soap. And her lips look made for kissing."

"Jesus, Pap," Frank choked. "What's the matter with you?"

"Nothing. I've just been thinking. I'm going to be forty this year, and it's time I find myself a wife. Me and Miss Marshall have a lot in common."

Frank said sarcastically, "You don't have hair the color of Cobb's mule, and frankly, your skin looks sun-weathered."

Pap put an empty fly trap back on its hook. "I know I'm nothing exceptional, but Miss Marshall needs someone. Especially after you took her piano."

Frank jerked his legs off the table, his boots thumping onto the floor. "That's a line of bull. I didn't steal the piano from her." He ground his cheroot under his heel. "And who the hell are you to talk? You've been drooling ever since you got that upright out of the crate. Guilt hasn't stopped you from playing it nonstop for the past nine hours."

"Who said anything about guilt?"

"You did."

"No I didn't. I don't have anything to feel guilty about. I didn't take the piano away from her." Pap walked toward a tall cupboard in the corner. "But you must be feeling guilty since you brought it up."

"I didn't bring it up."

"Well, you must have felt some kind of remorse, else you wouldn't have said she could use this one."

"I was trying to be accommodating," Frank insisted, unable to cover his annoyance. "She looked like she was going to cry."

"I hope you don't have a call to make her want to cry again, Frank, now that you know my intentions."

"I . . . hell. Yeah, right." Frank went for his glass, then remembered the mug was empty. He considered pouring a second Hennessy, but he'd set his limit on one per night. Any man surrounded by liquor for a living could easily suffer from bottle fever, so he never swilled on the job. An evening cognac quenched his thirst, and an occasional beer tasted too good to resist with his breakfast-lunch when the afternoon heat took him two hours to blow a cup of coffee cool.

Though Pap had riled Frank, he wasn't going to break his self-imposed rule. Besides, he wasn't feeling guilty about Miss Amelia Marshall. He'd nearly succeeded in not giving her a second thought—until Pap had decided to make an issue out of her. Amelia Marshall's troubles weren't his concern. The town had temporarily rectified the piano company's mistake, and he had made allowances for her.

"I'm a student of musicology," came Pap's steady voice, his words drawing Frank from his thoughts. "It's our common thread—Miss Marshall's and mine. We both play the piano." Pap took a broom from the cupboard and began to sweep the dirty sawdust into neat piles. "Tell me, Frank, can you read sheet music and draw a treble clef?"

Frank stood with agitation. "No, but I can read the top of a bullet box and draw a Smith and Wesson No. 3 revolver. I suggest you button your lip on the subject of Miss Marshall, or I'll be forced into proving my reading and drawing skills."

Pap laughed without interrupting his sweeping.

Frank went behind the bar, dunked his mug into a round tub of cold dishwater, then headed for the swinging front doors. "I'm locking up." He put his hand in his trouser pocket and felt for the Yale key he kept on a silver ring. Then he remembered he'd taken it off to give to Amelia. Feeling inexplicably short-changed, he ran his fingers through his hair. "Hey, Pap, give me your spare key."

Pap set the broom handle against a table. "What happened to yours?"

"I gave mine to your wife-to-be."

Pap's eyes held a faint glint of humor as he said, "You better not be planning any funny stuff with her, Frank."

"I'm not planning on doing anything with her," Frank replied as he took the key from Pap.

Frank strode through the saloon's entrance, stepped outside onto the boardwalk, and put his hand on one of the seven-foot doors he closed over his fancy ones. Leaning into the roughened wood wall, he pondered Pap's choice of words. *Funny stuff with her.* Frank hadn't counted on making a running commitment to Miss Marshall when he'd given her the key to the Moon Rock, but that's exactly what he'd done. How the hell was he going to deal with her taking over his domain every afternoon with a barrage of kids?

He hadn't really thought things through at the time, and too late after the fact, he realized he'd be keeping close company with a woman whose glance seemed to be accusingly cold, but he still found her attractive. To complicate matters, Pap had gotten the foolhardy notion into his head she was the girl for him. Any trifling Frank would have tried with Miss Marshall was now off limits.

Moving one of the heavy doors into place, Frank slipped a long rod into a hole in the plank and contemplated the situation. He was a mixologist and supposed to be a native philosopher. He knew how to listen for hours to endless monologues and be an impartial umpire of wagers and disputes, as well as a peacemaker, never an egger-on. He solved the drinkers' problems of heart and mind, or at least pretended to. He never discussed religion or politics, but stuck to sex and sports.

He got along with most everyone. He and Pap had never had a major disagreement, and not under any condition had they fought over a woman. They never would because Frank's attention wasn't engaged on the passionless Miss Marshall. So he had no problem to solve. No astute advice to offer himself.

Why, then, did his barroom wisdom fail to convince him otherwise?

Amelia held on to the key with a black ribbon she'd tied through the hole, in lieu of a ring. Self-conscious, she looked over her shoulder to check if anyone watched her. She'd waited until noon to come to the Moon Rock Saloon, praying all of Weeping Angel sat at their tables eating their lunches.

Swallowing her apprehension, she fit the brass key into the lock. Her fingers trembled so, she couldn't keep a firm grasp on it. She pulled her right glove off and stuffed the fingers into her waistband.

She grabbed the knob and pulled the tall door outward as quietly and as quickly as she could. A showy swinging partition blocked her way, and she had to push on the beveled glass to get inside. Though the afternoon was bright and sunny, the interior was dim, at best, and as suffocating as a hothouse. The air smelled of stale smoke, liquor, and sweaty men. She shivered and tried not to breathe too deeply.

With the door at her back partially open, she couldn't see the details of the interior clearly. She didn't want to imagine what it had looked like when Silver Starlight had been in this very room. But she was helpless to stop the flood of memories from assailing her. She was ashamed to admit she'd been taken advantage of by her trusting nature and had since set about building a new life for herself.

Holding her petit point music bag with one hand, Amelia took a tentative step, her eyes wide, as she tried to adjust to the murky shadows. She walked toward a long counter to her left, passing numerous hardwood tables where chairs had been stacked upside down on the tops. The floorboards beneath her feet had been swept clean.

She ran her hand along the edge of the counter, surprised to find the surface had been waxed. She couldn't see well at all and felt around for a box of matches or a lamp. Coming up short, she bit her lower lip.

Setting her bag down, she went behind the counter to look. Feeling around the shelf, she lifted a box and held it toward the meager stream of sunlight to read the label. *Old Virginia Cheroots.* She hadn't found matches; she'd found vile cigars. Putting them back, she continued to forage through Frank Brody's things. She hated spying on him. He should have left her a lamp and matches in plain view. Instead, she had to degrade herself in such a manner as to plow through his personal belongings. Her hand touched a hard square shape.

Something fell down and metallic rolling sounds invaded the narrow space. Lifting her head, she waited for Mr. Brody to come busting in on her and demand to know what she was doing. Knowing he occupied the room off the saloon made her uneasy. He was in there now . . . sprawled out on a bed . . . sleeping like the dead. As soon as she would hit the first note in her four-four time drill, she dreaded he'd wake up.

When Amelia felt along the floor, she couldn't find what had spilled. Returning to the shelf, she touched a narrow barrel of steel like a plumber's pipe. She inched her fingers across a fluted piece of metal, hook and handle, then froze.

"Oh, dear me," she whispered, and jolted her arm away from the revolver. Tears gathered in her eyes and she was on the verge of crying. How had this happened to her? Being in the Moon Rock was going to dredge up her disgrace all over again. She was an upstanding woman with morals and principles, not some dance-hall girl who felt comfortable in this sort of setting.

To her annoyance, Amelia concluded Silver Starlight would have known where to find a lamp.

Perspiration dampened Amelia's face and she felt flushed. The room's stuffiness threatened her with an attack of the vapors. She took several cleansing breaths, trying not to choke on the odious smells. It simply wouldn't do to swoon and have herself be found prostrate by Frank Brody. The shame would ruin her from ever coming back. And it had taken her two days to get this far.

Feeling slightly better, Amelia forced herself to look one more time and was successful in finding matches. She struck one and walked with the fuzzy light until she found a kerosene lamp on the bar. After removing the globe and turning up the wick, she put the flame on the burner and the saloon came to life.

She could see clearly now. Everything.

Amelia didn't pause to make an assessment. Rather, she headed straight for the door posthaste and closed it. Afterward, she leaned against the jamb and viewed the room detail by detail.

Behind the carved bar, a great mirror shone gloriously, and at its base, at least fifty cut-glass decanters were filled with warm hues of liquid. Never before had she seen such an array of glasses, or such vivid colors, or such huge carved and polished pillars and beams, or such enormous vessels of brass as the spittoons.

She rested her gaze on the numerous wooden cubbies composing the framework for the mirror. Curios and ornate pearl-shaped light globes filled most of them. She lightly studied the bric-a-brac, then saw the infamous, fist-sized rock—the one Mr. Brody touted to Weeping Angel as being documented by a German geologist as coming from the moon.

Three signs hung on the wall behind the bar.

> Biggest 10¢ Beer In Town
> In God we trust—all others pay cash.
> Anyone Violating the Rules Will Be Shot

There were only a smattering of gilt-framed oils depicting patriotic and sportive themes. Her vivid imagination had always conjured Dante-esque illustrations ablaze with decadence and lascivious oleographs portraying naked women in abandoned poses.

Viewing the grandeur, her hellfire and brimstone pictures vanished, and she forgot to wonder about shootings and stabbings. Overhead, six-branched chandeliers with crystal prisms caught the soft light of the lantern and made rainbow patterns. Through the sea of upturned chair legs, a gleaming black brilliance against the wall beckoned.

The New American upright parlor piano.

Despite her resolve to resist any enjoyment out of the upright until she had her own, a spark of excitement heightened her pulse. She was certain once she sat down at the keys, everything her teacher, Miss Lovejoy, had taught her would come flying back.

Amelia hurried to retrieve the lantern and her bag, in which she'd packed everything musically essential she could think of. Threading her way around the tables, she put the lamp on top of the piano. She stood back to admire the beautifully carved panels, Queen Anne trusses, and exquisitely finished hardwood case.

The Rogers & Company catalog drawing didn't do the New American justice.

Amelia ran her fingertips over the music desk, then set her bag on the floor. Taking a seat, she lifted the nickel-plated hinge on the fall board. Ivory keys and polished ebony sharps spread in seven and one-third octaves. She removed her other glove and positioned her hands in the proper fashion, with wrists high, and a delicate curve of her fingers. Her right thumb on middle C, she ran through her drill.

The piano was a little out of tune from being jostled in the shipping, but still, the notes were full and round. She tried the three foot pedals, prompting the chords to be first *mezzo piano,* then *mezzo forte.* Caught up in the practice piece, she forgot about Frank Brody being in the next room. As soon as she finished her four-four time drill, she went on to her second drill of three-four time. Smiling, she let the music tingle through her fingers. She hadn't played a piano in nine years, and much to her delight, she remembered how.

As her recital selection, Miss Lovejoy had made her memorize a Bach Minuet in F-sharp. Amelia concentrated, and after a few tries, the melody came back and she was able to play the notes through to the end. On the final chord, she softly giggled and folded her hands in her lap.

Loud clapping erupted to her left. Startled, she swung her head toward the applause, distressed to find Frank Brody lounging in the open doorway to his private quarters. She shot off the stool, reached for her music bag, and took a step backward. Clutching the handle to her breasts, she stammered, "W-What are you doing here?"

He shoved his tousled hair from his eyes, but the lengthy black locks tumbled back to tease his brow. "I live here."

"Of course . . . it's just that you surprised me. I . . ." She fumbled for the proper words, but there were none appropriate for a lady to say to a man half-naked.

Chapter

4

$\mathcal{M}$r. Brody wore no shirt.

The five pearl buttons down the front of his white vest with navy polka dots were unfastened, and Amelia couldn't help staring at the smooth skin showing through the gaping opening. She'd never seen a near-naked man before, and the glimpse of taut flesh made her throat go dry.

Sleep like the dead, indeed! Trying to keep a modicum of decorum, she said, "I thought you'd be sleeping."

"I woke up." He shifted his stance, and the waistband of his white duck trousers slackened and she saw his navel. She darted her gaze to the floor, unable to meet his eyes. A mistake. His feet were bare and not unattractive, as she'd assumed men's feet would be.

The pressing heat of the saloon seemed to thicken. Feeling light-headed, she blinked.

"What do you have in the bag?" he asked.

She lifted her chin and replied, "My busts."

Frank lifted a brow. "Miss Marshall, I make it my

business to stay on top of the complexities of women's clothing, and I've never heard of the need to carry around a bag of falsies in case something happens to the real things."

Amelia's face grew hot. "N-Not my—my—my—*those!* My *busts*. My replicas of the masters."

"Yeah." Frank's gaze swooped across her neckline. "I've seen the shape yours are in. They look like masters to me."

Aghast, she blurted, "I was referring to Mozart, Bach, Wagner, Mozart, Beethoven, and Verdi."

"You said Mozart twice."

"I know. He had a father—Leopold. His son, Wolfgang Amadeus Mozart, is more widely known," she rambled, trying to keep from gawking at his indecent, muscular composition. The music bag in her hand began to weigh her shoulder down. Not only had she lugged her miniature marble busts, she'd packed a silk piano scarf, metronome with fixed key, and Kinkel's Piano Folios No. 1 and No. 2. "Amadeus lived only thirty-five years, but in his short lifetime he wrote over six hundred compositions—operas, symphonies, chamber music, a great deal of piano mus—"

"Whatever." Frank pushed away from the door frame. "Give me that bag. You look ready to pass out."

Amelia begged to differ with him but didn't have a chance as he grabbed the handle from her hands. Black spots clouded her vision, and she had to sit down on the piano stool to catch her breath. "It seems I've developed a sudden headache."

Frank tossed her petit point bag aside and knelt down in front of her on one knee. She stared at him, embarrassed by the wave of dizziness incapacitating her.

"It's no wonder you have a headache, Miss Marshall. Seems like you overdress pretty often," he said as he rubbed the stiff cotton of her jacket sleeve between his thumb and forefinger. Though he didn't directly touch her skin, the friction he created by his fingertips set off warning bells in her head. "The other day on the train platform, you almost fainted, too."

"I assure you, I'm not going to faint." But she wasn't all that sure. Frank Brody was caressing her sleeve. Her insides burned; at the same time, a dull throb fixed on her temple.

"Well, if you do, I'm going to unbutton your dress and loosen your corset so you can breathe."

She definitely would not faint!

"I think you better sit here for a minute," he suggested.

Amelia nodded, but he didn't move away from her. He had a truly handsome face, even though he needed to shave the dark shadows of a beard; she regarded his generous mouth and rugged but classic nose. The man had a monopoly on virility.

She swept her gaze downward, unable to ignore the contours of his chest, nor the flat nipple peeking out from the edge of his vest.

Managing to find her voice, she said, "I would appreciate it if you dressed, Mr. Brody, while you're in my company."

"I did." His bright blue eyes were direct. "I put my vest and pants on."

"You're barefoot."

"That's not all that was bare a minute ago. Damn, it's hot enough in here to peel the hide off a Gila monster."

"I don't believe in monsters, He-la or any other sort, Mr. Brody. Even Shelley doesn't frighten me," she countered, wishing she had her fan.

His expression grew serious. "Is she real ugly?"

She massaged her forehead, not in a frame of mind to explain Mary Shelley's *Frankenstein* to him. "Never mind, Mr. Brody."

"Why aren't the front doors wide open?" Frank rose and began to walk toward the entrance.

Amelia stood—too quickly. The room spun. "I didn't want anyone to see me."

"Why the hell not?"

How could she explain that being in this room made her embarrassed? That she was loath for anyone to see her in the saloon and remember the incident with Jonas Pray. "You wouldn't understand," was all Amelia replied, bracing her hand on the edge of the piano.

"You look like you're going to keel over, sister. Let me make you a Baptist lemonade." He headed for the bar. His back to her, she took the opportunity to wave her hand in front of her face.

"Mr. Brody," she tartly addressed, "you keep misinterpreting my religious affiliation. I'm neither a sister of the order nor a Baptist. If you must know, I'm a Methodist."

He went behind the long counter. "Sweetheart, a Baptist lemonade is nothing but pure lemonade. No liquor." Walking to the center, he let out a painful yelp. "Dammit to hell!"

Amelia's ears burned. "Mr. Brody, may I remind you—"

"What are all my forty-fours doing on the floor?"

"Forty-fours?"

"Yeah, the bullets for my Smith and Wesson American."

Bullets? Amelia forced an expression of innocence on her face. "I wouldn't know."

"Somebody dumped the carton over. It wasn't Pap." Frank crouched down and his voice grew muffled. "He would have cleaned them up. He's always cleaning up after me."

Amelia feigned a great fascination with one of the hunting paintings on the wall. She tried to watch him without being obvious. She didn't dare confess to being the culprit, afraid he'd change his mind about her giving lessons in his saloon.

Frank surfaced with a handful of bullets; he dumped the silver cartridges into the empty box, then put them away. "Did you happen to knock the carton off the shelf when you took that lamp for the piano, Miss Marshall?"

"Me?" she squeaked. "Heavens no. I . . . I . . . No."

"If you did, it wouldn't matter." He procured a cutting board, knife, and lemon. "But you should have left the doors open so you could see what you were doing."

She nodded but still didn't admit her guilt.

Frank's movements were fluid and concise, as if he could operate his bar tools blindfolded. He sliced the lemon through the middle, then squeezed the juice from each half into a glass. Producing a block of ice, he began to chip pieces off with a pick. He glanced at her, and she changed the direction of her gaze, not wanting to be caught staring at him. Again.

Looking directly ahead, she realized he'd left the door to his apartment wide open, and from where she sat, she could see the messed-up bedclothes of his iron bedstead, a pair of drawers on the floor, and discarded boots. She leaned a little to the left to get a better view, but the hip pocket on Frank's white trousers and the outline of his hip blocked her view. Slowly tilting her head up, she forced herself to smile at his face while sitting straighter.

"See anything unusual?" he inquired, stretching his hand out to offer her the drink.

Amelia felt heat steal onto her cheeks. "N-No."

"Here's your lemonade."

She eyed the glass; beads of moisture formed on the outside, hinting the drink inside was cold and quenching. "Thank you," she murmured, taking it from him. Not fully trusting the ingredients to be wholesome, she sampled only a small sip. She couldn't find any fault in the blend of sweet and sour. The drink was perfectly mixed.

"It's just lemons, sugar, and water," he elaborated with irritation in his voice, apparently seeing she was skeptical over the contents. "If there was liquor in there, you'd have all the sensations of swallowing a lighted kerosene lamp."

"Why, then, would a man possibly want a drink?"

"Having the fair assumption you've never been drunk, Miss Marshall, that's something *you* wouldn't understand. Sometimes there's no better exhilaration for what ails you. Booze brings on a good-natured, easy friendliness if you don't let it pickle you."

Frank padded silently to the doorway of his room. "I'm going to open the back door. Generally, no one ever walks by there."

She watched as he stepped over his wrinkled underwear and unlatched the door, which had a wire-cloth screen. Almost instantly, she felt relief from the stuffiness.

On his way back, Frank kicked his drawers aside, then entered the saloon. Stepping close to the piano stool, he stared at her a long moment, as if he were contemplating asking her something personal. She waited, searching his thickly lashed eyes . . . waited as her heartbeat tapped out an uneven rhythm. Waited like a silly ingenue at her first dance. But she knew better. She would not be putty in his hand. *She would not!* He'd refused to let her have the piano. She didn't like him. Not at all. He was the type of man who hired Silver Starlights so they could ride away with book and Bible salesmen. . . .

He leaned forward, and to her dismay, she unwillingly swayed toward him. Frank's lips moved, and he merely whispered, "Drink your lemonade, Miss Marshall, so I don't have to dump you in the horse trough to revive you from a dead faint."

Amelia straightened. "Well I like that."

"I thought you might," he drawled with a hint of devilment. Before she could respond, he repeated, "Keep drinking your lemonade. Your cheeks are still flushed."

"Are they?"

"Yes. The color of sloe gin. Now drink."

Swallowing a delicate quantity of lemonade, she hoped slow-pouring gin wasn't a flaming red concoction.

Frank went to his icebox, pulled out a bottle, then grabbed a large box of animal crackers. He proceeded to pull the chairs off the table closest to her, and when they were all on the floor, he sat down. A *phisst* sound came from the bottle's neck when he popped the wire cap off. He held on to the beer in a most peculiar manner—with the neck between his middle three fingers. She wondered how he could perform such a trick as he took a drink. An obviously satisfying one, from the smile on his lips. Then it dawned on her he was drinking liquor in broad daylight.

She gave him her mother's most reprimanding frown as she glared at the beer bottle. "Really, Mr. Brody, have you no control?"

"With all the liquor in this place, I could be a drunkard. Seeing as I'm not, that says something for my control." He took another leisurely swallow, then added, "I'm sure Budweiser wished I did have less control."

"Mr. Budweiser must be a good customer."

"Yeah. He and Jim Beam are popular."

"I've never heard mention of Mr. Budweiser and Mr. Beam. They must not live in Weeping Angel."

"No, they only come up the first and third Friday of the month. Fisk at the Short Line handles them with kid gloves."

"What profession are these gentlemen in who need to be handled with kid gloves?"

He smiled easily when he said, "Spirits."

"The spirits of the Lord," she interpreted with offense. "And you allow them to partake in liquor?"

"I've heard it said, some men claim to see the Lord when they're in Mr. Beam's company."

"Disgraceful." She *tsked.* "I most heartily disapprove."

"I was certain you would." Frank brought the beer to his lips. "Now that we got Mr. Budweiser and Mr. Beam out of the way, I'm ready, so go ahead," he said, opening the crackers and eating one.

Baffled, she stared at him. "Ready for what, Mr. Brody?"

"Ready to listen to you play the piano."

"I beg your pardon—"

"There you go again. We've gone through this already. Women don't beg for my pardon."

"Well!" she declared. "Why must you twist my words to suit your vulgarity?"

"Because you're fun to tease, Miss Marshall."

There was something warm and enchanting about his humor, despite her being the object of his amusement. He had an arresting smile that touched her every nerve ending and put her senses in disorder. Normally, she was quite restrained around men. But Mr. Brody's magnetism turned her to mush.

Amelia was no longer in a frame of mind to continue her practice. "I'm finished." She stood and set the remainder of her lemonade on his table, then picked up her music bag.

He continued to munch on his animal crackers without making a move to stop her from her prompt departure. "You never took out your busts."

She gave him a sharp look. "My busts will have to come out another time."

"I'll be waiting to see them."

Feeling herself blush profusely, she strode toward

the entrance on her no-nonsense heels. "Good afternoon, Mr. Brody." Though she didn't wish him one at all. She hoped the remainder of his day turned out perfectly horrid.

Frank never slept until noon on Sundays because he wasn't open for business those nights. He'd tried keeping gospel hours a few times, but he hadn't been able to attract any customers—not even the Basques who periodically came into town for supplies. And if he couldn't tempt the loner sheepherders, he sure as hell couldn't entice the men of Weeping Angel— piano or not. Even Lloyd Fairplay shut down the Palace on Sundays. The womenfolk kept their men on short lengths of chain after church, and Frank had to give in to the day of rest, going as far as carrying his relaxation through to Mondays while he was already in the mood for recreation.

While everyone else clustered in the Christ Redeemer church listening to Thorpe sermonize something fierce, he and Pap spent Sundays shooting up empty bottles and swinging a baseball bat at cans in Reverend's Meadow. When they were finished blowing glass to smithereens and whacking tin, they waded hip-deep in Tadpole Lake and whipped their silk fishing lines over the glassy water. The rainbow trout took to their feather flies so readily, there was no need to pursue grasshoppers over the hillsides.

When Frank felt the cool water surrounding his legs, heard the choking squeals of blackbirds, and smelled the wintergreen, there was no greater heaven to him. He didn't need Reverend Thorpe's preaching to convince him otherwise.

"Did you bring the Ethel Mays?" Pap asked Frank as they walked the boardwalk on Divine Street carrying their tackle, poles, revolvers, and a gunnysack of empty food cans and beer bottles.

"I brought them."

"I wonder who thought to name trout flies Ethel May."

Frank hiked his left shoulder to more firmly secure the strap of his creel basket. "I suppose somebody who thought Ethel May looked like a trout fly."

"Yeah . . . I reckon."

They turned right at Dodge Street and went past the church just as the morning service let out. Frank never saw more suits in one place than Sundays at eleven o'clock. With their souls saved from sinful annihilation for another six days, the congregation milled underneath the shade of maple and cottonwood trees shaking hands as if they'd never met before. They talked in voices loud enough for Frank to hear bits of their conversations as they discussed the Sears, Roebuck & Co. catalog items, recipes, and making plans for Sunday suppers. But as soon as he and Pap were upon them, octaves lowered to whispers.

Frank was fairly certain he became a more pressing topic than the price of dress goods or the *Farmer's Almanac*. He wouldn't have minded so much if the men didn't act differently when they weren't under the preacher's thumb. They had no problem bellying up to the bar with a congenial how-do-you-do during the week; and it seemed to Frank more than a little hypocritical that they would view him in a less favorable light on the seventh day.

Thorpe must have spread the covenant of darkness on them real thick this morning.

Striding by sporting an expression of what he hoped to be measurable affability, and with an obligatory nod now and then, Frank caught a glimpse of duck wings through a sea of millinery trimmings. He kept his gaze directed on the feathered ornamentation, and as soon as the wearer separated from the churchgoers, he caught sight of Amelia beneath the notable hat. She'd efficiently pinned her shiny brown hair in a sort of springlike twist at the nape of her slender neck. Had he not seen the strands of hair tease her brow the day she'd played the piano in his saloon, he would have assumed her coiffure never rumpled; had he not listened to her feminine and breezy laughter after she finished her musical piece, he would have assumed she kept her voice in a bland tone befitting a school-marm.

But he had seen and heard otherwise, and viewing her this way—all coiled and subdued—suddenly didn't seem natural anymore.

Amelia paired up with Narcissa Dodge and smiled at something the mayor's wife told her. There was something appealing about the way Amelia smiled, and Frank figured Pap must have seen Miss Marshall smile once before he made up his mind to give her the chase.

Looking up, Amelia's eyes met Frank's and the animation left her face. The softened curves of her mouth were suddenly replaced by a wary line. She kept her expression under stern restraint when gazing at him, and it bothered him that she felt the need to bottle up her smile when he was around.

Frank let his glance travel from her to Pap. He barely had time to wonder if his friend had seen Miss Marshall, too, when Reverend Thorpe made a special point to single Frank out.

Dressed in a black vicuña suit more appropriate for coffin wear than a summer day, the preacher greeted, "Mr. Brody," in a tone too Bible friendly to keep Frank at ease.

He nodded tightly, his eyes shaded from the sun's brilliance by the brim of his panama hat. "Rev."

"Are you going fishing?"

Frank gazed at the fishing pole in his hand, then back at the reverend. "Looks that way."

"A blessed, beautiful day for it, too."

Sunlight caught on the gilt-stamped cross gracing

the cover of Thorpe's Bible. He held the round-cornered book in his large hands, front forward, and pressed to his chest. The holier-than-thou position was wasted on Frank; he didn't bow under scriptures anymore.

Reverend Thorpe smiled, showing his mouthful of big teeth. He didn't make a move to let Frank by, and kept on smiling until Frank got to feeling itchy under the collar.

"Anything you want, Rev?" Frank asked too late. The parishioners had circled around like a wagon train—him and Pap in the middle as if they were Indians waiting to get shot at by a hundred primed rifles.

"As a matter of fact, I did want to extend an invitation to the Lord's house."

Frank could feel the expectant gazes boring into him. "I don't accept invitations to ice-cream socials, tea parties, or church. Especially not church."

"I hope you'll change your mind, Mr. Brody. I do believe you are a Christian, despite your unsuitable occupation. After all, you're sharing the piano with Miss Marshall."

Uncomfortable with the crowd, Frank needed breathing room. "It doesn't take a Christian to do that. Now if—"

"I don't believe I've been introduced to your friend," the preacher said in a rush.

Pap shifted his feet. "O'Cleary. Pap O'Cleary."

The reverend kept his stronghold on the Good Book, aiming in Pap's direction. June's devouring sun reflected off the gold cross like a mirror and beamed a spiritual effulgence on Pap's face, as if he were being baptized without water. Thorpe didn't switch the angle of his Bible when he said, "I'd like to invite you to services as well, Mr. O'Cleary."

Squinting and trying to duck, Pap hastened to reply, "Go ahead."

"Would you come to next Sunday's services, Mr. O'Cleary?"

"Hell, no."

A rolling gasp emanated from the crowd, only to be broken by a boy's query near Frank's trouser leg.

"Hey, Mr. Brody, is that a real Spalding baseball bat you're holdin'?"

Frank gazed at the bat in his left hand, then at the freckle-faced kid at his hip. "Yeah. A genuine league model."

"Holy smoke!"

"Daniel Beamguard, you mind your phraseology!" clucked Mrs. Dorothea Beamguard. "Especially in the company of Reverend Thorpe." She gave Pap a severe glare. "Unlike others who have no manners at all."

Pap took offense with a snort, then skewed up his face in a heated shade of bully red. Those standing at his right abruptly disbanded, and Pap took off before Frank could escape through the gap after him.

Neither the disruption, nor the reprimanding from his mother, had any apparent effect on Daniel. He kept right after Frank. "Hey, Mr. Brody. Would you ever let me try it out? Huh? I'd be real careful. I ain't never hit off a genuine Spalding. All my Pop sells at the mercantile are handmade bats out of maple."

"Don't you downtalk your father's merchandise, young man," Mrs. Beamguard chastised, grabbing hold of her son's broadcloth collar and giving him a firm yank toward her.

"Ah, gee!" Daniel squirmed away from his mother. "You're embarrassin' me, Ma!" He broke loose with a jerk and kept on after Frank. "Them maple ones are sissy bats, Mr. Brody. I can't hit nothin' but fly balls with 'em. Can I try it out, huh? Huh?"

Frank felt extremely uncomfortable. All eyes were on him. If he told the kid to get lost, he'd look like a spoilsport. On the other hand, if he promised the kid, he was certain there'd be a good number who'd take offense over a bartender teaching an impressionable boy the fine art of baseball hitting.

Either way, he'd lose.

"Well, boy," Frank mused aloud, "I'll have to think on it."

There. No commitment in any direction.

"Think long, Mr. Brody," Daniel pleaded. "Drink a lot of hard stuff while you're thinking. My ma says that all you do in that saloon of yours is think up smut and drink hard stuff while you're thinking."

"Daniel!" Dorothea cried.

Frank's nostrils flared and he felt that damn tic—the one even the nuns hadn't been able to whop out of him—kick up at his jaw. "Well then, *ma'am,* I'm sure you won't be allowing Danny-boy here to take lessons from Miss Marshall in my smut hall."

"I-I—" Dorothea stammered, then straightened her shoulders. "One must make amends, Mr. Brody. Of course my Daniel will be taking lessons. I'm going to personally escort him to and from them to see for myself the inside of that bar of yours."

"You do that. And I'll make sure it's worth your while. I'll keep all my smut in full view. Now, if you'll excuse me, folks," Frank said, and nudged his way past Thorpe who had dried up speechless. "I've got to be moving on."

Frank glanced around for Pap but didn't find him. He did make eye contact with Emmaline Shelby, though. She stood off to the side, her black hair all done up in pretty waves, and with a silver cross dangling from the lace pin on her collar. He'd never seen her dressed up for religion before. Prior to their beginning a relationship, he'd known she was a churchgoing woman, and he'd asked her if she'd get all righteous and weepy on him with regret after they started something. She'd sort of shocked him with her reply of, "I know how to handle this type of situation. I have before." Then she'd gone on to say, the Lord need only know her business on Sundays; what she did with the rest of the week was strictly her own. So he'd let the subject go, but he hadn't counted on seeing her in the clutches of the Christ Redeemer right under his nose. It left him feeling rather unscrupulous about diddling one of their own.

Esther Parks, the ticket agent's wife, made her way to Emmaline's side, and the two of them went off before Frank could make heads or tails out of what Emmaline could be thinking about him. She'd made it quite clear two days ago when he'd brought his laundry in for cleaning—and some steam put in his pants—she hadn't been too happy about his consideration for the piano teacher. One look at the business-like pinch on her face as he'd set his clothes bag on the counter, and any thoughts of extra starch fled his mind. She'd politely asked if he wanted his muslin shirts laundered with blueing or borax. He'd stated bleach, then after an awkward lapse of silence, he'd left.

He couldn't understand why Emmaline was so agitated about the situation. Amelia Marshall wasn't a hot commodity type of woman. True, she was pretty, but not with the same passion as Emmaline.

As he walked toward Gopher Road, Frank saw Pap loitering in front of the mayor's house. A cast-iron railing surrounded the lawn and front border of curly pink rose bushes, and Pap had his foot propped up on the mud scraper. He'd ingratiated himself into the company of Amelia and Mrs. Dodge. The two women stood on the other side of the closed gate while Pap gave his jaw plenty of exercise by planting a crop of words on his plaster-smiling audience.

As Frank approached, both women looked up, but Pap kept on talking.

"I played an upright in the El Dorado. You've heard of the El Dorado, haven't you, Miss Marshall?"

"I'm afraid I haven't," she replied, turning back to face Pap.

"Why I'll be ding busted, Miss Marshall," Pap said, shaking his derby-topped head. "Everybody's heard of the El Dorado down in San Francisco. It's the best damn gambling house I ever played in." Pap shifted his stance and brought his foot down.

Frank noticed Amelia grew visibly embarrassed over Pap's brash language. But Pap didn't back off. He kept right on, and both ladies were apparently too cultured—and perhaps too perplexed by his attentions—to stop him.

"What all can you play, Miss Marshall?" Pap asked while adjusting the gunnysack of bottles and cans slung over his back. They made a trash-sounding noise, as if Pap were hauling a bin of garbage. "Any ballads? Popular tunes? *Love* songs?" He gave her a broad, infatuated smile, and when she didn't make a comment, he went on. "I know a few orchestral pieces by the Greats. You know, like Back and Vagger."

Amelia nodded and corrected. "I believe you mean Bach and Wagner."

Frank couldn't figure out what had gotten into Pap. Pap O'Cleary was running at the mouth like a braggart full of more verbal lather than suds in a shaving mug.

"Yeah, I mean those fellows," he amended, then kept yacking. "Say, do you know how to play 'The Band Played On?'"

Amelia gave Frank a short glance, Pap still unaware of his approach, then she shook her head.

"Ah, I'm sure you've heard it." Pap started to hum the tune, then sang, "Casey would waltz with a strawberry blonde, and the band played on . . . hmm-hum-hmm-hum-hmm-hmm . . ." Pap swung his arm a bit, his fishing pole hitting the fence. He put the words into baritone. "He'd glide . . . hmm-hum-hmm . . . But his brain was so loaded—"

"Bust your talkbox, Pap," Frank said, striding up to the trio. "Can't you see you're wearing the ladies out?"

"Huh?" Pap whipped around, the superfine hook on the end of his line slicing through the air. It snared Amelia's hat, and as Pap inadvertently jerked the pole, he pulled her toward the fence.

"Ow! Get it off me!" Amelia braced herself against the black iron spears and stood immobile.

"Oh, dear!" Narcissa cried and went to Amelia's side.

"What in the hell?" Pap's eyes widened as soon as he saw he'd hooked a hat and the woman beneath the brim. "Why, I'll be damned! I've caught you, Miss Marshall." He didn't give the line any slack when he added, "Now all I have to do is reel you in."

Amelia obviously didn't appreciate Pap's humor. "Unhook me right this minute!" She looked at Frank when she spoke, but he doubted she was talking to him. Just the same, he dropped his baseball bat and pole and took several strides to reach her side.

"Tip your head a little," he suggested.

She lowered her chin a bit. In a quick examination of her hat, he found a lot of ribbons, feathers, and pieces of green stuff. A gleaming gold-filigree knob caught his eye.

"This fancy gold thing your hat pin, Miss Marshall?" She started to nod, but he stopped her by cupping her cheek with his left hand. "Don't move your head."

"Yes . . . that's my hat pin," she whispered in a voice that broke. He noticed she kept her eyes downcast so he couldn't see their color. But he remembered they were brown. She sure had soft skin; she felt like velvet beneath his palm. And Pap was wrong, she did have freckles. Three. On the bridge of her nose.

"What are you waiting for?" Mrs. Dodge inquired. Pap piped in, too. "Yeah, Frank. Just yank it out."

"I will." Frank grasped the pin and eased the eight-inch length of wire from her hat. As soon as he had it in his hand, Amelia skirted out from under his touch. Her eyelashes flew up, and she stared at him as if he were on fire. He lifted his gaze to her uncovered hair. He liked the color brown. Not too plain and with threads of gold woven throughout.

"Thank you," she supplied, keeping that peculiar look on her face as he handed her the pin.

The duck-wing hat dangled from the end of Pap's hook, and he had to dump the sack of bottles and cans in order to grab hold of the brim to assess the damage. "Never caught me a mallard before. I'll unsnarl it for you, Miss Marshall." He wiggled the hook out without any regard for the delicacy of the hat's ornaments.

Narcissa Dodge laid a hand on Amelia's shoulder and spoke in a quiet tone. "I'm not feeling well, Amelia. I think it's the heat. I want to go inside and lie down before we start the chicken."

"Of course. I'll go with you." She took her hat from Pap, who offered no apologies. Then, shifting her head at a slight angle, she returned, "It's been a . . . an experience, Mr. O'Cleary."

"That it has, Miss Marshall. I'm anxious to see you at the saloon for your first lesson." He picked up the gunnysack. "When do you think that will be?"

"This week I'm sure."

"Hey! Tomorrow's the start of this week. So I'll see you soon, *Miss Marshall.*"

"I . . . yes, I suppose you will." Amelia turned, put her arm around Mrs. Dodge, and the pair walked toward the house.

Pap smiled after them, and Frank bent down to retrieve his bat and pole.

"What do you think, Frank?" Pap asked with moon eyes. "Did I make a good first impression?"

"Well, Pap, if you're asking my opinion, I don't think you ought to aim for a summer wedding."

Chapter

5

❧

The sun mercilessly beat down on Amelia's hat as she struggled to push her Acme lawn mower across the carpet of lush grass in her rear yard. She shouldn't have let seven days lapse between the cuttings, but the mix-up with the piano had thrown her off schedule. And now the lawn had grown too tall, and she had to use every muscle in her body to maneuver the unwieldy machine.

She would have adjusted the cutter bar, only she wasn't sure how to or if she had the right tool in her household set. Most likely, Coney Island Applegate would know. He was the towheaded nine-year-old boy who used to mow her lawn for a nickel. That was before a nickel was a nickel saved.

As the four blades sliced the grass, Amelia let her mind wander to Narcissa. She was worried about her. Lately, Narcissa's health had been failing. At first, she had only complained of dizzy spells; but now, it seemed as if she didn't have any energy left, and her appetite had dwindled to almost nothing.

Last night after Sunday supper, when she and

Narcissa were in the kitchen washing dishes, Amelia made Narcissa promise she would visit Dr. White for a check-up. Narcissa had sadly waved off Amelia's concern, stating she was nearly twice Amelia's age and her body was slowing down. The disclosure had hurt her friend, for Amelia knew how much Narcissa wanted a child; but she and Cincinatus had never been able to conceive one.

Amelia didn't want to believe Narcissa. Even the change in a woman's life didn't make her deteriorate in just a few months. No, something was wrong; and as Amelia huffed to turn the roller and wheels around the trunk base of her silver linden tree, she began to fear the worst for Narcissa.

The branches provided a canopy of welcome relief, and Amelia paused to revel in the linden's offered shade. Its creamy white flowers scented the air, and the peaceful drone of bees flitting about provided Amelia with music. She leaned her back against the smooth bark and wished she was finished with the sizable lawn so she could sit on the veranda and sip a glass of lemonade as cool and refreshing as the one Mr. Brody had made her.

Thinking of the quenching drink, Amelia slid her backside down the trunk and sat on the cushion of her two petticoats. She placed her feet apart, then hiked her pale blue percale skirt above her knees in an unladylike manner. The air felt good on her legs. She counted herself lucky she'd worn her short muslin drawers, only thigh high, and lightweight cotton hose.

She closed her eyes and promised herself she'd get up in just a minute. She hadn't slept soundly last night, her slumber distracted with thoughts of Frank Brody. She kept on reliving that fleeting moment on Narcissa's walkway when he'd removed her hat. She'd been thrown willy-nilly into a whirlpool of feelings outrageously different from the ones she'd felt for Jonas Pray. Her every nerve ending had focused on the way Frank had held her cheek in his strong hand; the way he'd taken charge. Thinking about the familiarity of his conduct brought tingles across her skin. What had possessed her to stand idle while he plucked the pin from her hat?

She knew better than to get caught up in a man's presence. She had prior experience with the spell of attraction. Her world had gone up in a poof the last time she went under. She had to be strong and resilient, just as Mother and Aunt Clara would have been and would have expected from her. No more backbone of jelly. From now on she would be firm and impenetrable because people tended to make the same mistakes over and over if they didn't nip them in the bud.

That decided, Amelia vowed to attack the lawn without bending to the power of the tangled green turf. She would cut the whole of it in no time flat. All she needed was another minute to gather her strength. She was feeling rather drowsy and enjoying the shade too much to leave it just yet. She would . . . soon. When her feet didn't hurt anymore. . . .

Sometime later, Amelia felt a tickle on her leg or, actually, her skin where her stocking ended in a roll and her embroidery-hemmed drawers began. Too sleepy to move, she dozed off again and hoped whatever it was would stop. It didn't. She lifted her hand to swat at that spot; then in the recesses of her mind, she came awake with the thought of insects. Perhaps ants, or worse yet, a big hairy spider.

Her eyes flew open and she bit back a scream when she gazed at her leg only to find nothing there. But *someone* was next to her, and from the pristine white of the trousers, she knew exactly who before raising her chin to see her guest.

"Frank . . ." His name left her lips in a rather sleep-scratchy voice, and too late, she realized she'd been dreaming about him and inappropriately called him by his first name. When he said nothing in return, she followed the line of his intense gaze.

He stared at her exposed legs . . . her drawers and her hose. In a scant second, she grabbed hold of her skirt and sailed the fabric across her limbs in a flurry of starched white and blue. Thoroughly embarrassed, she scrambled to her feet—or at least tried. She became entangled in the volume of material and stumbled. She felt a supportive grip on her upper arm, but slapped at Frank's hand.

"You needn't concern yourself, Mr. Brody. I'm capable of standing on my own."

He merely laughed and let her go, only so she could sway toward the tree and push off from it with disgust at her sudden clumsiness.

"You caught me unaware," she snapped, feeling undressed. Her resolve to be firm and direct seemed to be melting under the hot sun. Bringing her trembling hands upward, she adjusted the cockeyed tilt of her gardening hat. What must he think of her? Napping outside with her limbs exposed. Surely her face outshone the red cherries in Beamguard's Mercantile. "I thought there was a spider on me."

"There was," he stated in a rich voice, "but I flicked it off with my finger."

Her eyes narrowed, and she suspected the story he gave her was far from the truth. *"Humph.* I was mistaken. There *was* a big spider on me. The kind with," she paused and looked into his smiling gaze, "blue eyes and black hair. I believe Beadle's Gardening Handbook calls them wolf spiders."

"I think you're right."

"I know I'm right." She took hold of the handle on her lawn mower. "One thing about these Acme mowers—they're big enough to run over either a wolf or a spider."

He laughed deeply, then stepped aside.

She swept her gaze over him, once again reminded of his good looks. But she wouldn't waste thoughts on such silliness, so she checked the time from the chatelaine watch pinned to her bodice. "It isn't noon yet. You should be sleeping."

"I don't sleep in on Sundays and Mondays. I'm closed for business."

"Oh." She lifted her brows but refused to be taken in by the easy smile on his nice lips. "Is there something I can do for you, Mr. Brody?"

"Not really," he admitted. "But from the crooked rows in your lawn, it looks like you need me to do something for you." He lounged next to her linden tree with his arms crossed over his chest. "Did you do the front yard by yourself?"

"I did," she challenged. She'd thought she'd done a darn good job of the lawn, this being her first time behind the Acme. So she'd run over the flower head of her cobalt hydrangea, fleeced the tops of her forget-me-nots, and nicked the thick base of her pecan tree. And maybe the perimeter of the yard still had green fringe six inches tall in a two-inch width where the right wheel of the mower prevented her from cutting a clean edge. She'd clip the rest with her grass shears when she got a chance.

"You should have one of the boys in town do this for you."

"I did. Titus and Altana's son was cutting it for me, but—" She stopped herself short. She couldn't tell Frank Brody she'd run out of money. Neither could she think of a good excuse why she'd let the boy go. "But . . . never mind, is all. The reasons are my own reasons."

"Their boy's the one named after that amusement park in New York?"

"Yes, he is. Coney Island."

"Yeah, that's him. Coney Island. He owns Hamlet."

"Unfortunately," she countered, thinking of the

black Hampshire boar with a white belt, who periodically came through her fence and rooted up her petunias for a shady place to sleep.

"I kind of like Hamlet. He comes around the saloon every once in a while sniffing for slop."

"He should be kept in a pen, just like any other pig," she replied. "Now I'm sure you didn't come to discuss Hamlet or my lawn, Mr. Brody. What *did* you come for?" She eyed him with subtle curiosity.

He stretched out his arm and she refrained from taking a step back. "You left your glove behind in the Moon Rock a couple of days ago."

Looking at the scrap of delicate white in his large hand, she took the glove from him and stuffed it into the band of her yard apron. "Thank you. It wasn't necessary for you to come over."

"I wasn't sure when I'd see you next." Frank slid his hand into his trouser pocket and came out with a tissue-wrapped fancy candy. "You want a lemon drop?"

"No, thank you."

He removed the paper and slipped the hard candy into his mouth. Rolling it around his tongue while he sucked on it, he said, "You haven't come back to the saloon to take out your busts, and frankly, I'm concerned."

She knew he was teasing her. He had to be. No man would make mention of such a thing if he weren't trying to get her goat. She wouldn't let him see he was unraveling her. She'd simply ignore him.

But she couldn't stop staring at his lips . . . the way he licked them . . . the way he made a faint suction sound with his tongue around that blasted piece of candy. The smell of sugary lemons lingered in the air, and she felt the pinch of steel from her corset cut into her ribs.

"Are you sure you don't want a lemon drop, Miss Marshall?" he drawled.

"No," she shot back, gripping the mower's maroon handle more resolutely. "I don't want a lemon drop. I want my piano."

There, she'd said it.

The gist of the situation hit her as if she'd been smacked on the top of her head with a walnut. The only reason he unnerved her was because of the upright. Because he had it and she didn't. That's why she put so much stock into watching him . . . having sordid thoughts about him. It was only natural she think about him when she was really thinking about the New American.

"I figure you do," was all he offered.

Amelia didn't want to dawdle with Frank anymore. He'd gotten her upset when she told herself she wouldn't let him upset her further. She'd mapped out the next few months, resigned to giving lessons in his drinking parlor. She hadn't penned in time for arguments with the saloon's owner.

"If you'll excuse me, Mr. Brody, I need to get back to work. Again, thank you for bringing my glove by." She wouldn't be rude to him, despite the temper he put her in. "Good day."

Holding tight to the handle, she shoved off. The *whir* of the blades thankfully snuffed out the wild pounding of her heart. There was something about Frank Brody that put her into a tizzy every time she was near him.

Amelia had barely gotten a few feet when he stepped beside her and plucked her hands off the bar. "Slide over, sweetheart. This is a man's job."

"I'm perfectly capable of—"

"—going into the house and getting me a glass of something cold to drink."

Her mouth slacked open as her mind fumbled for a fitting retort. She watched him retreat, his long legs making fast work of the row she'd started. He made the job look so effortless, it pained her to think of the aches her joints would have tonight when she soaked in her tub.

Words to make him halt were on the tip of her tongue. She'd tell him to stop and let her do the rest. But when she took a deep breath and saw the expanse of the yard left to mow—over a half acre with a colorful border of flowers, vines, shrubs, and shade trees—and all she'd done was a twenty-yard loop . . . well, pride sort of simmered away to steam.

Just this once.

"All right, Mr. Brody," she called after him over the grind of well-oiled gears. "You may cut my lawn, but remember"—she raised her forefinger—"I started it for you."

With that, she turned and headed for the white-washed steps leading to her kitchen to make him a strawberry shrub.

An hour later, Amelia stood with her hand on the outdoor pump while Frank stuck the revolving Crown lawn sprinkler into the ground. "Okay, prime it."

She pumped the handle vigorously, and water immediately shot through the hose and sprayed a wide stream of water. "Uh oh . . ." she murmured. She forgot she'd already primed the pump when she watered the front lawn.

Frank jumped back and ran, but too late. His shirt received a strong dousing, so did his pants.

"I'm terribly sorry," she offered. "I had the hose out in front before."

"I gathered that." Frank shook off his hands. The fabric of his light blue striped shirt had turned transparent, and she could see the mold of his chest; the way his flesh sculpted the strong bones and sinewy muscles that made him a man. "Damn good thing it's a hot day and I could use a cooling off." He plucked the gusseted row of buttons away from his skin.

Amelia fought the urge to stand over the sprinkler and cool herself off. She noted the way droplets clung to the ends of his hair and glistened along his jaw. He removed his hat and slapped the band on his thigh. Then he used his bare forearm to wipe his brow, the movement prompting her into action.

"Let me get you a towel."

"Don't bother." He put a light hand on her wrist. "I'd rather drip dry."

She looked down where he touched her, mesmerized by the warm summer-hued color of his skin. She recalled watching him through the mesh of her screen door while he'd stopped his mowing to roll up his sleeves in a casual manner. Nothing about him spelled formality, but it was his lack thereof that had her entranced.

Amelia withdrew her hand. She felt a moment's awkwardness while looking up into his face. She couldn't think of a thing to say to him. He'd done a fine job on the yard—better than she ever hoped to do—and she didn't have any spare money to pay him for his trouble.

Frank didn't seem in a hurry to leave. He splayed his fingers, combed them through his wet hair, and put his hat back on. "Do you have any more of that red stuff to drink?"

"Strawberry shrub." Her voice was shakier than she would have liked.

"Yeah, that stuff. How come it's named after a plant?"

Amelia thought a moment, then lifted her brows. "I don't really know. I never questioned my aunt Clara or my mother why. They always called it a strawberry shrub. Or a raspberry shrub or currant shrub."

"Whatever's in it tastes almost as good as a sling."

"A what?"

"If I told you the ingredients of a sling, it'd ruin this conversation."

She croaked, "No doubt liquor."

"No doubt."

Frank headed in the direction of the veranda, and Amelia was helpless but to follow. She wasn't sure if she wanted him on her porch or not. Her nearest neighbors, the Applegates, lived two vacant lots over, and Altana sometimes called on Amelia when she sought gardening advice. How would Amelia explain Frank to her?

On one hand, it was Amelia's Christian duty to be neighborly in return for his charitable act; but on the other hand, he held her New American parlor piano hostage in his whoop-it-up joint.

In order to keep up with his full stride, she had to be quick on her feet; her tiny steps kicked the flounced hem of her petticoats as she narrowed the margin between them. She had every intention of bringing to the surface the strife between them with a staunch reminder of his position in their battle.

But as she neared the fragrant trumpet vines climbing through the slates of her porch, she caught sight of a patch of navy fabric. Frank had removed his silk vest halfway through cutting the grass and slung it over the railing. The garment was still there, a vestige of raw masculinity amongst the backdrop of her potted pink begonias and the apple green rattan porch furniture she kept arranged in a semicircle.

For some reason, her resentment waned, and she felt a warm glow radiate from deep inside her. There was a certain amount of intimacy about a man's article of clothing draped over a woman's honeysuckle.

Frank seated himself in her scroll-backed receiving chair; the cane made a protesting squeak under the pressure. He looked too heavy for the petite reed furnishing, and she hoped the legs wouldn't give out while she mixed another glass of shrub.

"I'll be right back." Did her voice sound breathless, or was she imagining it? Amelia shook off the thought, grabbed hold of the screen door handle, and let herself into her kitchen.

The room was large and meticulously organized. She didn't tolerate anything less than neat as a pin. Her pantry closet was in order at all times. Kettles, stew and sauce pans were of quality tinned ware, and her galvanized sink ample. Her Sunshine range came with a hot-water apparatus, and her floor was covered with a good oilcloth.

Amelia took a clean water glass from her shelf and went to her icebox. She opened one of the upper doors and picked up the ice scraper. She ran it over the block of ice, all the while casting furtive glances out the door. All she could see at this angle was Frank's left leg. As soon as she'd shaved enough ice, she closed the door and set the glass on the counter. She'd just poured the syrup and water over the ice when the screen door opened.

Turning with a start, she said nothing as Frank entered her kitchen. No man had ever seen this part of the house. Not even Reverend Thorpe. The farthest a person of the opposite sex had ever gotten was her dining room and front parlor. But never her kitchen.

"Which way is the bathroom?" Frank asked as calmly as if he were inquiring for the time.

The teaspoon fell from her grasp and clattered to the counter. "I . . . that is . . . my . . ." What she really wanted to say was, *"Are you sure?"* but didn't. If a man had never been in her kitchen, there may as well have been a moat around her bathroom, for that space had *never* been occupied by *any* caller. "Thr- Through," she cleared her throat, "through the doorway and to your left. Down the hall and up . . . up the stairs. The first room on the right."

"Thanks."

Frank strode under the doorway casement, his athletic build filling up the narrow opening. All

Amelia could do was stare after him, her mind whirling in the tense silence. She heard his footfalls over the floorboards, then the muffled clomp of his boots over her tapestry carpet in the hallway. The house seemed to creak in protest when he ascended the staircase. And finally the bathroom door latched into place.

Amelia let out her breath and remained rooted to the spot. The ensuing quiet was deafening. She absently picked up the spoon and stirred the strawberry shrub, lifting her gaze to watch the ceiling. He was up there. Not ten feet from her bedroom. Using her water closet to . . . to do whatever.

Suddenly, a warning voice whispered inside her head as she remembered what she had hanging in plain view on her adjustable clothes bar.

Snatching up the glass, she took off for the parlor. Once at the base of the stairs, she clutched the oak banister in her free hand and started climbing the risers. When her foot hit the fifth tread, the wooden joints beneath her shoe moaned, and she froze. Her eyes darted to the landing, and she gasped softly, "Mr. Brody. You're out." Her heart beat faster than a bird's, and she made a quick recovery by extending her arm. "I have your strawberry shrub ready." The cold glass in her hand was sweating, and the surface began to feel slippery.

Frank sauntered down the stairs to meet her, his fingers brushing the balustrade. "Did you want me to drink it in the bathroom, Miss Marshall?"

"Heavens no!" she cried. "I was just . . . just." She was floundering like a fish. "I just . . ."

"Just wanted to make sure I hadn't seen anything I wasn't supposed to," he supplied, and she felt her face flame. "Don't worry, sweetheart. Nothing inside your bathroom shocked me. I've seen it all before. You women have a lot of doodads." He took the glass from her. A good thing, too. She was on the verge of letting it slip through her fingers with humiliation. "I'm glad I don't have to use all that stuff."

Amelia wanted to crawl in a hole. He'd seen them. How could he not? He'd probably had to swing the clothes bar toward the window in order to . . . to . . . do whatever. She backed down the stairs, settled her footing on the floor, and held on to the newel post as if her life depended on it. Frank joined her and strode into her light and cheerful parlor.

Both she and her aunt Clara had chosen the furnishings, buying them piece by piece, not in a set. Her comfortable easy chairs and sofas were in pink hues. A light-colored paper of no pronounced pattern lent a rich air to the walls. The wooden mantel above the fireplace was filled with heirlooms placed on either side of a porcelain clock. But it was the oriel that caught his attention, and he walked toward the large bay window filled with vibrant leather ferns, philodendron, herbs, and her prized phalaenopsis orchids.

"Did you grow all these yourself?"

"Yes."

"Damn. I doubt I could grow weeds." Frank brought the glass to his lips, and Amelia found herself transfixed on the way his Adam's apple gently bobbed when he swallowed. He looked over the rim at the east wall and she followed his gaze. A waist-high area of wallpaper to the left of her fireplace was noticeably faded. She used to have her Turkish parlor suit situated there, but had moved the silk brocatelle tête-à-tête to make room for the piano. She hadn't gotten around to shifting the small sofa back into its old spot.

She'd been too depressed to even look in that corner of the room at night while she did her mending or reading.

Seeing the eyesore now, she became vexed, her feelings sensitive anew to the bruising Frank Brody had given her when he'd stolen her piano.

"I hope you're satisfied," she remarked briskly.

"Yeah, the drink tastes good."

"Not that, Mr. Brody. You know very well what I'm talking about."

"The damn piano."

"Refrain from cursing my piano."

"The piano isn't yours, so I can curse it if I want." He shoved his empty glass at her and tugged on the brim of his hat. "That New American came to me fair and square, Miss Marshall. I guess you're going to hold it over my head for the rest of my life."

"I guess."

He gave her a bitter glare. "I meant what I said. You can give lessons in the saloon for as long as you need. I didn't mean to scare you off, and I give you my word not to bother you anymore while you're practicing. Far be it for me to stand in the way of a woman's busts." On that, he went to the front door and let himself out.

Amelia stood in the middle of the parlor, watching him through the jungle of plant leaves in her oriel. She saw a glimpse of white leave through her gate, and it reminded her he wasn't wearing his navy vest. She turned to run into the rear yard to fetch it, went only one foot, spun back to look out the window, and stopped.

He was already gone.

It would seem they were both destined to leave articles of clothing at the other's residence. Whatever would the Thursday Afternoon Fine Ladies Society think of that, were they to find out?

Shaking off the thought, Amelia deposited the glass on a side table, plucked up her skirts, and bounded up the stairs. She stopped at the water closet doorway. The room didn't seem to be out of order or show any signs of disturbance; but she wasn't looking all that closely at her toilet articles. Her eyes were pinned on the pair of lisle hose, two snowy chemises, and a corset cover trimmed with Valenciennes lace dangling from her clothes dryer.

He'd folded the hardwood arms back next to the wall in order to use the necessary. She wanted to die. Of course he'd seen her most private attire. How could he miss them? And even more humiliating, twice in one day!

Amelia slumped next to the doorjamb, lowering her gaze with a deflated sigh. It was then she noticed the pull-chain fixture commode. The closet seat was up.

Now why on earth had he done that?

Chapter

6

⤳

*H*ere she comes!" Pap exclaimed from his vigil at the bat-wing doors of the Moon Rock. One side flapped into place as he let go and ran to stand by the piano with a Cheshire cat grin on his face. He'd been hovering around the entry since nine o'clock waiting for Amelia.

Behind the long bar, Frank rubbed a bourbon glass to give it polish. Pap had awakened him hours before he would have on his own, and he was damn tired.

He yawned, shook the sleep from his head, and opened his eyes as wide as they would go. "I'm going to have another key made for this place so you can have yours back, Pap. I could kill you for waking me," Frank muttered, setting the glass down to take a lengthy swallow of black coffee. His fourth cup, and without a single jitter. He definitely wasn't a man for mornings during a work week.

"Don't kill me now, Frank." Pap whisked the lint from the lapels of his pincheck coat with his finger-tips. "I've got plans."

"Yeah, so now what?"

"I'm going to charm her."

"Well, I guess I didn't get up for nothing then."
Frank picked up a chamois and wiped the beads of
water from the bar top. "This ought to be a good
show."

One of the swinging doors pivoted inward, and
Miss Marshall peered around the edge, key in her
extended hand. Seeing Frank, she couldn't hide the
disappointed look on her face; then moving her gaze
to Pap, she smiled weakly. "Mr. O'Cleary," she said,
stepping inside. "And Mr. Brody."

Frank didn't like the formal way she enunciated his
name, so he figured he owed her just a tiny ribbing.
"'Morning, there, sister."

She let out a disgruntled little sniff but didn't reply.

Frank gave her the once-over. She hadn't paid his
commentary about overdressing any attention. She
was buttoned up from top to bottom with a hat,
parasol, gloves, high shoes, and all. She'd brought
back her bulky bag of busts and held it as if it were
anchoring her to the floor. He'd grown rather curious
about them.

"Come on in, Miss Marshall." Pap swept his arm
over the piano stool. "I've been warming it up for
you."

Amelia deposited the key into the purse dangling on
a chain at her waistband, then strode forward. "That
wasn't necessary, Mr. O'Cleary. Really." She gave Pap
a quick look, then Frank. "I didn't think anyone
would be occupying the premises so early."

"Oh, I sometimes get up and compose songs."

Compose? Frank arched a brow. About the only
thing Pap ever composed were the uncouth poems he
wrote on the inside walls of the outhouse.

"I see." Amelia stood still, clearly at odds.

Frank set the chamois down and went for the tin
coffeepot he kept on a single oil stove behind him.
Clutching the handle with a burnt towel, he warmed

up his coffee. "Would you like a cup?" he asked Amelia. "It's probably not as aromatic as you're used to."

Pap laughed. "No, ma'am, it ain't. You don't want to drink Frank's coffee. It looks like tobacco juice spit. Tastes damn close to it, too."

Amelia touched her lacy collar. "No, thank you."

"Well, now," Pap exclaimed in an exuberant tone and rubbed his palms together. "Allow me to take your bag, Miss Marshall, so you can set yourself up." He went to take the petit point carryall from her, and she swiftly brought the handle to her waist.

"That's quite all right."

"Leave her alone, Pap," Frank said, holding on to his cup while the steam evaporated from the coffee. "She's got her busts in there. She's particular about them."

Amelia glared at Frank. "I thought you said you were going to behave, Mr. Brody."

He shrugged. "Yeah, you're right." He put his lips together and blew—not necessarily on the coffee. "Ignore me. I'm just going to keep on washing last night's glasses. You won't even know I'm here."

"Why *are* you here?" she asked.

Frank shot Pap a questionable look. "Why am I here, Pap?"

"Because," Pap's voice grew exasperated, "because I had to wake you to tell you we was all out of whiskey. You needed to get over to the Wells Fargo office this morning and send an invoice out before the stage left. *Remember?*"

"Oh, yeah." Hell, he never ran out of whiskey.

"That's strange, Mr. Brody," Amelia remarked. "I was speaking with Mr. Tindall at the Wells Fargo earlier, and I didn't see you there."

"I went right when he opened."

"So did I."

"Aw, hell." Frank set his cup down after a hot

swallow. "I don't know what time it was whenever Pap woke me up. I didn't check my watch."

"I did," she persisted. "I was speaking with Mr. Tindall at precisely nine thirty-one. And would you like to know the details of our conversation?"

"I would not." Because he knew damn well what she had to talk to Tindall about.

"I knew you'd be interested." Amelia walked to the New American and set her bag on the stool. "I was inquiring as to when your piano would arrive in Weeping Angel so I could have it, since you've seen fit to claim mine while yours is still in Boston."

Frank fished out another glass from the dishpan and let the cold water trickle onto the floor. "I figured that's what you'd say."

Pap's eyes darted between them before he spoke eagerly. "Miss Marshall, please allow me to help you with your bag." He went as far as trying to open the catch.

"No!" she replied, and stopped him cold with her harsh tone.

The room went still.

Even Miss Marshall could see she had wounded tough-as-nails Pap O'Cleary's pride. "I'm sorry I was short with you, Mr. O'Cleary. I . . . I'm not myself today. I'm upset because I've lost my . . . my favorite writing pen. I think I left it behind at the Wells Fargo office." She gave him a soft, apologetic smile. "Would it be very much of a bother for you to see if I did?"

"No bother, Miss Marshall." Pap tipped his derby. "It's all right if you were crabby with me. A woman's got the right to have her moods."

Amelia licked her lips. "Yes . . . well." She seemed a little at odds. "The pen is in a blue steel holder."

"I'll go check."

"Thank you."

"Be back in a minute, Frank."

"Yeah."

As soon as Pap was gone, Amelia turned toward Frank.

He frowned. "Did you have to be so hard on him, sweetheart? All he wanted to do was help you unpack your busts."

"I wouldn't care if that's all that was in my bag, Mr. Brody."

"You have unmentionables in there today?"

"That's not funny."

Frank cracked a half smile. "I thought it was."

"If you must know," Amelia informed him, opening the clasp, "I have your vest." She withdrew his navy vest and walked toward the bar. "I couldn't very well explain why I had it in with my personal belongings, could I?"

"I could."

"Well, I couldn't."

She came up to the bar and set the garment on the counter.

Frank slid the vest toward him and pitched it underneath the bar on top of his Smith & Wesson.

"I hope I didn't hurt his feelings," Amelia said with slight dismay in her tone. "It wasn't my intention."

"It takes a lot to insult Pap." Frank put a shine on the glass. "Nothing much ever gets him mad. Especially when he likes the person," Frank added, waiting to see her reaction.

Her facial expression didn't show much. He wondered what she would do if she knew just how much Pap liked her. Was there a chance she would return Pap's affection if she knew he was romancing her? At this point in her life, an unmarried woman Miss Marshall's mature age might accept courting from any man who showed some interest.

For some reason, Frank hoped she was more selective. Not that Pap was a bad sort. Pap was just too anxious and awkward for someone like Miss Marshall. She needed a man who knew how to flatter a woman slowly. Smoothly. A man who could kiss those pretty lips of hers and get her to kiss him back.

"Is there something wrong, Mr. Brody?" Amelia asked, her eyes narrowing suspiciously. "There's a challenge in your gaze. Have you changed your mind about my using the piano?"

Frank cracked a smile, thinking she was good at reading his expression, but not what was on his mind. "I gave you my word."

"And I gave you my piano."

Frank set the clean glass down. He kind of liked talking to Amelia. In the few conversations they'd shared, she was good at bantering with him. She had a sense of humor, and that surprised him. He figured her to be as stiff as her clothing but her ability to banter belied that, and the contrast intrigued him.

"Dare I ask," Frank began, "what did Tindall have to say?"

"Nothing informative." She affected her put-upon face. "He hasn't received a reply from Boston, yet— as I suspected. To clear this matter up may take weeks."

"Then I'll be enjoying your company for a few more weeks."

She looked at him askance with liquid brown eyes. "You can't be serious."

"I'm very serious."

She kept her features deceptively composed, but he noted a lightness to her breathing. He didn't have time to dwell on her because Pap returned, and Amelia abruptly turned away from him as the bat-wing doors bolted open on either side, crashing against the walls.

Pap sucked in gulps of air. "T-Tindall didn't h-have your p-pen, M-Miss M-Marshall."

Amelia gasped. "Mr. O'Cleary. You ran."

"Yup." He slid around the bar and snatched up the

glass Frank had just cleaned. He dunked it into a bin of melted ice and took a long drink. Wiping the water from his mouth with his hand, he smiled at Amelia. "I didn't want you to have to wait too long."

"You needn't have gone to so much trouble, Mr. O'Cleary."

"For you, Miss Marshall, I'd run clear to Boise and back if you wanted me to."

She grew flustered. "Well, I don't want you to."

Amelia left the bar and strode to the piano. Pap dashed from behind the counter and chased after her. "If I hear of anyone finding a pen in a blue steel holder, I'll make sure to get it for you."

"You're too kind."

"You're kind enough to let me."

Pap stood next to her and Amelia stopped. He blocked her way to the stool, and she had to go around him.

Frank absently drank his coffee, thinking Pap was making an ass of himself. Swallowing the bitter brew, Frank reckoned if he had any sense, he'd get the hell out of here and go on over to the laundry to check on his clothes. He should have picked them up yesterday, but he'd been mowing Amelia's lawn and forgot.

He smiled in remembrance at the way she'd tried to conceal her embarrassment over him seeing her underwear in her bathroom. He hadn't really thought anything much on finding it in his way. He'd been more occupied by the way she kept all her toiletry articles in neat rows on the shelf of her cabinet. There was an efficiency about her that fascinated him. Why would anyone go to so much trouble to be so organized? He probably should be more like her. He was always losing things.

"I was going to begin lessons tomorrow," Amelia was saying, "and wanted one good day of practicing, but if you and Mr. Brody—"

"Don't give us any never mind, Miss Marshall," Pap quickly replied. "We won't get in your way. Go right on ahead. I've been wanting to hear another person play this piano besides myself. I was hoping we could do a duet."

"I didn't bring any duet music with me."

"Damn." Pap snapped his fingers. "Next time you bring some, and we'll give these ivories what for."

"I'll try and remember." She stood poised by her bag a long moment, as if she was deciding what to do next. Frank saw her hesitation and felt he should say something to make her stay.

"Hey, Miss Marshall, you go on with your practicing if you need to. Pap has some things to do for me, so he won't be in your hair."

She frowned. "I haven't played in front of an audience—"

"Since you played in front of me," he finished.

"Damn," Pap swore again. "Seeing as you played in front of Frank, you need to play in front of me, Miss Marshall. He said you up-and-downed real good."

"Up-and-downed?" Amelia squeaked, giving Frank a wide-eyed stare.

"You know." Frank placed his hands in the air like he was playing a piano, then he moved his fingers from left to right and right to left. "Up and down."

"My scales."

"Yeah. What did you think I meant by up and down?"

"To be sure, I wouldn't know."

"Do your scales, Miss Marshall," Pap urged, "and forget we're here." He left Amelia alone and went to the bar. "What do you want, Frank?"

"I want you to . . ." Frank thought a minute. He really didn't have anything for Pap to do. "To clean my gun."

"Clean your gun?"

"Yeah. Cobb was giving me some trouble last night. I just want to make sure it's in firing order."

"I can't believe Cobb Weatherwax would be giving you any trouble. His brain cavity ain't big enough to start a fight."

"All the same, could you oil the gun for me?"

"Sure."

Pap came around the back side of the bar. He bent down at the waist, halting his movement midway. "What's your vest doing under here?"

"I pitched it there," Frank replied casually.

"I told you not to be hurling your clothes and whatnot all over the place." Pap grabbed the vest and folded it over his arm. "You've got to run a clean business. Junk all over the place ain't the way to go."

"My vest isn't junk."

Pap set the navy garment on the bar. "No, it ain't junk, but it don't belong with the glasses neither. I pity the poor woman you marry, Frank. She's going to have to be cleaning up after you every second."

"Who said anything about marriage?"

"Every man wants to get married, whether he admits it or not. It's the natural way of folks to pair up." Pap glanced at Amelia, who'd sat down and began running through her scales. "It takes some men longer than others to figure this out. You'd be smart to think about getting hitched while you're still good-looking enough to have your pick."

Frank snorted. "I'll be damn sure to keep all your philosophy close to mind, Pap."

Pap picked up the revolver and cleaning box, then went to a table and began taking all the paraphernalia out, all the while casting furtive glances at Amelia.

Frank leaned on the bar and watched Amelia, too. She hadn't taken a thing out of her coveted music bag, which she'd set on the floor by her feet. He figured she wasn't planning on sticking around too long.

Grabbing another glass, Frank set to work on the rest of the dishes, pondering Pap's advice. Frank had thought about having a wife every now and then. But the harsh realities of his childhood prevented him from thinking very long on the subject. Marriage and children were something he didn't think well of. His parents, Jack and Charlotte, had merely been spectators in his youth before leaving. The real adult had been himself, and the responsibility of the family had fallen on his shoulders. The fate of his brother, Harry, had been left up to Frank.

And Frank had failed.

From that day forward, reality had been caned into him. Life was cruel, and only those crueler would survive it.

He'd lived by that credo for as long as he had to in the orphanage, for without those words embedded in his mind, he would not have survived without Harry.

The music Amelia played softened, and Frank looked up. She'd changed directions in her scales and now ran through a beautiful melody. Some kind of orchestral piece. She was a damn good piano player, and he liked listening to the change of pace from Pap's tromping. Not that Pap couldn't hold an audience; Pap was the best. Amelia was just different.

Frank glanced at Pap, who tapped his foot on the floor to the tempo, a smile from ear to ear as he disassembled the gun. There was something about the harmony of the room that made Frank feel good. Not at all suffocated by the camaraderie.

He could have listened to the piano for hours. But Ed Vining burst in, and Amelia swiveled on the stool to see what Ed was babbling about.

"Miss Marshall!" Ed exclaimed. "I ran to your house and you weren't there. I was hoping you might be here when I heard the piano. I was right. I was—that is—I hope I'm not too late!"

"Slow down, Ed." Frank slipped from behind the bar and went to Ed. "What the hell are you trying to say?"

Ed swept off his hat. "Beg pardon, Miss Marshall. It's just that I'm . . . I'm . . ."

"Spill it, Vining." Pap had shoved the revolver aside to stand.

"I was sweeping off the boardwalks when I saw Mayor Dodge carry Mrs. Dodge into Doc White's office."

"Narcissa," Amelia gasped, her face going pale.

"I'm sorry, Miss Marshall," Ed continued. "She was passed out cold. I went in to see if there was anything I could do, and Cincinatus hollered for me to go fetch you, Miss Marshall." Ed crumpled his hat brim in his hands. "It looks bad. Real bad. I didn't see much, other than Mrs. Dodge's face was whiter than I ever seen a sheet. It . . . it looked to me as if she was dead."

Dr. Francis White's practice was only two doors down from the Moon Rock Saloon, and Amelia entered the reception room with fearful images built in her mind. Mayor Dodge occupied the waiting area with his pacing. The normally impeccable center part in his pomaded hair was not so orderly; both sides ruffled above his ears.

Upon seeing Amelia, he nearly broke down and cried. His eyes were rimmed with tears, and his face was the color of ashes. "Amelia . . ." he choked. "The doctor won't let me be with her until he's finished his exam."

Amelia clasped his hands in her own and squeezed. "What happened?"

"Narcissa came to the city offices to bring me lunch. I don't know if it was the heat, or the walk, or . . . I don't know. But she fainted in my arms." Cincinatus pulled out his large handkerchief and loudly blew his nose. "I carried her here, and as soon as Dr. White saw her, he ordered me to put her on the examining table and leave the room. That's all I know."

Amelia bowed her head and tried to calm the waves of apprehension running through her. "It's all my fault. I should have insisted she see the doctor before this. I knew something was wrong with her, but she denied feeling ill. She said she was suffering from her age."

"Balderdash!" Cincinatus blazed. "My Narcissa is not feeling her age at all. She's spry and lovely and . . . and—" His voice broke off in a pitiful crack. "If anything were to happen to her . . . I wouldn't want to go on living."

"Don't talk such nonsense." Amelia lifted her chin and looked the mayor in the eyes. "She's fine. She has to be. I'm sure it's nothing more than . . . the heat. I know I've been feeling the effects of it."

"What's taking so long?" he asked, wiping his eyes with his pocket kerchief. "Doc's been in there forever. Why doesn't he come out?"

"I'll see." Amelia rushed passed the handsomely appointed furnishings and raised her hand to knock on the closed cherrywood paneled door.

"Dr. White?" Her voice sounded distant to her hear ears. "It's Miss Marshall. I've come to see about Mrs. Dodge."

After a moment there was a click, then the door opened, and the doctor admitted Amelia.

The consultation room was large and the east window covered with sheer curtains to filter the light. Amelia went straight to the overstuffed chair Narcissa occupied by the doctor's pigeonhole desk. She was fully dressed, sitting up, and quite conscious—though her color was anything but rosy.

"Narcissa!" Amelia exclaimed, and knelt to take her friend's hand in her own. "You gave us all quite a scare. My goodness, Ed Vining said you were dead!"

She laughed a little hysterically. "Remind me to reprimand him for frightening me so." Putting soft pressure on Narcissa's fingers, Amelia smiled. "I told you to take better care of yourself. Why didn't you listen to me?"

Narcissa said nothing, and it was then Amelia noticed the far-off smile on her friend's mouth. The mayor's wife was anything but distressed. Although she didn't appear to be in exceptional health, she was taking the whole matter in stride. Actually, Narcissa looked almost giddy.

"Narcissa . . . ?" Amelia whispered. "What's wrong with you?"

Dr. White sat at his desk and picked up his ink pen to scribble notations on a piece of paper. He looked over the wire frames of his glasses at Narcissa and, with a scholarly nod, remarked, "You can discuss your condition with anyone you please, Mrs. Dodge."

"I'd like to tell Amelia," Narcissa said in a dreamy voice. "But I have to tell Cincinatus first." She looked at Amelia. "You'll understand once you hear. Can you get him for me?"

"Of course." Amelia stood and went to the door and opened it. "Mayor Dodge, your wife wants you."

Cincinatus came running into the room, leaving the newly arrived Ed Vining behind.

Ed seemed perplexed, but asked, "You want me to get Titus Applegate, Miss Marshall?"

"Good heavens, no! We have no need for the undertaker."

"Titus'll be sorry to hear that."

Amelia gently closed the door in place and walked toward the leather exam table, frowning at the mention of Mr. Applegate. He'd laid out her aunt Clara in a tasteful fashion, but few others had surrendered their lives since. Titus's funeral parlor was starved for customers, so he'd gone into the furniture business to tide himself over until someone else passed on. It was a good thing he'd ventured into retail, because Amelia was sure he wouldn't get Narcissa for a long, long time.

Dr. White remained sitting, but stopped writing and removed his glasses. Narcissa embraced her husband and put her cheek on his. Tears shimmered in her blue eyes, and Amelia felt like an intruder. She wanted to slip away, and even moved a step toward the door, but Narcissa stopped her.

"No, stay, Amelia."

Cincinatus pulled back slightly and caressed his wife's shoulder. "What is it, dear?"

She smiled genteelly, a lovely woman with her auburn hair and matronly features of her figure. "How many women desire a firstborn love?"

"You are my first love, my dear."

"Yes, but not my firstborn love. I'm speaking of the idol of a woman's waiting heart—a soul which shall be begotten within, clothed with my own nature—and yours," she spoke softly, "and yet immortal."

"I don't know what you mean, dear." Cincinatus placed a wispy curl behind her ear and stroked his thumb on her cheek. "What are you trying to say?"

Amelia knew. She felt her own tears gather, and that same nurturing need Narcissa was speaking of wrapped itself around her heart, and the emptiness inside hurt. There would be no scenes like this for her because she'd had her chance at marriage, and that chance had run off. No one had asked since. And in all probability, no one would ask again.

Narcissa's expression beamed. "You know what a natural instinct it is to yearn for offspring. We've both had the desire, but after so many years . . . we gave up hope. I gave up hope." Narcissa stood and took Cincinatus with her, her hands clasping his. "All that is beautiful and lovely in a woman finds its climax in motherhood. For what earthly being do we love so devotedly as our mother?"

"Narcissa . . . are you going to be a mother?"

She nodded. It took a few seconds for the words to sink in, and then he crushed her to him. But just as abruptly, he put some distance between them and handled her with a kid-glove touch. "My Lord, that means . . . that means . . . I'm . . . I'm . . . I'm . . . I'm going to be a . . . father."

"That's right, dear. In about seven months, you'll be able to hold your child."

"But . . . but . . . but . . . I'm fifty-two." He tottered. "I never thought . . . never figured . . . after all these years . . . I just never . . . we never . . . I'm fifty-two."

"Yes, my dear." Narcissa smiled. "And I'm forty-two. The Lord has decided to bless us with a miracle."

"I'm fifty-two," Cincinatus Dodge repeated. Then the town's aspiring orator was at a loss for anything else inspiring to say.

He passed out cold.

Chapter

7

Before Amelia reached Narcissa's house, she heard the joyful screams of children running through the well-kept yard. Not five hours after Narcissa had seen the doctor, the illustrious ladies of Weeping Angel had apparently closed in on her, children in tow, to see what needed to be done in the household.

Amelia kept the handle of her basket in the crook of her arm as she stopped at the gate and put one hand on the latch. She wondered if Narcissa could see what was happening on her property; surely, she could hear the chaos. The Reed twins, Walter and Warren, ran through the oleander bushes; a group of girls played tea party under the shade of an elm; and boys shot marbles on the walkway. It galled Amelia a little that the women would be so careless.

Narcissa took great pride in her home. The Dodge residence was the first to have been built in Weeping Angel and, by far, was the most opulent. The Queen Anne style house was painted terra-cotta with bronze green trim and shutters. The gables were old gold and the sashes black, and the latticework grills beneath the porch were flesh.

Fingering the latch, Amelia let herself in. She skirted the youngsters, all of whom she was generally fond of. In most cases, it wasn't their fault they weren't trained in courtesies. Some of their mothers put blind tolerance before firm discipline.

Daniel Beamguard looked up, a wedge of rusty hair dusting his eyebrows. "Hi ya, Miss Marshall," he called, then shot his glass marble through the ring, knocking out Jakey Spivey's blood agate.

She curtly nodded, ever the teacher that commanded respect, keeping her stride brisk over the flagstones.

"Hello, Miss Marshall!" cried Altana Applegate's beribboned girls, Bessie Lovey and Mable Dovey, as they dangled their fine bisque dolls over the exuberant balustrade which made the front of the house grand.

"Girls," she replied primly, lifted her skirt hem a few inches, and took the wide steps.

"Our mother is inside with all the other ladies," Bessie Lovey said in a proper voice.

Mable Dovey's springy blond curls bounced as she walked to Amelia. "We're playing house. I'm the mother and Bessie Lovey is the aunt."

"That's very nice," Amelia remarked, then twisted the knob on the bell.

"What did you bring Mrs. Dodge?" Bessie Lovey asked, her tiny nose twitching as she tried to sniff what Amelia had in her cloth-covered basket. "Mother brought cold ham."

Amelia didn't answer, wondering instead which one of the ladies would be in charge of receiving callers.

The neatly painted portal swung wide. "My dear!" Luella Spivey clucked upon seeing Amelia. "Come in! We've all gathered to see our poor Narcissa." Mrs. Spivey practically snagged Amelia's sleeve and reeled her in through the front door before slamming it closed.

Once inside the spacious foyer, Amelia was bustled into the sitting room through the lavish French-striped portieres that swagged either side of the double-door opening.

"Our Amelia is here," Luella announced.

Amelia looked around the room decorated in gray-ish blue with sage accents and Nottingham lace curtains covering the windows. She took in all those who were in attendance: Mrs. Dorothea Beamguard, Mrs. Esther Parks, Mrs. Viola Reed, and Mrs. Altana Applegate.

Mrs. Parks sat on the ottoman, her ample bosom straining the bodice fabric of her dress. She balanced a teacup and saucer on her lap while she discreetly adjusted the front of her brown puff-bang wig. The most nosy and interfering of the group, she spoke first. "My dear Amelia, we're so glad you could come and see Narcissa. We've all been beside ourselves with worry. She won't tell us a thing."

"It's awful not knowing," chimed Mrs. Reed. She chose a cucumber sandwich from a plate on the side table. "But you did know she was in poor health. You were with her at the doctor's office."

"Of course," Mrs. Parks said, resuming her tea. "Do tell. What is the matter with Narcissa? She's being so vague."

The plump Mrs. Beamguard helped herself to a chocolate cream arranged on a candy dish. "Narcissa is upstairs and won't say what's wrong. Simply put, she insists she's merely tired. I don't believe her. I say it's her gall bladder."

"My guess is gout," Mrs. Spivey put in, strolling into the sitting room. She plopped her wide bottom onto an overstuffed chair and pursed her pink lips—a jarring contrast to her frizzy orange hair. "I think

Narcissa has too much free time on her hands. That's the problem. She doesn't exercise enough. You know what Dr. Pierce says in *The People's Common Sense Medical Advisor*. Exercise sends sluggish blood through the veins and arteries to keep one fit."

"I disagree with your diagnosis." Mrs. Reed nibbled on the crustless edge of her bread. "If she had gout, we'd all know it. But I do agree she doesn't take in as much fresh air as she ought. I'm not talking about garden or home exercise, either. Our children put the bloom of color on our faces. In order to keep after them, we must take in air. She doesn't have children like the rest of us, so she—"

Mrs. Parks was waving her hand to silence the woman, her wig shifting. "My dear," the ticket agent's wife whispered, "aren't you forgetting our Amelia doesn't have children either?" Then added on a flip note, "Or a husband, for that matter."

Viola Reed glanced at Amelia who stood in the doorway, hat in place, gloves on, and still clutching her parasol. Amelia didn't feel the sting of the gossip because she knew the women for who they were. Mostly well intended, but with little care as to the other's feelings when curiosity abounded. The lot of them—except, perhaps, Altana, who generally remained neutral and quiet—had come to feast on Narcissa's ailment and make of it what they would. And should they not be able to guess the extent of what was making Narcissa ill, they would invent something just to fuel their conversation.

"Don't worry about me," Amelia said at length. "It's no secret I'm not married, and it's certainly out of the question that I would have a child." She didn't bother to enter the room entirely. "But I think you would all do well to remember our Narcissa isn't feeling well, and any comments made in haste would upset her." Glancing around at the faces, Amelia couldn't help adding, "I'm glad Narcissa isn't amongst you to hear your prattle. I'm going up to see her."

The women stood in unison, eagerness in their expressions. "We'll go with you," the five of them replied together.

"By myself, if you please," Amelia stated, and turned on her heels to take the stairs. Lightly touching the railing, she ascended to the second floor. She went past several doors, then came to the third on her left. It was ajar, but Amelia raised her hand and knocked.

"Who is it?" Narcissa asked, her voice sounding weak.

"It's Amelia."

"Come in."

Amelia went inside the light and airy bedchamber and found Narcissa at her writing desk, having changed into a white sateen wrapper. Her hair was unplaited and fell loosely about her hips.

"Thank goodness it's you." Narcissa set her pen in the inkwell. "I was afraid one of them had come back to see if I'd eaten the tray they left. Why is it when women come together, they have to bring food?"

"Because," Amelia replied, setting her basket down on the desk, "we want you to keep your strength."

"Not you, too?"

"Yes, me, too." Amelia lifted the red gingham cloth. "I brought you biscuits and honey. I heard the doctor say you must keep up your meals to regain your strength."

"Biscuits and honey are one of my favorites."

"I knew that."

Narcissa rubbed her temple. "Dr. White said it would be another month before the sickness comes to pass. I feel . . . well, not at all what I thought I would feel like to be carrying a child. I thought I would be full of energy and full of life. I'd heard stories of sickness, and here I am suffering from an upset stomach. But you know, it's not at all bothersome. I'm just so glad . . ." Tears welled in her eyes. "So glad I have the chance to throw up. Do you know what I mean?"

Amelia wished she could offer a counter opinion, a different point of view on the subject. But she could not. Unfortunately, the ladies downstairs were far more experienced with pregnancy than Amelia ever would be.

"You'll be feeling better soon, I'm sure," was all Amelia could advise.

"Dr. White says in another month I should feel more like myself." Narcissa sipped a glass of water, then stood. "I was writing down words of inspiration for Cincinatus. He hovered over and pampered me after seeing me home. I couldn't stand it. I sent him back to his office to work on his Fourth of July speech, but I'm certain he isn't worth a whit. He kept jabbering and carrying on, so when he left, I gave him the bottle of smelling salts Dr. White gave me before we left his office."

Amelia smiled.

Narcissa glanced out the window and said vaguely, "Can you imagine . . . my yard will have *my* child playing in it one day. I won't have other women's children to mess up my planters, or play in my tree, or spill dirt on the porch. It will be my son or daughter, and I won't be angry because I'll love them so much."

Amelia swallowed the heaviness in her throat. She couldn't imagine. Blinking rapidly, she tried not to let Narcissa see her hurt.

Narcissa turned from the curtained window. "Amelia . . . I'm so sorry! I didn't mean . . . oh . . . how careless of me!"

"It's all right. I'm happy for you, Narcissa. I truly am."

Narcissa embraced her, and it was all Amelia could do not to cry. Narcissa, on the other hand, had no trouble letting the waterworks flow. Easing back, she dabbed her eyes with the corner of a lacy handkerchief she'd produced from the pocket of her wrapper. "I don't know what's gotten into me. I'm happy and sad all at once. I can't seem to control my tears, and at the same time, I'm laughing."

The ring of the doorbell echoed through the house, and Amelia sighed. "Who else could be calling?"

"I wouldn't know." Narcissa sniffed and ran her fingertips under her eyes. "Widow Thurman hasn't been by." Then, as if remembering something, she gasped, "But do you know who came to call? Emmaline Shelby."

The name sort of sliced through Amelia. She suspected the laundress had a severe case of infatuation for Frank Brody. Just like everyone else in petticoats. "Whatever did she say?"

"Nothing much about me. She wanted to know about you."

"Me?"

"Yes. She wanted to know what your relationship with Mr. Brody is."

Amelia's heart tripped in her ribs. "My relationship with Mr. Brody is purely business."

Narcissa furrowed her brows. "From her tone, I would guess she thinks otherwise. She kept asking me—in a roundabout way—what you do in his saloon."

"All I've done is practice on my piano." Amelia held fast to the handle of her sun shade. *"The* piano," she rephrased. "He insists it's his, and I've grown weary of arguing with him. But I know it's mine—even though he won't admit it."

Growing thoughtful a minute, Narcissa said, "I wasn't going to mention this to you, dear, as well you know I voted against the piano going to that saloon. But I did hear why the women voted in favor of the upright being moved to the Moon Rock."

"Why?" Amelia countered with interest.

"Because, Esther Parks confided in me, they want to see for themselves if Mr. Brody really can slide a beer mug along the bar and make the glass stop wherever he wants."

"You've got to be joking!"

"I'm sorry to say I'm not."

"I suspected there was more to their change of hearts about the lessons, but I didn't want to accept they'd do it just to be able to see the interior of that saloon," Amelia said. "I was here in Weeping Angel when they did everything in their power to shut down Charley Revis's shebang and were very close to succeeding when . . . well, you know what happened." Amelia put her fingers on her forehead. "Oh, I knew they were enthralled by Mr. Brody's showplace, but I never thought things would go this far. Besides, who's to say he'll perform that little trick for them—if indeed he can?"

"Dorothea Beamguard can be very persuasive when she sets her mind to it. She's a shrewd businesswoman. You know it's really her that runs that mercantile. She has Oscar on puppet strings."

Amelia took in a long breath. "I'm appalled. Pure and simple. Why if I didn't need the—" She stopped herself short. Even her best friend didn't know she needed money. Narcissa would insist she take a loan if she knew. Amelia was better off not telling a soul.

"Need what, dear?"

"Need the diversion," she offhandedly rephrased. "I would call a stop to the entire thing. I wouldn't give lessons. Then where would they be? Certainly not inside that saloon."

Narcissa didn't speak for a moment, then said, "Forgive me for asking . . . oh, blame it on my condition if you must . . . but what exactly does it look like in his saloon? Are there naked ladies on the walls?"

"Not a one."

"You sound disappointed."

"Perhaps a little." She sighed. "I wanted to find fault with his establishment. Actually, the interior is tasteful—for a saloon. Not that I've been in any others."

Narcissa went to the window again and pressed her palm on the glass. "Whoever came hasn't left yet. It must be Widow Thurman, and the ladies are giving her an earful. I suppose I'll tell them all tomorrow and be done with it. Today I want to keep the news to myself—and those dearest to me."

"Well," Amelia said, "I'll leave you to your rest and see whoever it is out the door. Would you like me to clear the house?"

"No. I'll leave that to Cincinatus." Narcissa turned to face Amelia. "He gets great pleasure in ousting them from the parlor with a stern voice that fairly shakes the rafters and leaves their feathers flying."

Amelia laughed. "I'll come back for the basket tomorrow."

"Do."

"Good-bye, Narcissa. And, I am happy for you. Truly."

Narcissa smiled and Amelia took her leave. She went down the hallway feeling exhausted and angry all at the same time.

So, now she knew for certain.

The ladies voted against her because of their fixation on Frank Brody and his high-class *parlor*. If only Frank had been a mangy old coot . . . that upright would have been in *her parlor* this very moment. Amelia wasn't sure Dorothea Beamguard even liked the man. Dorothea may have thought he was a handsome devil, but the woman still had a low tolerance for drinking halls. That conviction sure hadn't stopped her from wanting to peek into one, and the piano had given her the perfect excuse!

As Amelia reached the landing, she was building a fine speech on the bonds of female loyalty, but all words fled her mind when she heard Frank's laugh coming from the sitting room. She took the stairs swiftly, paused in the foyer, and peeked around the edge of the thick portieres.

Frank sat in the center of the silk damask sofa, tiny plates of food balanced on each knee—a mound of sandwiches on his left, and a pile of confections on his right—while holding a cup of tea and saucer. His fingers seemed too large to keep the English china handle steady, but he was managing. He took a sip, then before he could figure out where to put the cup, Luella Spivey whisked it from him to set on the service cart.

"Mr. Brody," Viola Reed chirped, "you haven't taken a bite of the watercress. I made them."

"And I made the cucumber," piped Dorothea Beamguard, her lips thin and eyes a vivid blue.

Frank selected one of the small squares of bread on the top and ate it in one bite.

Luella Spivey sat forward from her place in a wing chair. "Try mine. It's that one." She pointed, and Frank obliged by picking it up while still chewing on the first.

Amelia watched for long minutes. Watched as Frank cleaned the entire plate of sandwiches, ate every last chocolate and molasses brittle, and washed it down with two cups of tea that had to be room temperature.

He was grabbing the crisp serviette off his thighs when Esther Parks called out, "Amelia, dear, is that you lurking in the portieres?"

Amelia stiffened, feeling like a mouse caught in a corner by half a dozen cats. Backing away from the curtain's edge, she took a small step forward. "Yes, it's me."

"Whatever are you doing hiding?" Luella asked, but

didn't give Amelia the opportunity to reply. "Look who's come to pay his respects to our Narcissa."

"I can see."

Frank gazed at her, and Amelia refused to meet his eyes. What was he doing here—besides feasting on loaves of finger sandwiches and boxes of candy? The last she'd seen of him was when she'd gone back to the Moon Rock to collect her music bag. He'd been sitting at one of the tables doodling in a ledger book and hadn't paid her any mind accept to say good-bye.

"Mr. Brody brought Mrs. Dodge cattails," Altana Applegate said in her naturally soft-spoken voice. She was thin and tall, with prematurely gray hair matching the color of her eyes, but she was still pretty, and Amelia liked her.

"How nice." Amelia glanced at the jardiniere stand and the cupid vase full of furry brown cattails with long flat leaves. "I'm surprised to see you here, Mr. Brody. Socializing. I would have thought you would be socializing in your saloon."

"Pap's tending the bar while I'm gone." Frank leaned back, soaking in the attention with his long legs stretched out before him. He overpowered the room, making everything inside seem dwarflike. "I would have left right away, but the ladies insisted I eat a few sandwiches. They were real good."

They tittered—all accept Altana. And Dorothea Beamguard who kept her skeptical facade up, but Amelia knew better. Dorothea may not have approved of Frank's occupation, but she knew an opportunity when one presented itself. Her petite sandwiches were her pride and joy and had gained her entrance to many a parlor. She was probably on the verge of asking Mr. Brody about the beer mug stunt, stuffing him with food so he'd do as she asked.

Agitation worked through Amelia. Why, of all the two-faced, dirty tricks! The ladies were consorting with the enemy, conversing around him, feeding him, and giving him flirtatious glances despite not wholly approving of his establishment. These were the same ladies who'd shunned any saloon in town, other than Lloyd's, and had forbidden their men to set one foot through the doors of the Moon Rock until all the fancy furnishings began arriving. Each day as lavish and expensive decor had passed through those cut glass doors, their curiosity had mounted. And now because of the piano, they'd apparently found exactly what they'd been searching for—a respectable excuse to view a disrespectable saloon.

"I thought bachelors preferred their independence," Amelia commented. "To live by self-sustenance."

"Who ever said that?" Frank meshed his fingers together. "A man who can't cook worth a damn appreciates the flavors that come from a woman's seasoned kitchen. Take Mrs. Beamguard's cucumber sandwiches."

Dorothea sat straighter, her chin high. "What about them?"

"They were my favorite."

Dorothea shrugged, but couldn't contain a blush. "There's nothing to them, really. Just sliced cucumber —from my garden, of course—a dash of salt and pepper with mayonnaise sauce. No trouble at all."

"Just my point." Frank crossed his leg, putting his foot on his knee. The polished black of his boots shone, the leather looking comfortable and supple. "I wouldn't go to the trouble of slicing cucumbers. I'd be more inclined to open a can of beans." He regarded the women in the room carefully, omitting Amelia from his perusal. "You know, that's one reason a man gets married. So he can have someone cook for him."

Altana stood with haste, her fingers covering the gasp on her lips. "My goodness! I should have been home to start supper an hour ago."

"What time is it?" Mrs. Parks asked.

Viola Reed exclaimed, "Half past four!"

"We must be off!" Luella rose.

"Ladies, you're too late." Frank's voice made them freeze. "I saw your husbands heading over to the Chuckwagon for something to eat."

"What?" they cried.

"Yeah," Frank replied without inflection. "One-Eye Otis's special tonight is cowboy beans and red bean pie."

"Egad!" Luella cried. "I'll have to give Saybrook peptonic bitters for certain. Beans in moderation are good for the digestive system, but anything in quantity begets dyspepsia."

"Grenville's stomach can't withstand the Chuckwagon. I've lectured him not to eat the food there."

In a flurry of skirts, the five women rushed into the foyer. They plucked the hall tree bare—except for Mr. Brody's panama—and hastily collected hats, gloves, parasols, and baskets.

"Give Narcissa our best, dear," Viola Reed said to Amelia.

"Yes, Amelia," Dorothea hastened. "We'd tell her ourselves, but we've got to rescue our men from sour stomachs."

The door flew open, scattered children were collected, and the exasperated entourage walked swiftly down Dodge Street in the direction of Divine.

Amelia looked at Frank. He'd remained sitting, one corner of his mouth lifted in a half smile.

"Really," she chided. "Are their husbands at the Chuckwagon or is there a reason you wanted them out of the house?"

He stood and pushed his hands deep into his linen trouser pockets. The front of his cream-colored silk vest was buttoned for a change. As he strode toward her, his head nearly hit the bottom of the bronze extension chandelier in the center of the sitting room's ceiling. "I didn't make it up. I saw the men when I left the Moon Rock to come here."

Amelia frowned. "You could have mentioned that before you ate."

"And have to eat at the Chuckwagon myself? Hell no." He stepped around her, snagged his hat, and fit it on his thick black hair. "Even I only eat there when I'm desperate, which is twice a week. More often than not, my culinary creations aren't fit for consumption unless they come out of a can. I have to prepare everything on a single burner. It doesn't leave room for creativity." He began walking toward the open front door, taking her along with him, his hand on her elbow. She wasn't aware of his steering her until she was on the stoop with him.

"Let me ask you, Miss Marshall," he said, "what kind of a cook are you?"

The question took her aback. "I'm useful in the kitchen."

"That's not an answer. What I want to know is, can you make fried chicken?"

"Of course, I can. Why do you ask such a thing?"

"Because every Sunday when I come back from fishing, all I smell on the walk to the Moon Rock is fried chicken. If I don't get me some soon, I'm liable to bust in on someone's Sunday supper and demand to be fed."

"Why don't you have One-Eye Otis make you some fried chicken if you crave it so much?"

"Sweetheart, have you ever eaten at the Chuckwagon?"

"No."

"The extent of his menu consists of sonofabitch stew, cowboy beans, sourdough biscuits, red bean pie, and vinegar pie. That's it. From Sunday to Sunday. You try eating that several times a week, and you'll see what I mean about fried chicken."

Amelia went down the steps with Frank. She had no choice. He was still holding her arm. "Just what do you think you're doing, Mr. Brody?" she asked.

"It would appear," he replied, opening the gate to let her pass through, "I'm walking you home."

"I protest."

"Go ahead." But he didn't give up his hold.

She tried to free herself by wiggling her elbow. He only held tighter. If anyone saw her walking arm in arm, with him, down the street *to her house,* they might misconstrue the meaning. They might think she was attracted to him, just like all the other ladies. They might think she was falling for the wrong man again . . . just as she'd fallen for Jonas Pray. "I protest," she repeated in a firmer tone.

"And I said to go ahead."

"Humph," she mumbled, realizing it was no use. He wasn't letting go.

"How come you always do that?" Frank propelled them around the corner of Divine Street toward her house on Inspiration Lane.

"Do what?"

"Make that croaking sound."

She felt her cheeks heat up. "I make no such noise."

"Yeah, you do."

"I don't know what you're referring to. My vernacular is faultless. My deportment strictly enforced."

"I noticed that, too."

Amelia didn't like the tone of his remark. It certainly wasn't spoken in a complimentary manner. As they passed the numerous vacant lots filled with knee-high grasses and sprawling elms, she decided to comment on his goodwill gesture toward Narcissa. "Why did you bring Mrs. Dodge a bouquet of cattails?"

Frank gave her a lazy smile that made her pulse race with an irregular beat. "She was under the weather."

"You're not telling me the truth."

"Nope."

Ducking the overhanging branch of a gnarled oak, Amelia waited for him to confess. When he didn't, she prodded him. "Oh, for heaven's sake, I told you I could make fried chicken, the least you can do is tell me why you gave Narcissa cattails."

"Making fried chicken is no secret." He grinned. "But the reason I gave Mrs. Dodge cattails is."

"Then suit yourself and don't tell me." This time she caught him off guard and wrenched free of his grip. She picked up her pace, practically setting off in a blind run. Let him keep his secret why he gave a married woman marsh stems. No man had ever given her a present, and perhaps the lack thereof was showing like a shiny penny on her face.

"Slow down, dammit." Frank chased her up her walkway and onto her porch.

Amelia opened her purse and fumbled for her door key, but not until Frank put his hand over hers. She didn't want to meet his gaze.

Frank took her chin in his fingers and lifted her head to face him. She stared into the depths of his blue eyes and felt an inexplicable jolt of her heart. "I gave Mrs. Dodge the cattails because her husband signs the permits that keep me in business."

Her chivalrous illusions of him shattered. He gave the gift because he wanted something. Or rather, wanted to keep things running smoothly. "Now I wish you hadn't told me," she said.

"Why not?"

"Because giving a gift for self purposes isn't heroic."

"Sweetheart, I'm not the hero type." He gazed at her, his expression unreadable. She wasn't sure what he was thinking. A man like Frank Brody could mask his emotions well, and she wasn't experienced enough to read between the lines.

"W-What?" she stammered. "Why are you looking at me like that?"

"I was just thinking."

"Th-Thinking what?" She couldn't breathe. He stood so close. Close enough for her to smell the sun-baked straw on his hat, the shaving soap clinging to his skin.

"About your fried chicken." Closer. . . . Then he gave her a kiss on the lips. Not really on the lips, but rather the corner of her mouth . . . the place where she had a very slight dimple when she smiled. There was nothing romantic or passionate about the kiss; it was more brotherly than anything else. But intimate just the same.

Amelia wasn't prepared for the gesture, and she didn't know what to do. She stood there like a statue, eyes wide and heart thumping. He pulled away, letting go of her hand. "You better get inside."

She couldn't find her voice as he turned to leave. Her eyes followed him through her picket gate and beyond until she couldn't see him anymore. How could she have allowed him to take such a liberty? She raised her gloved hand to her cheek . . . to the spot his lips had kissed.

As the sky deepened to dusk, and the evening call of crickets began their symphony of chirps, she couldn't help wondering . . .

Would he kiss her dead center on the mouth if she made him fried chicken?

Chapter

8

As the laundry shop bell tinkled above Frank's head, the smells of Roseine washing powder and borax pressed upon him. Though the two windows on the northern walls were open, the air in the receiving area was pungent and suffocating.

He shut the door and strode into the room. Balls of fuzz were prevalent on the floorboards and they scattered like pale chicks when he walked. His gaze landed on the name-labeled cubbies that had been built in back of the front counter. He looked for his and found a neatly wrapped bundle inside, then he waited for Emmaline to appear from behind the chenille drape. He leaned his hip against the hinged top of the counter, glanced at his pants leg, then plucked the lint off the dark material.

Fighting the need to breathe fresh air, he slid some of the stamped denim laundry bags bulging with clothes out of his way so he could rest his arms on his elbows. He drummed his fingertips on the surface, glancing at the bolt of manila paper and cotton twine.

He hadn't seen Emmaline since Sunday after church. Usually, he came around the laundry twice a week— once to drop off, once to pick up, sometimes a third time if he happened to run into her on the street and she invited him.

"Emmaline," he called out over the hiss of a steam generator when she hadn't appeared after a few minutes. "Hey, Em."

Nothing.

Straightening, Frank looked over his shoulder. Late in the day, the boardwalk wasn't overly used. Most of the businesses had two hours left until closing. Shrugging, Frank lifted the counter piece up and slipped through. He paused at the curtain, caught the edge in his hand, and glanced around the large area. Looking like a hydrant, the nine-hundred-pound generator spit vapors through cracks in the seams; white mist rose in clouds. There was a hand cylinder washing machine with a hose attached to a spigot running through the open back door. He still couldn't see Emmaline, so he entered the workings of the laundry to look for her.

He went around numerous clothes bars and a shelf lined up with Kingsford silver gloss, celluloid starch packages, a half-pound case of Roseine washing powder, Chinese laundry wax, and bottles of blueing, lye, and borax.

"Emmaline." His voice carried over the *shist-shist* of the steam.

He rounded a laundry stove with two boiler holes and space on the sides for nine irons, all of which were occupied with sadirons in varying sizes. A hand fluter with ridges rested in its cradle on the edge of one of the burners.

Figuring she was outside hanging clothes, he went in that direction. There was a double-wide door to his right, just behind the Jewel Collar and Cuff Ironer and Economic Starcher. He'd asked her once what all the gadgets were, and she'd proudly told him the names. He'd been interested in the flip-down lid on the sink, and she'd showed him that many times over since.

Frank reached the doorway and put his hand on the frame.

Emmaline stood next to a basket crammed with sheets, her cheeks a high pink from the heat. She'd plaited her hair in a loose braid, and black tendrils framed her face. Her apron pocket swelled with clothespins, and she fit one over the fold of un-bleached sheeting and into the taut clothesline. He hesitated, measuring her for a moment. She appeared much younger than the twenty-five years she'd told him was her age. He felt a queer flinch bunch his muscles, and a flicker of scruples swept through him.

As she withdrew another pin, she sang, "Ere my verses I conclude, I'd like it known and understood, though free as air, I'm never rude—I'm not too bad and not too good! Ta-ra-ra-boom-de-ay! Ta-ra-ra-boom-de-ay! Ta-ra-ra-boom-de-ay! Ta-ra-ra-boom-de-ay! Ta-ra-ra-boom—"

"Emmaline."

"—de . . . ay. . . ." Hearing Frank, she turned. An unsure smile curved her lips. "Hello, Frank."

"I waited for you to come to the counter, but you didn't hear the bell."

"I can't hear it when I'm outside." She fit the pin into the end of the sheet, then came toward him. An awkward tension stretched between them. "I have your laundry finished."

She made a move to go inside, but he touched her arm and prevented her from passing by. "I saw." She glanced at his hand, then at his face. "Are you still mad at me?" he asked, holding her captive with his gaze.

She shrugged softly. "I suppose not."

"Good." But oddly, he didn't feel any sense of

relief. He leaned in to kiss her, but instead of seeing her hazel eyes and ebony hair, he pictured tones of brown. Eyes the color of walnut and hair like shiny sienna. Rather than capture Emmaline's lips with his, he gently caught her jaw in his fingers, turned her head, and kissed her cheek. When he backed away, disappointment clearly showed in her gaze—as well as puzzlement. He let her go, but she didn't readily move away. Perhaps she thought he was waiting for her to invite him to spill some suds.

He felt a pang of guilt—for what, he didn't care to analyze. He didn't want to look at her as if he were weighing the question of doing it with her on the drainer lid. Dammit to hell, he wasn't in the mood for no good reason he could find to give her.

Brushing his knuckles under her chin, he gave her what he hoped was an easy grin. "I've got to be opening up the Moon Rock too soon to enjoy kissing you the way I like." He rubbed his thumb on her soft skin. "Next time, sweetheart."

Emmaline blushed. "Let me get your shirts for you."

Frank followed her around the equipment and through the curtain where he ducked underneath the counter to stand like an ordinary customer in front of her. She went for the cubby in which she'd chalked his name and withdrew his crinkling brown paper-wrapped parcel.

Shoving his hand in his hip pocket, Frank took out his leather flap book.

"That's all right, Frank." Emmaline's voice stopped him. "There's no charge."

"Why not?"

"Because I got mad at you when you invited Miss Marshall to give her lessons in your saloon." Emmaline fidgeted with the leaves of her sales book. "I shouldn't have. I . . . I guess I was jealous until I realized she's not the type of woman to turn a man's head."

Frank's misgivings were increasing. "I haven't noticed anything wrong with Miss Marshall."

"There's nothing wrong with her. It's just that, well, you know, the scandal and all with the book and Bible salesman left her rather . . . cold. She's not a very warm person, especially toward men."

"I think I should pay you for the shirts," Frank commented, not wanting to hear anything further on Amelia Marshall's character.

Emmaline traced the lettering on the cover of her book with a slender finger. "Well, there is something you could do in lieu of payment."

"I told you, sweetheart, I don't have time today."

"Not that." She gave him a beckoning smile. "The Fourth of July picnic is coming up in a couple weeks, and you could take me."

A tightness strained Frank's shoulders. "I don't go to town functions, Em."

"But it's not sponsored by the church, or anything," she rushed. "It's going to be fun. There'll be a box lunch raffle, booths, and games."

"I'm sorry. I don't like crowds."

Crestfallen, her chin lowered. "I'm sorry, too."

He grappled for an alternative to placate her. "Why don't you ask one of the boys who work at Reed's sawmill to take you?"

Her head lifted and her eyes shot him a glare. "No. A lady doesn't do that sort of thing. It was hard enough for me to ask you."

Frank selected a dollar from his wallet and set it on the counter. "I think you're a beautiful woman, Em, but I thought you understood I'm not a man for social functions."

"Yes . . . you told me. I just thought . . . oh, never mind."

He picked up his package, feeling like a pile of dog crap. "I'm sorry," he said again, then exited the laundry.

The boardwalk planks rang hard under his heels. He should have left Emmaline Shelby alone because she was beginning to want more from him than a casual affair. Well, he wasn't a courtship kind of man. He'd sooner buy his own casket than enter a church, stand in front of a reverend, and get into a matrimonial neck yoke.

As Frank walked to the Moon Rock, he kept seeing Emmaline's sad eyes. He'd thought he'd made himself clear before they'd started up. Emmaline might have been willing, but he shouldn't have allowed anything to happen between them. She lived in a respectable boardinghouse on Holy Road, went to the Christ Redeemer, and had parents living somewhere in Kansas—or so she'd said. She never told him why she'd left home, only that she had, and that she'd made some mistakes.

Hell, he really should have gone down to Boise once a month where the lights were red and the beds soft. Instead, he'd gotten tangled up with a girl who'd strayed off the main trail, but was an honorable woman just the same. He liked Emmaline and couldn't find a single fault in her. She deserved better than what she was getting from him.

As Frank neared his saloon, he heard the sour notes of his upright wailing for mercy from the lessons. Amelia had begun at one o'clock, and apparently the torturous noise hadn't let up since, this now being 3:15. Earlier in the day, he'd awoken to the god-awful sounds of *do-re-mi-fa-so-la-ti-do—do-ti-la-so-fa-mi-re-do*. Over and over and over and over, and not necessarily in the right order. He'd been so agitated by the time he'd swung his legs out of the bed, he'd gotten dressed in the first things he could find, and hightailed it out of his saloon. He'd eaten a dissatisfying meal at One-Eye Otis's Chuckwagon, then headed over to the laundry to see Em.

He'd been hoping the Moon Rock would be cleared out by the time he got back, but the ineptitude of the loud scales told him otherwise. Seeing twin boys with steel-framed eyeglasses sitting on the split log bench in front of the saloon didn't lighten Frank's dark mood. The bibs of their overalls were unfastened on one side and they were licking chunks of melting ice; dribbles of water trailed down their elbows and puddled on the boardwalk.

Spotting Frank, they snickered. One picked up a King popgun on the bench, took aim and fired right at Frank. The small cork hit him on the shoulder, and with enough force to annoy the hell out of him.

"Bang!" the grubby bandit declared. "You're dead, mister."

Trying to remain in control of his temper, rancor sharpened Frank's voice. "What's your name, *son?*"

"Walter Reed."

The other giggled so profusely, Frank knew there was an inside joke he wasn't in on. "All right, kid, what gives?"

"He's not Walter," the boy said. "I'm Walter. He's Warren, and he's a pissant."

"No," Frank amended. "He's dead if he ever does that to me again. I've got a real Smith and Wesson beneath my counter, boys, and it's not there for decoration. You got that?"

Walter and Warren looked like they were going to wet their pants.

Frank shoved the bat-wing doors inward with enough force to make the girl in pink flounces sitting at the piano with Amelia jump. Amelia gave Frank a quizzical gaze, then swiveled on her chair and returned to tutoring her pupil.

Rounding the edge of the bar, Frank ignored Pap

and made a beeline for his icebox. He put his hand on a beer, then changed his mind. He wasn't going to have a drink just before opening; it went against his principles. Shutting the door, he strode to the counter and grabbed a glass. He filled it with ice, then shot a stream of seltzer over the chips Pap had recently dumped in the dishpan underneath the bar.

Frank took a long swallow of the cold drink, the bubbles cooling him off. The piano-playing continued and he watched Amelia instruct the girl. Miss Marshall was looking a little taxed. Her neat and tight bun seemed to be pulling loose on top of her head, and her normally erect posture had begun to fade. Despite her flushed state, he found her a tempting sight.

He'd tried to shrug off why he'd kissed her, having no viable answer other than he'd felt like it. She'd stood there on her porch, still as a lake at noon. He wondered how many times she'd been kissed. If that salesman had put his lips on hers before he decided to leave her. That thought didn't set well with Frank.

"Ain't she a pretty sight?" Pap whispered, his face aglow with adoration.

Frank absently agreed, "Yeah," then remembered he needed to tap a new keg of beer. A good thing, because he needed a diversion. He looked for his bung starter—a heavy wooden mallet—on the shelf. Just as his fingers curled around the handle, a woman's voice carried from the boardwalk right in front of the saloon.

Her greeting contained a strong suggestion of reproach and was interspersed with the brassy rattle of a cage and the frantic chirps of a bird. "When you left the house, I told you boys to wait for me inside if I wasn't back from the veterinary on time!"

"We were finished," Walter and Warren said together.

Chirp! Chirp! "I distinctly said, if I'm late, you wait inside and I'll come in and get you."

"It was too hot in there," Warren complained.

"Yeah, too hot." Walter defended his brother.

The high-pitched tweet of the bird seemed distressed, but Viola Reed overlooked it. "Well, you're going back inside this saloon right now. You forgot your sheet music."

"Did not."

"Yes you did." *Chirp! Chirp!* "We need to get it from Miss Marshall." Her words were stern and spoken without margin for an argument. "Come along!"

Frank lounged against the bar as Mrs. Viola Reed poked her out-of-joint nose through the seam in the bat-wing doors. She swept her gaze around the room, her brows arched high, her lips pursed. The boys erupted on either side of her and shoved their wet hands into their pockets while slouching.

"My, my," she mused aloud, over the trill of a blue parakeet in her bell-shaped cage. As the bird flitted inside the limited space, tiny down feathers flew between the thin brass bars. Birdseed scattered from the twin cups as the parakeet lighted on the perch, then flapped its wings, and took off again toward the swing. "My, my," she repeated and took mincing steps into the saloon, the handle in her hand swinging the cage.

The crunch of seeds under her patent-leather shoes rankled Frank. The lady was making a mess on his clean floor.

"Mrs. Reed." Amelia stood from the stool. "Is there something I can do for you?"

"My boys," she said, not making eye contact with Amelia, rather taking in every detail of her surroundings, "forgot their sheet music."

"I gave it to them." Amelia looked at Warren and Walter. "Where did you put your Kinkel folio?"

Warren pushed his glasses higher on the bridge of his nose while Walter yanked his hand out of his pocket to show Amelia a paper folded in eighths. "Right here."

Amelia groaned.

Mrs. Reed shrugged. "I guess you did have it, after all."

"Miss Marshall," the girl at the piano whispered. "Am I finished?"

"Oh." Amelia turned and set the pencil she'd been holding on top of the piano. It was then Frank noticed the swatch of a tasseled scarf with fringy stuff draped atop the cabinet and the six statuettes of the masters lined up in official order.

The infamous busts.

Amelia fidgeted with a triangle-shaped thing with a long stick affixed to the front of it; there was a key on the side. He didn't think it was a clock, but it was ticking like one. She made the arm stop wagging back and forth by pushing a small weight down the stem. "Yes, Merleen. You may go. Don't forget your music."

"I won't." The little girl in pink gave Frank a shy glance, then headed for the doors. As she passed Walter and Warren, she stuck her tongue out at them.

The twins broke into peals of laughter, exciting the bird to dart around the cage. *Chirp! Chirp!* Seeds rained anew onto the floor.

This time Viola Reed took notice and pressed her nose next to the cage. "Bluebell, precious, calm yourself. Mama is going to take you home in a minute."

Walter and Warren laughed even harder at their mother's cooing. She shot them a disapproving glare, then gave Frank an unhurried gaze. "Tell me, Mr. Brody, where is it, exactly, my Wendell stands when he's at your bar?"

Frank drew another sip of a seltzer into his mouth, letting the cool liquid take its time sliding down his throat. "Well, Mrs. Reed, that all depends."

"On . . . ?" She hung on his every word.

"Depends on where the hell he wants to stand. Or

sit. I've seen him at that very table you're standing in front of, buying a few rounds for the boys from the mill."

"What?"

"Yeah. He's bought his men drinks."

"He's spent our money on liquor for the workers?"

"And they appreciated every drop." Frank set his glass down. "Not too many men as thoughtful as your husband, Mrs. Reed. It's a real pleasure to serve him."

Her jaw slacked.

"Now," he continued in a slow drawl, "if you were a man, I'd say you'd be just as generous. That's a rare quality in a person these days, and you'd best keep hold of that husband of yours. He's a mighty fine human being."

"Well . . . I . . ." She frowned, apparently considering Frank's monologue. "Yes . . . my Wendell can be . . . yes . . . he's . . ."

"A nincompoop," Walter snickered. "That's what you called him at supper last night."

"Walter Owens Reed!" Viola burst out. "You'd better be hungry, because as soon as we get home, you're eating soap!"

Warren bust up. "Hee haw, Walter gets a taste of scouring soap."

Frank ran his fingertips across his jaw, then his lips. He glanced at Amelia, who'd begun to tidy up. She seemed embarrassed by the family's bickering. She looked tired and in need of something cool to drink, but he knew she was too proud to ask for anything. So he decided to make the offer.

"Hey, Miss Marshall." She lifted her face from her music bag. "You up for a Baptist lemonade?"

Without cracking her teacher's facade, she nodded. "Thank you, Mr. Brody. That would be nice."

Viola's mouth turned down as if she'd bit into a sour grape. "Miss Marshall. You're a Methodist."

Amelia smiled ever so slightly. "Yes, you're quite right." But she didn't bother to give Viola Reed an explanation of the drink, instead choosing to keep its recipe a secret.

Frank liked the fact Amelia didn't divulge the harmless ingredients. It told him she enjoyed a gag as much as he did.

Amelia reached for one of the busts, the nile green fabric of her bodice stretching over her breasts. He admired her curves, while bringing his glass to his lips; he caught an ice chip in his mouth, the frosty coolness reminding him he'd thought of Miss Amelia Marshall as an icicle. Or, maybe he used to. After he'd kissed the sweet corner of her mouth last night, he couldn't exactly say she was cold. No. Her skin had been as warm as brandy. And she'd smelled nice. He couldn't quite put his finger on the scent, but it was pleasing. Not too flowery. Not too spicy. Feminine.

He crunched on the ice, letting the cold pieces melt on his tongue.

"Well?" Pap blurted, taking Frank from his thoughts.

"Well what?"

"Aren't you going to make Miss Marshall her lemonade?"

Frank moved into action, cursing at himself that he'd been caught up in staring at Amelia and forgot to make her drink.

The parakeet in Viola Reed's cage continued its nervous chirps, dropping more seeds. Frank glanced at the woman and gave her a hard stare, hoping she'd realize he was getting ready to give her the heave-ho if she didn't exit soon. As it was, Pap was going to have a hell of a mess to sweep up.

"Is there anything else you need, Mrs. Reed?" Amelia asked, and Frank was glad she did.

Viola pinned her gaze on the back bar, looking at

the knickknacks and especially the moon rock. "I suppose not. I'll have the boys come back next Tuesday at two-thirty."

"Yes." Amelia directed her next words at Walter and Warren. "Remember what I said. Hum the notes to each other."

"Yeah, we were going to," they snickered.

Frank could have whacked the boys on their butts. One thing he'd learned from the sisters was a form of respect.

Viola Reed turned to leave and had barely gotten out of the doors when Cobb Weatherwax came strolling in. As Frank sliced a lemon, he summed Cobb up with a nod of his head. There was only one word to describe the regular customer: hairy. He was tall, with an untamed mane of bark brown hair on his head and the lower half of his face. He seemed bigger than he really was, due to the bulky animal skins he wore even in the dead of summer. He carried his essentials: an out-of-date long Kentucky rifle, a bullet mold, and powder horn—of which he put a pinch of gunpowder into his drinks, a sharp ax, and a keen knife.

As Amelia finished her packing, securing the last bust into her bag, she looked up. Upon seeing Cobb, she bit her lower lip, and Frank figured she was stifling a gasp. Cobb could be a mite intimidating at first glance.

"How do, Frank," Cobb said, slipping off his battered felt hat and placing it on the bar in front of him. "I ain't got me no beavers today. Going to get me some, though. I like beavers. Better than I like coons. Do you like beavers?"

"I never thought much on them, Cobb," Frank replied, stirring sugar into Amelia's lemonade.

"It's a damn shame you don't."

Pap scratched his head. "Cobb, I've been wondering if I could ask you something."

"I don't see no call for you not to, Pap."

126

"How old are you?"

Cobb propped his Kentucky on the counter. "Twenty-seven."

"How come you're not married?"

"I ain't found no woman who would have me."

Frank finished Amelia's lemonade and walked around the bar to give her the glass. She accepted the drink from him, darting a nervous glance at Cobb. Frank said in a low tone, "He just looks scary. He's more hair than harm." Then more loudly, "Cobb."

The man at the counter turned. "Yes?"

"This is Miss Marshall, Cobb. She's a piano teacher."

"Howdy, Miz Marshall." To Frank, he said with puzzlement, "How come she's in the Moon Rock?"

Amelia swept a loose curl from her forehead. "Because Mr. Brody is using my piano while he waits for his to arrive."

"Huh?" Cobb replied.

Frank gave Amelia a thoughtful frown. "I thought you were over being mad?"

"Some things never die, Mr. Brody, they only flicker. But as soon as I'm reminded of my predicament, the resentment burns bright once again."

"Well unremind yourself while you're drinking that lemonade. I wouldn't want you to sour up." On an impulse, he whispered, "I'd have to squeeze you if you did."

She colored, just as he desired.

Pap poured Cobb a whiskey, the glass and bottle clinking loudly enough for Amelia and Frank to turn their heads. Pap's eyes were fixed on Amelia, and he awkwardly cleared his throat while he addressed Cobb in a voice strong enough for the whole room to hear. "Let's say you were to find the right woman, Cobb, would you marry her?"

Cobb unplugged the top of his powder flask and tapped some of the black flecks into his whiskey. "I reckon I would, if she'd have me. All men want a good woman."

Pap smiled. "I couldn't agree more." Grinning broadly at Amelia, he asked, "Miss Marshall, would you ever consider getting married?"

"I . . ."

Then as if realizing how literal his question came across, Pap quickly amended in a rush, "Not that I'm asking! I mean, not that I wouldn't ask a fine woman such as yourself. I doubt you'd have me—or would you? That is, what I'm trying to say is, what I mean is, I was referring to the institution itself." Gasping for breath, he asked, "Are you opposed to marriage, or do you like living by yourself?"

The longer Pap talked, the worse he sounded, and Frank could feel the tension in Amelia from a foot away. She gave an anxious little cough, then took a sip of her lemonade. She stole a look of indecision at Frank over the rim of her glass before hastily glancing away. Putting the lemonade down, she said with reserve, "I have adjusted to living alone, Mr. O'Cleary, but I believe most women would like the opportunity to be a wife."

A general answer, Frank thought, spoken with humility and effectiveness. But did she really mean it? He suspected she did and felt lacking for not having achieved the title of missus herself. Well, he couldn't help her there. He'd give her use of the piano; he wasn't giving her use of his name, though Pap sure seemed intent on hitching his after Amelia's.

Frank had never seen Pap acting so much like a horny bull penned up in a pasture. His behavior bordered on pathetic. At least Pap shut up after Amelia's reply.

Amelia put the last of her things away, drank more of her lemonade, and stood there with her glass half full, looking very out of place. Frank guessed the hour close to four. Some of the stockmen came in about now, and a gentleman guest or two from the hotel wanting to have a snort before dinner. Cobb generally left and came back near closing.

"Getting to be that time," Pap remarked offhandedly, but with an inflection of forced casualness only Frank saw through.

Pap O'Cleary wanted to show off his piano-playing.

Meshing his fingers together, Pap stretched his arms. His joints cracked, and Frank noticed Amelia shuddered. "I'd best be warming up."

Pap rounded the bar and stepped on the birdseed. The hulls crunched and he looked down. "Confound it." Blustering over to the corner, he snatched up the broom and began vigorously sweeping the seeds underneath the one-foot gap of the bat-wing doors.

"Thank you for the lemonade, Mr. Brody," Amelia said, pressing the glass into Frank's hand.

"Any time."

She fingered the gold watch on her bodice and read the round face. "It's eight minutes after four. I'm on your piano time. I'll be going now."

"Who counts minutes?"

"I do."

Slipping her gloves on, she picked up her bag.

"Did you get everything?" he asked, stalling her departure. "All your busts?"

Giving him a lift of her brows, she clipped, "All eight of them."

Frank couldn't contain a burst of laughter as he set the glass on top of the piano. "Goddamn, you can be funny."

"Don't damn God for my humor, Mr. Brody. In all likelihood it was my aunt who instilled a fraction of wit in me. She was very skilled at repartee—dry, especially. I think you would have liked her, but I'm not sure if the opposite would have rung true. She was very selective about her company." Amelia nodded curtly. "Good day, Mr. Brody."

"Wait," he said, surprised by his own voice. "I want to talk to you."

"I believe that's what we've been doing."

"This is about the lessons."

"What is it you have to say?"

Pap chose then to walk up to them and sit down on the piano stool. He gave his knuckles another bone-jarring snap, curved his fingers over the keys, paused, then burst into the chorus for "The Cat Came Back." He went as far as singing along in a baritone laden with staged emotion.

"But the cat came back, couldn't stay no longer. Yes, the cat came back the very next day. The cat came back, thought he was a goner. But the cat came back for it wouldn't stay away."

Amelia stared at him.

Under Pap's guidance, the piano strings worked into hard chords and set a brisk melody. The loud notes left no room for Frank to speak with Amelia, so he took her by the elbow and steered her out the front doors.

Once on the boardwalk, the song didn't seem so potent. But it still was noisy, and Pap didn't let up on his vocalizing.

"I don't know what gets into Pap when he's around you, Miss Marshall," Frank remarked. "He's normally not such a buffoon."

Amelia made no comment on that but did address Frank with a certain amount of appeal. "What is it you needed to say to me, Mr. Brody?"

Frank crossed his arms over his chest. In doing so, the gravelly sound of discarded birdseed beneath his boots made him frown. "I hope you don't take this the wrong way, sweetheart, but I think you're going to have to tell your pupils' mothers they can't hang around. I saw them gathered in front of the Moon Rock while I was over at the Chuckwagon. Parks's wife stayed inside for fifteen minutes before she left.

Then she came out to report to Mrs. Beamguard." Frank crossed one leg in front of the other. "Now, I'm not one to complain about women in the saloon—if they're the type of woman you'd expect to see in a saloon. But birdseed spilled on the floor doesn't make for a good impression, not to mention, that Reed woman is obnoxious."

"When the novelty wears off, I'm sure they won't come anymore." Amelia looked him straight in the eyes, and he felt the afternoon sunlight pouring over his back. "You wouldn't have to be concerned over this if I had the piano in my home."

"If you had the piano in your home, you wouldn't be talking to me, now would you, Miss Marshall?" He took a step closer to her. "And I rather like talking to you."

"Since we are talking," she noted in a cool, impersonal tone, "I've been thinking about what transpired between us yesterday."

"So have I."

Her eyes brightened. "You have?"

He nodded.

After a moment's pause, she sobered and cleared her throat. "It has to be said, what happened between us must never be repeated. I wouldn't want you to get the wrong impression of me. Just because I'm accepting your hospitality doesn't mean you can take liberties on my person, Mr. Brody. I won't allow it. Do I make myself clear?"

"Crystal. It won't happen again."

She seemed surprised, and a little disappointed, by his reply. "W-Well, then . . ." she stammered, making a move to leave. "I'll be going now."

He stopped her with a hastily put together question. "When are your eager students going to play something that doesn't sound like scratches on a chalkboard?"

She cracked a slight smile, as if gaining some

satisfaction that the poor skills of her pupils bothered him. "Don't you like their diatonic scales in solmization?"

"About as much as I like popguns shot at me. Kids aren't my favorite thing in life."

Her expression grew subtly serious. "You dislike children?"

"I have no feelings either way. They remind me I was little once."

"We all were."

"Yeah, but my childhood was fleeting."

"How very awful for you," she said softly. "What happened?"

He was uncomfortable with the sympathy in her tone and mad that he'd allowed her to maneuver their conversation onto a topic he'd only discussed with Pap. And that had been hard enough. The moods were rare that he spoke about the orphanage and Harry.

"There are some subjects, Miss Marshall," Frank said, his palm on the door's frosted glass, "that are better left undiscussed."

He pushed the door in and damned himself for bringing up old memories—however elusive. He recognized the fact that, for whatever reason, Amelia Marshall could bring his childhood memories to surface. A very dangerous feat to a man who prided himself on not needing anyone.

What he did need, however, was to concentrate on the do-si-do girls. The upright piano wasn't enough. Charley had said he'd been able to pack the place when his girl had been dancing to a banjo and harmonica. First thing tomorrow, Frank would send an open telegram to several papers advertising for saloon girls. He disregarded Pap's warning about the town women not going for the idea. He'd been doing what he wanted to up until this point, and no one had slung any fire and brimstone at him.

He had nothing to lose and everything to gain.

Chapter

9

Amelia sat at the table in her formal dining room, hands clasped on her lap, and a hot dinner of one pork chop, boiled red potatoes, and garden peas in front of her. She'd put a fresh-cut bouquet of fragrant pink peonies in the center of the table with two paraffin candles in glass candlesticks.

The pendulum on the black walnut regulator moved to and fro, counting out the seconds. When the striker hit the gong bell five times, she withdrew her flatware from her damask napkin. She aligned the knife to the right of her anemone-patterned semi-porcelain ware, the fork to the left. Opening the bleached linen square, she smoothed the napkin on her lap, picked up her fork, and began to eat her meal.

Alone.

Amelia didn't care for Saturday evenings. The unmarried ladies fortunate enough to have gentlemen callers were taken on sunset picnics or to a restaurant dinner at the Chuckwagon. The men at Reed's saw-mill never came to call on her; men didn't ask her if she wanted to go on a twilight buggy ride, or to have One-Eye Otis slice her a piece of vinegar pie. Instead, she had a pork chop on Saturday nights and ate in unaccompanied silence.

At least on Sundays she felt included. For the past two years since her aunt Clara had died, she'd eaten her Sunday suppers with Narcissa and Cincinatus. The couple had been the first Idahoans she and her aunt had met upon reaching Boise.

Amelia and her mother's sister, Clara Davenport, were newly arrived from Denver, and her aunt had been uncertain where they would settle. She'd decided to make the capital city their roosting spot while she studied prospective areas within the state to relocate. They'd met the Dodges in a Boise dining room; Cincinatus and Narcissa spoke of a small town to the north called Weeping Angel, that would be celebrating its founding on the Fourth of July. The couple had lived there for a year and had told her aunt it was still quiet, quaint, and had a reverend who could preach a mean streak.

Aunt Clara said that was just the type of town Amelia's mother had wanted for Amelia.

So Amelia and Aunt Clara had come to Weeping Angel and stayed at the Oak Tree Hotel while a house could be built for them on Inspiration Lane. Aunt Clara thought the street name befitting a home for her sister's only child.

Amelia pushed her peas around on her plate, thinking about her mother. Ida Marshall had died six years ago and had been a staunch Methodist. A singing Methodist—that denomination of pious people prone to vocalizing their way through the gospel. Amelia couldn't remember her father. He'd died when she was five and they lived on their farm in Lone Rock, Wisconsin. The details of his face had faded, and with no pictures of him, she wouldn't have known him if she passed him by in heaven.

Lifting a glass of milk to her lips, Amelia drank. The clock kept its steady beat; somewhere in the rafters, the house creaked.

Amelia reflected her childhood hadn't been really sad after her father died. From the farm they'd moved to Larimer Street in Denver to live with Aunt Clara and the two elderly ladies, the Wooten sisters, her aunt cared for.

Smiling in recollection, Amelia set her glass down. She'd liked the Wooten sisters, Cille and Cea, after she'd gotten used to them. They'd smelled like thyme and mint, glycerin, and rose vinegar. Amelia was given the task of making the sisters' beds each morning, and the toilet bouquet of old ladies lingered on the bedclothes. As she grew older, kitchen duties were added to Amelia's chores.

Although Amelia and her mother weren't well off, Amelia couldn't remember ever lacking for anything throughout her adolescence. The Wootens lived comfortably and shared their monetary security with those who resided in the house. Not through cash compensation—for Amelia and her mother were never paid—but by their prosperous surroundings.

Though Baptists, the Wootens loved singing and music as much as Ida Marshall. The sisters insisted Amelia take lessons, and for the next ten years, every Wednesday Miss Lovejoy came to instruct Amelia promptly at three o'clock—to the delight of Cille and Cea, who on those Wednesdays took their tea with musical accompaniment. It was only after Amelia's mother fell ill with chronic bronchitis, that Miss Lovejoy stopped coming, fearful of Amelia's mother's disease.

Sighing, Amelia took up her knife. The sisters both died in their seventies within two months of each other during the spring of 1890. Their house and their holdings had gone to Aunt Clara and, in an indirect way, to Amelia. For it was the Wooten money that built the very house she lived in now. It was the Wooten money that had kept her sheltered and financially secure after Aunt Clara passed on.

But it was the same Wooten money that was running out.

As Amelia put a small piece of meat into her mouth, she almost wished she could go back to her childhood when worries were not as pressing, when the worst thing to happen to her was Horace Button teasing her in primary school because she lived with smelly old ladies.

Thoughtfully setting her fork down, words came into Amelia's head. *My childhood was fleeting.* That's what Frank had said to her.

There are some subjects, Miss Marshall, that are better left undiscussed.

Despite all her trials and tribulations, she could look back with a semblance of fondness and talk about her growing-up years.

What had happened to Frank Brody when he was little? She couldn't picture him helpless or vulnerable. Or sad. He always seemed so casual. So disarming.

The chaste kiss he'd given her had stuck in her mind. She'd been uncertain how to conduct herself when in his company next, and decided to be cool and disciplined, yet approachable—the perfect definition of a teacher. He'd acted as if nothing intimate had transpired between them when he spoke to her about Mrs. Reed. It was only after she'd censured him on his behavior that he acknowledged the kiss at all. She should have been relieved he'd agreed with her.

But she still thought of the kiss often, putting more into it than she should have. She was acting foolish, she knew. No matter how fleeting, his mouth had brushed hers. She couldn't make that go away, no matter how sternly she willed herself to put it out of her head. . . . Well, it wouldn't occur again, so she needn't bother herself over foolish reactions to him.

She was being silly and out of character. She knew better.

My childhood was fleeting.

Why did his words keep coming back to haunt her?

Suddenly, Amelia wasn't hungry anymore. She pushed her plate away and stood. She didn't want to feel sorry for Frank Brody. It was a lot less complicated to feel sorry for herself. And right now, she could find a major reason to be morose: the chicken pox.

It had struck the second day of her lessons, hitting Elroy Parks smack on the neck and hairline. Had he not worn his hair slicked back with his father's brilliantine mustache oil that day, she might not have noticed the scattering of red dots on his forehead and behind his ears.

Taking her plate into the kitchen and setting it in the sink, Amelia knew the chicken pox never struck once. Soon most every student she had who had not had the chicken pox yet would get it. And quarantined students meant no students. No students meant no money.

Would her troubles never end?

Leaving the dishes, Amelia went to the back door and put her palm on the screen. The evening was lovely; the summer smells of grass and gardens and flowers drifted to the porch. The distant croaks and chirps of frogs and crickets sounded tranquil. A faraway coupling of laughter came from Divine Street . . . no doubt just outside the Chuckwagon.

Letting her hand trail the mesh, Amelia wondered . . . did anyone else notice these things, alone, and feel even more excluded than ever?

Frank lay on his bed, the much-worn copy of *A Tale of Two Cities* draped facedown over his bare abdomen. He'd left the door to his room open, and a light summer breeze stirred the warm air scented with his snuffed cheroot. He took a slow swallow of cognac, then set the near-empty beer mug on top of the dresser next to his bedstead. He'd closed the Moon Rock hours ago and sleep still eluded him. Sometimes he was plagued with fits of insomnia that lasted weeks. Mostly, the sleepless bouts came on him for no apparent reason. But tonight he figured he was suffering from wakefulness because his saloon had been raided by kids all week.

Kids made him think of his brother Harry. And the home.

Turning onto his side, Frank slid the Dickens story closed and ran his hand across the scarred leather top. He'd had the book for eleven years. His parents' theatrical troupe, the Merry Tramps, had been performing at the Vioget Theater in Frisco when he'd found the discarded volume in the alley behind the dockside playhouse. He hadn't been able to read the book then. It was many years later, when he and Harry were in the orphanage, that he'd been taught to read by the sisters.

Frank closed his eyes, not wanting to relive the pain of that wintry day in 1877, but could no more shut it out than he could open the window to his heart. At the age of nine, he'd been institutionalized because his parents didn't want him anymore. He and his little brother had been abandoned at St. John's Catholic Orphanage for Boys.

The first year was hell. The inmates were ruffians of sorts by day, but at night wept openly in their beds. Their sobs frightened Harry who . . . Frank took in a steady deep breath until he felt his lungs burn with the need for release . . . Harry who never was, or had the capabilities of being, like other boys.

Frank exhaled, his chest tight with pain. Blinking his eyes open, he refused to think about the past. He could not dwell on what had been or could never be.

Harry was dead.

If there was one thing he truly wanted to believe from his religious upbringing, it was that Harry was in a better place. A place where he couldn't suffer, a place where Jack and Charlotte Brody couldn't touch him.

Frank sat up and brought his feet onto the hard-wood floor. He ran his hands through his hair and rubbed the tension at the back of his neck. Flipping the lid on a box of Old Virginias, he took up another cheroot. He pulled the band, snipped the tip, and brought the end to his lips. Lighting the thin cigar, he stood and walked to the doorway. He put his hands on the frame above his head and stared into the back alley.

It was darker than pitch outside, without a sliver of moonshine to cast even the slightest shadows. Frank puffed on his cheroot and thought of all the other places he could be now. His mind wandered to the open desert and freedom. Endless space dusted with sage; cantinas with fine women worth their weight in gold. He knew just the place down south where to buy good horseflesh. And then there was that stream north of the Rio Grande where the rainbow trout bit on his flies like they were prime rib to a lumberjack. He could see—

Frank shook his head. Damn, he was thinking about leaving again. Why couldn't he stay and be happy here? Pap had settled in. Frank doubted he could convince his friend to come with him this time. Pap was taken with Weeping Angel and Miss Marshall. He'd settled into the men's dormitory on Gopher Road as if he'd lived there all his life; and he was making plans to move into Amelia Marshall's house by summer's end as her husband.

Unhooking the latch on the screen, Frank stepped outside. He put his hands on the split railing and hopped up to sit on the round post. The wood was smooth. His butt had worn away any splinters from many sleepless nights on this, his favorite do-nothing-in-the-middle-of-the-night spot.

Frank pulled in smoke from the cheroot, exhaling it in a slow, steady stream of gray. Then the cold hard truth hit him in the gut—even though he'd known it all along.

Pap really was planning on asking the piano teacher to set up housekeeping with him. Pap O'Cleary, confirmed bachelor and a man more in a saddle than not, wanted to hook himself up with a wife and stay put.

Resting his bare feet on the second railing, Frank had to admit there were worse things to want out of life if you were the sort of man who wanted a family. But he wasn't because he didn't know the meaning of the word.

"Walter and Warren can't come today, Miss Marshall," Daniel Beamguard informed Amelia as he rolled a large hoop across the floor. "They've got the chicken pox."

Amelia sat on the piano stool in the Moon Rock Saloon, having just finished instructing Jakey Spivey, when the mercantile owner's son came in to broadcast the news. News she didn't find surprising. Though the loss of her wage would be double given both boys were under the weather, giving up the dollar was easier knowing she wouldn't have to deal with Walter and Warren for the next two weeks. The Reed twins weren't exactly prize pupils.

Jakey rolled his sheet music down his thighs into a tight cylinder; she'd never be able to uncurl it next week, even if she brought her iron with her.

Amelia allowed Jakey to ruin his Excelsior Juvenile Collection, knowing her energies were wasted on a ten-year-old boy when it came to prudent advice concerning the care of sheet music. Instead, she stopped her metronome and turned to Daniel. "Thank you for telling me about Walter and Warren."

"Sure, Miss Marshall."

"Oh, and, Daniel, have you ever had the chicken pox?"

"Yep. When I was six." The boy steered his toy with a short stick by pushing its flat end on the inside of the hoop to make the hoop go around. He circled a table with ease, then stopped by Jakey to fit his flannel cap more securely over his hair. "Ma's making me practice on our defective piano, Miss Marshall, since we're the only ones in town who's got a piano besides Mr. Brody."

Amelia pictured the old upright in the Beamguard home. It had barely survived the Wells Fargo, having made the trip before the railroad had been put in. The notes were horribly out of tune and missing several strings in the middle C octave. Since there was no piano repairman in town to tune and restore the instrument, it remained in the condition it first arrived in: Awful.

"Ma says we're rich because we own the mercantile," Daniel stated. "The Dodges are rich. How come they don't have a piano, Miss Marshall?"

Amelia tucked her folded piano scarf into her bag. "Mrs. Dodge says she's not musically inclined."

"Oh," Daniel replied, but the inflection in his tone told Amelia he wasn't quite certain what "musically inclined" meant. He shrugged. "We may be rich, but that dumb mercantile doesn't even carry real Spalding baseball bats." Daniel balanced his oversize hoop, then propelled it toward the bar. "Hey, Mr. Brody. When are you going to let me hit off your bat, huh?"

Amelia glanced at Frank who'd laid out tiny drab feathers on the counter and was sorting them. He'd been there for the past hour rummaging through his tackle box. "Kid, I haven't got the time today."

"Tomorrow."

Looking up, Frank frowned. "Tomorrow's no good either."

"Can I borrow it, then? Jakey can throw some balls at me." The hoop got away from Daniel and crashed into the front of the bar; wobbling, the round piece of wood spiraled to a stop. "I'd be real careful, I promise. I wouldn't break it. I can't hit that hard. Well, I can hit pretty hard, but not hard like you. Have you ever broke a bat, Mr. Brody?"

"No."

Pap, who was sipping a beer next to Frank, gave Frank a dig in the ribs with his elbow. "That's a damn lie, Frank. You broke that pine bat in Tucson when we played at the Overland Stage picnic."

Daniel's face lit up like a firecracker. "Holy smoke!"

"Don't let him fool you, boy," Frank remarked, picking up a speckled feather no bigger than Amelia's thumbnail. "That bat already had a crack in it before I swung."

Wiping the foam off his full red mustache, Pap said, "It did not. Unless," he glanced at Amelia, and she quickly looked away, "I put it there before you hit with it. Now that's a distinct possibility."

Frank's low laugh made her smile and gaze at him. She was certain he did break a baseball bat. Having seen his bare arms in a vest, she could attest to the fact that his muscles were strong enough.

Daniel stared at Frank without saying anything further. The boy watched in fascination as Frank held the feather between his thumb and forefinger while he twisted something around it. The feather gadget looked extremely tricky to Amelia—an operation that required intense concentration and no audience to hinder the process. Keeping his head down, but lifting his eyes, Frank said to Daniel, "Kid, why don't you go help Walter and Warren scratch themselves."

"I don't need to do that," Daniel replied. "Those

boys do everythin' together. They can even fart at the same time."

Frank's right hand quivered; his left dropped the tiny feather as a broad smile cracked his mouth. "Shit," he muttered, and began to laugh. "Let one go at the same time, huh?"

"Yep. I've heard 'em myself."

Pap gave Amelia a hasty glance, then slugged Frank on the shoulder. "There's a lady present, you jackass. Watch what you're saying."

Amelia turned away before Frank looked in her direction. Feigning involvement in putting away her things, she could feel his gaze on her. She was angry at herself for being embarrassed by the talk. She was in a saloon and should have expected the colorful language.

"Daniel," she heard Frank say. "Pap's right. A man never discusses subjects in front of a lady he couldn't talk about in front of his mother."

"Ah, gee." The sound of a shoe dejectedly scuffing the planks made Amelia's lips tremble with the need to smile fondly at the boy. But, of course, she didn't. A well-schooled teacher never let her guard down in front of her students.

Amelia cast a quick look toward the bar out the corner of her eye. Frank was cleaning up his feathers and fishing things when Daniel Beamguard stood on his tiptoes to lean over the counter. Frank slid the tackle box out of the boy's way.

"Teach me how to be a man, Mr. Brody. I want to know how to order a drink."

Frank looked Daniel directly in the eyes. "I'll teach you to order a drink, but never confuse manhood with drinking."

"What do you mean?"

"There's more to being a man than drinking."

"Yeah, like baseball."

"Well, that's not exactly what I meant," Frank mumbled. "There's the husband part and fatherhood, if you're cut out for that kind of thing. You know, responsibilities and all that stuff."

"Yeah, I know what you're talkin' about. I have to run my father's general store when I'm old enough." Shrugging, Daniel dropped a cork float into Frank's tackle box. "Sooner than that, if he dies or somethin'."

Frank shut the lid and put the box under the counter. "Well I hope you're not wishing he'd die. Death isn't an easy thing to handle. Even for a man." Frank grew quiet and Amelia sensed he was thinking of someone dear to him who'd passed on. His reverie didn't last long before he snapped out of his thoughts and asked, "Do you know what it means to nominate your poison?"

"Huh?"

"Name your family disturbance," Frank rephrased. "That's barroom talk for ordering a drink."

"It is?"

Frank rapped the palms of his hands on the counter and shot a glance at Pap. "Shall we let the kid lay the dust?"

"With what?"

Jakey Spivey left the piano and ran to the bar to stand next to Daniel. "I want some dust, too."

"You boys put your feet on the rail."

Daniel and Jakey stepped on the brass rail and grew five inches taller. They bounced their shoulders a little and giggled at each other. Daniel pounded his fist on the shiny surface and lowered his voice to say, "I want a whiskey."

"Gimme a beer," Jakey hollered, then laughed behind his cupped hands.

"If you want to order a whiskey," Frank told Daniel, "say you want it neat."

"I want a neat whiskey, mister," Daniel said, cocking his narrow hips to one side. "I don't like my whiskey messy."

Frank smiled. "Neat means you want it straight. No water in it."

"Oh."

Jakey copied Daniel and swaggered his hips, his sheet music peeking out of his back pocket. "Gimme my beer neat, mister."

"No," Frank corrected. "Say you want a beer to shake you down to your gizzard."

Jakey pealed into laughter and hit Daniel in the arm with his fist. "Gizzard!"

Frank bent down and came up with two clean beer mugs from underneath the bar. Amelia didn't think he would really serve them, so she hadn't said anything. But now, she headed to the long counter. "Mr. Brody, surely you're not going to give these two boys something to drink."

"I am," he drawled. "A beer and a whiskey."

She opened her mouth, but he winked at her and she closed her lips.

"Belly up to the bar, Miss Marshall, and I'll make you a Baptist lemonade."

Trying to contain the spiraling of her pulse when he smiled at her, Amelia knew it was a bad influence for her to accept a drink—no matter how harmless—from him in front of the boys; on the other hand, it was all in fun.

"All right, mister," she played along, much to the giggling delight of Jakey and Daniel. "I'd like a lemonade, please."

"Sissy stuff, Miss Marshall!" Daniel teased.

Amelia took a place next to Daniel and up the heavily waxed counter from Pap O'Cleary. He'd been hovering close and stammering at her since she'd arrived. Just when she thought he'd break down and speak his piece, he was off again to the bar, or out the bat-wing doors, then back again as if he'd never been by her at all. He kept looking down at the tips of his boots, up at her, then back to his boots. Once she looked at his boots, too, just to see if something was the matter with them. There was nothing she could see. She wondered what he wanted, but at the same time wasn't eager to know.

Frank made a big production out of mixing up some "drinks." He tossed chunks of ice into the boys' glasses and caught them midair; then he shot some seltzer in them and gave each a slice of lime to float on the bubbles. "Put your hands back," he said to the boys, then at her. "You, too, Miss Marshall."

She tucked her hands toward her and waited while Frank took the two mugs to the end of the bar where it curved. "Who ordered the tangle leg?" he asked.

"I did." Daniel jumped up onto the balls of his feet. "I did, mister."

"Here it comes."

Setting the mugs down, he held the handle of the first, angled it just so, then with a loose pivot of his wrist, sent it down the glossy bar top. From the speed of the mug, Amelia thought the glass would sail right off the end of the bar, but it stopped directly in front of Daniel with hardly a drop spilled. If she hadn't seen it with her own eyes, she wouldn't have believed Frank could do such a trick. Dorothea Beamguard, should she ever coax Frank into a repeat performance, would be utterly impressed.

"Holy smoke," Daniel whistled.

"Mine!" Jakey exclaimed. "Do mine!"

Amelia gazed at Frank, noting the easy expression on his handsome features. This time, his eyes met hers and her heart turned over in response. She grew entranced by his compelling manner. She couldn't tear her gaze away from him as he said, "Who ordered the dust-cutter?"

"I did! I did!" Jakey shouted.

Frank slid the second mug the same way he had the first; it stopped in front of Jakey, and he whooped with delight.

"Drink 'em down, boys." Frank went to the center of the bar again. "And don't forget to tip the bartender."

"But we don't got any money," Daniel said after a drink of his seltzer.

"I don't need money," Frank replied. "Practice your lessons for Miss Marshall and don't give her any trouble."

Amelia was shocked that Frank would suggest such a thing. She didn't think he put much stock in learning the piano. That he would want the boys to respect her made her feel warm all the way down to her toes. "That's very commendable of you, Mr. Brody," she said, her pulse dancing with gratification.

As the boys drank their faux liquor, and Frank set out to make her a lemonade, Pap moseyed down the bar to stand in front of her. He made a big to-do about wiping the counter with a damp chamois. He didn't say a word. Keeping his head down and rubbing the surface vigorously, all she could see was the black top of his derby. When he looked up, she noticed his eyes were green, and his full mustache had a few gray strands in the ruby red bristles. He grinned at her, showing front teeth that had been cared for; none were missing.

Amelia was at a loss to say anything.

"Did you know," Pap began after taking a visible breath into his chest, "the Fourth of July picnic is on the Fourth of July?"

"Ah, yes."

"Do you like the Fourth of July, Miss Marshall?" he asked as if he were offhandedly commenting about the weather.

"I suppose I do."

"Have you ever made pyrotechnics?"

Amelia glanced at Frank, who didn't notice her, then back at Pap, who waited with hopeful eyes for her reply. "I'm not quite sure what they are, Mr. O'Cleary."

"It isn't fried chicken," Frank commented as he walked past to open the small icebox. "Pap, just ask her and get it over with."

Amelia darted her gaze to Frank's back, then at Pap's pained face. Frank had apparently said something to agitate him. *Ask her what?*

Pap looked at her as if he were weighing his options. "I . . ." he began, then shook his head and frantically wiped the counter as if he were trying to make a hole in it.

Frank butted in. "He wants to ask you—"

Pap cut him straight off with a hot glare. "I w-want to ask you if you order your sh-sheet music through Sears and Roebuck or Montgomery Ward."

Perplexed, Amelia shook her head. "Neither, Mr. O'Cleary. I order all my folios through the Whippoorwill Music Company in Chicago."

"That's all I wanted to know." He chuckled with a forced tone, then made a hasty retreat to the end of the bar, where he lifted the lid to a bin and began sprinkling sawdust onto the floor.

Amelia was bewildered by his behavior. She was certain he wanted to ask her something else, but what, she hadn't a clue. Frank sidled up to stand across from her. "He'll cough it up when he gets up the nerve."

"What do you mean?"

The brilliant blue of his eyes pierced the distance between them. "Think a while when you're drinking your lemonade. You'll figure Pap out." He gave her a tall glass, then backed away to toss an ice pick underneath the bar. "Next time I'll make you a Baptist sling. I think you'll like it."

Amelia knew she would as she brought the rim to

her lips and took a slow sip. Undoubtedly, Frank could make mud taste good.

Frank turned away and put lemons in a dish while the boys made slurping noises. Pap gave her a sidelong glance, and Amelia tried to portray an ease she didn't necessarily feel. She forced herself to smile politely at him before taking a second taste of her lemonade.

"Miss Marshall," came Pap's call, a little too loud and with a crack in his voice.

She gazed at him. "Yes, Mr. O'Cleary?"

"I can play 'Camptown Races' as a duet." Dropping a handful of sawdust, he brushed his hands off against the side seams of his pants. "And that song ain't offensive, so I'm sure you'll know it. Come on, Miss Marshall, you play high and I'll play low."

Pap came toward her, but Amelia didn't move. "I really don't know how the song goes anymore. It's been a long time since I learned the piece. It's such a nonsense song."

"That's the fun of it, Miss Marshall." Pap took her by the elbow and steered her toward the piano. His touch was light and cordial, nothing demanding. Perhaps it was because of his lack of pressure, she allowed him to guide her onto the hardwood piano stool. He quickly grabbed a chair from a table and scooted it next to her.

"I don't remember how it begins," Amelia said, trying to summon the tune in her head. "Perhaps we shouldn't—"

"It starts with an A chord and has E and C sharps." Pap ran through the opening notes, his short fingers nimble on the keys. Playing the chorus, he sang in a clear baritone. "Gwine to run all night! Gwine to run all day! I'll bet my money on de bobtail nag, somebody bet on de bay."

Amelia couldn't help smiling at the silliness of the words Stephen Foster wrote. "I remember now. The tune is animated—*moderato con spirito.*"

"That's right." Pap's expression became lively, and his eyes twinkled. "On a two-four time, Miss Marshall. Ready?"

Amelia curved her fingers over the keys. "I'm not certain how the beginning goes."

"Follow my lead. And don't stop if you make a mistake." He grinned at her, his big mustache slightly lifting with his lips. "It'll come back to you."

She nodded.

"On three." Pap tapped his foot on the floorboard. "One. Two. Three."

Pap set the meter, and Amelia fumbled into the opening of the tune. She concentrated on the melody, trying to remember the words as she went. Pap began to sing, and she put every effort into keeping up with him, even when she struck the wrong notes. Halfway through the second verse and into the chorus, she felt her confidence build, and she made no mistakes in the third verse. Only then, did she allow herself to relax and enjoy the music.

Amelia heard the two boys dancing in circles behind her, laughing and stomping their feet as Pap's voice rang through the room. Frank approached the piano and stood at its side, resting his arm on the top to watch her. She momentarily grew distracted and hit a sharp instead of a flat. Wincing, she chided herself for letting his presence get to her. Pap didn't miss a beat and broke into the last verse. She focused and matched him note for note, ending the song in a silly abandonment of modern chords Miss Lovejoy would surely have reprimanded her for.

Out of breath, Amelia put her hand to her collar, suddenly embarrassed over her abandoned behavior. But Frank didn't seem to notice. He put his hands together and clapped, as did Jakey and Daniel. Pap was adding his own applause just as someone pushed the front doors in and greeted, "Howdy, Mr. Brody."

Amelia recognized the familiar voice. Flushed from

the exertion, she turned to see Mr. Tindall from the Wells Fargo office. He had tiny eyes and a scraggly beard, but he was a good businessman and reasonably honest. "I thought I'd find you in here, Miss Marshall. I knew you'd want to read this right away."

Tucking a fine wisp of hair behind her ear, Amelia tried to compose herself. Mr. Tindall extended his arm and handed her a letter. "The mail just came in on the stage."

Taking the envelope, Amelia read the address in the corner. Rogers & Company, Piano Manufactory, Boston, Massachusetts. She opened the seal and scanned the contents.

"Who'd ya get a letter from, Miss Marshall?" Daniel asked.

Amelia glanced at Frank, but addressed the general room when she spoke. "I've gotten my reply from Boston. They found the shipping mistake before the piano even arrived. They've already sent another one, and it should be here on Friday."

Frank's eyes became as unreadable as stone. "That's two days away."

"Yes . . ."

Pap groaned.

"Then," Frank said with quiet emphasis, "this is going to have to be a going away from the Moon Rock celebration instead of a sing-along, Miss Marshall."

Folding the letter into thirds, she replied softly, "I guess it is."

Chapter

10

❦

*W*arm rain fell over the eaves of the depot's awning as Amelia waited for the three o'clock Short Line. The train was forty minutes behind schedule. Standing on the platform, Amelia worried about how she would get the New American home. Though the summer shower wasn't a downpour, the streets were muddy enough that her shoe heels sank into the soft ground. Mr. Fisk and Mr. Parks wouldn't be able to roll the crate across Dodge Street and Inspiration Lane unless they put boards down in the road.

Holding the closed-loop handle of her folded black umbrella, Amelia listened for the locomotive. All she could hear were the muffled male voices coming through the doorway of the station office and the distant baying of Jakey Spivey's hound, General Custer.

As the Short Line's delay wore on, Amelia grew more anxious. If something happened to this piano, she couldn't go back to the saloon. Not now. Not after what she'd gone through emotionally trying to distance herself from it since Wednesday night. She'd gone back yesterday, out of a sense of duty to her pupils, but her heart hadn't been in her lessons. Throughout her classes, she reasoned she'd talked herself into the Moon Rock Saloon when she'd had no other option, she could talk herself out of the drinking parlor now that she'd have her piano.

But she hadn't counted on feeling welcome in the establishment; she hadn't counted on feeling like a part of something when she'd played a duet with Pap O'Cleary while the boys jumped up and down, and Frank Brody gave her applause afterward. It wasn't supposed to have been like that. She wasn't supposed to have any attachment to the place. Or to Frank.

She'd been having a recurring dream about him lately. She was in her dining room with the table arranged just right. Only instead of one place setting, there were two. She wore her best Sunday dress and her finest white Swiss mull apron. She would come into the room carrying a heaping platter of fried chicken, which she would promptly put in front of Frank, who sat at the head of the table wearing nothing but his navy vest and pleated, white duck trousers. She'd wait by his side as he selected a thigh with his fork, took one bite and chewed the succulent meat with relish. Then he'd stand. Once on his feet, he'd sweep the table clean with his hand. Chicken, plates, flatware, flowers, and candles would fly. He'd take her into his arms and bend her backward over the table until she was lying on the rumpled tablecloth. His mouth would come down on hers, and he'd kiss her over and over. Kiss her until she was breathless with passion. She never knew how things ended though, for even in her dreams, she swooned into darkness from the excitement. When she awakened, she was dewy with perspiration and her stomach ached below her navel. It was dreadful. She felt restless and agitated, hot and cold, all at once. And no amount of milk seemed to calm her. It took her at least an hour to fall back to a sleep that was fitful and never satisfying.

It upset her to no end that Frank Brody could make her feel conscious of him, even when she wasn't in his company. She'd been determined to put him out of her thoughts, but he always managed to drift back into them. She began to wonder if she was strong enough to fight her attraction for him.

Sighing, Amelia didn't want to think about the Moon Rock or its owner. She couldn't afford to be distracted by romantic notions. Taking a punctuated breath for fortitude, she smelled wet wood, leaves, and bark. The fragrance of rainwater-dappled carnations growing in the flower borders of the station wafted through the breezeway, and she struggled to accept the end of her short-lived time at the saloon. She was going to have her own piano, and her life would take the direction she'd planned. She would support herself honorably and not fall into the poorhouse. The children would recover from the chicken pox and her home would be brimming with students. By the summer's end, she'd be ready to have the children give their first recital.

Yes, she told herself as she smoothed a wrinkle from her damp mackintosh coat, everything was going to fall into place now.

The chug of the No. 1's engine broke through Amelia's musings, and she walked to the edge of the platform to watch the Short Line approach the depot.

Frowning, Lew Furlong stuck his head out the cab's window after yanking on the steam whistle chain to clear the tracks. Amelia's ears rang from the racket, and she glanced at the rails in front of the locomotive. Coney Island Applegate was hunkered down in the oiled roadbed lining pennies up on the iron track. As soon as Lew blew the whistle again, Coney Island backed away to wait for the Short Line to flatten his coins.

Amelia shook her head in disapproval as the engine's driving wheels slowly rotated forward; the pennies disappeared under tons of steel, then reappeared as Coney Island quickly snatched the thin metal circles before the second set of wheels could roll them under their pressure. One of these days, Coney Island was going to lose a finger if he wasn't careful.

Grenville Parks came out of the station and caught Coney Island as the boy was bouncing the hot pennies in his hands. "You little devil!" Grenville barked.

The boy jumped and swung his head around.

The ticket agent put his hands on his hips. "How many times have I warned you not to put money on the tracks?"

"A dozen or more."

"At least. I'm going to have to tell your papa if I catch you one more time!"

Coney Island shrugged, pocketed his coins in his knee pants and mumbled, "I ain't a scare-baby," before running off.

Adjusting the short navy visor of his railroad-issued cap, Grenville stepped toward the train. He shoved his fingers into his vest pocket, drew out his watch, then flipped the case open on the timepiece. "You're forty-seven minutes late, Lew. What was there this time—a bear carcass on the tracks?" he asked with a chuckle.

"No," Lew fumed, letting go of the throttle to jump down from the cab. "The Oregon Short Line derailed on the Idaho side of the Wyoming border."

Grenville grew appropriately somber. "Anybody killed?"

"No, thank the Lord," Lew replied. "But everything is in one big metal scrap."

Mention of the derailment caught Amelia's attention. The word spelled disaster in more ways than one. She tightly clutched the knobby wooden handle of her umbrella and took a step forward. "Mr. Furlong, please tell me you've brought the shipment from Boston."

"I don't have a thing from that back east, Miss Marshall. Everything on board was mangled. All I have is the freight that was in Boise for me from California." Lew stuffed his rawhide gloves into his pocket. "At first, me and the other engineers thought the Number Fifty-seven was late. Then word came in on the telegraph wires about the derailment. Her link-and-pin couplings snapped on the downgrade near Bear Lake. Free-running cars coast faster than any engine can run them, and eight of the freight cars, the mail car, and an empty coach flipped off the tracks. It's going to take them a good few days to clean up the mess."

What did it matter how many days it took to clean up? Amelia thought, biting her lip until it hurt. Her piano was smashed to pieces. Swallowing the sob that rose in her throat, she felt as if the breath was being squeezed out of her. She needed to sit down.

She tried to walk with stiff dignity, not wanting Mr. Parks or Mr. Furlong to see just how devastated she was. They wouldn't understand that her life was over; they didn't know she was just about out of money. And now she was doomed to the most supreme humiliation of her twenty-four years. Just thinking about having to ask Frank Brody to take her back made her sway. She couldn't. She wouldn't.

Never.

Her body wavered, her knees grew weak. Before she knew it, she was abruptly caught by the elbow and firmly escorted to one of the green benches on the platform. Sitting, she looked up through teary eyes and gazed into Frank Brody's concerned face.

"Sweetheart, it's not even an oven-cooker today. How come you're going to faint this time?" He brushed his fingers over her gloved wrist. "The hot-house air getting to you?"

"The piano . . ." was all she could muster, her mind swirling with horrible pictures of shiny ebony wood all splintered and gnarled.

"What about the piano?"

"Gone."

"Gone where?" Frank crouched down on the balls of his feet, his gaze level with hers. "What do you mean it's gone?"

"Broken."

Rubbing his clean-shaved jaw, Frank asked, "Did Fisk bust the crate?"

"The train derailed and wrecked it."

Frank shot a glance at the Short Line over his shoulder.

"Not this one," Amelia grumbled. "The Number Fifty-seven."

Frank faced Amelia. "Shit."

"Mr. Brody, may I . . . I . . ."

". . . remind me," he finished when her voice cracked, "I'm in the company of a lady. I never pegged you for anything but."

Amelia buried her face in her hands, not wanting to see him; not wanting him to see her. She had to think. Clearly. Not in the presence of a problem who was just one of many on her long list of problems.

She was close to broke.

She had no piano—again.

And if she wanted to use a piano, she'd have to ask a man she liked far more than she should. A man she seemed fixed on dreaming about.

She couldn't suppress the comment he'd made to her their first meeting. His voice echoed in her mind. *"I don't begrudge you your hobby."* Hobby. She hated the word. Teaching the piano was not a pastime. Perhaps if she told him the truth about needing the money . . . Perhaps he'd let her take the piano from the saloon.

Over the past two weeks she'd gotten to know him.

He wasn't an awful man. To the contrary, Wednesday's display with the boys proved he wasn't all disreputable. He had admirable traits. And now that he'd had the chance to see she was accommodating, he would be just as much when she explained the situation.

Opening her eyes and bringing her hands down, she came back to reality. He was still bent down before her, gazing at her speculatively. She had a hard time organizing her words when he looked at her so directly. His eyes were too magnetic, too blue. There was a rakish tilt to his panama, his black hair appearing darker under the contrast of the natural-colored straw.

Wetting her lips, she had to speak before she lost her courage. "Mr. Brody, I think I've been a very good sport about the New American being at the Moon Rock for such an extended period." Fidgeting with a black button on her mackintosh, she struggled to maintain an even, conciliatory tone. "I think it's time we made other arrangements. I've—"

"Hey, Mr. Brody," Herbert Fisk called, interrupting Amelia's speech. "Got your order loaded up. Do you want me to take it on over to the saloon without you?"

"Yeah." Frank turned back to Amelia. "What are you trying to say?"

"What I'm trying to say is," she said as the porter steered a handcart past them loaded with four moderately sized crates. She never would have paid the boxes any mind at all if they hadn't been burned on the sides with names. Names that were familiar to her, but she couldn't place from where. Trying to shake the thought, she went on with what she was saying. "If I don't get a piano for my own, Mr. Brody, I'm going to be—" She cut herself short, stood and blurted, "Mr. Fisk! Stop!"

Herbert practically went over the double handles to do as she bade. He set the foot rest down, and swung around to face Amelia. "Miss Marshall, you put the fear of God in me. What's the matter?"

Amelia walked forward. She bent slightly at the waist to reread the markings on the crates, then straightened. Turning toward Frank, she said stiffly, "If you'll excuse me, I have to go home."

Then Amelia dashed off in a brisk walk. Her blood pounded at her temples. To think, she'd been ready to bare her heart, to tell him the truth, to implore him to give her the piano. How could she ever have thought he'd do the decent thing?

"Amelia!"

Frank called after her, but she didn't stop. She lifted the volume of her shepherd plaid skirt in her hand and descended the platform. Rain sprinkled her face. The heels of her shoes sank deeply into the soggy ground, and her feet were instantly cold. In her agitated state, she opened her umbrella with aggressive force. Rather than the dome of fabric covering her, the ribs shot up the axis and bent backward.

"Amelia!"

Her mind was a thundercloud, dark and stormy. She ended up holding what had to look like a black tulip over her head as she proceeded. There was no helping traipsing through a patch of mud to escape. She set a course through the empty lot adjoining the depot and behind Emmaline Shelby's laundry shop.

"Amelia, why are you running away from me?" Frank was by her side in a few strides, but she kept on walking. He caught her lightly by the single cape on her coat, making her slow down to his pace.

"Please unhand me," she said crisply, not directing her gaze toward him. Raindrops blurred her vision. Or they could have been tears. Either way, she blinked them off her lashes as she attempted to cross the street.

"Look, I'm sorry about your piano," Frank offered. "We could work things out—"

"I don't wish to be rude with you, Mr. Brody," she said as the downpour intensified, "but if you insist on expressing your false sympathy, I cannot be held accountable for my actions."

"What the hell are you talking about?"

She stopped midstride and turned to face him. "Today is the first Friday of the month, Mr. Brody."

"So?"

"So," she replied, "you'd better greet Mr. Budweiser and Mr. Beam. I've just had the unfortunate pleasure."

They stared at each other across a sudden ringing silence. Her face heated, and she knew her cheeks had grown red from anger and embarrassment. If she hadn't had such a horrible day, she might not have been so upset. But the fact was, she had, and she was feeling the tension of her financial circumstances and having her hands tied to do anything about it.

Frank still held her coat when he explained, "I didn't intentionally lie about the Budweiser and the Beam. It's just that you were acting as if I was—"

"You duped me, leading me to believe they were real people. And men of calling, to boot!"

"It's not what you think."

She was in no frame of mind to hear him out. Her shoes were ruined, her umbrella broken, and she was soaked. "I have to go home."

"Amelia—"

"Hello, Frank." Emmaline's voice caught Amelia by surprise, making her turn her head.

Emmaline stood in the doorway of her laundry, one hand poised on the frame. Her hair wasn't properly pinned up, and the damp weather brought out tendrils of jet curls to frame her face. "I thought that was you." Then out of apparent courtesy, she greeted, "Hello, Miss Marshall."

"Miss Shelby," Amelia mumbled, not at all in a sociable mood. "If you'll excuse me."

"Amelia," Frank said, "we need to—"

"Oh, Frank," Emmaline cooed. "I have your laundry finished. You may as well pick it up since you're right here. I did your shirts just the way you like them."

Amelia glanced at Frank, saw the uncomfortable hesitation in his expression, then went ahead without him. She felt the gentle pull of material slip free of his fingers as she hurried toward the other side of Dodge Street.

The last thing Amelia heard was Emmaline Shelby fussing, "Why, Frank, you're soaked through. You better step on in and change out of that wet shirt and . . ." Amelia couldn't make out the rest, and she was glad. She wanted to forget every single detail of the past hour.

The talk in the Moon Rock Saloon on Saturday evening was the mud brought on by the prior day's rain.

"The streets were so muddy in Sacramento," Pap embellished to a circle of drinking men from his stool in front of the upright, "that it looked to be a head was at the door of Sutters Mill Saloon asking for a drink. The bartender obliged him one, then asked if the man needed any assistance. The fellow said, 'No thanks, mister, I got my horse underneath me.'"

Frank listened to the conversation from behind the polished bar. He took a sip of tea the color of aged bourbon. Despite what looked like a piece of ice in the tumbler, the drink was room temperature. He kept a rubbed smooth fragment of glass in the drink, which never melted, to make it appear as if he were indulging. On duty, he never accepted liquor; and if he had to, he resorted to his snit—a special bottle he kept under the counter that gave the impression of red-eye.

His tale complete, Pap went on to play "Lily Dale," then in the spirit of the cowboys who'd come into the saloon, broke into song with, "Oh, Cowboy Annie was her name. And the N-Bar outfit was her game. We'll work a year on the Musselshell, and blow it in, in spite of hell. And when the beef is four years old, we'll fill her pillowslips with gold."

"Another Old Gideon, Frank?" Cobb Weatherwax asked above Pap's singing.

Standing in front of Frank on the opposite side of the bar, Cobb slid two coins across the counter with dirty fingers. As usual, the man's facial features were mostly hidden by hair; hair the color of sludge hung past his shoulders, covered his jaw, obliterated nearly all of his mouth, and winged above his clear hazel eyes. And what didn't naturally grow on him, he wore in skins.

Frank made idle conversation while mixing Cobb's drink. "How're the beavers, Cobb?"

"Few and far between. Going to get me some though. Beaver is what makes the most money. Beavers are . . ."

Frank let the rest trail from his mind. He wasn't really interested in beavers or barroom chat this evening. Throughout the night, his thoughts had been turning to Amelia. A heaviness had centered in his chest, awakening an emotion buried deeply inside him. Farfetched as it was, he was going soft for her. He should have let her think the worst of him; he'd never cared what people thought about him before. But he wanted to explain why he'd let her think Bud and Beam were customers at the Moon Rock.

He'd been borderline chasing after her yesterday, even with Emmaline watching on, but he'd decided against it. He didn't want to spur any fights between the two women.

". . . I caught a mink in a beaver runway once," Cobb concluded as Frank handed him his Old Gideon. "Then another time I . . ."

It wasn't like Frank not to concentrate on the bar. He'd even spent the past two days immersing himself in his work: balancing the books, cleaning out the underside of the bar, polishing the curios in his altar, and he even scrubbed the whole damn floor. But those tasks hadn't straightened out his mind. His gut felt tight, as if he'd eaten a fried egg sandwich too quickly and washed it down with a keg of beer. Most likely, there was only one way—besides taking a Bromo—to get rid of the feeling.

Confront Amelia, apologize, and get her out of his system.

As Pap finished his tune to the clunk of coins in his money jar on top of the New American, Frank spoke in a loud voice, but not as offhanded as he would have liked. "Pap, mind the bar for a while."

"Pap's no bartender," one of the cowhands grumbled.

Frank wiped the bar top, then flung the cloth aside. "Pap's expandable. He's like an accordion."

"If Pap's tending bar, who's going to play piano?" Wendell Reed articulated his query in a slightly slurred manner.

They had him there. Frank shrugged, seeing no other alternative. "Liquor at my expense. One short bit each."

A hoopla rose, but Wendell cut into it. "That's only a dime's worth," he complained. "A dime drink without piano music . . . I don't know."

"Make it a long bit, then," Frank recanted with an edge of annoyance. "Let's see how far you can make fifteen cents last."

"Not as long as he's got left in the saloon," Grenville Parks guffawed. "Viola expects you home at nine o'clock. You've got two minutes to drink your fifteen cents' worth and get on home."

Pap's easy gait to the bar was light and enthusiastic,

and a smile inched up the sides of his mouth. He rounded the corner with a little hop, then addressed Ed Vining, who stood at the end of the counter.

"Will you drive a nail in your coffin this evening, good sir?"

"A pair of overalls," Ed replied, going along with Pap who knew damn well who he was.

"Ah, two shot glasses of straight rye. Definitely coffin nails." Pap glanced at Frank. "Where are you going?"

"I've got something to do."

Pap's brows lifted. "If he's got something to do, it has to involve a woman."

Frank made no comment. If Pap O'Cleary knew he was going to have a talk with Amelia, he'd bust a seam. Pap still had wedding bells in mind for Miss Marshall. If only he'd get over his stage fright and ask her to the Fourth of July picnic, he might be able to start something with her. But for some reason, Pap acted like an imbecile around the piano teacher.

Parley Hawkins, one of the young cowboys who herded cattle for the big ranch north of town, sat at a table with six of his companions. All of them had baby white foreheads above their brows; and their skin was sunburned and leathery below.

As Frank dumped the rest of his tea into the dishpan, he called to Parley while he remembered. "Quit whittling on the wooden posts upholding the awning above my boardwalk. I'm going to have to replace them if you don't."

One of the boys at the table ribbed Parley. "He's making hearts with Earline's name in it."

"Shut up," Parley cautioned.

"Both of you shut up," came a third voice from a table in the corner. "We're trying to look at something here."

"What?" someone from Parley's crowd asked.

"Orlu Blue brought in a stereoscope," was the general reply.

"Big deal," Parley snorted, drinking the chaser of cold beer for his shot of whiskey. "Who wants to look at National Parks from the Monkey Ward catalogue?"

"It ain't parks we's looking at."

"But it's got hills and valleys," chimed another with a deliberate laugh.

"What is it?" Parley asked, a spark of inquisitiveness in his tone.

"Naked ladies." The man lifted the viewer by its folding handle. "This'n has a woman with a pair of bosoms that look like two gingersnaps."

"What?" blurted the six men in unison, scraping their chairs back so quickly, several toppled over. They stampeded to the neighboring table like cattle in search of a watering hole after a long trail drive.

The others in the room converged in a shuffle of boots, Pap O'Cleary included, all elbowing each other to get a better look at Orlu's girlie cards.

Shaking his head, Frank pulled the strings on his white apron and laid it on the counter. "Pap."

"What?" Pap replied without turning, standing on tiptoe for a look-see over the other men's heads.

"I'm going now."

"Yeah, Frank, I got everything handled." He absently waved. "Goddammit, Parley, you're stepping on my foot."

Frank pushed the crystal glass bat-wing doors and stepped onto the boardwalk. Rather than go straight down Divine Street to Amelia's house, he went through the narrow alley between his establishment and Titus Applegate's Furniture and Undertaker Emporium. He hadn't wanted Pap, or anyone else, to see what he was retrieving from the porch off his bedroom at the rear of the saloon. After he collected a long box, he headed for Amelia's.

He didn't bother opening the lid to check the contents in the box; the pungent smell of freshly cut cattails told him the boys had done their job. Jakey Spivey and Daniel Beamguard had been hanging around the Moon Rock all morning, pestering him while he was cleaning. After lunch he'd had enough and told them to go and pick some cattails for him. They'd asked what he needed the marsh reeds for, but he wasn't about to tell Jakey and Daniel he intended to give them to Amelia as a present. He'd said he was partial to cattails. When they didn't readily believe him, he'd had to embellish by saying he was thinking about setting up a frog terrarium.

The boys bought the lie for a dime apiece, and he'd finally been able to get rid of them for a good two hours. When they returned, their smudged faces proud, they told him they'd gotten *extra special* cattails just because they liked him so much. It had been opening time, so Frank hadn't questioned them about their exact meaning; he'd paid the boys and sent them home.

As Frank walked, he listened to the sounds of insects filling the warm night air with songs. He felt a certain contentment in the evening. He liked summer most of all because he wasn't a constricting clothing man—the less worn the better. On the job, he never succumbed to a coat but only went as far as a vest. Tonight he'd chosen a fancy red brocaded vest; underneath, he'd put on a pristine white shirt, his sleeves held up by women's garters. This particular pair of silk elastic garters with solid silver clasps had come from a pretty waiter girl named Kate in the El Dorado.

As Frank walked, he thought about the men who were converged in the Moon Rock. One thing about his saloon, he pretty much knew every patron by name now; he couldn't boast that same fact for the El

Dorado, where a man's face could be as fleeting as his prospects. It was a good feeling to be able to call a man by his name instead of mister. He'd never had the opportunity to do so before.

Weeping Angel had its advantages in being a small, close-knit community; but by the same token, it had its disadvantages. In a town this size, most people knew what their neighbors were doing and with whom. It was that thought making him shy away from Emmaline Shelby. He wasn't the right man for her, and any hopes she was apt to pin on him were wasted hopes. He was willing to take full blame for the situation and back off, but Emmaline had other plans.

Yesterday when she'd caught him trying to talk with Amelia, it had been apparent Emmaline knew there was more between him and Amelia than a casual disagreement. The tension surrounding them must have been as noticeable as sparks because Emmaline shot hers right back. Not by way of fire, but rather, with a smooth sugary persuasion that he would have had to be stupid to ignore. Under all that sweetness lay sour grapes. He knew if Emmaline thought he were interested in Amelia, Emmaline wouldn't let him go.

He'd done his best to appease Emmaline in the laundry shop, but he hadn't touched her. He wouldn't anymore, and he felt bad he'd ever done so in the first place. She'd gone on some about the damn Founder's Day picnic on the Glorious Fourth, and he let her talk because talking about him going was the only connection he'd have with the town gathering. There was no chance in hell he was showing up, pretending to be a regular member of the community.

A pig's low grunt caught Frank's ear. The streak of white on Hamlet's haunches tipped Frank off to the boar rooting through the Applegates' flower bed as he passed the home. The lights on the lower level were extinguished; only one remained lit on the second floor, and Frank figured the mister and missus were getting ready to retire while their boy's Hampshire boar wreaked havoc in his mama's pansies.

Hamlet lifted his chunky black head and snorted at Frank in recognition; then the pig went right back to nosing in the flowers. Frank had fed the pig his leftover scraps when Hamlet came sniffing around the Moon Rock. Having a three-hundred-pound swine as a pet never would have been Frank's first choice, but he did think the boar had character a dog didn't.

Frank unlatched Amelia's gate and let himself into her yard. The lawn was looking pretty high for a Saturday, and he knew she'd have a hard time mowing it come Monday. He couldn't understand why she let Coney Island Applegate go. Women like Amelia didn't get the calling to do hard labor. Women like Amelia puttered in gardens and arranged flowers. They didn't shove an Acme mower across an acre of turf for the enjoyment of it. Something wasn't right, but he couldn't second-guess her.

Approaching the steps, he quietly took them, not wanting to announce his arrival but not wanting to scare her either. He needed a minute to figure out what he was going to say to her and how he was going to say it.

Frank deposited his parcel on the porch, noticing lamplight spilling out the parlor window. He tread lightly to the medium olive-trimmed window casement. Feeling like a young degenerate didn't stop him from peeking inside. He couldn't see much through the screen because her forest of plants occupied most of the view. He'd never known a woman to grow so many houseplants. And grow them well, too. He had to peer through a jungle of orchids and ferns just for a glimpse of the sofa, and then the pink cushions were empty anyway.

Straightening, Frank went for the front door. He

found the bell and turned the handle twice. From within the house, he heard footsteps on the bare floorboards. It took a while for her to reach the door, and when she opened it, she only did so a marginal crack. She put her face close to the thin space to see who'd come calling past nine on a Saturday evening. Even with the interior glow of a lamp behind her, he couldn't tell what she was wearing; but from the dismay in her eyes, he doubted she was dressed for callers.

Recognizing him, she went to close the door without a word, but he shoved the toe of his boot in the way.

"Amelia, let me in."

"I will not," she whispered, as if someone would hear her—hear them.

"I've got something to say to you."

"I can't talk to you right now." She put pressure on the door. Slight as she was, he hardly felt the movement, but he heard her breath go *oomph* as she tried to smash his toes. "Remove your foot immediately."

"I could force my way in, Amelia. I don't want to, but I'm not leaving until you've heard me out."

"I'm still too upset about my piano to hear you out. Go away."

"Then the Applegates will have to listen in because I'll be yelling at you through the door."

Her eyes widened in alarm. "You wouldn't."

"I would. Now let me in."

She worried her lower lip with her teeth. The door's force on his instep didn't ease up when she said, "I'm not decent."

"Neither am I, but I promise to behave myself."

"I meant I'm not properly dressed."

"And I meant I'm not proper." He wedged his foot in farther. "If I was, I wouldn't be here at your bedtime. But for you, sweetheart, I'll remind myself

I'm in the presence of a lady and conduct myself accordingly."

Amelia opened the door a fraction wider, enough to poke her face through and glance toward the Applegate residence. "Did anyone see you?"

"Yeah, but he won't talk."

"Who?" she asked in a voice tight with dread.

"Hamlet."

"You pig."

"*A* pig."

"No, you're the swine leading me to believe you were seen."

"I will be if you don't let me in."

At that moment, Titus Applegate ran the sash up the second-story window, stuck his head out, and bellowed an expletive at Hamlet.

Amelia withdrew, stood behind the door, and opened it barely enough for a cat to fit through. "Come inside. Quickly."

Frank nudged the entrance with his shoulder. The hard edge rammed into his upper arm as Amelia practically shut the door on him as soon as he'd stepped inside.

The linen shade over the lamp on a stand in the entry didn't lend much light to the small receiving space. She'd already turned the wick low and made no move to bring it back up. She eyed him with a critical squint, but he barely noticed. All he could do was stare at the waves of burnished brown that tumbled to her hips.

Amelia Marshall had very long hair.

He must have caught her in the middle of brushing it. Her hair was parted in the center and very full on either side of her face. He couldn't imagine how she managed to pin all that volume up underneath a hat.

"Let's go into the parlor," he suggested, not because that was the general room for conversation but because he wanted a better look at her unbound hair.

Hers was the kind he fantasized about having spread across his pillow.

"No. I'd rather stay here."

If she'd wanted to keep the intimate details of her attire hidden from him in the half dark, she was fooling herself. Here, in the veiled light of the foyer, she looked far more provocative to him than she would have in a bright, open room.

She wore a wrapper of a light and sheer material imprinted with pale pink flowers. The collar was wide and reminded him of a sailor's, only with a point directing his gaze to her slender waist. The sleeves were large and gathered in at the wrist, with fancy trimming and wide flowing cuffs edged in lace.

"Well?" she prompted, the toe of her felt house slipper tapping an even meter like that metronome thing she had for the piano. She crossed her arms over her bosom, as if to shield them from his view. Even without a corset, she had a nice shape; her breasts didn't sag, nor did her waist seem too plump—a hand span at the least, nor were her hips too wide or too narrow. Miss Amelia Marshall was full of surprises.

"Yeah, well . . ." Frank shrugged, then crossed his own arms over his chest. So it was to be a standoff. She'd make this as difficult as she could for him. "Did you talk to Tindall and send another letter to Boston?"

"I did. But I shan't hope for a reply in anything less than two weeks."

"If we had a telegraph, it'd be a lot quicker."

Her ire was transferred to the lack of wire communication in town. "Weeping Angel will have telephones before we ever have a telegraph. Mayor Dodge doesn't like that kind of progress. Why, we never would have had the Short Line spur if it hadn't been for the fact he wanted a billiard table too big to disassemble for the Wells Fargo. If he wasn't the citizen to foot most of the city's bills, we'd—" She cut herself short. "Mr. Brody, I doubt it was your intention to come here and discuss the town's lack of utilities."

"You're right."

"What, then, have you been trying to explain?" Her hair fell across her cheek, and she had to unfold her arms in order to tame the rich mass over her shoulder.

He darted his gaze upward to her eyes before she caught him staring at her unrestrained curves. "I know who Shelley is."

"Excuse me?"

"I know who Mary Shelley is. She wrote *Frankenstein.* I read the book. I've also read Dickens, Cooper, Verne, Melville, Hawthorne, and Twain—just to name a few. I don't care much for Emerson or Brontë. I used to tolerate Sand's novels until I found out he was a she. Now I don't have to like reading them anymore."

Amelia discontinued tapping her toe, and for a long moment, studied him as if deciding whether he was telling her the truth or not.

"Just because I serve liquor for a living doesn't mean I'm illiterate. You treated me as if I were, so I let you think what you wanted about Budweiser and Beam. If you recall, I never said outright they were men of the cloth who drank in my saloon. That was your idea."

"Do you want me to feel bad because I found out your little joke?" she asked, her voice a flat tone.

"Hell, no. You had good reason to be mad at me. I can see now that I made light of something at your expense. But it's like I said, you were treating me as if I were stupid."

A few seconds passed, then she raised her gaze to his. "I apologize if I made you feel inferior. It's just that I've been under a great deal of stress lately."

He raked his fingers through his hair, relieved they'd at least straightened something out. But there was one problem still standing between them. "I'm sorry the piano was wrecked, Amelia. You're more than welcome to use the one at the Moon Rock again until another one arrives."

"I'd rather not."

"I wish you would."

"I wish you'd give me the one you have," she said softly.

Frank shook his head, glanced at the floor, then back at Amelia's face cast in shadows. "Sweetheart, you make twenty-five cents a lesson for thirty minutes' effort. Right now, I'm making that in five minutes. It's not as if you need the money. You have a fine house here."

Even in the gloomy entry, he could see her expression change to resentment. She wanted to pop him. Why, if she was only teaching the piano as an accent to her socializing?

He decided to do something that could change their situation by way of flipping a coin to fate. "You tell me why you won't pay a kid to mow your lawn anymore and that upright is yours." He tipped his head meaningfully. "Right now, Amelia. One answer. That's all it takes. I'll have Pap and the boys bring it to you tonight. Just tell me why. Do you need money?"

The muscles in her neck seemed to tense along with her jaw. Her nostrils widened a bit, and her breathing grew unsteady. For a minute, he thought she might just wallop him.

"My aunt left me financially sound, Mr. Brody, so I most certainly do not need any charity from you." She brought her arms down, her delicate hands clenched by her sides. She took a step toward him to reach for the doorknob, and he could smell the faint scent of some kind of floral perfume on her skin. "Now, if you're finished—"

"No, I'm not."

He slipped his arm around her waist and gathered

her into his embrace. Holding her snugly, the diaphanous fabric of her wrapper felt like polished stone under his fingertips. The curtain of her hair teased the skin below his shirt cuffs; he entangled his fingers through the silkiness, rubbing the texture between his thumb and fingers. Before she could protest, he kissed her on the lips. Nothing lingering; nothing deep. Just long enough to taste the flavor of teaberry tooth powder on her startled mouth. Just long enough to make him realize a quick kiss wasn't going to satisfy him. Just long enough for him to change his mind and give her something lingering and deep.

When she didn't make a move to hit him, he slanted his mouth over hers. She did taste good, and he was suddenly starved for her. He held the back of her head with his hand, feeling that hair of hers. It was as soft as her lips, and so thick, he was stunned. He loved a woman's hair, but he'd never seen or felt anything like Amelia's. The texture of it was erotic, making him kiss her harder. Making him want to . . . damn.

He backed away before he'd do something he'd regret—like tug on the half belt keeping her wrapper together in the front so he could see what she had on underneath. So he could back her onto the stairs and lean over her and . . .

"Christ," he muttered, and shook his head, needing to clear his thoughts.

He didn't need a glaring lamp to tell him her face was flushed. He heard her breathing as if she'd run up and down the steps a hundred times. She'd raised her hands and put her palms on her cheeks. "Mr. Brody," she gasped, her bosom rising and falling. "Mr. Brody . . . Well . . . I . . . I like that."

"I was hoping you would." He turned and opened the door to let himself out. "I was hoping I wouldn't."

Once on the porch, he bent to lift the box he'd carried over. Amelia stood in the doorway, one hand on the jamb, the other still covering the curve of her cheek.

"Here." He gave her the present. "I got these for you."

Amelia stared at the box he'd pressed into her grasp. Without a word, she lifted the lid. "Why . . . they're cattails." She put her fingers on the fuzzy brown tops, then suddenly pulled back as if she'd been bitten. "Wh-What's this?"

"What?" he asked, leaning forward for a look.

"Th-There's a . . . a frog in here."

"Ah, Jesus," Frank swore. He was going to kill Jakey and Daniel.

"You got me a frog?"

Frank grappled for an appropriate response. There was none. If he told her he hadn't thoughtfully picked each cattail himself and admitted to paying two kids, she'd be more insulted than she would be if he said he'd intentionally gotten her a frog.

"Ah, yeah." Frank tapped the side of the box. "It's a leopard frog. I figured you might like a pet."

"A pet frog?"

"Yeah, well, you won't have to housebreak it or anything." Frank shoved his hands into his pockets, wishing there was a hole he could drop into.

"Mr. Brody," she moaned, "whatever possessed you to give me a frog?"

He kept his face toward her, but backed down one of the porch steps. "At this moment, I really couldn't say." Then he swung around, jumped over the last two steps, and was gone before he could make more of an ass of himself.

Chapter

11

⤜⧽⫘

*T*he congregation of the Christ Redeemer church rejoiced in the news of Narcissa Dodge's blessed condition. After the mayor was allowed to make the announcement, everyone broke into the next hymn with extra glee while singing "Bringing in the Sheaves."

Amelia only pretended to sing. She had other matters on her mind. She tried to ease open the spring clasp on her chatelaine bag without being noticed by Narcissa, who sat next to her. Amelia's fingers slipped on the catch, not because of the gloves she wore, rather the dampness her palms seemed to give the thin fabric encasing her fingers. She never perspired in church, even though the house of the Lord was often as hot as His adversary's during the months of June, July, and August.

Elroy Parks and Daniel Beamguard pulled the ropes that operated the palm leaf paddle fans above the parishioners' heads. A gust of warm air traveled over Amelia as she was able to undo the clasp; but the bag still remained anchored to her belt by a short length of decorative chain.

Even with a beacon of stained-glass light to brighten the interior of her purse, *it* happened again. That awful sound. And of course, right at the end of the song when the church went holy silent—except for someone's cough, which didn't disguise the croak.

Rrrribbbittt.

Narcissa glanced at Amelia and whispered behind the screen of her silk fan, "Didn't you have breakfast, dear?"

Shaking her head, Amelia let Narcissa believe she hadn't eaten this morning. How could one tell one's friend—during Sunday services no less—the guttural croak wasn't her stomach growling?

It was a frog in her pocketbook.

The clucking notes came again. This time Viola Reed turned her gigantic-hatted head from her seat in the pew in front to give Amelia a polite, but reproaching, upturn of her lips.

Amelia smiled back, acting as if nothing was wrong. The frog croaked again, but this time Amelia coughed behind her hand through most of it.

Her eyes widened as she saw the frog moving around underneath the supple calfskin of her purse. She'd dumped everything out, of course. Even her embroidered handkerchief. She'd had to use her sterling sugar tongs—which were disinfecting in hot soapy water this very minute—in order to get the frog out of the cattail box. All the while she prayed she wouldn't squeeze it to death; she'd shivered at the thought of actually having to touch it.

Rrrribbbittt.

Amelia cleared her throat to the multiple stares of those sitting around her. She kept her face forward, watching Widow Thurman at the organ as she shuffled blindly through her sheet music, dropping half of it while Reverend Thorpe took his place at the pulpit to deliver his sermon.

Amelia's pulse raged as swift as a river's spring thaw. Perhaps she shouldn't have brought the frog with her. But how else was she going to give it back to Frank? She knew he passed by the church every Sunday just as the service was letting out. She planned to have a very brief word with him, make him take the plum-sized, green-spotted frog out of her purse, then be on her way. She could have brought it back in a box, but the only ones she had were her hatboxes. And the ladies would have insisted on a peek. They would have seen she had a frog, wonder how she'd gotten it, why, from whom, and what was it doing in her hatbox? This way was better. More discreet.

Too bad she hadn't counted on the frog to think the dark interior of her purse was nighttime and begin to croak.

The frog continued to wriggle. Amelia didn't dare open the purse any further; but she did unhook the chain from her belt in order to put the bag on top of her pocket Bible, which lay on her lap.

While Oscar Beamguard read the gospel lesson aloud, Amelia's concentration was tugged in a different direction. To be sure, not down the path of righteousness. She was thinking about Frank Brody's lips covering hers with velvety warmth.

She'd relived last night a dozen times over in her mind. She hadn't slept much thinking about the kiss Frank had given her. The passion of their lips joining put her fried chicken dream to shame; she didn't dream the dream that night. But she'd thought about the kiss while she lay awake in her bed. She'd thought about the kiss in the bathroom first thing this morning as she went through her ablutions. She'd thought about the kiss in the kitchen while she ate her breakfast. And now she thought about the kiss in church.

She'd been kissed squarely on the mouth only one other time. Jonas Pray had given her a dry, closed-lipped kiss the evening he'd presented her with the Legacy Collection—right before she'd handed him her money. She hadn't really thought much of it and, actually, had felt disappointed when his mouth had touched hers. But she'd talked herself into thinking it was more wonderful than it was because she'd assumed she'd have to kiss him for the rest of her life.

After sampling Frank's method of kissing on the mouth, Amelia was glad she didn't have to endure dry lips from Jonas. She wondered if there were other men who could kiss as dreamy as Frank. She doubted there were. His kiss may have been short, but it had been chock-full of wonderful sensations. She'd felt transported on a cloud, and too radiated with pleasure, to remember exactly what she'd said to him afterward.

She should have reprimanded him severely. He'd broken his word about not kissing her again, and she, too taken by the romance of it all, had allowed him to turn her to putty. What was done was done, and she couldn't wipe away the kiss. But what she did know was, she couldn't keep his gift—no matter that it was just an eye-bulging frog. The cattails, however, were another matter entirely. She hadn't been able to fit them in her purse, so she was reconciled to keeping them. Even so, a lady never encouraged the addresses of a gentleman unless she felt she could return his affections. And as long as Frank made a living out of a saloon—the very one that had once glorified Silver Starlight—she couldn't see any hope for their relationship.

Not only did the New American upright parlor piano stand between them, she wasn't even sure Frank liked her. He was ever teasing and trifling with her. Sometimes she would catch him giving her long stares that made her feel naked, and other times, he acted as if she weren't in the same room with him. She couldn't imagine him ever asking her to the Chuck-wagon for supper or renting a buggy for a Sunday afternoon ride. Frank was not made of the stuff for courting, and that was what she wanted. His passionate kiss had left her reeling and mixed up. It could not, and would not, happen again.

The frog had quieted, and now Amelia feared its suffocation. She vented the opening on her purse a little more, then lifted her gaze to the front of the church, determined to put her effort into the Sunday message the reverend was about to deliver.

Dressed in a somber-cut black suit with a bow band necktie, Reverend Thorpe held on to the edge of the pulpit, staring out at his flock. He made eye contact with each and every last one of them. When his gaze bored into Amelia, she swallowed hard but remained still in her seat. Others did not take the reverend's weekly inspection so well. There were muffled coughs amongst them and the squeak of wooden joints as people shifted uncomfortably in their mahogany pews. Coney Island's sisters, Mabel Lovey and Bessie Dovey, had to be scolded in a harsh whisper for kicking their brother on each of his shins.

This whole process of scrutinizing the congregation took no more than sixty seconds, but when one was counting them off, it seemed like an eternity. When the reverend finally finished, he remained silent, his lips pursed, his brows jutting downward in a frown. Then, since he only had his audience captive once a week, he struck zealously hard.

"Prepare yourselves to meet your maker!"

Reverend Thorpe's booming voice startled Amelia, and her chatelaine bag and her Bible bounced to the floor.

Narcissa turned her head to stare at her. Amelia mumbled an apology, then as casually as she could, leaned over to pick up her purse and thin black book. Once they were safely back in her lap, she smoothed her hand over the calfskin to feel for the lump of the frog.

It was flat.

The clammy thing had escaped!

Horrified, she quickly inclined her gaze over her knees to see if she could spot the frog on the varnished floor. Nothing. She tilted her head both left and right, frantically searching for a glimpse of green through ankles of polished black and brown shoes. Nothing.

Straightening, Amelia held herself erect. Where did it go?

All she could do was sit and wonder as Reverend Thorpe spoke of an abyss of despair and the covenant of darkness. Seconds rolled into minutes, minutes rolled into a quarter of an hour.

"So I say to you, my friends," the preacher decreed, raising his right fist to the rafters, "live each day as if it were your last. Do not stray from the Lord on Thursday thinking to redeem yourself on Sunday. Friends, I could be officiating at your wake on Friday." He lowered his arm, perspiration running down the sides of his red face. "Prepare to meet your maker and—"

A woman's scream cut short Reverend Thorpe's dissertation. Luella Spivey, who sat in the third-row pew, shot to her feet and pointed at the aisle carpet runner. "Which one of you heathen boys," she exploded, "set that frog loose?!"

Amelia shrank.

Daniel and Jakey traded glances, as if to ask the other, "Did you do it?" Both shrugged.

In spite of the pink pox scabs healing on their pale faces, Walter and Warren Reed were each cuffed on the ear by their mother. Together they declared, "We didn't do it!"

The frog hopped toward the pulpit risers; it made a low croak lasting about three seconds, followed by several clucking notes. Ladies' fans snapped open to fan flushed faces; men who'd dozed off opened one eye. The boys, and even most of the girls, erupted into squeals of laughter. They all knew they didn't have to claim responsibility because they weren't responsible; therefore, they could abandon themselves to the pandemonium of one of the better pranks ever pulled off during a Sunday sermon.

Amelia might have been inclined to laugh herself, but the trouble was, someone had to confess to being the culprit.

"Friends!" the reverend cried. "Come to order!"

As the frog leaped on the pulpit landing, Reverend Thorpe chased after it. Amelia stood, along with everyone else, to watch their minister bound helplessly after a zigzagging frog. The reverend fell to his knees, sprawled out on his stomach, and cupped his hands over the floor. "I got it!" Scrambling to his feet, he kept his fingers locked together. A shock of his oiled hair hung over one eye, as he said, "All those not guilty, sit down. Those who are, stay standing."

Feet shuffled, pews creaked, whispers mounted, and the only one left standing was Amelia.

"Sit down, dear," Narcissa said softly.

Amelia shook her head.

The reverend frowned. "Miss Marshall, you may take your seat."

"I can't, Reverend." In the scuffle, Amelia had reached for her purse and now held it by the chain. "I . . . that is . . ." She excused herself and went around Narcissa and Cincinatus. "It's mine, Reverend." She met him at the base of the pulpit. "If you would be so kind as to put him in my bag."

Old Widow Thurman was the only one who made a sound. Air whistled through her false teeth as she chuckled in an aged tone from her place at the organ. Nobody chastised her, of course. At the ripe age of seventy-eight, she could do and say whatever she wanted.

Amelia snapped her purse closed as soon as Reverend Thorpe dumped the frog safely back inside. Turning, she couldn't meet the stares; she kept her head down as she resumed her seat. She wanted to die. She should have just let the frog go in her yard. But she'd had to stand on ceremony of returning "the gift." That, and the fear the frog would take up residence on her property and hop out at her when she least expected it to.

As the congregation settled in once again, Amelia sat through the rest of the service without blinking an eye—even though nearly every pair strayed to her. At last when it was over, she stood with as much dignity as she could muster and strode out with everyone else.

"Why didn't you tell me you had a frog in your purse?" Narcissa whispered behind her gloved hand.

"Would you have sat next to me if I had?" Amelia whispered back.

"Of course I would have." Narcissa nodded politely to Mrs. Spivey as they crossed paths. "Why *do* you have a frog in your bag, dear?"

"It doesn't belong to me." The plaster smile on Amelia's lips began to hurt her cheeks as she moved through the narthex. "I'm returning it to a friend."

"A friend? Who?"

"Mr. Brody."

Narcissa tilted her head. "Mr. Brody gave you a frog?"

"Yes."

That was all they could converse. They'd reached the doorway where Reverend Thorpe customarily stood after each service to shake hands and greet his congregation. After the mayor and his wife had exchanged pleasantries with him, he received Amelia with a question in his eyes.

"Miss Marshall, do you require extra spiritual counseling? I could come calling this week." He gripped her hand. "Monday if it's an emergency."

"No thank you, Reverend. I'm quite fine." Then she

made a hasty retreat before he could say something further.

As she stepped into the sunlight, she opened the sunshade she'd had hanging by the radiator. She would have spoken with Narcissa further, but her friend was swarmed upon with well-wishers.

With her Bible in one hand and her purse affixed to her belt, Amelia strolled toward the big elm to watch for Frank Brody. Several of the ladies inquired about lessons now that her piano would be delayed. Amelia held them off with vague replies, knowing as soon as she squared up with Frank, she had to speak with Mrs. Beamguard. She didn't want to, but she had no other choice in the matter.

Standing in the shade, Amelia gazed down Dodge Street in the hopes of spying Frank. She'd been waiting all of a few seconds when Emmaline Shelby sauntered toward her. They eyed each other like two cats before an alley fight, this seeming ridiculous to Amelia. She wasn't quite sure why she was on the defensive; all she knew was, of late, Emmaline rubbed her the wrong way.

Emmaline sported a new suit of Scotch taffeta with a French lawn waist. "Who are you waiting for?" she asked in a tone that was less offhanded and more nosy.

"No one in particular."

"Well, if you're waiting for Frank, I can tell you, you'll have a long one. He went to Boise early this morning. He won't be back until tomorrow."

Amelia hoped she hid her disappointment from the woman. "It doesn't concern me in the least where Mr. Brody travels."

Twirling the handle of the parasol resting on her shoulder, Emmaline said, "We don't have to stand on ceremony, do we?" She gave Amelia no opportunity to reply either way. "I'd like to make one thing perfectly clear. You may have the advantage of being in his saloon all morning and afternoon, but I launder his clothing. His *intimate* clothing."

Amelia made no remark; she picked up on Emmaline's meaning, but wasn't clear how to translate how washing underwear could give her the upper hand.

"If Frank Brody were the marrying type—which he's not—*yet,*" Emmaline stated, "I'd be the one he'd choose."

"Shall I offer my congratulations?"

"In due time."

Amelia maintained an air of calm self-confidence, even though scalding fury was blistering her nerves. "I'm certain you'll be very happy tied down to a man like Frank. Myself, I'm doing just fine being on my own. I intend to keep my living arrangements as they are."

"And a very wise choice. Why, everyone in town knows you'll never get married—even if you wanted to. Not after the shameful behavior you displayed toward that book and Bible salesman from California two years ago."

Amelia felt the sting of Emmaline's unveiled barb pierce through her armor.

"Besides," Emmaline went on, "you're too old to get married to someone as virile as Frank anyway. You'd do better with an elderly gentleman. A widower with a passel of grandchildren—your own age."

Emmaline finally managed to shatter Amelia's complacency. "If you'll excuse me," Amelia mumbled, needing to get away from the woman before she forgot she was a lady.

Amelia made her retreat with as much decorum as she could salvage. How dare Emmaline take notice of her unmarried state. Why, the woman was near her own age and not married either. Emmaline Shelby had never been outright mean to her before. They'd met on the street with a passing "How do you do?" or in the Wells Fargo picking up their mail, but they'd always had a civil, social word for one another.

Emmaline's attack had stirred bitter jealousy in Amelia. She knew she shouldn't feel that way, but she did. Emmaline had strongly hinted she was doing more than just washing Frank's dirty clothes. Had Frank kissed her, too? Given her cattails? Put his hands in her unbound hair?

Amelia suddenly felt sick at heart.

"Amelia, dear! Over here!" Mrs. Beamguard called with a wave. As she advanced on Dorothea, Amelia took a quick inventory of the other women in the group. Mrs. Spivey, Mrs. Applegate, and Mrs. Reed. She would have liked to speak with Dorothea alone, but it might work to her advantage if she had the endorsement of the others.

"Amelia, dear," Mrs. Beamguard cried, "we were just speaking about you! We've had the most wonderful idea. Let me tell you every sumptuous detail!"

Amelia listened, nodding when appropriate. But all the while she was thinking, her troubles were worsening by the minute.

Frank wouldn't have gone over to Amelia's house on Monday afternoon if Coney Island hadn't told him she let a frog loose in the Christ Redeemer on Sunday. He doubted her actions had been planned and wondered why she'd brought the frog to the church in the first place. For some reason, he figured it had something to do with him. And he wanted to find out what.

As he walked across town, he lost himself in the reverie of a striking bloomer girl he'd met in Boise last night at the Can-Can Revue. She'd been corsetless and wearing bloomers instead of chaste pantaloons and layers of petticoats. With a cigarette between her blushing red lips, a shot glass of bourbon in her hand, she'd dealt him cards most of the night; then, later, when she'd offered to play a one-on-one game of her own with him, he'd been too drunk to comply.

Maybe he'd gotten hammered on purpose. So he could have the excuse he couldn't do it when all along he knew there was no reason he shouldn't. But, hell, that didn't make any sense. He didn't owe anyone in Weeping Angel anything. He was a free man. He did as he wanted, when he wanted.

Why, then, was he feeling guilty as sin?

He'd run into Emmaline in Teats's livery yesterday morning when he was renting a horse. She'd gone on, in as subtle a way as possible, about all the events that would take place at the picnic coming up. He'd shrugged off her hints as best as he could, seeing he'd already told her no dice, then rode out of town.

In hindsight, it wasn't Emmaline's pouting expression bringing out his guilt. It was because he'd kissed Amelia. He'd looked back to that night more than once while fighting off his attraction toward her. It had been harder than he'd thought to leave her porch that evening.

She'd felt so good in his arms, he'd been more than a little shaken up. She was certainly not the cool, disciplined woman she appeared to be on the surface. No, Amelia Marshall had the potential to be a real firecracker.

On the ride home from Boise, with his head splitting from a hangover, she was all he could think about. Her smile. The sweet perfume on her skin. That glorious hair of hers. He'd almost gone straight over to her house when he'd returned to Weeping Angel but hadn't because he didn't know what to say to her. Damn, he'd really messed up with that frog. But that wasn't really his fault, and he didn't know how to explain it without looking like a bigger idiot.

He'd been searching for an excuse to see her, and

Coney Island's description of what happened in the church was a good enough reason to Frank.

He let himself through the picket gate at Amelia's house. The front lawn looked like hell. The grass was chewed up in patches that would take more than a week to grow out. He should have paid Coney Island to do the yard for her. Stubborn as she was, she'd clip her toes under that mower before she gave in and let him pay for the job to be done.

Taking the porch steps, Frank rang the bell. When no one answered, he decided to investigate the backyard. He found the Acme mower in the side yard butted up against a half-trimmed hedge of boxwood, where leaves had been defoliated by a pair of hedge shears that had been pitched in the dirt, their blades obliterated from his view underneath the shrub.

Standing there, he removed his hat, absently ran the back of his hand across his brow to collect the sweat, then fit his panama over his forehead. Maybe she was sitting on the lawn furniture drinking something cold.

He'd just taken a step when he heard the sobs. A kind of instinct for trouble kicked in, and he ran toward the pitiful wails coming from deep in the rear of the yard. Sprinting through the calf-high grass, he saw her sitting by the edge of her thriving garden. Her shoulders shook and she was clutching her stomach, rocking back and forth.

"Jesus." The word whooshed through him before he realized he'd even called for higher help. She must have accidentally cut herself with the shears was all he could think of. "Jesus," he said again, this time knowing full well who he was calling upon.

Reaching Amelia's side, Frank dropped to his knees and tried to pry her hands from her abdomen to assess her injury.

She gazed at him through tear-swollen eyes, not allowing him to examine her; her muscles were locked, and he couldn't budge her arms. Her sudden burst of strength amazed him, and he tried to compose her with his voice. "Sweetheart, let me see what you've done to yourself."

"I . . . I . . . I . . . I . . ." She tried to speak but was so upset, she seemed on the verge of hyperventilating.

"Calm down. Take a deep breath," he ordered, gripping her shoulders with his fingers. "That's a girl. Slow and easy."

"I . . . I . . ." A sob choked her throat, then in a hysterical voice she blurted, *"I've killed it!"*

"Killed what, honey?"

"Ffffffffffffffff . . ." Her bosom rose and fell with so much distress, he felt sick for her. "Ffffffffff . . ."

"What?"

"Frog!" she sobbed. "I've killed the frog." A torrent of fresh tears streamed down her blotched cheeks. "I didn't mean to. I—I didn't hate it. Honest! I should have"—her breath hitched in her chest—"should have let it go. I wanted to give it back to you yesterday, but . . . oh . . . the poor thing." Then looking at him through long wet lashes, she suddenly punched him in the upper arm. "Why did you have to go to Boise? Frog would have been alive and eating . . . eating . . . eating flies in the pond . . . instead . . . instead . . . instead of being . . . d-d-d-dead."

Then she cried even harder, the pain in her voice slicing him in two. Damn, she was on the worst crying jag he'd ever seen. Even the bed wetters in the home hadn't cried this hard after a bare-butt whipping.

The fingers in her left hand were closed in a soft fist. Call it a hunch, but Frank figured he could lay a sure bet on what she held.

Frank was at a loss over what to do, considering why she was lamenting. He'd never dealt with an overwrought female before whose frantic raving was caused by a kicked-off leopard frog. He reached out and awkwardly stroked her fist. "Why don't you let me take it for you, sweetheart?"

"No!" She clutched her fist to her breasts. "I'm going to bury it."

She was more distraught than he thought. At the sight of her woebegone face, his thoughts fragmented as something clicked in his mind: He wanted to take care of her. "I'll bury it for you."

She looked at him as if he were an angel. "You will?"

"Yeah."

"All right." She sniffed and slowly extended her hand, unfolding her fingers. "H-Here he is." Seeing the limp, spotted green leaper in her dirty palm made Amelia weep anew. "M-M-Make a marker for him, too. There's wood by the shed."

Frank nodded. "Do you have a cigar box I can put him in?"

Her shoulders trembled as she blew her nose into the lace-bordered handkerchief she'd plucked from her apron pocket. "I don't smoke."

"I'll just put him in the dirt then."

"No!" she protested, then bit her lip in thought. Gazing at the square of dainty white in her hand, she gave her hankie to Frank. "Put him in this."

Frank took the soggy square of linen, laid the frog in the center, and began to fold up the scalloped corners.

"Wait!" she exclaimed. She leaned forward to snip a drooping peony with her fingertips, then rested the fluffy pink flower next to the frog. "This, too."

Frank finished doubling the fabric. "Where do you want it buried?"

Amelia's brows knit together, then she stood. "Over here. By the corn where I won't accidentally dig him up."

Frank followed her between furrows of carrots and tomatoes, past bush beans to a three-row block of six-foot-tall cornstalks. The brown silks brushed his arms where his sleeves were rolled up; the air around him smelled sweet and rich with minerals.

As Amelia walked in front of him, the heavy ears and green spears cloaked them from the rest of the garden. She wasn't crying anymore, but every now and then, her shoulders quaked and he could hear her tear-spent sigh of exhaustion through the rustle of cornstalks. The pleats on the backside of her skirt sported a grass stain; the thick twist of wavy hair on top of her head was askew, and only one loop in the bow on her apron was knotted.

In short, Amelia Marshall wasn't herself.

He somehow doubted her accidentally killing the frog was the sole cause for the change in her behavior, and he guessed before he left, he'd find out why.

"Right here." She pointed to the ground at the edge of the corn. "That's where I want him."

"Is the shovel in the shed, too?"

"Yes."

Frank obtained the appropriate tools for the job, put the sole of his boot on the edge of the shovel, and turned out a big scoopful of dirt without any effort. "I don't think I need to go too deep." Crouching down on the balls of his feet, he picked up the handkerchief he'd set aside and placed it on the bottom of the hole. Just as he did, Amelia began to cry all over again. Fat tears splashed off her lashes, down her high cheekbones, and put wet spots on her green-and-white shirtwaist.

"I'll n-n-n-never forget how it looked in the b-b-b-bottom of the box."

Frank bet it looked dead.

"The poor thing j-j-j-just laid there." She hiccupped. "I poked a hole in the lid and kept the box on the porch so Frog could catch flies." She glanced at him with eyes so sad, he wanted to wrap her in his arms and make her hurt go away. "Do . . . do . . . do you suppose he ate a p-p-p-poisoned fly?"

"Well, sweetheart . . . I don't think so."

"Neither . . . neither . . . neither . . . do I." She buried her face in her hands while he buried the frog. "I killed it," she moaned through sobs.

He smoothed the dirt over with the palm of his hand, made a marker, and hammered the point into the ground. The deed done, he hoped she'd snap out of her wails of woe. She was melting him down faster than a candle, his body and soul aching for her. Instead of calming, she grew much worse, trembling so badly his heart went cold.

Rising, he walked to where she stood between the corn, took her in his arms, and held her so tightly she had to stop shaking. Her arms remained at her sides, and it felt as if he were hugging a post. "Dammit, Amelia, you're scaring me. Do you need me to get the doc?"

"N-N-No."

"Then why won't you stop crying?"

"I can't h-h-h-help myself."

Frank felt the white-dotted muslin of his shirt dampen over his collarbone from her tears. He splayed his fingers and ran them up and down her spine in a soothing motion. "Hold on to me," he whispered in her ear, wisps of her hair tickling his lips. After a moment, she did as he asked, but her wrists slumped indifferently over his shoulders.

Massaging the heel of his thumb at the nape of her neck, he asked, "Amelia, are you in some kind of trouble?"

"No."

"Do you need money? I could lend you—"

"No, I don't need money, and I wish you'd stop asking me if I do!"

Drawing her slightly away from him so he could look into her brown eyes brimming with tears, he murmured, "Then what's wrong? Sweetheart, is it your monthly time?"

Her gaze blazed up at him, but surprisingly, she didn't slug him. "No." Her voice cracked, and he sensed he'd struck a chord. "But I don't have m-m-m-many left! I'm a sour grape withering on the vine to a dried-up, wrinkled old raisin!" Then the mother of all torrents was unleashed.

Amelia bunched his shirtfront in her fists and hid her face next to his chest. He never would have believed one person could cry so much. "You're not a wrinkled old raisin, sweetheart."

"Oh yes, I am!" Her voice came out muffled.

"What makes you think that?"

"It's obvious."

Frank stroked her back, feeling the corded edge of her corset underneath the callous pads of his fingers. He ran his fingertips higher until he met the soft percale of her shirt and the vague impression of eyelet chemise straps. "It's not obvious to me." Then he confessed before he thought better, "I think you're pretty."

"Ewooh dah?" He felt the vibration of her mouth moving against his chest.

"What?"

She raised her chin and gazed at him; her lashes were spiked with dewy tears. "You do?"

There was no sense in taking it back. He'd spoken the truth. "Yes, Amelia, I do."

She gave him a soft smile and a cute sniff. But then a pitiful frown. "But you'll probably marry Emmaline Shelby and I'll . . . I'll . . . I'll still be a wrinkled old raisin!"

"Ah, shit," he cursed. "Where would you get an idea like that?"

She wouldn't give him an answer.

"I'm not in the marrying market, and whoever told you otherwise is deluded. Hell, I have enough trouble figuring out what to do with my life. I don't need to worry about somebody else's."

"Well," her voice broke with teary emotion, "I'm glad you set me straight on that subject. Neither one of us will ever get married."

Frank was startled by her declaration. "Don't sell yourself short, Amelia."

"Why not? I'm a . . . spinster." She cringed when she said the word. "I'm destined never to marry."

It angered Frank she would think so bleakly about her future. Holding her chin with his fingers, he said, "You shouldn't worry about something that's not true. You've got a lot to offer the right man, only you just haven't found him yet. Someone is going to snap you up." Pap came to mind, and Frank tried to stifle his critical squint. "Sooner than you think," he went on without much enthusiasm. "So you can stop wasting tears on spinsterhood."

"I'm not," she spoke with denial in her tone. "I'm mourning the frog."

"Well, don't." He brought his hand down and put his arm around her waist again. "I have to tell you, I didn't intend to give you a frog."

"You didn't?"

"Naw. I sent Jakey and Daniel to pick the cattails, and the frog was their idea."

"You didn't pick the cattails?"

"I'm sorry. I didn't."

"I see," she said in a flat tone. "Why did you bring me cattails anyway? I don't sign your business permits."

"Because I thought you'd like them."

"I see."

"Why do you keep saying that?" Frank asked, drawing his brows down.

"I can't help wondering about your ulterior motives. You yourself more or less admitted you never give out presents for nothing. So it's only natural that I wonder."

Frank felt uncomfortable. "I gave them to you

because I was apologizing for Budweiser and Beam, and because . . ." He was on the brink of admitting more to her than he was ready to admit to himself. "Well, Amelia, there's something about you that—" He broke off his thought, not liking the direction he was headed. "You're something, is all, Amelia."

She opened her mouth to speak, but he went on. "And another thing, you're coming back to the Moon Rock to give lessons. I don't want to hear any argument, so don't give me one."

"I won't."

"You won't?"

She blinked a crystalline tear off lower lashes. "No. And you can thank 'The Star-Spangled Banner' for my answer."

Baffled, he asked, "What does 'The Star-Spangled Banner' have to do with anything?"

"I'm supposed to play it at the Fourth of July picnic and have my students sing. The problem is, Mrs. Beamguard is the only one in town who has a piano besides you, and she won't let me use hers. I asked her, but she refused. Her excuse was the racket would upset the store. But I knew better when she advised me to go back to your establishment, or Daniel wouldn't be taking lessons anymore. She gets an illicit thrill of stealing into that stale drinking parlor of yours every week." Amelia pulled back to gaze at him. "When I think of all the times I let her add the points in her favor during our Thursday Afternoon Fine Ladies Society canasta games. I would have said something if she hadn't been my partner." Then from out of the blue, "Do you *really* think I'm pretty?"

He gave her a half smile and a scowl. "Pretty enough to get me into trouble."

Her face brightened. She tilted her chin higher, closed her eyes, and made her full lips part.

Seeing the expectant expression on her face, he was tempted. The idea of recapturing the pleasure he felt while kissing her pulled at him stronger than he would have liked. Cloaked in the cornstalks, it would be so easy to give her slow, shivery kisses without anyone seeing.

Staring at her inviting mouth, he lowered his head a few inches. He paused, contemplating the taste of her mouth against his. She'd be soft and damp, salty and sweet. He'd tease her lips apart this time, kissing her with more intimacy.

That last thought sobered him.

Intimacy. As in a very close association, familiarity and devotion. Words he couldn't promise. Not to a woman like Amelia. And especially when Pap O'Cleary was counting off the days until he would marry her—never mind the man hadn't bucked up enough nerve to ask her to the Fourth of July picnic.

Frank dropped his arms from around Amelia's waist and took a step backward. "I think you better get inside. It's too hot out here for you."

Her eyes fluttered open, and she stared at him with a bewildered sparkle in her gaze.

"I'll send Coney Island over to finish your lawn." Frank steered Amelia out of the garden and across the grass toward her back porch. "I'm going to pay the kid to come once a week. Consider it a gesture of goodwill on my part with absolutely no strings attached." He propelled her up the painted steps, deposited her in a green lawn settee, and stood over her. "If Dorothea Beamguard says the only way Junior will play the piano is at the Moon Rock, then that's how it'll be for now. I expect to see you there tomorrow at whatever the hell time it is you arrive. I won't hear you come in, I sleep—"

"—like the dead," she quoted him.

"Yeah." He laughed in a low voice. "You know the routine, honey." Adjusting the angle of his panama, he tipped his hat at her. "I have to confess, the place hasn't been the same without you. I got used to having you around. So did Pap."

A small, shy smile touched her moist lips.

Frank was frozen for a long moment by the expression on her beguiling face. Unbidden, he slowly leaned forward. But when her lashes began to lower, he realized what he was thinking and curbed his impulse to kiss her. Straightening, he shoved his hands in his pockets. He couldn't keep doing this to himself. To her. Why was it, he had this need to get close to her? He'd never felt this way before about a woman, and it unsettled him.

"I have to get back to the Moon Rock," he mumbled. "I'll be seeing you."

She nodded, but he barely noticed. As he walked down the steps, he began to wonder if it would have been better for him to concede the piano and cut his losses. Continuing to see Amelia Marshall five days a week could cost him a lot more than being minus a New American upright.

Chapter

12

On Monday, Amelia went to the mercantile to inform Dorothea Beamguard she was back teaching at the Moon Rock. The woman had been ecstatic and once again proposed Amelia give a small concert before the fireworks on the Fourth of July. Amelia went along with the idea to keep the peace.

Her first day back at the Moon Rock Saloon, Amelia was tense and nervous. Something special had sprung into existence between her and Frank in the corn rows of her garden, and she was reluctant to put a name to the intangible feeling. Friendship would have been the safest answer, but she knew there was more to it than that. She sensed Frank did, too.

Rather than sit in his favorite chair, drink a beer, and eat crackers during her practice time, he didn't show his face until four o'clock—the designated hour he had occupancy of the upright. When she looked up at him from the piano stool, his gaze met hers. His eyes were a blue so familiar to her, she didn't have to be close to him to recognize their dazzling color. He didn't say a word and just studied her with unhurried intensity. She did likewise, noting he was freshly shaved, wore natural linen trousers, and sported a peacock green vest with gilded threads. His hair was damp from a comb and styled straight back from his forehead. Knowing he'd kissed her, and knowing how wonderful his mouth had felt on hers, she was hard-pressed to control the butterfly-like flutters in her rib cage.

Frank broke away first. He crossed to the bar, zipped some seltzer into a glass of ice, and drank it as if he were parched. Cobb Weatherwax came in with a few of the boys from the mill, so they had no opportunity to converse. But she felt him watching her back while she packed up her music bag. Just before she left, their eyes met over the hatted heads of men lined up at the bar. His parting look was so galvanizing it sent a tremor through her.

That Tuesday Amelia was afraid she was falling in love with Frank.

Wednesday she suspected her fears were sure.

On Thursday she made the hard-fought decision to make herself available to him . . . should he inquire. Which she almost hoped he wouldn't. Thoughts of what happened with Jonas Pray were too fresh in her memory for her to jump blindly into another relationship. Though all men weren't the same, Frank's vocation paralleled a part of her past. She couldn't ignore the pain and humiliation she'd suffered. If she lost her heart again, she would have to be sure she wouldn't be hurt.

She and Frank had been treading lightly around each other all week, careful to be polite. Yet there was an underlying current that seemed to charge the room whenever they occupied it at the same time. Even so, she could practically count on one hand the number of times Frank spoke to her. What he lacked in conversation, Pap O'Cleary made up for tenfold.

Pap bragged about himself so much, Amelia was

sure he had calluses on his hands from patting his own back. At first, she found his flagrant regard for her distressing, though not because she didn't care for him. Like a barbed-wire fence, he had his good points. But she could not encourage him because she had strong affections for another tugging at her heart-strings.

Friday, Amelia decided to test those feelings. She dressed in her very best Eaton style summer suit of imported navy cloth. The skirt was lined with rustling taffeta and interlined with crinoline, and every step she took whispered like fall leaves. She had chosen a smart scarlet four-in-hand scarf for her neckwear and a hat of her aunt Clara's she'd restyled with wired wings of lace and pretty bunches of wildflowers on the right and left sides.

Her first lesson was at one o'clock, and she'd finished her lunch early so she could go to Beamguard's Mercantile to purchase red, white, and blue paper festooning to decorate the piano on Sunday.

Opening the door to the general store, the pleasant smells of new merchandise and old wood wafted in the air: the pungency of ripe cheese and sauerkraut; the smell of bright paint on new toys; kerosene, lard and molasses, poultry feed, gun oil, calico, coffee, and tobacco smoke.

The right side of the store contained dry goods: shelves of yardage, ready-mades, and the cabinet of Clark's Our New Thread. On the left was the grocery section: barrels of flour, sugar, and crackers, glass cases for cigars and penny candy, and a good array of cans, kegs, bottles, boxes, and bins. At the center stood the black potbellied stove gone cold for the summer. The chairs still circled around it with a chipped spittoon for the loungers.

Mr. Oscar Beamguard had been stocking jars of his wife's fresh strawberry preserves for sale when she'd entered the store. He wasn't nearly as skeptical as his wife—nor as round. In fact, he was slim as a bed slat, probably only producing a shadow when he faced west or east.

"Good afternoon, Miss Marshall." He set up his last jam-filled mason jar, then climbed down from his stepladder. "What can I do for you?"

Amelia peered through the curved glass display at the Independence Day decorations of red, white, and blue items and the shining stars surrounding them. She wished she could afford handheld flags for all her students, but they were a penny apiece. Lifting her gaze to Mr. Beamguard, she said, "May I buy the paper festooning by the yard, or do I have to purchase the roll?"

Mr. Beamguard stood over the case, absently adjusting the knot on his black tie. "It comes ten yards to a roll for twenty cents."

"Oh." Amelia did some quick calculating in her head. "All right. I'll need a roll of each color."

Oscar dropped open the lid on the case back and went to work. Amelia wandered through the store, looking at the various buttons and sewing accessories, thinking by next year she would be able to afford some of the more frivolous items.

The door opened, and she glanced up to see Emmaline Shelby coming inside. Amelia had to concede Emmaline didn't appear wilted from the heat, even though she manned a washer and iron all day. Her black hair curled around her face beneath a straw bonnet tied under her chin with pretty yellow ribbon. Her cheeks had just the right amount of natural pink.

"I'll be with you in a minute, Miss Shelby," Oscar said as he began to wrap Amelia's items in brown paper.

"I'm in no hurry," she replied. "All I need is some blueing. While I wait, I'll just look around."

Amelia didn't say a word; she pretended to be

engrossed in a box of safety pins, hoping to avoid a confrontation.

"Miss Marshall," Emmaline stated in an oh-so-casual tone. "I thought that was you. I recognized your suit."

Amelia had to gaze at the woman and force herself to smile.

"I've always admired that color on you when you've worn it." Emmaline paused, her voice too sweet.

Amelia felt herself stiffening, waiting for the blow.

"And you have worn that suit often. How long now?" Emmaline tapped her chin with a slim finger. "I think I've seen you in it for the past five years. At least."

Before Amelia could launch a counter retort, her opponent was firing again. "And that hat. Is it new? No . . . I don't think so. Why, it reminds me of the one your aunt always wore." Emmaline took a step closer. "I can see now that it is. How clever of you to remodel it. Why I wish I was as creative as you."

To anyone with any reason to listen—solely Mr. Beamguard—their conversation would have sounded like one woman complimenting the other. But Amelia knew an insult when she was the object of one. She racked her brain for something offensive, yet pleasant-sounding, to hit Emmaline with.

"Thank you, Miss Shelby," she said with mock cordiality. "I do believe your sunburn is looking much improved today."

Emmaline raised a hand to her cheek. "I don't go in the sun without a bonnet."

"Excuse me." Amelia sounded appropriately apologetic. "It must be the heat of your washer, dear, that's making your face so healthy."

Emmaline squared her shoulders with a tiny squeak. "If you don't mind, Mr. Beamguard, I'll just help myself to the blueing and you can put it on my account."

"Very well, Miss Shelby."

Emmaline took the bottle from the shelf, then gave Amelia a silent glare. In a lowered voice, she warned, "Don't think I'm not onto you. Fancying yourself up in Sunday clothes and dousing yourself with lemon verbena isn't going to make him notice you. Frank doesn't like a woman who's not modern—modern in fashion, thinking, *and* music. He told me all you play are songs from dead people. Well, let me tell you, I know gay tunes and I sing them for Frank all the time."

On that, she left energetically humming, "Ta-ra-ra-boom-de-ay!"

Amelia was so vexed, she saw stars without having to look at the festive case of decorations. Ooh! That Emmaline Shelby was fast becoming a thorn in her side. It wouldn't have been so bad if the woman hadn't read her like the *Gazette*.

"Is there anything else, Miss Marshall?"

"Yes . . ." she said tentatively, thinking she would have to take drastic action. "I'll be just minute."

Amelia put the pins aside and strode to the wooden stand of sheet music. The selection wasn't very large —there being only two pianos in all of Weeping Angel. But the owner of the Oak Tree Hotel, Eugene Thistlerod, did own a zither. And Saybrook Spivey had an accordion he'd play at social functions. Not to mention there were countless harmonica players in town.

She thumbed through the scant folios. At a glance, "Daisy Bell" looked complicated. There were many left-hand chords, and the song was spread out over five pages. Biting her lower lip, she set the music aside and continued her search. "In the Baggage Coach Ahead" had four flats. "Oh, Promise Me" had just as many flats—the same ones as "In the Baggage Coach Ahead"—but the lyrics were romantic. "Rock-a-Bye Baby" would be pushing things a bit far. Catching the corner of another she saw "Sweet Rosie O'Grady." Then, just what she was looking for seemed to pop out at her, and she grabbed the last folio with a broad smile.

In the end, she chose six *gay tunes* she would have normally frowned upon. Setting them on the counter next to her streamers, she did frown when Mr. Beamguard totaled the cost of the music. She tried not to worry about it too much. Her students paid her on Friday and that was today. She'd just have to be more frugal on her grocery bill.

After exchanging money with Mr. Beamguard, Amelia gathered her parcel and departed. As she crossed Holy Road, she glanced down the street. The men's dormitory that housed Reed's sawmill workers and a few of the bachelors was that way on Gopher Road. She never would have paid it any mind, if not for the fact Pap O'Cleary resided there. As of late, he seemed to come out of nowhere to walk her to the saloon. It didn't matter where she was coming from, he'd find her.

Stepping onto the corner, she gave the street one more gaze, just to make sure. She didn't see a trace of him. She passed the doctor's office, and as she did so, she thought of Narcissa, who was blossoming in her condition. Her sickness had eased and her color had returned. It was amazing the difference three weeks could make on a woman almost four months into the family way.

Amelia used her key to let herself inside the Moon Rock, then closed the door. She knew precisely where to find a lamp now. And the smells of stale cigars and spirits didn't bother her as much as they used to. She still didn't find the odors attractive, but she wasn't sickened by them anymore.

After setting her music bag and package on the bar, she slipped off her gloves but kept her hat on. She went to the oil stove next to the icebox and lit the single burner. Then she prepared a pot of coffee so strong, the aroma of bubbling grounds was as thick as stew. Frank liked his coffee robust enough to float a silver dollar on it—at least that's what she'd heard him say to Mr. O'Cleary once.

She arranged her piano teaching necessities as she normally did, all the while casting furtive glances at Frank's closed apartment door. She couldn't understand how he could sleep so soundly while she was making noise. There had been those few times when he rose early and surprised her, though that hadn't happened recently.

She opened her parcel and shuffled through the music, knowing just the one she would select first. Putting it on the piano's music stand, she scanned the notes, trying to get a sense of the tune before she played it. Then, feeling ready, she went directly into the chorus. She played the song with as much airiness as she could muster. After stumbling through it once, she tried again. The second try was much smoother, and by the third, she felt breezy.

If she hadn't been blaring the piano keys, she probably would have heard Frank yelling at her. As it was, his shrill whistle between his fingers made her lift her head and take notice of him in the doorway. She stopped playing immediately, her eyes coming to rest on his exposed navel.

He wore a pair of form-fitting Derby ribbed drawers with three pearl buttons at the sateen waist placket— all of which were *un*buttoned. The fine combed white cotton had to be staying up by sheer will alone. Since he'd let her know he slept without the benefit of a nightshirt, he must have slipped these on while half asleep. Was he aware they weren't fastened?

"Hello, Frank." Despite her pulse speeding, she tried to sound very calm and matter-of-fact. "I didn't know you were awake."

"How could I sleep with you belting out that Tin

Pan Alley stuff?" His tousled black hair fell into his eyes, and he combed it back with his splayed fingers. "Damn, I dreamed Emmaline was out here. That's all she sings."

Amelia's nerves grew brittle, and she fought for a fitting reply. "Doesn't everyone appreciate the melody of 'Ta-ra-ra-boom-de-ay!'? I just bought the sheet music this morning, along with a few others I find very contemporary."

He hitched the band of his drawers higher on his hips, the sinewy cords of his legs stretching the thin material. Absently, he fit each tiny pearl button into its hole. A brief shiver rippled through her. She stared at his masculine hand, his powerful fingers as they worked to close the gap in his underwear. Even put together, she couldn't refrain from taking in the thick definition of muscle on his chest, the flatness of his abdomen . . . and even the outline of his crotch.

She averted her eyes as he stepped into the room wrinkling his nose. "What's that smell?"

Delighted, she said, "Coffee."

"I wasn't referring to the coffee." He sniffed and made a face. "What's that rotten lemons smell?"

Rotten lemons? On the pretext of smoothing her hair, she lifted her hand. She turned her nose into her wrist and quietly sniffed. No one had ever told her aunt Clara she smelled like a rotten lemon when she'd worn the perfume. Lemon verbena had a sweet lemony scent.

Amelia lowered her arm. "I don't smell a thing offensive. Your nose must be playing tricks on you."

"All I know is, I was in a deep sleep. Then I started dreaming Emmaline was out here singing her boom-de-ays off."

"No, it's just me."

Laying his palm on his belly, he stifled a yawn. "What time is it?"

She checked the hour on her chatelaine watch. "A quarter to one."

"You put coffee on." It wasn't a question, rather a statement of fact.

"Would you like me to pour you a cup?"

"I can do it myself."

Then he disappeared into his room, only to reappear a scant minute later in trousers—no shirt or shoes—and with his hair a little tidier.

While she put a new song on the music stand, she heard him pad to the bar. The clang of enamel, and the clink of a metal spoon against stoneware signaled he was stirring sugar into his coffee. As he did so, she broke into her second melody, "Oh, Promise Me." This popular tune was more suited to her classical background. There weren't nearly as many snappy chords.

She played the piece through once, Frank not interrupting her. When she was finished, she put her hands in her lap and turned to see where he'd gone. He sat at his usual table, his large hands corraling his coffee mug in his grasp. He would have been absolutely more handsome than a new catalog bonnet if he hadn't been scowling at her.

"Have you heard anything from Rogers and Company?"

"No." She felt crestfallen. "I just posted the letter four days ago. I'm sure they've been informed of the train accident and will expedite another New American posthaste."

"Yeah, let's hope so."

Amelia knit her brows. Well, he didn't have to sound so expectant. What happened to insisting she play at the Moon Rock? He acted as if he were counting the minutes until he got rid of her.

Their conversation, if Amelia could have called it that to begin with, came to a standstill. She tilted her head to one side, just enough for him to lift his gaze to her new hat.

He didn't say a word as he took a sip of his coffee.

She sat a little straighter, smoothing her navy skirt across her lap.

He seemed engrossed with the table's wood grain.

She stared at him.

He got up, took his coffee, and went behind the long bar.

She could have screamed her frustration. She might have, too, if Pap O'Cleary hadn't come in, causing both of them to shift their gazes on him.

But Pap only had eyes for Amelia, so she gave him one of her most charming smiles in the hopes of making Frank jealous.

"How do, Miss Marshall?"

"I'm quite fine, thank you."

Pap didn't acknowledge Frank as he entered the saloon and crossed over to where she sat on the stool. "I've been looking for you."

"Have you?" She wished he hadn't found her.

"Yup."

She waited, but he seemed to have nothing further to say. She didn't pursue the matter, knowing there was no point to it. Every time she'd tried to have a conversation with Pap O'Cleary, he turned it one-sided. With him doing the talking—more like rambling—while she lent a patient ear.

Amelia tried to include Frank before he could make his escape. "Mr. Brody and I," she began, gazing directly at Frank, "were discussing Dishpan Alley music."

"Dishpan?" Pap scratched the back of his ear.

"She means Tin Pan," Frank put in while he bent over his hot cup.

She inwardly cringed. "Yes, that's what I meant."

Pap cocked his chin to the side. "That's the only

kind of music there is, Miss Marshall. Now, I didn't want to offend you or nothing, but this dead guy stuff you teach the kids isn't up to snuff."

She pursed her lips. "Classical composition is the root of all music, Mr. O'Cleary." Then seeing Frank head for his room, she quickly added, "Mr. Brody, what do you think about dead composers?"

"Don't dig 'em up."

He was nearly at his doorway, and she was beside herself with a way to stop him. On impulse, she gathered her sheet music and pretended to "accidentally" drop it. But the folios were more apt to be described as sailing toward him. Whatever the case, he stopped in his tracks and looked at his bare feet where the sheets had scattered.

"Oh, I'm terribly sorry, Mr. Brody." She bent over in a ladylike move. Her motions were fluid and slow, a jaunt to her shoulders. The only comment her efforts gained her was Pap asking, "Do you have a creak in your neck, Miss Marshall? I've got some liniment—"

"No," she snapped.

Frank made no move to help, but Pap had dropped on his knees to gather the papers. Deflated, Amelia slumped on the stool as Frank went into his room and closed the door.

Pap read them as he picked them up. "'Her Eyes Don't Shine Like Diamonds.' 'Ta-ra-ra-boom-de-ay!'" Gazing at the other titles, he read those too, then gave her an approving grin. "These are all swell tunes." He rose to his feet and handed her the sheet music. His face was one big smile, then his crooked nose twitched. "Is that you smelling up the place, Miss Marshall?"

She simply nodded, seeing no point in denying it.

He let out an *ah* as he said, "I've always had a fancy for this perfume. My invalid grandmother used to wear the very same one."

Amelia wanted to crawl inside the piano. She thought she might have if not for the fact Jakey Spivey came in for his lesson.

And so her afternoon was spent playing "The Star-Spangled Banner" and coaxing her students to sing the words as if they meant them. Coney Island insisted on singing, "Oh, the rabbits we watched," instead of "O'er the ramparts we watched." By 1:45 she felt a dull headache forming behind her eyes. At least she had a reprieve between 2:30 and 3:00 when Lysbeth Foster didn't show up. It seemed the second round of the chicken pox was making its arrival. By four o'clock, Amelia must have played the national anthem forty times, and as Jessamyn Parks left, Amelia was ready for a Baptist lemonade.

Too bad Frank was nowhere to be seen. Perhaps she'd taken things a bit too far. She'd never been boldly flirtatious before. Her head swirled with doubts. Maybe Frank hadn't been aware of her in the same way as she had been aware of him. Maybe she'd imagined the whole thing . . .

Amelia pressed both hands over her eyes, then stood with a long, exhausted sigh. The saloon was empty, which was odd. As of late, Pap sat and listened to her giving lessons. Even he must have been feeling the chalkboard-like scratch of the children's voices, over and over and over, so he'd deserted the area.

"Lookee what I got."

The Appalachian-twanged voice made Amelia jump with a start. Turning, she gasped as she came eye to beady eye with a lifeless reddish brown rodent baring two front teeth from each jaw.

A little hysterically, she sputtered at the floppy creature swinging from Cobb Weatherwax's grubby hand, "M-Mr. Weatherwax, what is that?"

"Dead beaver."

"W-What's it d-doing in here?"

He gave her a lopsided smile, and she realized his

teeth were straight and white under his wiry facial hair. "I aim to skin it and make a poke."

"A poke?"

He looked at her with eyes the color of lake moss as if she were deaf, dumb, and blind. "A poke." Seeing she still hadn't a clue, he explained, "A bag."

"Yes, well . . . it's . . . a nice beaver, Mr. Weatherwax. I'm sure it will make a lovely bag."

"I thought so," he declared proudly. Bringing his arm down, the beaver's webbed rear feet and flat tail brushed the planked floor. "Where is everybody?"

"I wouldn't know." Normally by four, Frank was setting up tiny glasses and Pap was spreading sawdust on the floor.

Cobb plopped in a chair and sat the beaver on his lap like a baby. The finely tanned fringe on his buckskins fanned down his sleeves and pants legs, and as he crossed one leg over the other, he gave her a polite smile. Shrugging, Amelia glanced away and continued to fill her petit point bag.

"I think you play that pianner real fine."

"Thank you."

"I heerd music like what you do before, but none so good. You got a way about you, Miz Marshall." Cobb patted the beaver with the flat of his hand, then dumped the carcass on the tabletop.

He stood and walked toward her.

A burst of trepidation hit her, and she froze. But there was no need. He went right on by to stare at the piano keys.

"That 'un you did afore, on Tuesday, is my fav'rite. I don't know what you call it. I cain't read."

She felt sorry for him then, thinking it must be hard for him not to be able to read. But even harder for him to admit his deficiency.

He tapped middle C several times with his lean forefinger. Then it was as if he forgot all about her. He sat on the stool, gave the keys a thorough examination with his gaze, and began to play—note for *exact* note—Beethoven's Sonatina in G.

She was astounded, not believing what she was hearing. He used the *moderato* tempo, playing with a natural grace she'd never witnessed from any musician.

She allowed him to perform the entire piece, then exclaimed, "Mr. Weatherwax, wherever did you learn to play Beethoven?"

"From you, Miz Marshall."

"Me?"

"I heerd you play it, and I remembered." He put his finger to his head. "In here. That's where I keep the music." Then he broke into a Haydn minuet she'd taught last week.

"Oh, my," she said when he finished, laying a hand next to her racing heartbeat. "I'm awed, Mr. Weatherwax, truly I am. You're blessed with a gift."

"Only thing Cobb's gifted with is the gift of gab," Pap said as he strode into the Moon Rock hauling a gunnysack containing a block of ice over his shoulder.

"You're wrong, Mr. O'Cleary." Amelia grew flushed with excitement. She felt as if she'd made a historic discovery. "Mr. Weatherwax can play music in its entirety just by listening to me play it once." Then to prove it, she slid a chair next to Cobb's and said, "Listen. I'll play Bach." She ran through a few bars of a musette in D major. "Now, Mr. Weatherwax, you play." He grew suddenly bashful, and she placed her hand gingerly on his arm to encourage him in a soft and coaxing voice. "You can do it."

She was vaguely aware of Pap's growl. She cast a brief glance in his direction and saw his face had gone as red as his mustache. She disregarded him and encouraged Cobb once again. "Please, Mr. Weatherwax."

After a moment's hesitation, Cobb played the musette precisely as Amelia had.

She clapped with joy. "See! What did I tell you?" Then to Cobb, she fairly beamed. "Why, Mr. Weatherwax, this is the most phenomenal thing I've ever heard!"

"Big deal," Pap muttered. "Cobb can play the piano. So can I. So can you, Miss Marshall."

"But Cobb's talent is special."

Pap swore under his breath as he went to unload the straw-covered ice into the icebox. "Well, I don't see Cobb getting paid to play the piano. He ain't that talented at it."

Cobb got off the stool and hefted his beaver across his arm. "See this hyar beaver, Pap? I'm going to make a poke out of him."

"Big deal," Pap repeated.

"For you."

Pap straightened from the icebox. "Me?"

"Yes, sir. It's you who give me a free beer last week on account I was short a dime."

"Keep it up, Pap," Frank said from his doorway, "and we'll go broke. No offense, Cobb, but I'm in the business of selling liquor for money."

Amelia shot her gaze in Frank's direction, wondering just how long he'd been standing there. He'd changed into a fancy gold vest with a pure white shirt underneath and snappy black garters above his elbows. She should compose herself and act more refined, but she was too excited about Mr. Weatherwax to bother being demure.

"And I can appreciate that, Frank," Cobb said. "It's just that times are hard. Beaver are scarce these days. But I got this 'un hyar and he's a fine catch. I'm going to skin him now."

"Outside, I hope." Frank walked to the bar, his mood no more improved than it had been three hours ago.

Amelia watched him, thinking she wanted to hit him on the back of the head with her shoe. He didn't have to be such a crabapple. "Well, I have some wonderful news about Mr. Weatherwax," she said to Frank.

Pap shot in with, "Cobb isn't any kind of news."

"I think he is," Amelia countered.

Slamming the icebox door, Pap crossed his arms over his chest. "Frank doesn't care that Cobb can play music with his ear. He only pays those who play music with their fingers."

Frank nudged Pap. "Where's the sawdust?"

"In the bin."

"Why isn't it on the floor?"

"I ain't got around to it yet."

Frank leaned against the bar. He gazed at Pap, then Cobb, and lastly Amelia. "What in the hell is going on here?"

No one said a word.

Frank put his fingertips on the counter and drummed an impatient beat, then nodded. "I know what this is about. It's that damn picnic, isn't it, Pap?"

Pap grimaced. Amelia didn't know what he was talking about.

"Miss Marshall," Frank began, "Pap's gun-shy about asking you something, and my guess is all this attention over Cobb has Pap chomping at the bit."

Cautious, Amelia said, "What does he want to ask me?" as if Pap weren't in the room.

Pap remained buttoned up like a patent-leather shoe.

"Pap wants to ask you to the Fourth of July picnic."

Amelia couldn't disguise her surprise. "Oh." She knew Pap had been up to something, but she hadn't guessed he wanted to escort her to the picnic. She'd been hoping Frank—ridiculous as that might be—would ask her today.

She glanced at Pap. He was looking at her so longingly, she thought his tongue would lop to the side of his mouth. She wished Frank would intervene and say she already had a partner—him. But he didn't. So she was left to deal with the situation herself. She could decline politely, coming up with a few short excuses, none of which would be the truth. Or she could accept. In doing so, she'd be letting all of Weeping Angel—and most especially Frank Brody—know she wasn't a withered old raisin on the vine waiting for him to come calling.

"Mr. O'Cleary," she said in a clarion voice. "Is it your intention to ask me to the Fourth of July picnic? Or is Mr. Brody putting words in your mouth?"

Pap brought himself up taller—about as high as he could go, him being only five foot three. "Yes, ma'am. That was my intention, but I was too spooked to ask you."

"I don't know why you should be, Mr. O'Cleary. I'd be delighted to accept."

"Holy shit," he replied.

"I don't believe it is." She was proud of herself from holding back on reprimanding him for his colorful comment. She'd show Frank she could be very modern, indeed.

She grasped the handle of her music bag and nodded to all in the room. "I'll expect you shortly before one o'clock on Sunday, I assume."

"Ah, yes, ma'am. That would be the designated time, the picnic starting at one o'clock."

"Very well." She didn't dare look at Frank, afraid of what his expression might reveal. She'd just have to make the best of things with Pap O'Cleary. Who wasn't a bad sort, she rushed to add in her thoughts. He was just, well . . . rather eager.

And too short for her.

"Good afternoon, everyone," she said in an airy tone, belying the knots suddenly twisting in her stomach. She left before she could change her mind and tell Mr. O'Cleary she was otherwise engaged after all.

*T*here was something to be said about indoor plumbing: Frank didn't have any.

When he wanted to take a good long soak in a hot bathtub, smoke an imported Havana cigar, and read, he had to go to Barent's Bathhouse and Barbershop next to the men's dormitory located on Gopher Road—the road pocked with holes dug by the nuisances. So many, the public works office was on the verge of giving up trying to maintain a level surface and let the gophers have their way, since the town had already foregone naming the avenue something pious —there being nothing remotely inspirational about gopher burrows.

Be that as it may, Frank could have cared less about the gophers and their holes. As long as he could navigate his way to the bathhouse, he didn't care if they lived in the middle of the street.

Frank kept his stogie clamped between his teeth and his chin just above the soapy water level. His legs were too long to fit all the way inside the copper-lined tub, and he had to bend them at the knees. As he puffed, tiny clouds of smoke rose overhead. He lifted his gaze to the pine ceiling awash with an orange shellac varnish.

No cobwebs, spiders, or black ants.

Barent Bloodshine kept the place pretty clean. The Turkish towels were set aside to be laundered after every customer. You had to bring your own soap and shampoo paste, and a shower rinse was extra. Barent supplied poorly written pulp books and yellow-covereds—brochures of an obscene nature containing images of naked women and the stories of their exploits. Sometimes the gas burner heating the water would smoke and stink up the small, one-window cubicle, but other than that, the place wasn't too bad.

Frank had bathed in worse.

As he enjoyed his cigar, he closed his eyes and let his mind drift. The dancing girls would be hitting Weeping Angel any day now. He'd had a response within a week of posting an open ad to Wyoming, Montana, and Nevada newspapers. A reply came in to the Wells Fargo office from four girls, all former employees of the same hop joint, the Nockum Stiff in Helena. They'd written to say they were out of jobs since the saloon burned down.

He'd made up his mind without even leaving the office to think on it and wait for any more answers. He'd paid Tindall extra to have Boise City wire Helena rather than rely on the mail. The matter of having girls in the Moon Rock had become an urgent one.

If Frank had to keep on the way he was going with Amelia, he wouldn't have a clear mind left to run his business.

He hadn't missed the way she'd done herself up yesterday, dousing herself with perfume, and playing the songs she thought he'd like. Emmaline was the one who went in for all that modern gaiety; he was satisfied enough to hear Pap's versions of outhouse tunes. And though he didn't really hate lemon verbena, he'd had to say something to the contrary. If she knew he liked fragrance on a woman, she'd double up on the spray. And he didn't need any more distractions from her. Already he'd been noticing her clothes. He had never paid any attention to how her hat matched her suit before, or how the buttons on her bodice were so tiny, he'd pondered if his big fingers could ever get them undone. Then he'd realized he was in serious trouble. Undressing a woman like Amelia Marshall was not something he could afford to fantasize about.

And he'd been fantasizing about her a lot lately.

Keeping things simple between them was best. In an effort to cool his thoughts down, he'd been avoiding her. When he had to be in her company, he tried to keep his distance. He wasn't the right man for her, despite wanting her in the worst way. She was home and hearth, while he put in long hours serving liquor at a bar. She needed a man whose arm she could be on to attend the church and town social functions. Her acceptance of Pap's offer to that damn picnic drove him in the ground like a stake. He didn't want to go, but neither did he want her to go with Pap. He wasn't right for her either. It maddened Frank to think he was jealous. He couldn't be. Never had feelings of resentment taken him over. He didn't care to give the rivalry in his system an explanation. He knew if he did, he'd be sorry.

At least tomorrow he could get away and go fly-fishing.

Then he frowned on that thought and took another draw on his Havana. It was the Glorious Fourth tomorrow. Reverend's Meadow and Tadpole Lake would be overrun with kids, people, and noise.

After a minute, a smile worked its way on his mouth as he thought about the peaceful spot farther upstream, secluded by trees and a carpet of grass scattered with white daisies. Wild mint grew along the banks, and he'd hauled out more than one trout feeding in the watery marsh grasses.

Frank developed a cramp in his shin and lifted his leg up to straighten his knee. He made sure he didn't touch the water tank heater just above the faucets, having burned the bottom of his foot a few times when he wasn't watching.

He was about to pick up his book again when a knock pounded on the door. A quick glance at the lock, and he noted he hadn't put the hook in the eye.

"What?" he barked, irritated someone would disturb him when he was soaking.

"Frank?" came Pap's low voice. "Are you in there?"

"Yeah, I'm in here. What do you want?"

"I gotta come in, Frank. It's a hot emergency."

Having just been thinking about saloon conflagrations putting people out of work, Frank clamped the sides of the tub with both hands, slid his buttocks across the bottom, and sat up. "Shit, the Moon Rock's on fire!"

He was putting a leg out when Pap reassured him in a level tone, "No. The Moon Rock is fine."

Frank froze.

There was a dry pause.

"It's me, Frank, who's in trouble, and you're the only one who can help."

Slumping back, Frank grabbed the bar of Colgate floating on the surface of the murky water. "This better be good," he said around the fat cigar in his mouth. "Come on in."

The door opened and Pap staggered inside, nearly stepping on the novel Frank had on the floor next to the tub.

"Damn, Pap, watch where you're walking. That's *Oliver Twist* you almost kicked."

"Sorry, Frank," he said, and it sounded to Frank as if Pap's teeth were chattering. Though the day was warm, his sleeves were rolled down to his wrists, the buttons at his cuffs fastened with horseshoe-shaped links. He'd even put on his winter mohair coat, his derby hat, and had wrapped a blue bandanna high on his neck.

"Couldn't you have waited until I got out?"

"No."

"What's the matter with you?"

"I'm sick."

"You look sick." Frank propped his elbows on the sides of the tub and tapped the ash off his cigar. "Take the night off and go to bed. Did you think I was going to make you come into the bar?"

"N-No. 'Sides, I ain't that kind of sick." Pap shivered. He glanced for a place to sit. Seeing none in the bare bathing room, he slumped against the cedar wall and slid onto his backside. Wrapping his left arm around his middle, he scratched his ear with his right hand.

Frank took the situation more seriously once he got a good look at Pap and saw the red blisters on his forehead. "Son of a bitch, you've got scarlet fever."

"I think I got malaria."

"Hell, you can't have malaria. You wouldn't have spots if you had malaria." Frank puffed thoughtfully on his cigar. "But you would if you had the chicken pox."

"The chicken pox!" Pap exclaimed, moving his arm down and across the side of his neck after tugging at his bandanna. "Damn . . . I think I do."

"How in the hell did you manage not to get the chicken pox until now?" Frank absently soaped his chest. "This is something you're supposed to have when you're four—not nine days after you turn forty."

"I don't know," Pap whined, scratching at his underarm now. "I just don't know. Damn. I'm sick. I'm cold, my bones feel like they're all broke. Ah, damn. Shit." He raked the inside of his thigh with his fingertips. "Even my parts has 'em. I woke up this morning, and there they were. All over. You should see my back. Thank God I ain't got a mirror big enough, but I can feel 'em. It's like they're crawling, and my skin can't stop tingling." He rubbed his back and shoulders against the wall.

Frank let the soap slip from his fingers, and he ran his hand over his belly. "Stop scratching. You're making me feel itchy."

"I can't help it. I ain't never felt this sick in my life. It was all I could do to come on over here."

"Then why the hell did you?" Frank put out his cigar in the galvanized soap dish hanging over the side of the tub. "I would have known something was wrong with you and sent Cobb over to see what."

"Don't you ever send Cobb Weatherwax over to my residence."

Frank glanced at Pap. "You're still agitated with Cobb about yesterday?"

"Damn right."

"You think he's after Amelia?"

"I know he is."

"Well, Pap, I don't think Cobb is her type."

"I don't care." Pap's eyes grew tiny and his lip curled in a sneer; the red dots on his face grew prominent and deepened a shade with his aggravation. "I won't give him the chance to take her from me tomorrow, Frank."

"You don't even know if Cobb is going to that picnic."

"What else does he have to do?" Pap dug his fingers into the side of his boot and scratched his ankle. "He'll be there." He pointedly stared at Frank and said, "You've got to help me."

Frank didn't say a word.

"You need to take Amelia to the picnic for me."

"I don't need to do anything."

"Frank," Pap implored between scratches, "you're the only one I can trust."

"What makes you think you can trust me?"

"Hell, Frank, you're the best friend I ever had. I'd trust you with my life." Pap itched his brow. "I'd trust you with my girl."

Frank shot his gaze on Pap. "Saying she'd go with you to a picnic doesn't mean she's your girl."

"Close to it."

"Not close enough."

"Regardless, I'm thinking," Pap said, moving his fingers to rake his neck again, "Cobb's thinking, if I'm not there tomorrow, Miss Marshall is fair game. You saw for yourself the way she was mooning over him about his piano-playing."

Frank shrugged. "He impressed her."

"Now you know why I need you to do me this favor, Frank. I ain't ever asked you to do me anything as big as this. Not even when we were running shotgun for the Fargo."

Feeling his stubble-covered jaw, Frank tried to think of an excuse. He couldn't afford to be alone with Amelia Marshall. Not to mention if he did take her, he'd have to listen to political speeches, eat watermelon, be under the scrutiny of the old crow matrons, and feel obligated to socialize with the men.

It was one thing doing business with Fisk, Dodge, Reed, and the others in his saloon; the boundaries were drawn, and he knew where he stood. He was a businessman; they were the customers. When they exited through the bat-wing doors, so did their problems, and Frank was free of them.

He wasn't sure they liked him all that much but tolerated him because he served them right. Bringing one of their own to a town function—especially a lady as cultivated as Amelia—he'd turn some heads.

"I can't, Pap. I've got plans."

"Plans!" Pap's tone was dubious. "What the hell kind of plans? Going fishing?"

"So what if I do?"

"So what?" he huffed. *"So what?* So my life is flashing before my eyes. I could die of this, you know."

"I've never heard of a case of chicken pox death."

"Well, I could be the first. And if I did kiss off, I'd be eternally floating in heaven, wondering if Amelia was with Cobb Weatherwax."

"First, I don't think you're going to heaven, with some of the hell-raising you've done with me. Second, you're not making any sense, Pap." Frank sloshed the tepid water with his hands. "I think you're delirious."

"I am not." Pap stood. "I can't believe you're being such a hardhead about this. I ask you one favor, and you're acting like I asked you to go kill someone. It's for one day. A few hours of your time. Just make sure Cobb doesn't get near her. You've got to stick by her side, and above all else, make sure you're the one to buy her box supper. That's all I ask, Frank."

Frank inhaled and closed his eyes for a moment. He'd have to bid on a box supper. And Amelia Marshall had said she could cook fried chicken. How long had it been since he'd eaten some? Too long to even remember.

Opening his eyes, Frank gazed at Pap. "You look like hell."

"I feel like hell."

"If it weren't you asking, I'd tell them to go to hell."

"And I'd agree. But it is me, and I'm the only kin you've got. We're like brothers."

"True."

"Then you'll do it?"

"I guess I have to."

Pap frowned. "You don't have to look so pained, Frank. She ain't an ugly woman."

"I know that."

Twisting his arm to claw at his back, Pap stamped his foot like a dog whose belly was being scratched. "You won't regret it."

"I hope not."

"Go by her place tonight and tell her it's you that's taking her and not me. I'm ashamed to show my face. I'd scare her. I ain't ever itched so bad in my life. Ah, damn. I think my skin is coming off."

"Go home, Pap."

"You'll go over and tell her, won't you?"

"I'll try. I still need a shave."

Pap grabbed the knob. "I don't know when I'll be back to the saloon . . . them Reed twins wasn't around for over a week."

"Damn," Frank said. "That's right. I'll be out a piano player for a week."

"It weren't like I planned to get this."

"I know."

"I got to go, Frank. I'm sick." He rapidly blinked his eyes and rubbed at them with his left hand. "Even my eyeballs are itchy."

Pap let himself out, and Frank stayed in the bath, the water no longer soothing to his muscles. He pondered what he'd gotten himself into. He'd made a promise to his friend he'd make sure Cobb wouldn't get near Amelia.

The trouble was, who was going to make sure *he* didn't get too close to her?

Frank didn't have a chance to go see Amelia on Saturday. There was a line for the barber's chair, and he'd had to wait. By the time he returned to the Moon Rock, it was near his opening hour of four, and he'd had to do Pap's jobs on top of his to get ready.

The customers had been sorely disappointed to hear they'd lost their piano player to the chicken pox, but after a round of free drinks to toast Pap's speedy

recovery, most of the patrons were more than forgiving.

But that was one night.

Frank hoped he wouldn't have to dole out free suds
for the rest of the week just to keep the men at the
Moon Rock instead of bailing out in favor of Lloyd's
Palace. Iza Ogilvie could sing a passable tune when
she was encouraged, and Lloyd's clunker organ could
sound good to a man with a thirst for music.

This being Sunday morning, Frank had forty-eight
hours until Tuesday to figure out a way to keep his
customers coming back while Pap recuperated. But as
it stood now, tired as he was, his thinking wasn't
worth a damn. Having turned in somewhere in the
vicinity of three-thirty in the morning, he'd been
jarred awake just past nine by Dodge, Fisk, and Parks
to open the saloon so they could move the piano out
and into a gazebo that had been erected toward the
outskirts of town off Divine Street. He'd had five cups
of strong coffee since, but yawns were still creeping up
on him.

As he crossed through Amelia's picket gate, he
thought he should try and catch a quick nap before
having to take her to the picnic.

His twist on the bell ringer didn't bring her to
answer the door. He waited and rang again. She didn't
show up. Frowning, he ascended the porch steps and
headed toward the back, thinking this was the second
time he'd gone looking for her at her house. He hoped
he wouldn't find her crying in the grass again.

The backyard was empty, so he went up to the
veranda. The back door was open and the screen in
place to keep the insects out. The smells of a home-
cooked meal hit him at once, making his stomach
rumble—almost to the point of pain. He thought of
all that coffee sloshing in his empty belly and was
instantly starved.

He rapped on the door with his knuckles.

No answer.

He knew she was inside. She wouldn't have left her door open if she weren't.

He knocked louder.

This time, he heard her call from the interior of the house. He couldn't make out what she was saying, so he waited for her to let him in. Only after a long moment, did her voice drift to him more clearly.

"Come in, Coney Island. You may set your lesson money on the kitchen table."

Frank raised his brows inquiringly. "It's not Coney Island."

She must not have heard him, because she repeated her request. "Coney Island, dear, I'm indisposed at the moment." She sounded like she was talking from the stairs leading to the bathroom. "You may let yourself in and put your quarter on the table."

Shrugging, Frank pulled the handle on the screen and walked into the kitchen. He surveyed the room. Neat as a pin. On a rack resting on the sideboard was the most perfect pie he'd ever seen. Leaning over, he sniffed the fruity-smelling, buttery crust with the decorative fork markings on it.

Cherry.

Jackpot. He loved cherry pie.

Then he let his gaze wander over the rest of the fixings. There was a jar of homemade root beer. And she had a small wicker basket with a Turkey red fringed cloth neatly arranged and folded over a large lump. He couldn't help lifting the hem and checking out the contents.

Fried chicken.

Wings, drumsticks, thighs, and breasts—all perfectly golden. They looked light and crispy, and he detected a hint of cinnamon in the flour coating.

Biscuits.

Buttermilk from the looks of them. High and plump, with a crock of honey as an accompaniment.

Cole slaw.

He hadn't tasted that in years.

Indian pickles.

He could tell by the cayenne pepper and red pepper pods.

And she'd packed something with vegetables in a jar. Who cared what it was? It looked good.

"Coney Island?" Amelia called, and Frank straightened.

He didn't answer.

Footfalls came on the floor in the dining room, then a face peered into the kitchen from around the corner. Or at least he hoped there was a face underneath all that cream smelling like almond liqueur. She looked as if she were wearing a ghoulish mask, her eyes, mouth, and nostrils the only parts spared from the white paste. She'd put her hair up in rags and it stuck out all over with frayed ties keeping the knots in place. She wore the same floral wrapper she had on the night he'd kissed her in her foyer.

There wasn't a chance he was going to kiss her now.

"Frank!" she gasped, and immediately retreated behind the wall so he couldn't see her.

"Yeah, it's me."

"Where's Coney Island?"

"I wouldn't know."

"But you said you were he."

"Actually, I replied to the contrary. You just didn't hear me."

"Why did you come in?"

"You told me to."

"I said for Coney Island to come in."

"Well, he's not around."

"I can see that."

"I can't see you." Frank crossed his arms over his chest. "Why don't you come here?"

"No."

He decided to flush her out. "I've never seen a

woman have to use so much depilatory cream on her face before, Miss Marshall. I guess your facial hair is a real problem."

"Well, I like that!" she squeaked, and came around the corner once again.

He chuckled. "I figured you would, sweetheart."

She put her hands on her hips, and gave him a mad glare. "What are you doing here?"

"I came bearing a message from Pap."

"Mr. O'Cleary?" She suddenly looked alarmed.

"He can't take you to the picnic today."

He couldn't really tell because of the white stuff, but she didn't seem all that let down. "Did Mr. O'Cleary change his mind?"

"No, he's got the chicken pox."

"The chicken pox!" This time he saw her distinctly frown. "Oh, dear."

"Don't start making other plans. I'm taking you," he said before she could get too broken up.

Her gaze shot to his and she said incredulously, "You?"

"What's wrong with me?"

"Well . . . nothing."

"Good. I'll be back at one to get you. I hope you'll look more yourself."

Chapter
14

The Glorious Fourth brought out every able body in Weeping Angel to participate in the festivities. There wasn't a boy who didn't count the hours until he could shoot off his torpedoes and skyrockets—a high proportion of which were already aimed at the front porch of the dowager widow Thurman. When nightfall came around, the dogs and cats in town would be running for their hiding spots, the noise sending them to far-off places. Only Hamlet wouldn't be bothered by all the commotion. By dusk, he could be found passed out under the elm by the depot, having overindulged on fermenting melon rinds.

The parade started just after one on Divine Street at the Christ Redeemer, with the Odd Fellows marching in the front of the line. Erhardt Tweed wore his Civil War uniform—still a firm believer in the Confederacy after thirty-three years—while Verlyn Tilghman wore his Yankee colors. Both men had kept their weapons, each gleaming single-shot revolver primed and loaded in case such a cause came between them to start up a skirmish.

Had the town owned a hose carriage, as they did in Boise, the citizens would have decorated it with crepe paper; but having none, they decked out Titus Applegate's black-lacquered hearse with garlands of evergreens and blue-and-white columbines. A princess had been chosen, Lula Whitman, and she sat on top of the carriage waving to those standing on the boardwalks.

By two o'clock, the entire entourage converged on a stretch of grassland called Reverend's Meadow on the outskirts of town. The area had been decorated with Japanese lanterns, flags, and streamers. The Odd Fellows got busy cranking the dashers on ice-cream freezers, while boys and girls fished for treasures in a booth sponsored by Beamguard's Mercantile. The sack races were yet to begin, and there was some talk brewing to get a baseball game going, though no one could agree on who would captain each team.

Parasol poised against the sun, Amelia strolled through the jubilee with Frank at her side, the smell of corn on the cob wafting from big washtubs over open fires. He didn't offer his arm, but to those who said hello, it was obvious he was with her because he stopped to chat when she did. Not that he chatted. Frank kept quiet mostly, nodding his head or shaking it in appropriate responses.

Though she felt bad Mr. O'Cleary had come down with the chicken pox, she was relieved. Ever since she accepted his invitation, she'd been having second thoughts. There'd been no graceful way out of going with him once she said she would; therefore, she'd been talking herself into it for the past two days. But she hadn't slept much for worrying about accompanying a man she wasn't comfortable with as a suitor.

There were many female gazes on Frank, even from the budding young girls accompanying cowboys and lumbermen, and Amelia felt a happiness inside her that warmed her more than the July sun. She recalled the scene in her kitchen earlier in the day. She'd been surprised to see him, and even more so when he'd asked her to the picnic in Pap's stead. The question was on the tip of her tongue, but she couldn't very well have inquired if it had been his idea. She hoped it was.

She'd dressed in a salmon shirtwaist with narrow pleats halfway down the front and intermittently on the long sleeves. Her surah silk skirt was of a matching shade and had a shallow ruffle along the bottom. The fruity color reminded her of the peach Frank had been eating that day at the train depot, and it was by no accident she'd selected this particular outfit.

Smiling, Amelia kept the handle of her basket in the crook of her elbow. As they walked, her arm brushed his once and she felt his solid strength. It was hard to believe she was actually here, with Frank, at the picnic of all picnics.

"Hallloooo!" came Mrs. Beamguard's cry, and Amelia paused to return the greeting.

"Hello, Dorothea."

Dorothea's hat was so full of frilly plumage, Amelia waited for her to take flight. "Well, my goodness!" she said in a tone spiced by curiosity. "Imagine seeing the two of you together. I would have thought you'd tire of being in each other's company having to be in the same place every day, five days a week." She gazed at Frank who appeared to be brooding. "I didn't notice where you were during the parade. You are here *together*, aren't you?"

"Yes we are," Amelia replied when Frank didn't. "We're looking for the picnic table. I'd like to put my basket down."

"Of course, dear. It's over by the gazebo." Then to Frank, "Are you going to bid on her dinner, Mr. Brody?"

Frank scowled from beneath the brim of his straw hat, and Amelia waited just as anxiously as Dorothea.

He simply nodded.

"Isn't that wonderful?" she said, but she sounded hypocritical to Amelia. "Forgive me if I'm in a hurry, dear. I have to find someone." Then she dashed off.

Amelia knew she'd be ferreting out the other ladies to tell them every word that had been spoken by the three of them. Though she'd been hopeful he'd bid on her basket, she wasn't sure. This was the first time she'd ever made up a box to be bid on.

She looked at Frank. He watched the feather-hatted Mrs. Beamguard retreat, then he let his gaze slip to the watermelon stand where Elroy Parks was spitting seeds at anyone who had the misfortune to walk by.

"Come on," Frank said. "Get rid of your basket, and I'll buy you a cup of coffee."

"All right." She really wasn't thirsty for something hot, but she suspected he needed a drink to wake up. He was looking a little tired to her, and she wondered what time he'd gone to bed last night.

They came upon the New American, which she'd decorated this morning. Amelia angled toward the table designated for the box suppers, but Frank held back while she set her basket down and was assigned the number five. She'd just turned to meet Frank when Viola Reed and Luella Spivey came charging up to him, panting and threatening to expire in their corsets. Their cheeks were flushed, and they had overextended themselves to get a look at Frank and Amelia. Apparently, they'd gotten an earful from Dorothea.

"Good afternoon, ladies," Amelia said, her chin high. She wasn't at all ashamed to be seen with Frank, and she wouldn't be made to feel out of place by two of her so-called friends.

"Hello, Amelia," Viola replied, her dress appearing too tight around her middle from an overindulgence of sweets.

"Amelia, dear." Luella's red hair was poofed on top

of her head in a loose style with a smart felt hat over the frizz.

Both women stared at Frank as if they'd never seen him before. "Dorothea tells us you're here with Mr. Brody," they said in unison, then gave each other an exasperated glare.

Viola went first. "We mean, we didn't expect to see you with him. After all, he does own a saloon."

"Yes," Luella hastened to add. "We didn't picture you consorting with a man of his calling."

For the first time that afternoon, Amelia opened her mouth to speak, but it wasn't her voice she heard. Frank had taken hold of her elbow and broke in with, "Yeah, ladies, I'm the owner of a saloon. The same saloon you bring your children to each week for lessons. That fact doesn't much bother you when you're looking around the joint, sniffing the air for signs of booze, and hinting for me to slide a glass down the counter. And as for consorting with someone of my calling, at least I'm not trying to sell her a Bible before I run off without her."

Both ladies gasped.

"So maybe," Frank continued, "consorting with me isn't half as bad as you think it is. In fact, I think she might just have some long overdue fun."

He put pressure on her elbow and pulled her along. Amelia was at a loss over what to say. No one had ever spoken about her in such a way—especially to her circle of lady friends. And how exactly did he know about Jonas Pray? What had he heard? When did he find out she'd been made a laughingstock? He could have heard it from anyone.

She couldn't ask him now, not with so many people milling around. Amelia caught a glimpse of Narcissa and Cincinatus Dodge. The mayor was decked out in his best suit, this being the more important holiday in town at which he officiated. Narcissa was more radiant, more lovely than Amelia had ever seen her.

Amelia had dashed over to Narcissa's as soon as she pulled the rags out of her hair and wiped off her face to tell her about the change in plans. Narcissa had been concerned over her going with Pap O'Cleary, and her fears weren't quelled by the announcement she was now attending the picnic with Frank. She cautioned Amelia not to enter into anything with blinders on. Amelia had reassured her she wouldn't.

Narcissa gave Amelia and Frank a cordial smile, then kept walking through the crowd with her husband.

"I don't see any coffee to be had," Frank remarked, pulling Amelia from her thoughts. "You'd think they would have some."

"Why don't we get strawberry frappés instead?" she suggested.

"I've never had one of those."

"You haven't?" She laughed. "Why, my goodness. You've never had shrub nor a milk shake. Where have you been?"

"Here and there."

She smiled. "You'll have to tell me where exactly here and there are."

"I might."

Just within eyesight of the ice-cream stand, Amelia wished she'd never made the suggestion. Emmaline Shelby stood at the corner of the table with Orlu Blue, and she looked up at precisely the same moment Amelia noticed her. The woman's face turned white with astonishment.

Too late to steer in the other direction, Emmaline was coming right for them, leaving Orlu behind. "Well, as I live and breath, it's Frank Brody," she exclaimed. "What are you doing here? With her?"

Frank gazed over Emmaline's shoulder. "You forgot Orlu, Em."

"Orlu Blue?" She shrugged. "I didn't really come

with him. He met me here." She shot Amelia a withering glance. "Is that what happened with you two? You ran into each other?"

Amelia would have set the woman straight if Frank hadn't intervened and said, "Circumstances brought us here together."

"Well, then it wouldn't be imposing for me to steal him away from you, Amelia." She hooked her arm through his. "Why, Frank, honey, there's this darling bisque doll in the fishing booth you've just got to hook for me."

Frank didn't budge, and Emmaline tripped. She gazed at him with a frown worrying her lips. "What's the matter?"

"I'm with Miss Marshall, and it wouldn't be polite if I just went off and left her, would it?"

From the look on her face, Emmaline would have disagreed if not for the fact Cobb Weatherwax chose that moment to step up to the group. He'd prettied himself up in a scarlet linen shirt with neck lacings and frontier trousers made out of buckskin. He wore a fringed bag at his waist, and a stovepipe-shaped top hat made out of beaver felt on his mane of hair. He cradled his long Kentucky rifle.

"I seen you acrost the way thar, and I come to say howdy." Lowering the barrel of his gun, Cobb nodded at Amelia. "Miz Marshall. Yore looking fitten for the day."

"Thank you, Mr. Weatherwax."

Amelia noted Emmaline didn't hide the wariness on her face when it came to staring at Cobb. Her eyes roamed over his figure, pausing on the silt brown hair that covered most of his head. She stifled a shiver of revulsion, and it angered Amelia. Cobb may not look fashionable or handsome, but underneath all that hair was a true genius.

There was a moment's silence before Frank made

the necessary introductions. "Miss Shelby, this is Cobb Weatherwax. Cobb, this is Miss Emmaline Shelby."

"Pleased t'metcha, Miz Shelby." He doffed his hat. "Didje know the base of that perfume yore wearing comes from beaver's castoreum?"

Emmaline took a step backward so Cobb couldn't get close to her. "No, I didn't know that."

"Well, it is. Beavers are good for many things. Most of 'em yore not aware of, I'm sure."

"I'm sure." Emmaline kept backing away. "If you'll excuse me . . . Orlu is waiting."

Amelia watched the woman retreat, glad Cobb had come when he had. Emmaline wasn't giving up on Frank, and her gall put Amelia in a dour frame of mind.

Amelia said nothing further as Frank and Cobb purchased the strawberry milk shakes. She waited for Frank under the shade of an alpine larch, feeling good he hadn't gone off with Emmaline when she invited him. Whatever had been between them was apparently over—at least in Frank's eyes.

Frank returned, handed her a glass, and the three of them sipped the cool confections while watching the events around them.

Amelia's attention was pulled toward a group of men who'd converged next to the beer barrel, hotly debating the subject of baseball team captains again. It was fairly clear since Oscar Beamguard owned the mercantile, and he was donating the flour bags for the bases and the lines, he would be in charge of one team. Up for grabs was the leader of the opposing side, and thus far Wendell Reed was in the running, seeing that he had a healthy amount of recruits from his sawmill. In contention with him was Ilar Stock, owner of the Tumbling T ranch.

The two men shouted at each other, then suddenly Wendell punched Ilar in the nose hard enough for blood to dribble out of his nostril. Before anyone could blink an eye, Ilar got a lick into Wendell's bread basket.

"Oh, my!" Amelia gasped, horrified as all parties involved broke out in fisticuffs. "Someone should do something!"

"Like what?" Frank asked, obviously unaffected by the brawl. The tone of his voice suggested he'd witnessed such spectacles many times.

"I don't know," she answered just as a spry sawhand jumped on Ilar's back for a ride. "Something!"

"Hyar." Cobb Weatherwax shoved his glass at Frank and strolled toward the scuffle. He raised his Kentucky rifle to the air and kicked off a shot of black powder. The explosion tore up a Japanese lantern, and tiny pieces of colorful paper littered the air.

All those tangled-up men froze, and Cobb in his calm voice recommended, "I think there ought to be a better way to settle this hyar fight, gentlemen." When no one objected, he continued. "I don't think thar's a dispute as to who's going to head one team. It's t'other we got to worry over, but I cain't see no problem on that. I know yore man. He's Frank Brody."

Frank cursed under his breath, and while holding both his and Cobb's glasses, raised his hands. "Hell, no. I'm not playing ball."

By now, the fracas had collected a fair share of onlookers, one of them being Daniel Beamguard. "Come on, Mr. Brody. I want to see you knock the cover off the ball."

A few others joined in with their agreement, even those who were involved in the fight. The crowd pressed Frank to the point where he started glancing around for an easy escape.

Amelia couldn't understand his reluctance to play a harmless game of baseball. She didn't know much about the game other than the haphazard way the men of Weeping Angel ran around a square after swinging at a pitched ball, gave off mild oaths when they didn't hit the ball, and got dirty when they caught the ball.

Cobb said, "Frank, I really think you ought to show them ezactly what you can do."

"*Please,* Mr. Brody," Daniel begged. "It's the Fourth of July picnic, and it just wouldn't be the same without a baseball game. I've just gotta see you hit a ball. I won't hardly stand it if I don't get the chance."

A few of the other boys chimed in as well.

"Please!"

"Come on, Mr. Brody!"

Frank shook his head in resignation. "All right. One game."

"Hooray!" Daniel Beamguard exclaimed.

"If we're going to play, we'll play serious." Frank turned to Amelia after passing off the frappé glasses to the twins, Walter and Warren. "I'll be back in a minute."

He left and she followed the easy way he moved with her gaze. He had a tall grace to his stride, making him stand out from the other men. She wondered where he was going, but soon the crowd got moving, and she didn't have time to miss him.

While Frank was gone, the men set up the diamonds by laying a series of flour lines and using the remaining Pink Label sacks with just enough inside to be plump bases. Chairs were set up in a half square around the playing field, and the chalkboard from the schoolhouse was brought in. Reverend Thorpe was designated as the scorekeeper—he being the only trustworthy one in the bunch, while Daniel Beamguard complained about having to be in charge of his father's bats. He wanted to field for Frank, but Oscar wouldn't hear of that.

Teams were drawn up, most of the sawmill workers opting to play with Frank; the cowboys from the

Tumbling T hooked up with Beamguard's Mercantile after Oscar promised each man a free month's supply of canned beans if they played for him.

Then the sides were named: the Moon Rock Warriors and the Mercantile's Majors.

Frank was back in a matter of minutes. Amelia stared at him as he came toward the diamond, not prepared for the change in his attire. He wore a pair of blue, round-lens glasses—the kind the catalog sold for weak eyes—and a flannel cap that said *Chicago* rested on his jet black hair. He carried a uniform bag and had put on a funny pair of lace-up shoes. He hadn't given up his white shirt and the fine red brocade vest or his black linen trousers.

"Holy smoke!" Daniel said in awe. "He's wearing a Chicago White Stockings hat."

"What's the glasses for?" Oscar asked, scratching his head.

"So I can see the ball."

"You got eyesight trouble, Brody?"

"No."

"You'll cut your eye out with a shattered lens if you get hit in the face with the ball."

"If I get hit in the face with the ball, then I'm deserving of having my eye cut out," Frank said caustically as he deposited his bag on the ground. Turning, he sized up his players. He counted them off. "I'm short a man."

Daniel jumped up and down. "Me, Mr. Brody! I'll be your man!"

"No, you won't," Oscar bristled. "You get on over to the sidelines and wait until I call you."

Frank gazed at the spectators, especially Cobb. "Any man who makes his living by shooting ought to have a good eye and a steady hand—the two most important qualities in a pitcher. Cobb, come here and be on my team."

Cobb took a long moment to answer. "I guess I could try it. I ain't never thrown a ball afore. Thrown a line trap at a beaver on occasion."

"That'll do."

The men gathered around, and from where Amelia sat, she was able to hear Frank.

"All right. We'll play by Hanlon's basic rules."

"Who the hell is Hanlon?" Oscar asked.

Frank frowned. "Ned Hanlon." When that didn't get a rise out of Oscar, Frank clarified. "He managed the Baltimore Orioles in '94 and taught the players to back up bases and each other, and to change positions for cutoff throws."

"Huh?"

Frank adjusted the brim of his hat. "Aw, hell. Just go out there and shag some balls."

All the men nodded.

Daniel took a seat next to Amelia, and she smiled at him. "Do you know how to play this game?"

"Heck, yeah."

"Then perhaps you'll keep me informed as to when I should applaud."

"Sure, Miss Marshall."

At Amelia's left sat Narcissa and Cincinatus, and just five chairs down, Emmaline Shelby. Emmaline didn't glance her way, but Amelia watched her from the corner of her eye. The woman pretended to be enthusiastic about Orlu playing for the Majors, but her gaze was pinned on the man heading up the Warriors.

Reverend Thorpe flipped a coin, and Frank called it to hit first. The game began amidst a loud cheering. Amelia tried to follow what Daniel was telling her, but he used abbreviations that were confusing.

"He's ahead of the count, Miss Marshall," Daniel said when one of the Warriors was up to bat.

Just when she thought she could understand the

game, the rules appeared to change, and she couldn't keep track. The batters seemed to take a long time at the plate, shifting and adjusting their stance. It was a waste of time. For all the preparations and precautions, Orlu struck them out anyway.

Holding on to her umbrella, Amelia tried to remain sedate under the shade her parasol offered. But as soon as Frank went up to the plate, as Daniel called it, she sat straighter and waited for him to take a swing.

He fingered the bill of his cap, then bent down to rub some dirt on his hands. His flexing backside strained the fabric of his trousers; the cut of his clothing suddenly seemed too tight. Amelia felt a tingling consciousness of the strength of his muscles. She had to fight the urge to sway toward him. It was Daniel's voice that stopped her.

"Come on, Mr. Brody! Hit a good one."

Oscar glared at his son and shook his head disapprovingly.

Frank picked up his bat. He wasn't playing with one from the mercantile, but rather the Spalding Daniel had made a fuss over. Amelia couldn't see anything special about the wood. It looked like a bat to her.

The crowd began making calls, trying to rile the game. As far as Amelia could tell, nothing special had happened. Two strikeouts seemed pretty boring. She wanted to see someone connect with the ball.

Orlu tilted the angle of his cowboy hat, wound his arm back, and let the ball speed toward Frank.

Frank sliced his arm through the air, the tip of the bat catching a piece of the ball. It flew through the sky like a bird going too fast to see clearly at first. The two men standing in the outfield raced to catch the ball but crashed into each other while the ball landed and bounced toward their feet.

"He walloped a fast ball to the left!" Daniel screamed while he nudged Amelia.

The onlookers went wild as Frank tossed his bat and made it as far as third base. Amelia was just as enthusiastic as everyone else, frantically clapping.

Wendell Reed was up next and hit the ball up in the air; it arced, then slowly dropped into Orlu's bare hand.

Emmaline cheered for Orlu, and Amelia gave her a stern look. The woman stared right back in challenge. Then both women turned their attention to the game.

The Warriors took the field and it was Cobb's turn to pitch. He looked out of place in his frontier clothing, holding on to the ball as if he wasn't sure what to do with it. He turned it this way and that in his grime-stained fingers. Then finally, with Frank's coaching, he nodded and said he figured he could throw it well enough.

The first ball he pitched was wide and high and landed smack in the catcher's glove; the error garnered him a few laughs from the opposing side. This didn't seem to bother Cobb. He merely tried again. The ball bounced off the ground and sailed into the glove's center once more. Frank went out to have a talk with him, and Cobb shrugged, not too concerned.

Frank retreated, mumbling something unintelligible under his breath.

Amelia watched as Frank straddled a caned chair backward and gazed at the field from behind his blue glasses. The cloud-peppered sky was mirrored in the dark lenses, making his face unique to look upon and also wonderfully attractive. His profile was hard and his jaw set with concentration. He had a fierce intensity about him that she'd never seen before. It almost frightened her but was dangerously appealing.

"He does cut a dashing figure," Narcissa whispered to Amelia.

"Yes, he does at that."

Their discussion was broken when Cobb threw a ball the hitter swung at, and Frank made a fist while shouting, "Good throw, Cobb! Do it again! Over the plate. Pitch him out."

Unfortunately, Cobb wasn't able to, and the next few batters scored points, or whatever they called it, when the men ran across the hitting plate.

The game dragged for Amelia, even though Daniel chattered on about good fielding, swings and misses, hits on the grass, choppers, fouls off the bats, and a noise he made in the back of his throat sounding something like *sssssssttttttttttteeeeee!* She watched with as much enthusiasm as she could muster for the other players. The only one she focused on was Frank, and it didn't seem like he got the chance to do a whole lot. What she did notice was he yelled and cursed more than normal. He yanked his hat off once and went out to argue with Oscar Beamguard. Reverend Thorpe had to stand between them before they came to blows.

The sun sweltered down on the crowd, and by the time the score was six to four in favor of the Majors, there were only two boxes left on the chalkboard to fill in. Amelia waited for Cobb to take the pitching position again, hoping the end would soon be near. She was thirsty and coated with dust from all the earth-stirring the men were doing.

Cobb's expression was blank when Frank spoke with him in tones too muted for Amelia to hear. Cobb kept nodding his head and agreeing to whatever it was Frank said.

The first man up to hit, Cobb pitched too low, and the ball rolled in the dirt behind the catcher. Cobb held his hands up in a shrug and came to Frank at the sidelines. This time Amelia heard every word.

Frank took his cap off to smooth his hair from his eyes. "Look, Cobb, we're playing pretty good. Hell, we got four runs and that's not too bad. We're at the top of the game here, and we could win this thing."

Cobb kept nodding but didn't look too confident.

"You've got to concentrate. Hold the ball like I

showed you and give it a spin with your wrist. Aim for his groin, but for chrissake, don't hit him there."

"I'll try not to, Frank."

"You do that."

Then Cobb went to take up his place again, while Frank practically tilted in his chair. Cobb drew his leg up and let the ball fly. The batter, Orlu Blue, went down swinging as the ball whacked him in the inside of his thigh.

"You son of a bitch!" Orlu picked himself up and grasped his leg. "He aimed for my crotch!"

"You just didn't swing low enough," Frank said.

Oscar Beamguard went to argue. "It wasn't Orlu's fault. Your pitcher is throwing spitballs! I seen him do it!"

"That ball was dry as toast," Frank shot back.

"Bullshit!"

"My ass!"

An indignant gasp rose from the ladies, especially loud from Dorothea who shouted, "Oscar Howard Beamguard, you mind your phraseology!"

The reverend dropped his chalk on the ground and went over to referee. "Gentlemen, there will be no profanity in a game overseen by the Lord!"

"I don't see the Lord," Frank remarked, removing his cap to fit it firmer on his head for the dozenth time that day. "But if you do, Rev, send him over to help my team hit the goddamn ball."

"Mr. Brody, the Lord surely won't help a man who insists on taking His name in vain." The reverend pulled Frank aside, right in front of Amelia, and spoke prudently. "The way I see it is, your winning this game must be thought upon like my sermons." Thorpe put his hand on Frank's shoulder. "Seize the moment. Strike hard, young man. You've got to make the fear last for six days until next Sunday or they won't go beyond Monday before committing a sin."

Frank cocked his head. "I'm not sure what you're

getting at, Rev. I don't have six days. I've got about six minutes."

"Then send them a gale of asps."

"What?"

The reverend removed his hand and spoke bluntly. "Tell them to field and hit the ball, or else you'll charge double for drinks at your saloon."

"Now that they'll understand."

The men broke apart and Amelia gazed at Frank, waiting for him to notice her. To smile at her. To say he'd hit the ball for her. But he didn't. He was too absorbed in the game to give her even the slightest hello.

He called his men to order and obviously relayed what the reverend had told him about doubling the price of liquor. Amelia would have been offended by the reverend's advice were it not for the fact she wanted the Moon Rock Warriors to win so much. It kind of shocked her that Reverend Thorpe thought about spirits other than those which were godly.

The game resumed and Cobb pitched Orlu out; the next two men to hit never made it to second base off their hits. The players in the field had suddenly banded together to cut off throws. The side was retired without any more runs.

The first up for the Warriors was Owen Akin, a strapping boy who worked for Reed's sawmill. He took his position; he hadn't made contact with the bat the entire afternoon. So it was with much encouragement from the crowd that he finally smacked the wood dead center of the ball and sent it whirling through the air.

Cincinatus whistled. "There must be a mistake. Akin hit the ball."

Amelia applauded with a smile as Owen rounded all the bases to make the score five to six. "Yes, a wonderful mistake."

Cobb went up to bat. He tested the weight of the

pine in his grasp, stared at it a long time, then ran his bony fingers through his beard to fluff up the wiry bristles. He took a while to get into the correct body figuration Frank had shown him. When he was finished, he looked too stiff to move, but Amelia held out hope. Cobb glared at Orlu, then Orlu pitched the ball.

It hit Cobb in the shoulder and sent him down on the ground.

Frank was out of his chair and nose to nose with Orlu Blue in a matter of seconds. Both sides emptied their prospective sidelines, and a free-for-all would have commenced if the mayor hadn't threatened to call off the festivities.

Frank's face was animated as he walked toward Cobb who was still on all fours, a dazzled expression on his face. Frank helped him up. "Come on, Cobb. Shake it off, man. Shake it off. You'll be all right. Take your base."

"Take it?"

"Hell, yes. You earned it. Go on. Stand over there." Frank pointed him in the right direction and called, "As soon as I hit the ball, run like hell. You got that?"

"Yes, sir."

Frank rubbed his jaw with his hand and stooped to pick up his bat. The muscles in his forearms were tense and looked hard as wood. His shoulders flexed and moved with a fluid strength. The cords of his thighs were solid and bulging against the seams of his trousers. He hunkered down a minute to stretch his calves, his buttocks defined by a tight swell in the seat of his pants. Sweat ran down his temples, and he looked as if he were going to hit someone.

It was at that moment Amelia realized the game wasn't just for fun to Frank. He really wanted to win, and if he didn't, he'd be angry. She didn't understand his passion for the game or why he adjusted his cap so much.

As he took the plate, Frank kept stepping into the

dirt with those funny shoes of his. Dust clouds rose around his ankles, and he shouldered the bat high in the air. "Come on, Blue. Hit me with it."

Orlu spat around the wad of chewing tobacco in his jaw. "You can bet I will."

Only Orlu didn't hit Frank.

Frank hit the ball.

Hard.

The *thwack* was so piercing, it hurt Amelia's ears. The ball went sailing, higher and higher, farther and farther.

"Touch 'em all! Touch 'em all!" Daniel screamed while he jumped up and down.

Narcissa and Amelia clasped their hands and cheered.

The players in right field chased the ball down, but it was too late. Cobb ran over home plate with Frank not far behind. As soon as Frank's heel touched down on the flour bag, the crowd jumped from their seats and ran to congratulate him.

"Never seen anything like it!"

"What a hit!"

"You sure can play ball!"

"Best Fourth of July we ever had!"

"I'll never forget this game!"

And so the accolades went. Amelia stood back and watched with pride in her heart. He had hero written all over him, and the town acknowledged his feat. She would have been overwhelmed with happiness as his waiting heroine.

Too bad he'd kissed his baseball bat instead of her.

Chapter

15

$\backsim$

After the game, Amelia had gone off to the box supper table to converse with the ladies, but Frank slipped away from the crowd for a few quiet minutes to cool off. Putting his foot on the planked wall behind him, he drank a cold Budweiser on the unoccupied boardwalk in front of the mercantile.

He tilted the bottleneck to his lips, and the smooth taste of barley slid past his throat. He knew he got too emotionally involved while playing ball. He'd always enjoyed the sport, even when he was a boy in the home. He took the game to heart, and perhaps the reason for his fervor was due in part because all he'd had in his childhood outside the religious order was a bat and ball.

When his bottle was empty, and his temperament calmer, he went in search of Amelia. The past few hours, he'd tried to be just what Pap had wanted him to be—a fill-in. But trying to remain impassive toward her had been hell. He hadn't missed the way their arms had brushed, the looks she gave him through the fringe of her lashes, or the gentle softness of her laugh. He'd practically been ignoring her, but no more. Seeing her clap for him on the sideline, feeling her smile on his back, he gave in to what he really wanted: to spend time with her alone.

As he walked, men and eager young boys came up to him to recount in their own animated ways the ending home run he'd hit. Talking and joking with people he'd never met before got to him. He didn't feel as grossly uncomfortable as he had when he'd first arrived. Like a new mitt, the town was oiling his palm, and he felt that he was fitting in.

He wove his way to the box supper table, which was full of baskets and crates, some decorated with ribbons. The smells of hot wicker, breads, and sweets filled the air. The crowd pressed together as anxious ladies sought out their beaux in the hopes they would bid the highest for their box.

Frank found Amelia near the front, her parasol closed as the branches from a tree shaded this particular area from the Independence Day sun. When she saw him, she smiled, then returned her gaze forward. He was given a view of her profile as she watched two girls trying for prizes at the fishing booth.

He'd always thought her pretty, but today she looked beautiful. Dressed in peach, the fair color complemented her eyes and the upsweep of her remarkable hair beneath that duck-wing hat he disliked. She had a subdued tranquility about her. A sense of belonging.

She'd carried herself with grace, even when under attack by the busybodies and Emmaline. The probability of encountering Em had been too great for it not to happen. He hated hurting her, for in her eyes, she'd accused him of lying about his attendance to town gatherings. And he had. But not intentionally.

"Ladies and gentlemen!" Cincinatus called the

crowd to order, his celluloid collar and snappy scarf cutting into his neck. "It is my pleasure to commence the sales of these delectable dinners. Any man who's hungry won't be disappointed."

Frank turned to Amelia and whispered, "What's your box number?"

"I'm not supposed to tell."

"But you will."

"Five," she replied in a tone full of breathless anticipation.

The first several baskets garnered a nice amount. It had been decided beforehand, the proceeds would go toward a single-rail roundhouse so Lew Furlong wouldn't have to drive the Short Line backward all the way to Boise. Some had objected to this cause, saying a telegraph would be more useful to the town. But the majority had won, although the cost of such a renovation was more than the citizens could ever hope to furnish on their own. It would take a donation from a healthy bank account to see such an endeavor to fruition. And seeing as Cincinatus Dodge was in favor of the roundhouse, the popularity of it had gone in his direction.

When Mayor Dodge came to Amelia's basket, he held it up by the handle and lifted the cloth to peek at the contents. "Oh, gentlemen, gentlemen!" He wet his lips and made a big to-do over the offerings. "Box number five is a feast to fill a stomach starved for perfection. I won't hear of a bid less than seventy-five cents."

"Seventy-five," someone called.

Frank sought out the man through the crowd and recognized him as a cow runner from the Tumbling T.

"Seventy-five," Cincinatus said with a frown. "I couldn't on good conscience let this mouth-watering meal go for seventy-five. Do I hear one dollar?"

"One dollar," Frank bid.

Amelia gazed at him, a blush stealing into her cheeks.

"One dollar." The mayor looked over the men. "Gentlemen, are you going to let Mr. Brody walk away with this supper for a mere dollar? I can smell fried chicken and biscuits. And is this . . . ?" He poked inside with great melodramatics. "My word, it is. Cherry pie."

"One twenty-five," came another offer.

Amelia glanced nervously at Frank.

"One twenty-five," Cincinatus recorded. "At one twenty-five I would have to say this basket is being pilfered."

Frank cut to the chase. "Three dollars."

Amelia glanced at him, her expression bright. All around, women were awed by the charitable gesture.

Frank figured he'd aced the competition. It was only after Cincinatus was repeating "Three dollars going tiwce" that out of the blue a voice offered five.

All heads turned toward the new bidder.

Cobb Weatherwax stood off to the side holding up five dollar bills. Frank wondered where in the hell Cobb had found five green frogskins.

"Five dollars!" Cincinatus boomed, a shock of oiled hair spilling over his brow. "Five dollars for box number five seems like fate!"

"Don't go closing out anything yet, Dodge," Frank remarked, then proposed, "Eight dollars."

"Eight dollars!"

A gasp resounded.

"Eight-fifty," Cobb bid without hesitation, and Frank grew annoyed. Damn, maybe Pap was right. Cobb did have an infatuation for Amelia.

Frank clenched his mouth tight. "Nine," he counterbid before the mayor could firm up the prior offer.

"Ten dollars."

Frank gave Cobb a hostile glare that went unnoticed. Just what the hell did Cobb think he was doing? Cobb never had any spare money—much less ten dollars. That was why Pap spotted him drinks so often. Something wasn't right.

It was then, Frank spied Emmaline not far behind Cobb, an expression of forced innocence on her face.

"Ah, hold on there, Dodge," Frank called. "Don't pronounce anything final until I can count my money. I don't know how much I have on me." Then to Amelia. "Excuse me, sweetheart."

Amelia looked at him puzzled just before he cut through the throng to have a word with Emmaline, who'd stepped back from the proceedings and stood behind a tree.

He would have been inclined to apologize about not taking her to the picnic, but she'd resorted to using Cobb to play a dirty trick. That didn't earn her his respect, and any empathy he was feeling vanished.

She greeted him sweetly, and he bent his head to whisper in her ear, "Em, sugar, you got me."

"I don't know what you mean," she breathed in a light, airy tone.

"I think you do. Cobb can have Amelia's supper. Now you just tell me the number of yours, honey, so I can buy it for myself." He pulled back and gave her a lazy grin full of promise. "And we can go off somewhere and enjoy it."

Her lashes fluttered, and if he knew better, he would have pegged her for being coy. "Thirteen."

"Well, damn, who said thirteen was an unlucky number? I'll make sure no one else gets a chance with it." Frank winked at her and walked away to her sigh. As he did so, he motioned for Cobb to follow him.

"Mr. Brody," Cincinatus shouted. "Where are you? Have you come to any conclusions? I've got other suppers to sell."

Frank pushed through the crowd and yelled, "In a minute, Dodge. This is taking some thought." To Cobb, he frowned and nudged him behind the treasure-fishing booth. "What the hell's going on, Cobb?"

He gave Frank a blank stare. "I don't know what you mean, Frank."

"How much did she give you to buy Amelia's supper?"

Cobb looked as guilty as a kid with his hand caught in the cookie jar.

"I'm not stupid, Cobb. How much did she give you?"

He took off his beaver top hat and crushed the brim in his hand. "Ten dollars." He gazed down, then up. "You aren't mad at me, are you, Frank?"

"No." Frank dug into his trouser pocket and pulled out ten dollars more. "Here. Now you have twenty. When number thirteen comes up, go straight for the kill and offer twenty frogskins up front."

"I don't know . . ." Cobb glanced over his shoulder, but couldn't see Emmaline through the degree of hats. "That Miz Shelby said to buy number five."

"And I'm telling you to forget number five. Buy number thirteen."

Cobb's face grew indecisive, his simple mind working to comprehend it all. "I think I'll keep the twenty dollars."

Frank felt a tic twitch at his jaw. "Hell, no, Cobb. You bid the twenty on number thirteen."

Cobb didn't look convinced.

"Christ," Frank swore. "You bid the twenty dollars on number thirteen, and I'll give you free drinks every Friday night."

"Saturdays, too."

"Dammit, Cobb, but you're making me mad."

Cobb began to walk away.

"All right!" Frank hissed. "Saturdays, too."

Cobb grinned through his beard—a flash of white. "Thanks, Frank."

"Mr. Brody!" Cincinatus hollered. "I'm closing the bid right now at ten dollars."

Frank pushed through the throng and returned to Amelia's side. "Hold on, hold on. Since it's going toward a good cause, Dodge . . . fifteen dollars."

"Fifteen!" Cincinatus's silk hat practically fell when he tipped his head. "That's the most any basket has ever been bid for." He took up his gavel and slammed it on the table. "Going once, twice, number five, sold, for fifteen dollars!" He gazed at his wife. "And who is the maker of number five, my dear?"

"Amelia Marshall," Narcissa announced with a knowing smile.

Suddenly, the ladies in the Thursday Afternoon Fine Ladies Society had the need to flock together. It was as if a mound of birdseed had been dropped on a particular patch of grass, and thereupon a frenzy of chirping and picking began. And it was almost as certain, when they were through, there wouldn't be even a hull for Amelia to hang on to. She'd been plucked right in front of them by the enemy, that evil tipper of strong waters, and hadn't done a thing to stop him.

"Are you sure we should go this far?" Amelia asked while awkwardly traipsing after Frank. Laden with the supper basket and her open parasol while trying to manage her petticoats and skirt in the brush, she wasn't sure how much farther she could walk through the wooded terrain.

"We're within earshot of Reverend's Meadow."

Amelia doubted that. The sounds of the picnic had ebbed, and only the slow trickle of water over river rocks and the songs of sparrows were their company. She might have complained about the jaunt, but she wouldn't admit a physical weakness of any kind to Frank.

Besides, he was hauling more than her.

He'd returned to the saloon to drop off his baseball gear, leaving behind his White Stocking cap in favor of his straw panama. When he'd come out of his room, all she'd been expecting was a lovely picnic. She hadn't expected him to reappear with his tackle box, fishing pole, net, and a blue-and-white gingham spread. When she'd asked him about it, he'd said he didn't think she'd want to sit on any insects. She'd assumed they'd be dining with the others on the grass, but he had other plans.

And he hadn't been secretive about them either.

They'd walked right through the other picnickers and headed up a narrow trail until it thinned to nothing. Amelia had felt so self-conscious, she almost pleaded for him not to take her out of eyesight; but when she thought of all the stares she would attract, she conceded privacy might just be the best answer.

"Come on, sweetheart. We're almost there."

She had to plow between the heavy leafage, and once on the other side, sunlight dappled through the trees and made a bright circle in a scattered patch of yellow-centered, white daisies. The air smelled like mint when the wind blew ever so slightly. There was a peaceful spot next to the water where Frank spread out his blanket and deposited all his fishing paraphernalia.

He walked toward her and took the basket from her grasp; his warm fingers brushed hers. She felt his deep voice melting into her as he said in a resonant tone, "You look like you need to sit down, Amelia. I don't think you get out in nature too much."

"I go outside," she protested as she walked toward their picnic setup. "Last I checked, both my front and rear yards were outside."

"I'm talking about the wilderness." He set the

basket next to his fishing pole and gazed at her seriously. "Have you ever gone camping?"

"You mean with a bedroll?"

"Yeah."

"No."

"You ever want to?"

"No."

"Too bad."

Amelia grew somewhat flustered. What was he implying? That they go camping and share a bedroll? Inasmuch as she wanted to share his likes and spark his interest in her, she couldn't pretend to be enthusiastic about sleeping in the wide open. Bears were known to haunt the area, as well as huge black ants and big flying bugs with antennae that were as long as her fingers. She shivered from the thought of a winged insect getting caught in her hair.

She watched Frank as he sat on the spread, then patted the space next to him. "Sit down, Amelia, and take a load off."

It suddenly hit her, they were truly alone. This was their first outing together as a couple, and her inexperience blew up in her face. She'd wanted him to be attracted to her, but what was she supposed to do when he was? The tiny plot he wanted her to sit on was no wider than her broom and, not to mention, directly in the sun. The blue-and-white checked cloth was not overly large, and Frank was a tall man. He took up half of the coverlet with his long legs.

Drawing in a soft breath, she wouldn't show him her anxiousness. She was a modern woman; she played gay tunes on the piano. Still holding her parasol, she gathered the fabric of her skirt and sat beside Frank. The fullness of her petticoats puffed around her, billowing against Frank's knee in a sensual touch of sheer fabric against the coarse composition of his trousers. She grabbed a handful and tucked the salmon-colored silk toward her.

"Get rid of the umbrella. Take your hat and gloves off," Frank suggested, "and feel the sun on your skin. It's nice."

The propriety in Amelia fought against the idea for a moment, then she decided there was no harm. No one was in the vicinity to reproach her. She slid the long pin from her hat, removed her gloves, and put both next to her purse. Folding her parasol, she kept it by her side in case she got too hot.

Sitting with her knees bent and locked together was uncomfortable, and her corset stays were all but ready to snap in this position. It was her own fault for adjusting the laces on her corset this morning. But she'd wanted her waist nipped in just one more inch. As she'd made the necessary alterations, she'd noticed a fragile spot in the cording where it had rubbed in the eye, but she hadn't had the opportunity to replace it.

"What do you say we see what you have underneath all this?"

"W-What?" she stammered, having just been thinking about her clothing.

Frank gave her a curious smile as he extracted her hat and cloth from the basket. "The supper I paid fifteen dollars for. What do you think I was talking about?"

"N-Nothing."

He brought out all the items, lining them up in a neat row. If she'd been thinking properly, she would have gotten the plates right away; instead, she got them now and began serving him.

"I hope you like it." She handed him his plate.

Taking up a fork and knife, he crossed his legs and said, "I know I will. You told me you could cook fried chicken."

"Being able to cook it and make it edible are two different things."

She gave herself much smaller portions, the heat, her corset, and the company, factors for such meager amounts. She'd never eaten a meal with a suitor before, which was more than she could say for Jonas Pray. Oddly, in the short time she'd known him, he'd never taken her to the Chuckwagon for dinner. Nor had she cooked him a meal.

Frank had no problem consuming the large amount she'd given him. He devoured a drumstick in no time, and was working through his cole slaw and biscuit while she nibbled on a pickle. She was dying to ask him what he thought, but wouldn't press the subject. She knew she could cook a passable supper, in fact, a very satisfying one. Still . . . having Frank's stamp of approval . . . After all, he'd paid top cash for the dinner.

"Aren't you hungry?" he asked while reaching for another piece of chicken.

"Not very."

"I guess you don't need to eat like a horse. You can eat this good whenever you take a mind to fix it."

Her heart warmed. *He liked it.*

"Now, take me," he said after swallowing a mouthful. "About the only thing I can cook from scratch is a fried egg sandwich and open a bottle of beer."

"Opening a beer isn't cooking," she teased, taking a biscuit for herself. Maybe the bread would help settle the butterflies in her stomach.

"Well, this is some cooking. And speaking from a bachelor's point of view, being able to eat like this everyday would almost be worth getting married for."

Her stomach flip-flopped and she took a bite of the biscuit. The flaky dough tasted like dust to her, and she needed something to wash down the lump. Though he'd said he liked the food, her cooking was nothing worth getting married for.

She rummaged through the basket for her jar of root beer. Finding it, she uncapped the top and poured two glasses. She drank hers in slow sips until she was able to swallow the biscuit. Frank, on the other hand, downed his in several large gulps.

They ate the rest of their supper in companionable silence. Amelia didn't mind. She found she had absolutely nothing useful to say. She was giddy as a new bride, inexplicably shy all of a sudden.

As Frank finished off his latest helping, she hoped he wasn't going to search for more. After consuming two huge slices of pie, he'd just about cleaned out the basket. She'd managed to eat a biscuit and half her pickle. Perhaps she'd try the pie later when her stomach wasn't in knots. Maybe if she stood up, the pressure on her waist wouldn't be so bad.

Frank set his plate aside, leaned toward her, and before she knew what happened, he'd kissed her cheek. She sat there, shocked to her toes, and speechless.

"Amelia, sweetheart, that was the best goddamn dinner I have ever eaten in my life."

She floundered for her voice and murmured, "I'm glad you liked it."

"It was worth more than fifteen bucks."

"Really?"

"Yeah." Then he straightened his leg a bit and grabbed the heel of his boot. Pulling, he took first one, then the other off until all he had on his feet were his stockings.

"What are you doing?" she asked in a voice with controlled panic. Could it be, he'd eaten one dessert and was now looking for another kind? Inasmuch as she reveled in his kisses, she wouldn't go that far to make him like her.

"Going fishing," came his moderate reply.

Relief flooded her, but then a quizzical frown set over her brow. "In your socks?"

He laughed. A deep laugh that rippled through her and made her warm. "No. Barefoot." He peeled the black stockings from his feet and stuffed them in his tall boots. Rolling up his pants, he said, "Why don't you take your shoes off and try it with me?"

"Oh, no. I couldn't take off my shoes."

"Why not?"

"Because . . . I just couldn't."

"Ah, hell. Nobody's around to see. Take 'em off, Amelia, and roll down your stockings. Have some fun."

She sat straighter. "I have fun."

"None that I can see."

"I'm a lot of fun," she disputed. "You just haven't seen my fun side because we're usually at odds over the piano."

"Christ," he frowned. "Don't bring that up. We were having a good time."

"I wasn't bringing up anything. I was trying to tell you I can be fun."

"Then prove it." Frank stood. "Take off your shoes and come wading with me. I'll teach you how to cast a line."

Seizing on the one thing that would allow her to bow out gracefully, she said, "I don't have my button hook with me."

To her consternation, he replied, "I'm sure I have something in my tackle box that can take your shoes off."

Deflated, she murmured, "Oh."

He bent on one knee and lifted the lid to the box. She heard a lot of shifting and pawing through metal before he came out with a long metal thing. "Give me your foot." He held out his hand to hold her ankle.

Amelia really didn't want him to see her naked feet. She didn't think they were remotely attractive, while Frank's . . . she moved her gaze down . . . were quite handsome. This wasn't the first time she'd seen his feet bare. He had perfectly shaped toes, with nice nails and a little bit of dark hair on the tops.

"Give me your foot," he repeated.

Tentatively, she straightened her leg, discovering she'd developed a cramp in her shin. "Ow . . ." she moaned before she could stifle the whimper.

"What's wrong?"

"I have a cramp in my leg."

"No wonder, by the way you've been sitting." Frank took her foot and pushed her skirts higher on her leg. "I've told you, sweetheart, you need to loosen your corset."

Aghast that he would guess the nature of her discomfort, she did her best not to blush. Then she remembered his words on the train depot that first afternoon they'd engaged in a conversation, or rather, dispute. He'd said she was laced too tight—a reference to her stiff character. That had to be what he was implying now. Why, then, didn't she feel better knowing he thought she was rigid instead of wearing her corset too tight?

Frank worked the buttons on the sides of her shoe, freeing them with the rod. Once they were unfastened, he slipped the patent leather from her foot. She couldn't stop the reflex of curling her toes in her black lisle hose. She brought her leg down, wincing as she extended her other one. As he poked that contraption into the side of her shoe, she asked, "What is that you're using?"

"Sockdologer spring fish hook."

She grimaced. "Is there fish guts on it?"

"Nope."

When Frank was finished, he slid the shoe off and held her leg by the calf. His hands were large and tan against her stocking; he kneaded her flesh for a minute and the pleasure of it sent tingles darting in all directions of her body. She closed her eyes and imagined him rubbing her calf for the rest of her life. She'd cook him the best meals ever.

Sighing, she opened her eyes to find him watching

her. His gaze had darkened with emotion. He enthralled her. He also scared her. What would she do if he swept the picnic cloth clean with his hand and demanded to make mad, passionate love to her? It was what she'd dreamed about, but now that she was with his flesh and blood body, she didn't think she'd have the nerve to go through with it.

She waited for him to move, her muscles tense and unyielding. She wished she could read his mind.

He turned away and, without saying a word, leaned back on his haunches and went to his fishing box again. She watched his fingers shake and thought that it was a good sign. He wasn't so sure of himself. He wasn't so immune as he let on. He did feel something for her. He just was afraid to admit it.

Amelia unrolled her stockings from her legs, and not once did Frank glance her way. She folded the delicate hosiery and put it by her shoes. Then she brought her feet under her dress so he wouldn't see them.

He busied himself with the line of his pole, tying on some intricate feathers and a hook. She couldn't stand the silence any further and asked, "Don't you use worms?"

Lifting his head, he said, "No fly fisherman in his right mind would ever dirty his hook with a worm." He stood and held out his hand to help her up. She took the offering, fitting her fingers in his; electrical storm currents seemed to strike every time he touched her. With her pulse skittering, she looked at the connection of their hands. Her skin was pale as flour next to his. She bet he never once wore a pair of gloves.

He let her hand go sooner than she would have liked. The spread was toasty from the sun under her feet, and the first step she took in the grass felt cool and tickled her soles. Frank was already walking toward the water's edge. She took small steps, watching where she placed her feet. Even the smallest pebble felt like a stone on the sensitive bottom of her foot.

Frank paused at a knee-high boulder and assessed the stream. There was a pool that looked made for wading, and he began to walk into it. He didn't cringe, so she assumed the water would be warm as a bathtub.

The first contact with her big toe, and she knew the water was a far cry from warm. Brisk was a better adjective.

"How far out are you going?" she asked when he kept walking, the cuffs of his pants getting wet where he hadn't rolled them high enough.

"Not far."

She didn't continue, preferring to stand in the extreme shallow. She wasn't a swimmer, and the current, however gentle, looked deadly to her.

Frank flicked his wrist. She wouldn't have been able to see the fishing line if it hadn't glistened in the sun. The feather fly on the end snapped over the water in strokes so light, it seemed the lure barely kissed the sun-brilliant waves before he was moving it again.

She watched him, her heart heavy in her throat. He looked so peaceful, so serene, a startling contrast to the man he was at the baseball game. He never wore an expression like this in the saloon—a face of utter contentment, of relaxation.

As the sun poured over him in its golden glow, and the water bled into his expensive trousers, it struck her then that she didn't really know him at all. They'd been acquainted for nearly a month, and she couldn't remember any tales of his family nor his upbringing, save that he'd implied it was worth forgetting.

Right now she wanted to forget the piano stood between them, for suddenly, it didn't seem to matter who had it. The day was too joyous, the scenery too heavenly, to be troubled over finances and differences of opinion.

While he whipped the deceptive fly back and forth across the water, she held up her skirts and sloshed carefully toward the boulder to sit on its smooth surface. From there she could watch him better. From this height she could also see the tops of the red, white, and blue picnic canopies over the trees. In the distance the town continued to celebrate.

Cottonwoods lined the stream, and their buds had burst open, sending fuzzy, snowlike seeds through the lazy air. They fell around Frank, his arm stirring them as they landed on the water.

"Come on out here and I'll show you how to cast," Frank said without missing a whip of his fly.

"No . . . I don't think so." She felt safe on the dry rock and perfectly content to observe him.

He turned his head toward her, his eyes shaded from the woven brim of his panama. "Come on."

"I've never fished before. I'd break something."

"No, you won't." As he spoke, a bite on his line bent his pole. He whisked a shimmering trout from the river and into the air.

Amelia sat up. "You got one!" she exclaimed.

Frank held the fish by the gills. "Get me the creel, Amelia. I forgot it."

Amelia slid from the rock and stumbled to where he'd left his fishing gear. "What's a creel?"

"That basket with the strap."

She picked up the creel, went toward the water, and stood at its edge. "Here."

"Bring it out. Hurry."

She bit her lip, contemplating his request. She would have thrown the creel to him—if she'd been any kind of thrower. But she couldn't even hit Hamlet with an apple when he was turning up her flower bed with his snout, and he was a big target.

"Come here!" Frank urged, the trout wiggling to be free.

Dismayed, Amelia bunched up her skirts and took a

tiny step. The cold mountain water washed over her feet, and she sucked in her breath. She hiked her petticoats even higher as she went another foot, the sand rough with pebbles beneath her. She teetered precariously as she went ankle-, then calf-deep, holding on to the creel for dear life and her skirts at the same time—as if either would save her, should she slip and fall.

"That's it, sweetheart, keep coming."

Amelia glanced up at him, trying to save face by smiling as if she weren't the least bit nervous or frightened by the water whooshing between her legs. She had a yard to go and she'd be by his side.

Just shy of Frank, she slipped on a rock, but he caught her elbow before she could plunge into the water. Resuming her balance, she was proud of herself that she'd neither dropped the basket or her skirts.

She held out her hand and presented him with the creel.

"Thanks." He put the strap over his arm, unhooked the fish, and let it go.

She watched in disbelief as the trout swam from her view, then disappeared into the deep pool. Gazing at Frank, she said, "Why did you do that?"

"I wasn't fishing for a meal, just for sport."

"Sport?" She would have put her hands on her hips if not for the fact her dress would get drenched. "You made me come out here under the assumption you needed that basket for your fish."

"That I did."

"Why?"

"Because I wanted your company."

"Well, I like that," she complained. "I didn't want to admit this, but I can't swim. I'm sure that seems very ridiculous to you, you're apparently comfortable in the water, but I—"

Unexpectedly, he put his arm around her waist and pulled her close.

"I . . ." she trailed off, her mind muddled by the depths of his eyes. ". . . never had the opportunity to learn how to . . . swim . . ."

She still grabbed hold of her skirt, her arm crushed between them. He brought his head over hers, his mouth close. Closer. "Stop talking," he whispered.

Chapter

16

⟡

At the touch of Frank's lips, Amelia's eyes fluttered shut, and she stood there, immobile. The coolness of the stream and the warmth of Frank made her forget to be fearful of the soft current. Slowly, she began to relax against him as he gathered her closer. Ever so slightly, he bent her backward over his arm, and she hung on to him as his mouth slanted over hers. She tried to hold on to her slipping composure, but the kiss hit her with a stunning force. The sensation was dreamlike and not so very far from how she'd imagined a thoroughly passion-filled kiss would be.

She rested her fingers lightly on the top of his shoulder, her hand clenching her skirts crushed between them. Her senses were so disordered, she had to remind herself where she was lest her knees weaken.

He slid his hand through her coiffured hair, his fingers splayed. She felt the pins loosen under his firm coaxing, and since her mouth was otherwise occupied, she couldn't voice her protest. Wavy curls tumbled to her waist, and she knew she'd never be able to fix the damage. He cupped her neck, massaging and kneading the tightness from her muscles. She moaned, and her lips parted from the pleasure.

He claimed her mouth with his tongue, and a strange shiver shot through her. The textures and sensations were foreign to her—shocking, but pleasing at the same time. She would have panicked if it hadn't been Frank kissing her in such an intimate fashion.

She felt his scratchy beard against her chin and tipped her head. This inadvertently gave his mouth a much better fit over hers, and he deepened the kiss. His tongue touched hers and stroked the inside of her mouth. She met him, tentative and unsure of how to kiss this way. She heard him moan against her lips, and his fingers bunched her hair.

She quaked in his arms as he pulled her full up against him. The hand coveting her skirt threatened to release the precious fabric. Her breasts were crushed on the broadness of his chest. She was breathless. She was feeling passionate.

She was in love.

All too soon, he lifted his head, his grip on her hair gentle, but firm.

Her eyes were still closed, her mind whirling. It was only the sound of Frank's voice that brought her back to earth.

"Did he ever kiss you like that?"

"Whhhooo?" she sighed, not having the foggiest idea what Frank was talking about.

"The salesman."

The dreamy haze she felt lifted, and as she opened her eyes, the sky looked too bright. "Jonas Pray?"

"Yeah."

"Oh . . . him." It seemed odd after what she just shared with Frank, he make her recall someone he had all but erased to a dim memory. "Why do you want to know?"

Frank kept her close, his eyes hooded and dark; a

hint of brooding puzzlement filled them. "I just want to know."

She licked her lips, tasting the faint traces of cherries from Frank's mouth. "No. He never—*no one has ever*—kissed me like you did."

They remained where they were for a long moment, neither moving nor saying a word. Amelia wished he would forget about Jonas and kiss her again. But he didn't, and the water around her calves grew cold again. She shivered.

"I'll carry you out," Frank said at length.

"You don't have to."

"I want to."

Her hand slipped down his muscled shoulder. "How will you manage? You're holding your fishing pole."

His fingers left her hair. "It comes apart."

Their hips still touched.

To Amelia, it was a mixture of hot and cold. She looked into his eyes, feeling a blush creep over her cheeks. He gave her that rakehell gaze of his, then a slight degree separated them as he disassembled his line and made three pieces out of his pole and handed them to her. "Carry that for me."

She nodded, taking the segments, careful for the hook.

He put his arm by her behind and swept her into his embrace.

The wicker of the creel cut into her thigh, but she didn't dare wiggle for fear he'd drop her. Not that he wasn't strong. She felt every single muscle where her body pressed his; the hard definition of his chest; the tautness of his belly; the cords of his upper legs. With each of his steps, she grew a little breathless. The events were rapidly unfolding much like a poetic novel, and she was eager to read quickly in order to find out what would happen to the fated lovers.

As the river thinned and the shallows approached,

she felt more and more self-conscious. What should she do? What should she say? *"Pardon me, but I loved the way you kissed me. Can we try it again on dry land?"*

Frank set her down but didn't let her go. Flowers tickled her wet toes. She let her skirt and petticoats drop, the hems dusting the tops of the daisies. When he didn't move, she stepped out of his embrace with uncertainty. Outstretching her arm, she handed him his fishing pole. "Don't you want to fish anymore?"

His eyes probed hers with a smoldering intensity she felt in her very soul. "I think I've caught more than I can handle," he said as he took the rods from her and set them beside his tackle box. He stood and was about to flip the lid down with his bare foot.

"Wait," she said. "Could you get that sock thing and put my shoes on for me?"

"Sock thing?"

"Whatever you called that metal hook."

"Sockdologer."

"Yes. I'll need it to put my shoes on."

"Leave 'em off for a while." His big toe caught the lid, and he closed his tackle box. "It's too damn hot for shoes. I'll put them on for you. Later."

"Later?" She thought they would be rejoining the other picnickers now. At dusk she had to give her recital. "What are we going to do?"

"Sit and enjoy the sun." He sat on the blue-and-white cloth and put his long legs out in front of him. She couldn't see all of his face; his panama hid his eyes and nose in a gray shadow as he stared at the river. But she could see his mouth. Full. Chiseled. The color of pottery clay, sort of bronze and terra-cotta.

She swept her hair over her shoulder, but not before feeling for her crimped-wire hairpins. She came up with three. The others must have fallen in the river. She decided to try and repair her hair; she put the three pins between her teeth. Since she didn't have a brush, her fingers had to suffice. Once she got the small tangles in order, she began twisting the whole mass together to make a coil.

She'd just positioned the knot on the back of her head when she glanced in Frank's direction. She froze.

He was watching her.

She spoke around the hairpins to explain. "I have to try and fix my hair. I still need to play 'The Star-Spangled Banner.'" Shoving the pins in place, she felt for curl wisps. There were many. Too many to go unnoticed. People would know this wasn't the hairstyle she'd left with. Perhaps her hat could hide the imperfections.

She went in search of it and found the hat by the side of the picnic basket at Frank's knee. He followed her gaze.

"Leave it, sweetheart."

She lifted a brow. "Leave it?"

"I like you much better without that hat." His blue eyes traveled over her coiffure. "And without the hairpins."

Before she could lose her courage, she asked, "Is that why you took them out?"

Frank leaned back on his elbows. "This may surprise you, Amelia, but ever since that night I saw you in your nightgown, I've been crazy wanting my fingers in the thickness of your hair again."

"You have . . . ?" Her voice was small and threaded with the frantic beats of her heart pounding in her ears. This was not like Frank. Not at all. He rarely, if he'd ever, admitted anything to her.

Especially not a weakness.

She sat down next to him, following his suit by viewing the stream. Neither spoke nor moved. The fragrance of crushed flower petals surrounded them, and the trickle of water seemed the perfect music.

"I wasn't sure you liked me at all," she said softly when he remained quiet.

Her words broke through his pensive inattention, and Frank's shoulder bumped hers as he sat up. "I like you, Amelia. Too much."

"Really?"

"Yeah."

She smiled, blissfully happy.

"You know, there are others who like you, too," he began in a tone that was strained. "Certain people at the saloon."

"Yes," she agreed. "And I like Mr. O'Cleary and Mr. Weatherwax." She peeked at him from the corner of her eye through her lashes. "I also like you. Greatly."

His profile hardened. "I don't know why. I'm not much to like."

She had the strongest urge to put her hand on his arm, but refrained. "Don't say that. Why, I think you're very likable . . . at least after I got to know you I thought that . . . which isn't really true, is it?"

"What?"

"I don't know you." She hugged her knees to her chest and rested her chin on the top of her hands. She chose her words very carefully, trying to lead up to a question she wanted to ask him in a way he wouldn't balk at an answer. "When I was a little girl, we had to leave our farm and go to Denver to live with two elderly sisters, the Wootens. They smelled like medicine, but I got used to it as I grew up. We were all women in the house—just my aunt, my mother and I, and the two sisters." She lifted her chin. "Do you have a sister or a brother?"

Her subtle query was greeted with silence.

"I always wanted a sister," she continued, pretending not to notice his lack of a reply, "but my mother never remarried after my father died when I was five. When you're an only child, I think it's natural to want a sibling to play with. Did you, too?"

He wouldn't talk.

If she kept the conversation going in this direction, she would be forced to carry it. But the subject was worth pursuing, and she tried once more. "It would be nice to have family you could write to or visit. My aunt Clara was the last bit of close family I had. My father's side is spread out in the Midwest, and I don't really correspond with any of them. I can't imagine you writing a letter. But if you did, where would you post it? I mean to say, where does your family live?"

Frank snipped a daisy in his fingers, the petals looking fragile in his strong fingers. "I can appreciate what you're trying to do, Amelia, but my family is dead, so there's no sense in talking about any of them."

Her chin rose from her knees, and she turned her head to gaze at him. "I'm sorry."

"Don't be." Tossing the flower, he frowned. Then he met her sad expression and his face softened. "Ah, hell. You can be sorry for Harry, but not for Jack and Charlotte."

"Who's Harry?"

"He was my brother."

"Oh. . . . And Jack and Charlotte?"

"My parents."

"When did they die?" she asked, wondering how long he'd been alone. She still wasn't used to the emptiness of her aunt's house, even though Aunt Clara had been departed for two years now.

"Jack and Charlotte died when I was nine."

"And your brother?"

A play of emotion clouded his eyes. She felt his sorrow and knew that he must have loved his brother deeply. "Harry died when I was twelve."

"How awful to have lost him when you were so young," she sympathized. "Was he older than you?"

"No."

She dared to press the issue further since he was beginning to talk. "How did he die?"

"He drowned."

Growing reflective a moment, she did put her hand on his arm. "I'm sorry, Frank. Truly."

"Yeah." He shrugged with a forced lift of his shoulders; she sensed he was trying not to show his sadness to her. "Well, it was a long time ago. I've gotten over most of the guilt."

"Guilt?"

He gazed at her, as if realizing the implication of what he'd said after the fact. His eyes studied her hand on his white sleeve. Then he smiled and said, "Let's count clouds," as if their prior dialogue hadn't transpired.

"Count clouds?"

"Yeah." Tossing his panama by the picnic basket, he leaned back, and her fingers slid across the fine fabric of his silk shirt. "Lay down."

She did as he asked. She put her feet straight out and her arms at her sides, just like Frank. A lodgepole pine shielded the sun from her eyes, and she was able to stare at the cobalt sky without squinting. There were cottony billows of clouds. Some were defined with curving edges; some looked like marshmallows and whipped cream pillows.

"You can't count all these clouds," she said.

"No, but that one there"—he pointed—"looks like the Widow Thurman."

Amelia glanced at him. He was grinning.

"The Widow Thurman happens to be an acquaintance of mine." But she couldn't keep a straight face.

He kept the corners of his mouth turned up but said, "How come you don't have any friends your own age?"

She stared ahead again, her smile fading. "I don't have anything in common with women my age."

"Which is?"

"I'll be twenty-five this December. And you?"

"Thirty next month. Why don't you have anything in common with younger women?"

She was embarrassed to say, "They're all married and have children."

He grew quiet for a moment, then asked, "Did you love that salesman?"

She took her time answering, trying to figure out the best way to phrase her answer. "I thought I did."

"Pap told me what happened."

She turned her head toward Frank. "Mr. O'Cleary?"

Frank shrugged. "Pap can be nosy."

Amelia put her gaze back on the endless sky. "One doesn't have to be nosy in Weeping Angel to find out a person's life history. Just drop a name or a hint, and someone will tell all. The problem is, most times, it's retold in fabrication."

"Then you tell me. What happened?"

She wasn't sure she wanted to. It was humiliating thinking about being jilted, much less telling the details aloud. "Let's just say . . . I fell in love with the wrong man. Jonas wasn't in love with me, and I was too stupid to see him for what he was."

"He was the stupid one, Amelia, for running off with that dancing girl from Charley's shebang. Pray would have done much better to stay with you."

Gentle tears stung the backs of her eyes as Frank slipped his hand in hers. "I always thought Jonas Pray was a fine person because of his calling selling Bibles and books about scriptures. But now I recognize it doesn't really matter what a man does for his living that makes him decent. A true man is one whose goodness is a part of himself. It doesn't consist of the outward things he does but in the inward things he is. And no occupation can change that."

Frank was quiet a moment before saying, "You keep talking that way, and I might believe you."

"You should believe me." With her fingers entwined in Frank's, Amelia stared at the summer sky of clouds. "I saw the way you were with Jakey and Daniel in the saloon, letting them pretend they were grown-up. Most men would have been bothered by them."

"Who's to say I wasn't?"

"You can talk a good story, but you can't lie." She faced him. "Not even about cattails. I wouldn't have found out you weren't the one who picked them. But you told me."

He shrugged while gazing forward.

"And there's Mr. Weatherwax."

This time, Frank tilted his nose in her direction. "What about Cobb?"

"You don't really mean it when you tell Mr. O'Cleary not to give him free drinks. I myself have seen you slip him a few without any charge. Not that I condone what you're pouring. But I think you only pretend to be gruff with him to save face. You know he doesn't have anyplace to call home, so you try and make the saloon welcoming to him. And the reason you played baseball was because you didn't want to let Mr. Weatherwax down."

Frank skeptically arched his brows, then returned his gaze to the blue above. "Is that what you really think?"

"Yes," she replied.

"Nobody's ever taken the time to figure all that out about me before. You make me sound like a nice gent to know."

"You are, you ninny."

Frank's thumb grazed her finger. "The way you've got me pegged, I'll be hearing harp music when I kick off instead of smelling smoke."

"Well, of course you will."

A reflective silence blanketed them as they watched, hand in hand, the clouds move along. The sun's toasty rays melted through Amelia's clothes, making her tired and comfortable to just lie there in the serenity of the afternoon. She became drowsy and fought against closing her eyes.

"You mustn't let me fall asleep." Then with reluctance, she added, "We should probably go soon."

"I won't let you fall asleep," Frank assured her, but his voice sounded tired and peaceful to Amelia's ears. And for the first time, content.

Frank dozed off. When he awoke, he saw the sun had set. Hidden by the treetops, all that was left was its fiery orange glow in the remote distance.

Instantly awake, he turned his head. Amelia's eyes were closed; her breasts rose and fell as she took in soft breaths. He had to wake her, but was finding it difficult to disturb the mesmerizing picture she made. Her creamy skin was pinkened by the sun; her mouth rosy and full. He felt something stir deep inside him. The sensation pained him and left him hot, with a weight on his chest so tight he could barely breathe, even though he was sucking air into his lungs. Jesus . . .

He was falling in love with Amelia.

For a moment, he let the revealing thought govern his mind without diluting the emotional implication. The day Harry died, Frank had closed off the feeling part of himself. He'd buried his heart with his brother, thinking there would be no one else he could commit his love to.

Frank had been wrong.

Amelia's talk about goodness and decency had gotten to him. He hadn't wanted to consider what she was saying could be the truth. She had to be wrong about his character. Most of the time, he was irritated by Jakey and Daniel. And there was that remote possibility she could have found out he hadn't picked the cattails or gotten her the frog. As for Cobb, Frank only put up with him because he was amusing. Nothing more. The baseball game had appealed to him enough to go along with it.

There was an explanation for everything, and she couldn't make more out of him than he was. But she'd had him believing that no matter what he did for a living, he'd be worthy of her. In her view, he was kindhearted. Well, if he was so kindhearted, why didn't he just give her the upright?

Frank sat up and sank his fingers into his hair. There were some things about him that she couldn't gloss over. So where did that leave them?

Gazing at Amelia, Frank had no answer. All he knew was, he wanted to enjoy the present. He'd know how to manage the future when the occasion arose.

Frank plucked some of the yellow and white daisies and put the stems between Amelia's toes until she wore flower shoes. She twitched, then wiggled her feet.

"Amelia," he whispered, awakening her with the touch of a daisy on her cheek. "It's time to wake up."

"Mmmmmm?" she moaned dreamily.

"We fell asleep."

"We did?" she murmured, her eyes flitting open as he put another stem between her big toe and the one next to it. Her toes curled. "What are you doing?" she giggled. "That tickles."

He grinned. "Are you ticklish?"

"No."

"Are, too." Then he held on to her ankle and began to feather his fingertips on the sole of her foot.

Amelia screamed and laughed and squirmed. "Stop it! Stop it! Oh, let go!"

"Not until you promise never to sing 'Ta-ra-ra-boom-de-ay!' again."

"Y-You didn't like it?"

"No."

"But I thought—"

"Promise not to," he said through her giggles.

"I-I promise not to— Oh my goodness!" She stilled despite the fact he hadn't given up his assault. "Stop. Frank, you have to stop."

From the serious expression on her face, he did. "What is it?"

She sat up, her eyes wide. "Oh, my goodness . . . my corset." She put her palm on her stomach and averted her gaze from his. "My corset string broke!"

"How in the hell did it break? Aren't those things supposed to be indestructible?"

"No . . ." She shut her eyes. "I redid the laces this morning, and I must have made them too tight." Her lashes flew up. "What am I going to do? It's almost time to start the ceremony. I'm going to have to go home."

"From the look of the sky, you don't have time to go home and get another corset on. You're supposed to play the piano at sundown. It's that now."

"This is awful," she cried, a tremor to her voice. "I can't let anyone see me like this."

Frank crossed his legs and sat Indian style. "Undo your dress then."

A pink stain suffused her cheeks. "I-I beg your pardon?"

"Undo your dress, and I'll tie the broken lace in a knot."

"But you can't!"

"Why not?"

"Well, because you'd see me half undressed. And . . ."

"Sweetheart, I think I can control myself to tie the lace and have you put yourself back together."

"It's just that . . ."

"You don't have any choice if you're going to make it to that ceremony in time. Unbutton your bodice."

He saw the uncertain lump in her throat as she swallowed, then she raised her hands to her neckline.

Her fingers hovered over the decorative pearl buttons a moment before she got up the nerve to actually unfasten one. "Close your eyes."

"How can I see what to fix if my eyes are closed?"

"It's improper if your eyes are open." The slowness to which her hands were moving—obviously done to try and save her modesty—had quite the opposite effect on him. It was like a honky-tonk gal doing a strip down, teasing him with every slow and drawn-out move.

He couldn't tear his gaze from her hands. His own fingers started to tremble, and he knocked her hands away so he could unbutton the bodice himself. Quickly. "Christ, Amelia, you're not fast enough."

Her mouth fell open as his fingers brushed the warm skin where her breasts created a slight valley. He tried to think of something other than the smooth satin feel of her beneath his fingertips. He tried to keep his gaze from lingering on the neat blue ribbon bow nestled in her cleavage and the lace edge of her corset cover. He had to keep a level and calm head. Think about something distracting. Something safe.

Saloon fights.

Bare knuckles scraping skin. *He wanted to caress her sweet skin with his knuckles.*

Bloody noses. *His blood was boiling for her.*

Windows breaking and glass shattering. *His resolve was shattering like glass.*

"Hell, I can't do it!" he groaned, and pulled his hand away. "Finish it off, for chrissake."

There were only several buttons left, and she did so. "Turn around."

"What for?" he said through teeth clenched so hard, his jaw hurt.

"I have to pull my sleeves down to my waist."

"Oh, God . . ." That image did it, and he turned to stare into space. His pulse was pounding out of control. He tried to think of anything to make him blot out the scene taking place behind him. But he couldn't. So he reasoned with himself the best he could. If he touched her, he'd be a goner. Go over the line with this woman and the next step was marriage. She would expect it, and so would every gossipmonger in town if they found out. But the feel of her in his arms was almost worth the risk of discovery.

Anything and everything made him think about Amelia when he heard the rustling sound of fabric slipping from her arms, and no doubt pooling at her waist. Then came the quiet whisper of cambric as she took off her delicate corset cover.

"Okay. Turn around."

He did and was presented with her back. Her shoulders were naked except for the embroidered muslin straps of her chemise. He attempted to stay focused, but it was too much. Just too damn much. Without trying to talk himself out of it, he lowered his head and kissed the tantalizing bare skin at the nape of her neck where her hair was falling out of its twist.

She stiffened with surprise.

He stopped, his mind speeding like a kicked-off shot from a gun. Words like *danger* and *explosive* were flying through his head. If she hadn't swayed toward him, her neck arching against his shoulder, he wouldn't have kissed her again. But she did. So he did.

Jesus, her skin was sweet against his mouth. He slipped his hands around her waist, the fine satin of her corset sending an erotic tremor through his fingers. Turning her face toward his, a soft gasp left her throat. Their lips touched. He explored her curves, resisting the temptation of her breasts. If he touched her there, there would be no going back. Lowering his hands with slow exploration, he felt a daisy that had fallen in her skirt, and picked it up.

Leaving her mouth, he burned with fire. Her accelerated breathing made her breasts rise and fall seductively. He took the flower and dragged the ruffled petals across the milky white swells . . . higher, to the graceful column of her neck, and lastly, her cheek. He would have pulled her into his lap and pressed his lips over hers, had he not heard a rustling sound in the distance.

He froze.

Looking up, he peered into the brush. He found it empty.

Amelia didn't move, her body still touching his. Apparently she didn't hear the noise. But he'd been in this clearing too often to know the sound was not natural to the area. Something was there, but who or what, he wasn't sure.

He was thinking about investigating just when General Custer came trotting out of the shrubs and went toward the river. He lapped up some water and turned around to sit on the cool sand. The yellow dog was panting and probably would have laid down, but a pop-pop-pop from an exploding firecracker came from the picnic grounds and sent the dog off once more.

The distraction ended up being Frank's saving grace. "I guess I can't control myself. If that hadn't been a dog in the bushes, we would have been in deep shit." His heart was pumping double time, and he realized just how probable being discovered was. He had to get her out of here. Now. "Hold still and I'll fix the string," he said in a tone harsher than he intended. He needed to get a grip on his emotions and put a stop to his thoughts of pressing her down in the flowers.

Wordlessly, she turned her back to him. She shivered, and he felt as though he'd let her down. Was she crying? Scared? Angry with him? He would have given anything to pull her into his arms, but didn't. Couldn't.

Drawing on his willpower, he gazed at the double-knotted bow at the top of her corset. The frayed ends were out of several eyeholes, leaving a gap in the back.

Though he'd taken it upon himself to know the basic mechanics of woman's clothing, he'd never had to fix a broken corset string before. "What do I do with it?"

"Un . . . Untie the top," she breathed lightly, "and loosen the lacings. You'll have to bring the severed ends together and tie them in a knot."

He did as she instructed, keeping the conversation on anything other than what was really on his mind—like kissing her. "Why are the laces on these things in the back? You'd think they'd be in the front, where you could adjust them or whatever."

Her voice was still labored when she spoke. "Normally," she said in a feathery tone, "a lady doesn't have to do anything to the laces once she establishes them to the form of her body."

"Hell, I don't even know how you can wear this thing." He was coming back to earth, despite the raging tautness in his groin. "It's stiff as a railroad tie. No wonder you can't take the heat." He tugged on the strings. It was tough getting them to meet, and he had to pull hard.

"Ow!" she complained.

"Sorry." Pausing, he took in several gulps of air to cool his lungs. "This isn't something I've done before. Why can't you just take it off and work on it?"

"No! If I did that, I'd never be able to get the busks in place."

"What the hell is a busk?"

"I don't think that's something you need to know. Are you almost done?"

"Yeah." He gave the string one last yank, and the ends met enough for him to tie them in a reef's knot. "It should hold," he said. "You can get dressed."

"Turn around again."

Frowning, he complied with her wishes, thinking it ridiculous after what just transpired between them. He was tense and miserable; he felt strung just as tight as her corset. He needed a release, and he was aching to hold her.

A minute later, she told him he could face her again. "You're going to have to help me with my shoes, too."

She put her stockings on, and with no time for modesty, he was given an ample view of her legs as she rolled the black hose up over her thighs. He didn't have an opportunity to let his gaze linger because she flung her skirts over her knees and thrust her shoes at him. "We'd better hurry, Frank."

He made quick work of the job while she pinned on her hat. When he was finished, he put his boots on, then stood and helped her up. Just the touch of her hand in his almost set him off. They remained standing for a moment, gazing at each other; he thinking of doing so much more than he was, as the sun's radiance all but dimmed and twilight took its place. Time became meaningless. Stars peeped through the heavenly mass of sky; they shined and winked, growing bright, then fading.

"I'm going to be late," she whispered.

His voice was thick when he spoke. "You already are."

She gave him a small, intimate smile. "I'm sorry Mr. O'Cleary caught the chicken pox . . . but I'm glad he did. This was the best time I've ever had. Thank you, Frank."

He nodded. "Yeah, well, I was planning on having a much worse time than this," he admitted with quiet huskiness, "but you cheated me out of it."

Her smile widened, and he knew that if he didn't get out of here—*now*—he'd be in trouble. "We'd better go."

"Yes . . ." she replied, but with the same reluctance as he had.

As they left, Frank knew he would never be able to view his favorite fishing spot without seeing Amelia Marshall sleeping on a blue-and-white gingham cloth with white daisies between her toes.

Chapter

17

⤳

*F*rank poured several fingers' worth of Hennessy cognac into a beer glass, then lit a cheroot. Slumping into one of the Moon Rock Saloon's bow-backed chairs, he kicked his feet up on the table.

The Fourth of July festivities had broken up a short time ago, the hour nearing midnight. Dodge had gotten in a dozen or so sentences of the Declaration of Independence before a string of Red Devils had gone off underneath the gazebo. The mayor had let out a startled wail, and the consequences thereof had every boy in town being yanked upon the ear by his mother. No one would fess up, and since a culprit couldn't be nailed down, the fathers took charge and brushed the matter off as boyish shenanigans.

Frank would have liked to have seen the sisters in the home walk away so easily from disreputable conduct once in awhile. He'd had his fair share of slaps, even for crimes he hadn't committed.

Taking a draw on his cigar, he continued his reflection. Amelia had done her part by playing "The Star-Spangled Banner" and having her students sing along. Afterward, the kids disbanded to light fizzle sticks. As the glow of sparks illuminated their faces, Walter and Warren had looked at him as if they'd swallowed their mother's parakeet. Several of the other boys had gazed at Frank and snickered. Daniel and Jakey had guilt written all over their faces. Frank couldn't figure out what they were up to. Everywhere he turned, the hoodlums were whispering behind their hands. He had a hunch the boys knew something he didn't—probably some kind of prank yet to be played out against him, like firecrackers beneath his chair.

Frank inhaled, thoughtfully deliberating the way the evening had ended. Under a shower of skyrockets, he'd stood by Amelia and watched the show. He hadn't concentrated much on the magnificent colors raining from the dark sky. His mind had been occupied with the woman by his side. When the spectacle was over, he'd walked her home. He hadn't trusted himself to touch her—not even a handshake. Not when he had thoughts of daisies, bare toes, and smooth, sweet-smelling skin. Her expression had been puzzled, but he wasn't about to explain that kissing her wasn't enough anymore.

He'd returned to the Moon Rock and had given the place a hasty inspection. Finding no hidden explosives waiting to be lit when he least expected it, he'd decided to have a drink before bed.

Sitting in the dim solitude of his saloon, with a single chandelier lit, he could think more clearly. And the way he saw things was, he had two problems.

One, what exactly did he want to become of his affections for Amelia? She was held in high esteem amongst her social circle, a woman who had been in town long enough to be embraced in its bosom, despite her mistake with the Bible salesman. He, on the other hand, was popular with the men; but his saloon was not looked upon with much favor by the ladies, despite their curiosity. The novelty of the

Moon Rock was waning. Even Dorothea Beamguard hadn't hinted for him to slide a beer along the counter lately. What would these fair women do if he made it known he wanted their Amelia?

Two, and this hurdle was far taller—though not in a literal sense—was Pap O'Cleary.

Since Pap had confided to Frank he intended to marry Amelia, this posed a considerable obstacle in their friendship, not to mention, their working relationship.

There was a way to handle the issue. Tell Pap how he was feeling about Amelia. Pap wasn't going to like it. He'd goad him into a fist fight, and they'd have to bloody each other's noses. Giving him a bruising would make Pap feel better, but it wouldn't be a remedy. Frank wasn't sure what was.

"Frank? Is that you?"

Frank looked up and saw Cobb peering over the top of the bat-wing doors.

"Yeah, Cobb. Come on in."

He pushed the doors and slipped inside the saloon. Still outfitted in his best mountain attire, he walked across the floor on soundless moccasins. "Are you serving drinks?"

"No."

"Oh." Cobb's expression fell. "Well, you see . . . I was . . . that is, beaver being so scarce you know . . . and this being hard times and . . ."

"Get a glass, Cobb, and help yourself."

"Don't you want to hyar my hard-luck story, Frank?"

"No."

"But I've been practicing a good one."

"You save it for a night when I'm not feeling so generous, Cobb."

His eyes twinkled. "Thanks, Frank. That's right kind of you." Cobb went to the bar and came back a short minute later with a shot glass of Jim Beam. He sat at the table with Frank. "I didn't pour much. I'm not a charity man, you know. I pay for what's mine, but since you did make the offer." He took a taste. "And remember what you said about free drinks on Friday and Saturday."

"I remember." Frank brought his glass to his lips and let the cognac slip warmly down his throat. "What happened between you and Miss Shelby? I saw you during the fireworks, and she wasn't with you."

"I bought her supper like you said." Cobb rested his arms on the table, his hands wide and large around the squat shot glass. "She cooks real fine vittles. I et the whole basket."

"I'll bet that made her happy," Frank remarked, but Cobb didn't pick up on his sarcasm.

"She said she had no appetite. She's a small woman. I like small women."

"I wasn't sure you were interested in women."

"Well, I ain't interested in men, if that's what yore trying to say."

"No, Cobb, I wasn't." Frank puffed on his cheroot, the smoke swirling above his head in a slow-moving ribbon. Though he would have never thought to worry about Cobb pining after Amelia, Pap had put just enough doubt in his mind for him to ask, "Do you like Miss Marshall?"

"Yes, sir. I think she's purdy." Cobb drank a swallow of his whiskey. "She can play the piano good."

"She says the same about you." Frank tapped his ash on the floor and considered the best way to phrase his next question without scaring Cobb. There really was no other option other than to come out and ask, "Do you really think about getting married, or were you just trying to pull the wool over Pap's eyes when he asked you?"

"I think about getting married all the time."

Frank sat straighter. "No shit? Damn, Cobb, but I

didn't figure you thought about anything but beavers."

"I think about lots of things." His bushy brows rose into the tangle of hair on his forehead. "But I mostly talk about beavers cause they's what I know best. I can read them better than people. You take that Miz Shelby. I don't know what to make of her. I was polite and even said I thought she smelled better than a beaver."

Frank repressed a smile.

"She didn't like me saying that. I can't figure it out."

"Well, Cobb, next time you see her, tell her she smells like heaven."

Cobb scratched his temple. "I ain't never smelled heaven."

Frank crushed his cigar and tossed back the remainder of his cognac. "Lie." He stood, feeling the toll of the day in his tired muscles. "I'm going to bed. Finish off that drink so I can lock up."

Cobb tipped his head back and drained his glass, then he stood and tapped the top of his stovepipe hat. "I told Miz Shelby this hat was made out of a dead beaver. She doesn't like beavers. And she told me I was hairy as a grizzly bear."

They walked toward the door and as Cobb exited, Frank put his hand on the jamb. "Well, Cobb, I don't know what to tell you about Miss Shelby. She can be as sweet as any preserves ever put up, but she can also be as sour as a pickle. If you want her to like you, don't give up on her. Take some dirty clothes to her laundry and tell her you like starch."

"I ain't got no dirty clothes. All mine's broke in. Why would I want 'em washed? They'd lose their shape."

Frank rested his forearm on the top of the frosted glass in the fancy double doors. Sliding his hand into his pocket, he fingered two quarters. He tossed them at Cobb. "You go on over to the mercantile tomorrow and buy yourself a cheap shirt. Roll around in the dirt, then take the dirty shirt on over to the laundry to get clean."

Cobb thought on it a moment, his expression dim as the light behind Frank, then he cracked a smile. "That I will, Frank. Thanks for the ideer."

"Any time, Cobb." Frank stepped onto the board-walk to swing the large doors in place as Cobb mounted his short-legged mule and rode in the dark up Divine Street.

Frank put the tall doors in place, and bolted them to the boardwalk. He strode back to the table and picked up his and Cobb's empty glasses; then he moved to the bar. He dunked the glassware into the bin and, out of habit, began to wipe off the countertop.

His mind was cluttered with the conversation he had had with Cobb and the one he'd have to have with Pap. Both men were seeking a lifetime of companion-ship. He wondered if they knew what they'd be getting into when they married. Did they understand com-mitment and devotion? Two big words. Scary as hell words. Matrimony meant loving another person enough to spend the rest of your life with them. Once that ring was on, it was a done deal.

All of a sudden, Frank felt as if he were drowning. He went against his self-imposed rule by getting a fresh glass and pouring a second drink. A hazardous diversion for a man surrounded by liquor.

For a moment, as he swirled the pleasant taste of expensive cognac around his tongue, he tried to picture himself married. It was a hard canvas to paint. There was only one face that came to mind. Amelia's. She was an independent woman who was firm on principle. That self-reliant trait, among her individual mannerisms, was what drew him to her like no other woman ever had. She was sensitive, knew her own mind, and was witty. She could banter with him, make him angry, and have him desiring her all within a few short minutes. He could live with a woman like Amelia and never get bored.

That thought alone set alarm bells ringing and aroused old fears and uncertainties. He'd never envisioned himself married. Not when he'd had such poor role models in Jack and Charlotte. How would he know what to do to make a marriage work? He'd never been in a happy home. What did it take to create one?

"Dammit . . ." He breathed tightly and tipped his glass back to drain it. "I'm thinking seriously about asking her to marry *me.*"

Anxiety singed the corners of his control, and he poured another drink. Rubbing his fingertips over the rough abrasion of his beard, Frank wondered when he'd last truly enjoyed himself with a woman without romping in some sheets with her. To his recollection, he hadn't.

Unbidden, he pictured Amelia in his bed with white flowers between her toes and her hair spread across his pillow in shimmering waves of brown. He heard her laughter; he saw her smile. She opened her arms for him. . . . The image left a burning imprint on his mind and made him more troubled than ever.

He needed an element of danger to combat his restlessness, an outlet in which to vent his frustration. Since there was no one around to get into a fight with, he did the next best thing.

He got drunk.

Frank didn't wake until late the following afternoon, and when he did, he had a blinding headache. He brewed an extra strong pot of coffee, and after a half dozen cups, he decided he couldn't talk to Pap while he was in dull pain. He needed to take the edge off his throbbing temples by putting his mind on other things besides too much cognac and the probability of Pap hitting him. He figured his bedroom was due a cleaning since he'd scrubbed the saloon already. In between sips of coffee, he made his bed, pitched his dirty clothes into a laundry bag, and stacked the various dishes he found into a dishpan.

He'd just stepped onto the rear boardwalk off his apartment to wring his wet floor rag over the railing when Mayor Dodge approached him.

"Mr. Brody," Cincinatus greeted with a fair amount of soberness to his tone. As always, he was impeccably dressed in a fine coat and shirt, his hair parted to perfection and oiled.

Frank paused after squeezing the cloth. He leaned into the rail. "Dodge."

"I hope you have a minute to talk." Cincinatus took the few steps, clearly not wanting to be put off.

"What's on your mind, Dodge?" Frank asked, shifting so that his hip rested on the post of the boardwalk. "You look like you just lost an election."

"I feel like I did."

Frank slung the damp cloth over the rail. "Sounds serious. You need a drink?"

"No." The mayor frowned, his gaze troubled. "I was just at my residence for lunch. I do that these days. Take my lunch at home with Narcissa, that is. Ever since we found out she was expecting, I don't allow her to tax herself and come to the city offices with my lunch box."

Frank guessed there was a point to Dodge's rambling and gave the man room to speak.

"I came through the kitchen, as I normally do. No sense in wearing out the carpet in the foyer when I'm going directly to eat. When I entered my house, I heard female voices coming from the parlor." The mayor grimaced, his disdain evident. "This isn't unusual. Narcissa's friends have been coming over more frequently these days to inquire about her health. I'm not opposed to her socializing, but I've made it clear to her, I don't necessarily like all that cackling going on in the house when I'm there. You know, a man's home is his castle."

Frank crossed his arms over his chest, wishing Dodge would come out with it.

"I was just getting ready to push on the door to the parlor and clear the house, when one of their voices stopped me cold. It was that Spivey woman. She said something that made me stop"—his eyes narrowed —"and listen."

From the mayor's emphasized pause, Frank felt as if he were under attack.

"She claimed her son saw something untoward by the river yesterday when he was calling for General Custer. As soon as she mentioned the word 'untoward,' it was as if someone let a canary out of a cage. They all began to chirp at the same time, saying their sons were with him and saw the same thing."

The mayor gave Frank a condescending glare. It didn't sit well with him, and he tried to depict a natural ease he didn't feel. "Go on."

"The boys were witness to what you and Amelia were doing at the river. These women claim their sons saw some hanky-panky."

Frank shoved his hands in his pockets, and as casually as he could manage, asked, "What exactly did they see?"

"I don't even like to talk secondhand about it. A woman's reputation is on the line here."

"I didn't do anything to Amelia to damage her reputation."

"Then how do you explain why you were helping Miss Marshall take her clothes off?"

"Ah, hell," Frank mumbled, his wall of controlled nonchalance crashing down. "I wasn't helping her take them off."

"What, then, were you doing?"

"What Amelia and I were doing is nobody's business."

Cincinatus's face went a shade of red. "I ought to whup you for that remark. You're implying something I don't like."

"I'm not implying anything. I'm merely saying what she and I do in private is our own business."

The mayor ran his fingers over his lips, then pursed them. "I suppose what you do in private with a woman is. *If* you're dallying with that kind of woman. But Amelia is not. I think of her as a daughter, and my wife is quite taken with her. She's been through some trying times, and I do not want to see her being made fodder for gossip again."

Frank slipped his hands from his pockets and grabbed his rag. "Neither do I."

"Then you better set the record straight. Those ladies are in my parlor this very minute, thinking the worst. The last time something like this happened to Amelia, she almost didn't live it down. She's just started to get on with her life this past year." The mayor's brows pulled into a frown. "I trust you'll not make any false implications to the contrary of what transpired between you two. You can be smart with me and try and get me to think the worst, but I don't believe it of Amelia. She's not a loose woman. And I'll admit it, I'm glad Jonas Pray ran off. He didn't deserve her and—" He sliced his words short.

Frank finished Dodge's thought with a question to his tone. "And neither do I?"

The mayor stepped down. "I don't know, Mr. Brody. You tell me. Are you worthy of a woman good to the bone? Would you do the honorable thing to protect her? If not, then you're not the right man for her. If so, then I suggest you act quickly. Once this gets around—and you can count on it—Amelia is not going to be able to hold her head high. The rumors will send her running. Think about that," Cincinatus said, then walked away with a brisk gait.

Exhaling, Frank grabbed the railing with both

hands. The muscles of his forearms hardened beneath his sleeves from his tense grip. His heartbeat sped through him; his breath burned in his throat. *The rumors will send her running.* The thought froze in his brain. He didn't want to be the cause of Amelia hiding behind her door. Though he couldn't imagine her cowering. But he hadn't been here before when Pray had walked out on her; he hadn't been here to see her shamed and jilted. And he knew how biting the tongues of those gossiping women could be.

Frank pushed away from the rail and straightened. He went inside and threw his rag on the bar as he passed by. Dammit, he should have known if there was a dog around, the boys weren't far behind. Stupid! He'd been stupid to let things go too far yesterday.

He stopped at the end of the bar, hooked his boot heel over the brass railing, and hung his head. A wedge of sunlight lit the floorboards. He'd opened the front doors to air the place out. "Dammit," he whispered in a dull and troubled voice. He had a lot to figure out in a brief amount of time. A painful knot twisted his gut. He wasn't keen on rushed decisions, but he had some heavy trouble. The kind of trouble he couldn't just ride away from or pay cash to get out of. The kind of trouble he wasn't good at figuring out and usually had Pap think it through for him. Only this time, he couldn't talk to Pap.

He had to keep in mind that Amelia's integrity was what counted. If he came to her defense, his strong testimony opposing what the boys thought had happened might work to his disadvantage. Firm denial of the incident could possibly make things more suspicious and make the boys' story look all the more convincing.

Ideally, if he said nothing at all and made no comment to the contrary, there could only be speculation. But those boys did see Amelia and knew Frank had seen her in her corset. Just that fact alone was scandal enough for their meddling mothers.

"Mr. Brody?"

Frank lifted his head and turned around. Daniel Beamguard stood behind him, his hands stuffed into the hip pockets of his overalls.

"Not now, kid. I'm busy."

The boy hung his head low. "Oh . . . It's just that me and the boys . . . we were wanting to play some ball . . . I was hoping I could, that is, well . . ."

Frank rubbed the bridge of his nose. "What? You want to borrow my bat?"

"Yes, sir. Seeing how that bat's lucky for you, and all."

"I wish I could make it lucky for me, but the lady's not on my side." Frank looked into Daniel's expectant face, seeing a bit of Harry in the boy's expression. "Yeah, sure. You can borrow it," he said, then strode to his bedroom.

Daniel followed him and Frank crouched down to rummage through his leather-bound, brass-trimmed trunk. Finding the Spalding, he handed it to the boy. Daniel touched the smooth wood grip, but Frank didn't let the bat go. "Sit down, kid."

Daniel slumped onto the bed, his expression riddled with guilt. "I . . . Are you mad at me, Mr. Brody?"

Frank straightened his legs and scratched the back of his head before shaking the hair from his brows. He absently put the bat over his right shoulder and began to pace the short length of the room.

"You are mad at me, I know it."

Frank stopped in front of Daniel, lowered the end of the bat, and dropped the top in between the spread of his legs. Leaning on the handle, he asked, "Why do you think that?"

"Because of yesterday . . ." he mumbled. "I didn't tell my mother anything, I swear. But Jakey, Coney

Island, and Walter and Warren did. I said we ought to keep it to ourselves. I mean . . . we didn't really see nothing. We didn't mean to . . . I mean we were just looking for General Custer." He lowered his gaze.

Laying the bat on the bed next to Daniel, Frank sat down and put his forearms on his knees. He drew in his breath and looked at the tips of his boots.

"I'm not allowed to come here anymore for piano lessons," Daniel confessed dejectedly. "I don't mind the not-having-lessons part, but I'd miss coming to the saloon to belly up to the bar and have you horse around with me and the boys."

Frank made no reply.

"My ma told my pa if she ever caught him in the Moon Rock again, she'd go live with my grandmother." He cocked his head. "And she said she'd make sure none of the other fathers could come here anymore either."

Right now Frank didn't care if he lost the business. But the scandal would cost Amelia hers. He could still see the look of devastation on her face in the church when she lost the piano. Word of their so-called indiscretion was going to ruin her unless he did something to halt the rumors before they started.

Daniel glanced at Frank. "What are you going to do, Mr. Brody?"

Frank turned his head to gaze at the boy. "I'm going to marry Miss Marshall."

Daniel swallowed, his tiny Adam's apple bobbing. "Gosh, you are? Do you like her?"

"Yes."

"Do you love her?"

Frank inhaled slowly. "I think so."

Daniel meshed his fingers together, the nails soiled. "Then I guess you could marry her. You'd have to kiss her though, but I don't think she's ugly."

"Me neither."

They were quiet a moment before Frank asked, "Have you ever taken anything from your father's store without him knowing about it?"

"I've never stole from him," Daniel defended in a rush, then hastened to add, "Well, at least not *real* merchandise. Lickerish shoestrings and bellyburners don't count. Do they?"

"I reckon they wouldn't to a boy."

"Why do you ask, Mr. Brody? Do you want me to get you some candy?"

"No." Frank sat up. "But I would appreciate it if you could buy me something without your parents knowing about it."

"Why can't you come in and buy it?"

"I'd rather no one know about the purchase just yet."

Frank rose, went to the low bureau, and retrieved his wallet. He counted off some bills. "I want you to pick out the best ladies' ring in the store and pay for it with this. Put the money in your father's cash box. Can you do that?"

"Yes, sir." Daniel took the money and stuffed it into his pocket. "What kind do you like?"

Frank thought a moment. "I've always fancied opals."

"My father has a real nice opal ring with diamonds around it."

"That'll do."

The boy nodded. "When do you want me to bring it back?"

"Give me thirty minutes."

"Okay."

Frank picked up the bat from the bed and handed it to Daniel. "I'd appreciate it if you kept this between me and you. Man to man."

The boy stood. "I will."

"Good." Frank put his hand on the boy's shoulder. "And no surprise frog this time. You do this favor for me, and you can keep the bat."

"W-What did you say?" he stammered.

"You can keep the bat."

"Holy smoke . . ." Daniel breathed. "You mean it?"

"Yeah. I mean it."

Grasping the Spalding in his hand, Daniel put the bulk of the wood in the crook of his arm. "I don't care what my mother says. I don't think you'd ever do anything bad." He gave Frank a sheepish gaze from underneath the locks of sandy brown hair. "You're my hero, Mr. Brody."

Then he ran out of the bedroom, the heels of his plow shoes clopping over the floorboards.

Amelia had gone to Narcissa's house right after her breakfast, but when she saw the ladies converging on the stoop of the Dodge residence, she'd turned around and gone home. She longed to tell Narcissa about yesterday. A disclosure of this importance was a private matter between her and her best friend. She could never blurt out how she was feeling about Frank with the others sitting on the edges of their brocaded chairs, hanging on her every word. Though they wouldn't say so outright, most likely they'd think her foolish to become involved with the very man who laid claim to her piano; not to mention, he was a server of alcoholic refreshment. They'd started to gun down Frank Brody's occupation during their card games, despite having once stuffed him with finger sandwiches and candies. She feared the newness of Frank's arrival in town, and their inquisitiveness being sated about his showplace, had begun to ebb. Their acceptance of him and his establishment was dissipating, and it angered her they could be so fickle.

Since Amelia hadn't been able to readily talk with

Narcissa, she'd spent the morning ironing, took her lunch in the wicker settee on the back porch, and was now weeding the flower bed on the side of the house.

Humming a bright melody while the sun warmed her back, she felt a bottomless satisfaction and contentment as she worked. Last night she'd been so wrapped up in her cocoon of euphoria, it had taken her awhile to fall asleep. When she'd finally drifted into a light doze, she dreamed about Frank . . . about his arms around her . . . his firm lips on her own. She'd relived their kiss dozens of times in her sleep, and when she awoke at dawn, she was embracing her pillow. She'd stared romantically at the downy plumpness through half-closed eyes, imagining what it would be like to wake up and see Frank lying there next to her instead of a lump of feathers stuffed into a pillow slip.

A month ago she never would have thought such a thing, much less put a face to a man she was pretending to be sleeping in her bed. But now, things were different. She was different. She no longer projected her life to be lived in solitude as a withering raisin on the vine. Frank had made her feel pretty and desired. He'd given her hope, and in that, she'd found joy in his company, in his kisses.

She had fallen headfirst in love.

She wondered when she would see him again . . . be able to touch him again. Raking a dandelion with her weeder, she dropped it in her bucket. Amelia sighed, stood, and took her bucket of weeds to the rear of the house, where she put them on the porch steps. Then she reached for her watering pot and went to the pump to fill it. That done, she began to sprinkle the petunias growing along the walkway.

Immersed in her thoughts, she didn't hear Frank until he said her name. Looking up, she broke into an inviting smile as he walked toward her. He looked especially handsome in his black trousers, silk shirt, and blue vest. He'd combed his hair away from his forehead, his panama hat giving her a marginal view of his inky black hair.

His stride was purposeful as he shortened the distance between them.

"Hello, Frank," she greeted warmly. "I wasn't expecting you, but I'm glad—"

She was unable to finish her sentence. Frank slipped his hands around her waist, pulled her close, and kissed her hotly on the mouth. The sudden passion of his gesture caused her to drop her watering pot. At first she did nothing, but as his mouth worked over hers, as the heat of his lips melted her shock, she wrapped her arms around his neck and settled into the kiss that was divine ecstasy.

He parted her lips, his tongue seeking hers with tantalizing persuasion. She felt a quickening start in her ribs, spreading and warming her with delightful shivers. Her knees weakened; her pulse beat erratically. His arms tightened around her midriff, and he pulled her roughly against him. She felt the press of his shirt buttons on her collar, the solid muscles of his chest and the length of his long legs as they tangled in the soft gathers of her skirt.

His tongue stroked the inside of her mouth, and she melted into every rugged curve of his body. Her breasts were crushed, and a tingling radiated from her nipples as they tightened into peaks beneath her chemise. Groaning into his mouth, she slid her hand to the nape of his neck. His hair was silky cool, and she sifted the fine locks with her fingers.

"Marry me, Amelia," he whispered on her lips.

It took her a moment before the words sunk into her mind. "What?"

"Marry me." Brushing her open mouth with hungry kisses, he left her reeling. His lips caressed her along her jawline, and he breathed hotly into her ear, "Marry me and you won't be sorry."

She shivered as his deep voice vibrated through her, making her heart drum wildly. She couldn't believe what she was hearing and had to ask, "You're proposing?"

"Yes." His arms tightened around her, and he bent her back against his arm to kiss her once again. His possessive grip took her wits away. Her head whirled as she gave herself over to his kiss, aware she hadn't answered him.

Amelia couldn't think; she couldn't breathe. Every fiber of her being was focused on Frank—his body hard and firm against hers, his lips tasting and pleasing her to her toes.

"Marry me," he asked once again, the words fluttering over her kiss-dampened mouth. "Say yes."

"I . . ."

"Say yes."

"I want to." *And she did want to!* Her head was swimming; her gaze was locked with his. The startling intensity of his eyes told her he was serious.

Her frivolous side wanted to shout yes. But her reasonable side, the side she knew best, couldn't help wanting to know why he wanted to marry her. Did he love her? Did he feel the same things about her as she felt about him?

He must have sensed her hesitation because he said, "Don't think about reasons. Seize the moment, Amelia. Take it. You want to be happy. You can be happy with me. Marry me. Now."

"Now?"

"Yes." His palms slid seductively down her back, his touch evoking a shower of exhilarating tingles across her skin. "Let's go see the Rev."

"I . . ."

"Christ, Amelia. Don't make me keep asking." His hold on her tensed. "I want to marry you now, but if you keep making me ask, I'm going to—"

"You're unsure then," she interrupted.

"No, I'm not. I'm just impatient." His hands lingered at her waist, and he pulled her flush against him. The way he held her was indecent, but she wasn't shocked or repelled. Something deep inside her screamed for him to go further, to take her further. She wanted him to kiss her again, to touch his tongue with her own and feel her body respond to him.

Amelia closed her eyes and thought of her bed—the vacant place that was cold on winter mornings; the vacant place that had only been filled with her musings of a husband, and all the while knowing she would never have one. This was her chance. Her last chance. She'd taken the risk before with Jonas. She'd put her hopes into a wedding ring, but he'd tricked her. His deceit had hurt so bad.

But Frank wasn't like Jonas Pray.

Frank wouldn't lie about marriage. He wouldn't ask unless he truly wanted her to be he wife.

Opening her eyes, Amelia smiled tenderly at him. His face, the face she would grow old with, was looking down at her. She lifted her hand and put her palm on his cheek. Turning his head, he caught her fingers in his and brought them to his mouth for a kiss. "Yes," she said. "I'll marry you, Frank."

"Let's do it now." He sounded as if he had trouble getting the words out of his mouth, and he cleared his throat. "I've already talked to the Rev about marrying us."

"You spoke to Reverend Thorpe?" she said in disbelief.

"Yes. He's waiting for us at the church. I told him we'd be there in fifteen minutes."

Startled by his confession, she gasped, "You were that sure I'd say yes?"

"I hoped to hell you would." He kissed the corner of her mouth. "I would have convinced you even if you said no."

She didn't doubt that. The touch and expertise of

his lips could make her do crazy things—things her aunt and mother would have disapproved of. But they'd gone with the angels, and though her love for them was strong in her memories, she had to live her life without them. She had to ask herself what she wanted.

She wanted Frank.

She wanted him more than she'd ever wanted anything. Even more than that New American piano.

"Fifteen minutes?" She heard her voice go unnaturally high. "I can't get ready in fifteen minutes."

"You'll have to be."

Her mind was awhirl. She didn't have a wedding dress. She had nothing in her wardrobe that was all white. All her clothes were suitably drab, and those with color were in darker shades. She had shirtwaists in white and natural linen . . . perhaps if she put one with her Henrietta skirt. Glancing at Frank, she asked, "Why can't we wait until I can make suitable arrangements for a dress?"

"Because"—his head dipped and he kissed the side of her neck—"I don't care what you wear."

"But—"

He silenced her protest with his mouth on hers. She felt her resolve slipping, snuffed out by the heat of his kiss. "Oh, very well," she said in a wispy tone. "I don't care either."

Lifting his head, he caught her chin in his fingers. "I'll wait on the porch. You have ten minutes left."

She backed out of his arms, her gaze unable to leave his. Her heart soared with happiness, and she couldn't stop smiling.

She was going to be Mrs. Frank Brody.

Chapter

18

༄

*T*he Christ Redeemer church wasn't decorated with a marriage bell, white doves, or garden roses, or any of the symbolic tokens Amelia had envisioned having at her wedding. The smells in the air were not of fragrant petals but, rather, the Burnishine furniture polish on the wooden pews and a mustiness that exuded from the rafters. No one played the pipe organ to announce her walk down the aisle. The only music in her ears was the clamor of horse tack as wagons traversed Dodge Street, kicking up dust and sending it through the seams of the marginally lifted window sashes.

But she was standing next to Frank, and that alone dismissed her youthful dreams of a traditional wedding. The groom was all that mattered. He would be what she remembered most of all on this important day in her life.

Amelia felt Narcissa's presence; her dearest friend was at her left side acting as her bridesmaid. She'd been taken aback to find the Dodges at the pulpit with Reverend Thorpe when she and Frank had walked into the church. Frank had spoken in a low tone when telling her he'd invited Narcissa and Cincinatus to be witnesses for the ceremony. Amelia couldn't have been happier about the arrangement, and the couple gave them their blessing without a question as to the impetuousness of the nuptials.

The initial awkwardness of their quick arrival had faded, and now Reverend Thorpe began the ceremony with a winded sermon about the duties of a husband and wife.

Amelia did her best to fix her attention on the insightful words, but her mind wandered. *This is it. My moment. My wish come true.*

Standing next to the man she loved and taking her vows before God was what every woman desired. She didn't care that she was dressed in her Persian patterned shirtwaist and her black grenadine skirt instead of white silk with a long wide veil of tulle. She didn't care that she held a simple pink-ribboned bouquet of daisies instead of a wreath of maidenblush roses with orange blossoms. The daisies meant far more, especially since they'd come from Frank. So what if she hadn't had an engagement reception or a bridal party in which her friends would give her cruets, vases, figurines, and memory books. The intentions were here, and just thinking about Frank giving her his name made her overcome with emotion. She struggled to hold back the tears gathering in her eyes. She couldn't look at Reverend Thorpe or at Frank; if she did, she'd start to cry. She kept her gaze safely downward as the clergyman finished his speech on conduct and duty.

"Do you, Amelia Ruth Marshall, take Frank Wolfgang Brody to be your lawfully wedded husband?" Reverend Thorpe asked. "For fairer or fouler, for better or worse, for richer or poorer?"

Amelia was so stunned to hear Frank's unusual middle name, her reply wasn't forthcoming.

"Miss Marshall?" the reverend queried with a raised brow over the edge of his black Bible.

She wet her dry lips and swallowed. "I do."

Reverend Thorpe turned to Frank. "Do you, Frank Wolfgang Brody, take Amelia Ruth Marshall to be your lawfully wedded wife? For fairer or fouler, for better or worse, for richer or poorer?"

"I do." Frank's deep voice carried through the rectory without a hint of doubt.

"Is there a ring?" Reverend Thorpe asked.

Amelia gazed at Frank, wondering. He put his hand into his right trouser pocket and came out with a ring. "I have one."

The reverend took the ring, put it on his closed Bible and said, "Bless this ring and the linking of these two lives. The form of the ring being circular— that is round and without end—is important in this way: that mutual love and hearty affection should roundly flow from one to the other, as in a circle, continually and forever." He gave Frank the ring back. "You may place the ring on her fourth finger."

Amelia handed her daisies to Narcissa. Frank reached for Amelia's hand and took it firmly in his. Her fingers trembled as the gold band touched her fingertip. He fit the ring smoothly down her finger, pushing it as far back on her hand as it would go. She stared at the gems in awe. She wore an iridescent opal surrounded by eight petite diamonds.

Her throat closed, and she blinked. It was the loveliest ring she'd ever seen. And it was hers forever.

Frank meshed his fingers with hers and lowered their hands to their sides. He didn't let her go as the reverend concluded the ceremony.

"Inasmuch as you both have pledged your love and bequeathed your worldly goods to each other by way of the symbol of this ring, from this day forward, you shall have and hold in the bosom of your hearts the life of your mate, in sickness and in health, until death do you part. By the powers vested in me as a minister of God, I can pronounce you man and wife. Amen."

Amelia let out a sigh as Frank took her into his arms and kissed her softly on the lips.

Her first kiss as a married lady. It was different from his kisses before. This one tasted of love and comfort and the many promising years to come.

Frank sat on a cane-seat stool in Amelia's spotless kitchen, watching her fix dinner. Since they'd gotten married in the late afternoon, she'd insisted on making him a wedding supper.

He wasn't hungry but he let her go through the motions, having the suspicion she needed a diversion. It went unspoken that tonight they'd be sleeping in the same bed. She had a fragile panic written all over her lovely face, and it bothered him. He wondered how much she knew about wedding nights.

They'd left the church separately, he going off to the Moon Rock to pack his belongings, she to her house. While he was in the saloon, he'd poured himself a short bracer of straight bourbon to fortify his nerves. As soon as the Rev had pronounced them husband and wife, the enormity of what he'd done hit him like a fist.

He was married.

Bound to an institution for which he had no training. He'd never observed a loving couple; Jack and Charlotte had never been considerate of each other.

But Frank was man enough to know how to treat a lady. He was also astute enough to know there was a lot more to matrimonial living than considerate manners. Narcissa Dodge had been opposed to their spontaneous wedding and initially refused to stand up for them. It had taken his word of honor to convince Narcissa that he'd been seriously considering marrying Amelia regardless. Narcissa pointed out that damage had been done before the wedding ring was on

Amelia's finger, and there would still be gossip. Was he willing to put everything aside and make Amelia the most important thing in his life? He'd assured Narcissa if he wasn't certain he was the right man for Amelia, he wouldn't be marrying her.

"Do you like greens?" Amelia asked him from her position in front of the sink.

He lifted his gaze to hers, noting she was as nervous as a long-tailed cat under a rocking chair.

"Greens are all right."

"And ham?" she squeaked. "If you don't like ham," she went on in a rush, "I could prepare something else."

"Ham is fine."

"Good, because I baked a small ham the night before last." She efficiently pivoted toward her icebox and opened the door. Removing a covered pot, she took out the cold meat and put it on a pastry board. She cut a few slices, then dropped them into a hot frying pan on her range plate. The sizzling noise made her jump. "I could scramble some eggs," she offered with a faint tremor to her voice.

"I don't want any eggs."

"That's right. You said you make egg sandwiches." She kept her slender back to him. He let his gaze wander down the length of her spine, to the nip in her waist where the wide bow of her apron was tied, and lastly over the flare her skirts made at her hips. "I'm sure you're tired of eggs," she said with an airy laugh he sensed was artificial from tension. He studied her tidy hair in the sunlight, thinking he could unpin the curls and watch them tumble down whenever he wanted.

He wanted to now.

She had to lean a little to the left to reach for a utensil she had on the stovepipe shelf. He viewed the profile of her upper body, the outline of her breasts in the form-fitted shirtwaist she wore. He wouldn't have to wonder what she looked like naked. Now he'd be able to see the color of her nipples.

He wanted to see them now.

Using a two-pronged kitchen fork, she turned the slices of ham. "I'm sorry I don't have any cherry pie left. I could make a marble cake, but it wouldn't be ready to eat for a while."

"I don't want any cake."

"Oh. Well if you change your mind, it would be no trouble."

As she moved to the sink to rinse the salad, her skirts made a rustling sound he found sensual. The fabric of her petticoats whispered, no doubt caressing her bloomer-covered thighs with their satiny touch. He visualized the luscious flesh of her legs.

He wanted them around his hips now.

"I do have peach butter and some leftover biscuits," she chattered. "At least I think I have some peach butter left." Pausing, she pressed her forefinger to her mouth in thought.

He wanted to kiss her lips now.

"If I don't have any peach butter, I'm sure I have plum jam."

What he really wanted was her to stop talking. He might have told her as much if she hadn't suddenly turned to face him and announced, "Supper is finished. You may go to the table."

Frank stood, the muscles in his body burning from the blood pounding through him. The degree to which he was responding to her stunned him. He'd had women before. He'd felt the physical release of pleasure and knew the gratification of fulfillment. But for Amelia he felt a rush of sexual desire rising in him like the hottest fire, clouding his brain.

It took every ounce of self-control not to touch her.

Instead, he went through the motions of allowing

her to show him to the dining room, since she seemed determined to make him something to eat. But he didn't want food.

He wanted to devour his wife. Now.

Every last inch of her.

He chose the first chair his hand touched, hell-bent on getting the meal over with as quickly as possible. But before his behind could make contact with the cushion, Amelia cried, "That's where I always sit!"

Tilting his head, he stole a slanted look at her. Visibly distressed by her outburst, she wrung her hands together. "I'm sorry. Of course you may sit there. That's the head of the table, and you're the head of the household now."

"If this is where you always sit, Amelia, then this is where you'll continue to sit."

"But you're the husband."

"Yeah, well, I'm not really one yet," Frank remarked, the suggestive innuendo going over Amelia's head. She stared at him with wide brown eyes, and he still refused to sit in her chair. He picked the one across from hers, slid the legs out, and wedged himself into the seat.

Absently drumming his fingers over the tablecloth, he waited for her to move. She didn't budge. He spoke in an even tone meant to move her into action. "Is that the ham I smell?"

Her brows shot up, and she gasped, "It's burning!" Then she took off in a flurry.

He heard a lot of metal noise, the pump hinge drawing water, and Amelia's series of little coughs. The kitchen grew quiet after that. He waited a few seconds, the showy wall clock slowly ticking them off. "Sweetheart, are you okay in there?"

She didn't answer.

He wondered if she was crying and was just about to investigate when she came into the dining room. She held a tray laden with two plates, a strained smile taxing her lips. She set one before him, and he gazed at the smoking ham on the fine china. There was a biscuit next to the charred meat, and a salad without dressing.

Wordlessly, she took her seat.

He stared at her through the gap between the unlit yellowed candles and a centerpiece vase of drooping daisies. Her bridal bouquet, to be exact. With a punctuated sigh, she unfolded her napkin and let it sail primly to her lap. Picking up her fork, she gazed at her plate but didn't make a move to eat a thing.

A difficult silence cloaked the room.

"I'm sorry," she murmured in a thick voice. "It's not like me to burn something. It won't happen again." She sniffed, and he could tell she was holding back her tears.

Her show of brittle emotion worsened the situation, and he couldn't restrain himself any longer. He stood with a suddenness that made her chin snap upward and her eyes grow large. Bracing the tabletop with the flat of his palms, he put his weight on his arms. "Quit being so goddamn polite. I don't want to eat. You don't want to eat. We don't have to pretend we want to eat."

He saw her swallow hard, but once he got going, he couldn't hold anything back. "I don't want you to apologize to me. It's not flattering to you, Amelia. I like you better when you give me a piece of your mind, so stop being so considerate and keep your chair. I don't give a flying cocktail shaker where I sit."

"But—"

"But nothing. It doesn't matter. Nothing as insignificant does. So you burned the ham. Who cares? I don't."

Her shoulders quaked and he swore.

"Ah, Christ, sweetheart. Don't cry."

"It's just that I wanted everything so perfect," she said in a tiny voice.

Frank sharply nudged his chair back; it tipped over with a dry bang. He didn't flinch. He walked the length of the table, his mouth set in a tight line.

Amelia started and dropped her fork. The metal clinked on the edge of her plate before falling noisily to the floor.

Frank reached for her, took her firmly by the elbow, and made her stand up. He could feel her trembling. Goddammit, he didn't want her afraid of him. Moving with a definite gentleness, he tucked her into the protection of his arms. With restrained strength, he tenderly pushed her into him; her breasts were crushed against his chest. Pinning her between his legs, he cradled the back of her head in his hand and stared into her moist eyes. He felt an ache inside him; he felt her hurt, her fear. It pained him. Deeply.

Lowering his head, he consoled her, his lips brushing the shell of her ear. "Things are perfect." He kissed the arch of her silky smooth neck. She tasted so good. She felt so warm. "Relax, Amelia. It's me. It's Frank. You know I don't bite . . ." He lightly nipped her earlobe. ". . . unless you want me to."

He felt her breasts rising and falling; he heard her labored breath snag in her throat. He slid his hand up her back so he could hold her face between his palms and kiss her fully on the mouth. Her lips were parted, and she moaned as he met her. He kissed her a long time, savoring her, experiencing her. She clung to him, her arms wrapped around his middle, light and weak. He felt himself leaning into her, pushing her up against the table's edge for support.

The fullness of her breasts rubbed his shirtfront, the friction of fabric to fabric singeing his already hot skin. He moved his hands upward, the pads of his thumbs massaging, stroking the sensitive skin behind her ears. He felt her hair, his fingers reaching for the pins that kept it bound. He found several and plucked them from her carefully styled curls. The silken strands felt like the coolest ribbons around his fingers. He inhaled the feminine fragrance of her hair as it wafted around them. Kissing her deeper, harder, he bent her back a little further.

She spoke against his lips, her voice hitched and faint. "Are you going to sweep the dishes to the floor and lay me over the table?"

He inhaled sharply. "Jesus . . . do you want me to?" he asked while catching her full lower lip with his teeth and running his tongue over the velvety softness of her mouth.

She gasped. Her hands tightened to fists, bunching the thin linen of his shirt in her grasp. "I don't know . . . I didn't make you fried chicken . . . and the dishes . . . they're my best ones."

"Then I won't break them."

He stroked the inside of her mouth with his tongue, touching her, teasing her. She met him, reserved at first, then returned the kiss just as ardently. He moved his hand downward, over her breast, cupping the mound with his palm.

She didn't stop him, but she made a low noise. A groaning sound that dissolved on his wet lips. The heat that slashed through him was fierce. His mind was blinded. Their rapid breaths filled the dining room, a reminder of where they were. He broke his mouth from hers, and they gazed into each other's eyes for several frantic heartbeats.

Without a word, he bent slightly at the knees and scooped her into his arms. He moved under the wide archway curtained with glass beads and took long, purposeful strides into the parlor. The contact of her body, the imprint of her breast next to his ribs, and her fingers curled into his shoulder left him with only one thought in his head.

Getting her on the first bed he could find.

He took the stairs, went past the water closet, and nudged open the first door he came to with the toe of his boot. The small room was scattered with a miscellany of *objets d'art,* including a painted plaster bust of an Indian maiden. There was a marble-topped table, several plump sitting chairs, but no bed.

"This is my sewing room." Her words were husky, lower than normal.

Taking a step backward, he entered the next room down. The sunset filled the area with hues of orange, casting a large brass bed with plump pillows in beckoning brilliance.

He'd found the mother lode.

Barely planting his heel in the room, Amelia panted in a rush, "No! Not this room. We can't . . . not here."

Shafts of fire were shooting through his groin, and his brain wasn't up for a lengthy debate. "Why not?"

"This is my aunt Clara's bedroom."

"I don't want to sound crass, sweetheart, but she's not using it."

"Of course she's not." Amelia reacted with outrage. "But this was her bed, and I could never . . . that is . . . this was where she slept. Where . . . where she died."

Frank did his best to refrain from swearing foully. "I have slept in beds active with snakes, lizards, scorpions, centipedes, bugs, and fleas. I've slept standing, sitting, lying down, doubled up, and hanging over, twisted, punched, jammed and elbowed by drunken men, snored at, sat upon, rained upon, snowed upon, and bitten by frost. So I can honestly tell you, I have never been kept out of a bed because a dead woman used to sleep on it!" He squeezed his eyes closed, but feeling her struggle against his pelvis didn't help matters. The fullness of his erection behind the placket of his trousers was torture. He'd be damned if he'd put her down now. Not until he could lay her on a mattress and cover her body with his. "Where's your bedroom?" he asked, his voice hoarse.

"My bedroom . . . our bedroom is this one." She

motioned to the door across from where he was standing.

He was inside in a second, bumping the edge of the door with his elbow; the force reverberated the joints in the house.

The setting sun didn't lend much light through the eastern facing window. Dark shadows painted the flock-papered walls, but he could see the silhouette of a bed. It looked too delicate and narrow to hold both of them.

Regardless, he carried her straight to it.

His knee depressed the white crocheted spread; the woven wire mattress made a thirsty squeak from his weight. A lascivious thought flashed through his mind that tonight they were going to make the bed creak as it never had before.

Conjuring the image of naked legs, entwined arms, and fused junctions had him depositing her on the coverlet with a raw grunt. As her head met the pillow, her radiant hair fanned around her flushed face. She looked like an angel—pure and pale. Her lips were swollen from his kisses, damp and full.

His heart opened, and he let her enter him as physically as if he'd put his sex in her body. She was his.

Christ, what had he done to deserve her?

The Rev's words slipped into his thoughts. Thorpe had said love was the crowning grace of humanity, the holiest right of the soul, and the redeeming principle that reconciled the heart to life and eternal good.

Because religion had been beaten into him, Frank rebelled against believing in God. He took the Lord's name in vain all the time. It meant nothing to him. But looking into Amelia's eyes, searching their depths, he conceded that maybe there really was a place of infinity. If there was, he wanted to experience it now. He wanted to feel heaven, sheathed by Amelia. His wife.

"Have you changed your mind?" she asked in a tremulous whisper.

He answered her by dipping his mouth on hers. He kissed her as if he'd die if he didn't, reveling in her soft curves next to his hard muscles. She moaned but not with pleasure. It dawned on him he was too heavy for her, and he shifted his weight to his side. He skimmed his hand across her arm and over the gentle swell of her breast. He could just barely make out the pointed tip of her nipple through the layers of her clothing.

"Sit up."

He helped her, sitting up as well, and began working the cloth-covered buttons of her shirtwaist through the tiny holes. His fingers were large, and he felt clumsy. Amelia didn't offer to help him. She sat there, her lower lip caught between her teeth. He wasn't going to ask her to do anything for him. Not the first time.

Tugging on the end of her shirt, he pulled the silk free and unfastened the last small button. He peeled the sleeves down her shoulders, pooling the fabric around her waist. She wore a snowy corset cover with tiny roses embroidered around the neck. Slowly, he untied the three satin ribbons holding the front closed. She trembled. He reassured her with a fleeting kiss that turned into more because she gripped his shoulders and pulled him toward her. He guessed she was stalling, thinking perhaps a kiss would be enough.

But it wasn't.

And he intended to show her how much more there was.

He didn't break away from her mouth while he unclasped the long row of hooks keeping her corset tight around her slender waist. When he withdrew the heavy piece of canvas and steel, she exhaled into his mouth. Her open lips were too much of an invitation and he partnered his tongue with hers. Impatiently, he lifted the hem of her chemise so he could feel her bare breasts. His thumbs stroked her wrinkled nipples with a light graze.

Watching her face, he asked, "Does that feel good?"

She squeezed her eyes closed and mutely nodded.

"Then relax. It gets better." Without her being aware of it, he leaned her back onto the mattress. He laced his fingers through hers and put their hands over her head. His eyes fastened on the creamy whiteness of her breasts, the dusky nipples. He bent forward and took one into his mouth, rolling his tongue around the tight bead. She squeezed his hands with surprising strength.

The textures of her body, her erotic scent, swam in his head. He knew he should undress her completely. Hell, and undress himself. But the need to bury himself inside her pulled at him, stressing the cords of his taut muscles.

He rested his forehead between the valley of her breasts, his hair falling over his brow. Bunching the fabric of her skirt in his fist, he brought the fullness up to her waist. He pressed his palm on her flat stomach, lowering his hand until he came to the open crotch of her drawers. He instantly felt her stiffen.

"Don't," he murmured. "Don't." He nudged her locked thighs apart with his knee. He wedged himself between her legs, putting the bulk of his weight on his elbows so she could get used to him. When he felt the tension in her slacken, he began rocking his pelvis slowly back and forth over her.

The bed springs cried out in rusty protest.

Sweat collected on his forehead, but he kept the rhythm until Amelia groaned, clasped the back of his neck and brought his lips to hers. She kissed him, turning him to liquid fire. Still, he kept the same motion until she tentatively raised her hips to meet his. To match his tempo. He was so thick and swollen, he hurt.

"Do something," Amelia pleaded in a silky whisper.

Frank one-handed the buttons on his fly and freed himself without removing his trousers or drawers. He felt her entrance, felt the heat radiating from within. She was slick. He pushed himself inside her, slow and smooth, until he could go no further in the tightness surrounding him. There was no other way to go on other than to thrust quickly. He captured her mouth with his, silencing her cry of pain, trying to stay focused and move with control. He held himself back, poised on the brink of release. He wanted her to come with him, to be fulfilled.

"Let go, Amelia."

She said in a shaky voice, "I'm trying."

He moved—stronger, deeper. "Relax. Feel us. Together."

His hips began to move faster. He couldn't hold out much longer. As it was, he'd been so caught up in her, he hadn't even taken his clothes off.

He stared down at Amelia. Her eyes were closed.

The heat, the friction, his mind in a haze, he felt the last borders of his restraint crumble. He climaxed, pouring his soul and his life into his wife.

He collapsed on top of her, nestling the hollow of her shoulder with his nose. His blood pounded in his ears. Amelia lay beneath him, motionless. The air in the room was hot and moist from his labored breathing. Her heart tattooed in an even beat with his. Words failed him. He was a fool to the pleasure she gave him.

He slowly lifted his head and gazed at Amelia.

She refused to meet his eyes, but her expression was riddled with disappointment that speared him straight in the gut.

"Excuse me," she whispered brokenly. "I have to use the water closet."

Chapter

19

Amelia sat on the wooden lid over the water closet, her elbows digging into her knees, and her chin resting on the heels of her hands. Both the four-paneled entry doors to the diminutive chamber—the one leading to the hallway and the one leading to her bedroom— were shut and bolted. She'd changed into her cambric lawn wrapper and was debating taking a lukewarm bath. She was sore, but despite her discomfort, her breasts continued to tingle. Her mouth still craved Frank's dominating kisses. She felt as though she were blindly grasping for something but wasn't able to reach it.

The door connecting the bathroom with her room rattled. She lifted her gaze to the skeleton key in the lock. The white porcelain knob jiggled. Severely.

"Amelia, unlock the door."

"I'm indisposed." Without looking, she reached behind her and grabbed the chain pull above her head. She gave it an absent tug. The rush of water from the tank sloshed through the pipes in the wall and gurgled.

As she brought her arm down, her gown's flowing cuff fell back, exposing her wrist. She plucked the Valenciennes lace and rearranged the gathers. The last vestiges of daylight crawled through the windowpanes with just enough luminance to accent the fire of her opal and diamond ring. She held out her hand, fingers apart, and examined her wedding ring.

"Amelia." There was an impatient edge to Frank's voice, and he shook the lock in the jamb. "Open the door."

"I'm occupied." She rolled the Honest Count toilet paper backward for a few revolutions in its bronze fixture to make it sound like she was using it.

She didn't like deceiving him, but she couldn't face her husband.

Not yet.

She should have pretended. She should have made him believe she'd liked it. Actually, that wasn't true. She had loved—been thrilled by—everything he'd done to her up until he . . . when they'd joined. The knifelike pain, the largeness of him stretching her, had caught her by surprise. Even when he returned to the sensual tempo of his hips grinding into hers, she hadn't been able to relax.

She'd been scared to death he was going to break her.

Amelia stared at her bare feet, curling her toes under. She wasn't ignorant about sex. But she and Narcissa had never had a conversation about it with much depth. It simply wasn't a topic one lady discussed with another. The particulars of coupling were supposedly left up to a bride's mother to relate.

That thought saddened Amelia. Though she highly doubted Ruth Marshall would have reviewed boudoir conduct with her, at least she could have had the opportunity to ask her mother general details—if she'd gotten up enough courage. Which she probably wouldn't have anyway.

"Amelia," Frank called through the barrier. "If you don't unlock the door, I'm going to bust it in."

She rose from the water closet, unable to prolong her exile any longer. He would make good on his promise if she didn't let him in. Before clicking the key in the lock, she made sure her wrapper was demurely covering her up to her neck.

The door instantly swung inward as soon as she unbolted it. Frank filled up the opening with his great height. He was fully dressed and, she quickly noted, the closure to his trousers was buttoned in place. However, the masculine definition behind the placket suddenly made her feel very accessible. She shouldn't have taken her remaining clothes off, but she'd headed for the bathroom in such haste, she'd left half her apparel behind. Her only means of fully concealing herself had been her wrapper, which she kept hanging on a hook behind the door. Her Mother Hubbard nightgown was stored in her dresser.

She raised her hand to her throat, keeping the high collar in place. "Yes, Frank?"

Even in the barren light, she could see his scowl. "What were you doing in here so long?"

"I was conducting matters of a private nature." She walked around him with forced calm while her pulse strummed an uneven beat at her wrists. She wasn't the least bit tired, but what else was there left for them to do but go to sleep? Night had all but fallen outside, the broad branches of her linden tree snuffing out the sunset's fragments. She noted Frank had lit the kerosene lamp on her bureau, but kept the wick low. The light wasn't much, just enough for her to view her tousled bedclothes.

She was glad for the semi-darkness; it hid the hot flush of embarrassment burning her cheeks. The image of them paired on the cramped bed flashed through her mind. Veiled in soaring degrees of passion, she'd abandoned herself to his virility. She'd wanted . . . let him . . . reveled in . . . his mouth tasting her body. But without intense desire making her limbs weak, she'd grown suddenly, and horribly, self-conscious around him.

She felt Frank close in behind her. He slid his wide hands around her middle and put his chin on the curve of her shoulder. The stubby bristles of his evening beard caught in her hair, and he smoothed a curl over her ear. She shivered, fighting against closing her eyes; she couldn't help leaning into him, pressing her back against the supple muscles of his chest. His arms were like an iron vise, gently squeezing her waist, keeping her close and giving her a sense of protection.

He nestled his open mouth on the side of her throat, kissing her lightly. "Don't run away from me. I won't hurt you like that again. I swear."

She ached with an inner pain, a thirst left unquenched. "It's all right."

"No it's not."

His words of apology coiled around her breasts, disintegrating her willpower. Her eyes shut, locking out the flickering shadows; the flood tide of blackness behind her eyelids intensified her other senses. She could hear him breathing low and deep. She could smell the salt of his sated sweat and a vague trace of liquor and tobacco that lingered on his skin molded over the sinewy slabs of muscle and bone that defined his torso beneath his thin shirt.

The roughness of his hands snagged the delicate material of her wrapper. "This time, I promise, you'll feel like one of the skyrockets Beamguard shot up on the Fourth."

She responded to the resonant inflection of his voice; she angled her head back. The reaction was involuntary. She didn't think she could take getting all heated up again without letting go. Without finding some kind of release. Inasmuch as she wanted to believe him, she didn't think feeling like a shooting rocket was possible. "It's all right," she said again. "I can make us some tea and we can forget about it."

"*It?* It's called making love, Amelia." His palm supported her chin and he kissed her jaw. "And I don't want to forget. I want you to come apart, sweetheart. Let go."

A groan went by her throat. She wanted to let go. She'd tried to let go, but Amelia Ruth Marshall Brody was apparently too much like her mother and aunt. She was as rigid as a washboard and just as stiff as a collar with too much starch.

Rather than be unsatisfied a second time, she fought against Frank. Not very hard. She put her hands on his arms and tried to pry them off her. He only held on tighter, his lips searing the side of her neck.

"Frank . . . really . . . we don't have to."

Before she could realize what he was doing, he lifted her off her feet and carried her to the bed. "We have to."

The tired springs, the worn-in sounds that had been a nightly comfort at the end of a long day, now grated like a shameless hussy in her ears. She hadn't been oblivious to the noise they'd made when Frank had been moving above her.

He put his knees on either side of her hips, straddling her, but not lowering his weight on her. His thick black hair spilled over his brow and brushed her temple when he leaned over to kiss her forehead.

She shivered, the ends of his hair on her skin tickling her, exciting her. His thumbs and fingertips fell on her collarbone and shoulders, and he began to massage the tension out of her muscles. The urge to resist him reduced. The stiff way in which she'd locked her legs to keep them together tapered off. Her knees softened, hitting the insides of Frank's thighs.

She didn't want him to see her, so she closed her eyes tight. She felt the muscles in his legs as he moved his upper body; she heard the slow slide of linen as he slid his shirt down his arms. Then his lips were on hers. She opened her mouth in a last ditch effort to tell him this really wasn't necessary. Instead of words coming out, she felt a sleek texture, a sweep of her mouth with a tongue. He flicked her teeth, tasted and teased her until her hands rose to grip his straining biceps. His arms were smooth and cool as marble.

He caught her lower lip with his teeth. "Open your eyes."

She did. Her hands spread wide on his chest, her fingers twining through the coarse dark hair that grew around his flat brown nipples.

He leaned back on his knees and began to unbutton the waist of her wrapper. His knuckles skimmed her throat as the dainty lawn separated. She watched his eyes, staying focused on them as he pulled her gown open. His pupils grew dark, ringed by a blue that looked smoky in the skimpy light.

She reacted to him. To her embarrassment, her nipples turned tight and pronounced. He cupped her breasts in his hands, gently kneading them, intermittently flicking his thumbs over the hard areolas. Her back arched off the bed.

He bent his head and suckled her nipple, stimulating her with his tongue until she was helplessly squirming and moaning beneath him. She clutched at him, that fierce heat threatening to bubble over inside her again. She forgot to be modest and proper. Her hands came to rest in his hair, ensnaring the flowing mane between her fingers to keep his head close to her breast.

"Are you seeing any colors yet, Amelia?" he asked, his wet tongue darting over her, moist and hot.

"Y-Yes."

"Good." He kneeled back and tugged on the half belt that kept her wrapper together. She was barely aware of him pulling her arms out of the sleeves.

Her gaze fell to the indentation of his navel and the line of hair that dipped into his waistband. She saw the impression of his body, thick and long. Her pulse skipped a beat. She was hit with the strongest urge to tell him no.

The flat of his hands came to rest on her stomach, and she jolted when he lowered his fingertips to her most private place. She was too shocked to move. "You're so warm." He found the center and traced her with the pad of his thumb.

"You can't do that!" she gasped. She tried to sit up, but he put his hand on her shoulder to keep her still.

"I can." He began to rub her back and forth, in unhurried strokes.

She knew things weren't going to be any different this time. How could they be? She was feeling the same swirling sensations as before. And before she'd been let down by her own body. She wanted to hold back. She tried. But he kept touching her; that intimate part of her that was exposed and sensitive. He stroked her faster until her entire being was on fire. The flames fanned across her skin, assaulting her with a tide of heat that radiated from her every pore. She squeezed her legs together and grabbed for Frank. Her fingers gripped his waist while she struggled to capture and unleash the feeling that was at the threshold of her senses.

Just when she felt the first waves, he took his hands away.

She might as well have fallen off the bed when he ceased. "Why did you stop?" she panted. "I think I could have . . . I would have . . ."

"You will." The caress of his lips on her parched mouth didn't make her feel any better. "We will together."

Frank unfastened his trousers, pulled them down over his hips and kicked them off his legs. He wore white drawers. The crotch was tight, and the finely combed cotton cupped him like the palm of a glove. Her mind burned with the memory of seeing him in a pair similar to these with the buttons undone and fitting him so snugly, they stayed up.

Using just his right hand, he popped open the three pearl fasteners with his thumbnail. The first time they'd done this, she hadn't seen anything. She'd only felt him.

A dark wedge of tight curls contrasted next to the snowy band of his drawers as he slipped them lower. Before she could even think to breathe, he pushed his underwear off and pitched it over the side of the bed to the floor.

She hadn't realized she'd closed her eyes again until his low voice melted through her. "Look at me."

She gazed at his face, cast in half shadow, unable to look any lower. His chiseled expression encouraged her to explore. She didn't dare. Instead she said in a tiny voice, "Maybe if you kiss me . . ."

"Where?" he asked, changing the position of their legs and separating her thighs with his knees. "Where do you want me to kiss you?"

"Don't make me say it."

He held his upper body over hers, keeping his arms straight so the flat of his belly didn't touch her. His mouth came down on hers, his teeth nipped at her lower lip. "Here?" He bent his head lower, his tongue flicking over one of her nipples. "Here?" He moved between her breasts and kissed her breastbone. "Here?" He went lower and she suddenly realized his intentions.

"No! Not . . . no!"

"Don't you want to feel what it's like to be kissed . . . here?" His hands spread her inner thighs wide, his knuckles brushing her skin until they reached between her pliant legs.

"No . . . I . . . it's too . . . no. Don't."

"I won't if you don't want me to." His fingers began

to move over her nest of hair the same way they had before. He made swirling patterns with his thumbs, over and over, that made her blood pound in her head.

She braced her hands on his chest, her palms on his rigid nipples.

"Come apart, Amelia," he directed. "Let go." Sweat bathed his face, the hair crowning his forehead. The veins in his taut arms stood out on his tanned skin. She could see he fought to control the rhythm that was sending her over the edge. She struggled to take what he was giving her. She began to unravel; her desire overrode everything else.

She gasped when his fiery heat probed her entrance. He burrowed into her, and she waited for the discomfort. There was a moment's dull pain, but he kept massaging her, making her feel so good, she didn't recognize the soreness. He thrust again. She tried to keep her hips on the bed, but in an instinctive movement, they raised to meet him.

He fit neatly into her this time, rocking her against him. The friction of his movements, his body and hands, undulated through her. Each time he withdrew, he went deeper when he settled back inside.

It was his hoarse voice that finally broke her down. He kept urging her, "Let go. Let go. Let go," between the chanting squeak of the bedsprings.

At last, her breath came in long surrendering moans. His seduction had worked. He freed her in a bursting of sensations. She fell into a vortex of light, an explosion of dazzling color that had showered the Fourth of July night.

He lowered his head, kissed her hard, catching her sighs on his mouth. She wrapped her arms around his neck, holding him close. Groaning, he pushed hard, clinging to her. She felt the muscles on his back bunch and strain as he shuddered.

And then he stilled.

The tiny bedroom was filled with the sounds of their heavy breathing and rampant heartbeats; with the musky scents of their sex-spent bodies.

To Amelia's utter chagrin, she started quietly crying.

"You're not going to run to the water closet again, are you?" Frank had withdrawn from her and put the bulk of his torso on his elbow, his face creased with concern.

She shook her head no, but she was thoroughly shaken.

"Then why are you crying?"

She blinked her lashes, hot tears spilling into the shells of her ears and tickling them.

"What's the matter, sweetheart?" Frank pushed her rumpled hair from her brows. "Jesus. I didn't hurt you again, did I? I thought . . . ah, hell. I felt you . . . so I . . ."

She gulped loudly, trying not to outright sob.

"Amelia, Amelia, Amelia," he shushed. "Don't cry."

"I can't help it." She gazed into his eyes. "It's just that . . . I love you, Frank."

He stared at her, speechless.

It wounded her that he didn't say the words back, but she wasn't sorry she'd said them. "I just wanted you to know . . . that's all."

A tender smile lurked on the corners of his mouth as his thumb wiped her tears from her skin. "I'm glad you told me." His lips touched hers. Softly, warmly, barely brushing. Then he laid on his side, put his left hand on her shoulder, and turned her to face him. His fingers stroked her arm, caressing, cuddling.

The light from the lamp silhouetted him from behind. His hair appeared darker than pitch and fell over his neck. The shadow of his beard put a rugged strength on his face that she appreciated. The full lines of his brows bridged his mellow blue eyes. Within their depths, she saw fragments of all the emotion-charged expressions he'd ever given her.

It was easy to get lost in the way he looked, and it was no wonder every girl in town thought he was handsome. She felt a glorified sense of satisfaction knowing that when they stared longingly at him now, they'd be staring at her man.

"There's something I've been wondering," she said, reaching out to him, too tempted by his disordered hair not to touch the cool thickness.

"What?"

"How did you get the middle name Wolfgang?"

He laughed with a dry and mildly humorous sound. "That's what the Rev wanted to know when he asked me for my full name."

"Well?"

"Have you ever heard of the poetic drama *Faust?*"

"Is it about someone who enters a pact with the devil?"

"Yes. A magician, to be exact." He inhaled, his nostrils flaring. His deep breath sounded more like a shiver of vivid recollection. "Johann Wolfgang von Goethe wrote *Faust.* My parents were performing the play at the Haymarket Theater in San Francisco when my mother went into labor." His gaze lowered, as did his voice. "I was born in the orchestra pit. As my mother told it, my father cursed her ill timing and would have nothing to do with my delivery. So the conductor shouted for something to wrap me in. He was handed his stack of sheet music, and I was swaddled in the melody he'd written for the performance. For all I know, he was the one who named me," he said, trailing his fingertips down her forearm and raising her gooseflesh.

"Hmm." She longed to ask him other questions—personal ones about his childhood, why it had been cut short, and more about his parents, about Harry.

She sensed his mother and father held the key to why he'd said he didn't care either way about children. She didn't want to believe he wouldn't desire a child because she so hoped to have one with him.

Although she wanted to know all about Frank, she feared any interrogation, no matter how subtly phrased, would ruin this precious moment. Instead, she contented herself to touch him, learn him on the outside; touching and learning him on the inside would come later.

Her hand in his hair slid to the hard curve of his shoulder and down his solid bicep. The light covering of hair on his forearm didn't disguise the crescent-shaped scar that marred him. She ran her finger over the small protrusion. "Did a piece of the moon really come out of the sky and cut you on the arm?"

"No."

"So the rock in the saloon isn't from the moon?"

"No. I found it in the bottom of a Mojave crater."

She traced the mark on his skin. "Then how did this happen?"

"In a bar fight. A guy used my arm to shatter a liquor bottle."

"What were you fighting about?"

"A woman."

"Oh." She was sorry she asked.

"I can't remember her name. I was drunk. I don't do that much anymore."

"What?"

"Get drunk."

"Why not?"

He gave her a lopsided smile. "Because I own a drunkard's haven."

She grew thoughtful for a moment before sitting up. She would have been self-conscious of her nakedness if she hadn't had her hair to hide her breasts. She used the long brown waves to cover herself as Frank rolled onto his back. His hand came toward her and he playfully tugged on the ends of hair that fell to her waist. "Where are you going?"

"You reminded me of something." She tried to disengage her wrapper from them, but Frank was resting on most of it. He had no problem lying there completely nude, but she wasn't used to his lack of clothing. She kept an unwavering gaze on his face, certain he could tell it was no accident she didn't move her stare lower.

"Lift up so I can get my wrapper," she directed when he didn't budge.

"What for? I like you wearing just your wedding ring."

"You're incorrigible."

"I could be more than that if you give me a minute."

Through the din of his implication, she breathed one word. "Again?"

"Oh, yeah."

A new and unexpected warmth surged through her. "Could we wait until after I give you your present?"

"We have all night, sweetheart." Then his eyebrows slanted in a frown. "What present? You're going to make me feel bad I don't have anything for you."

"You're wrong. You already gave me my present." She held up her hand. "My wedding ring, silly. And besides, my present really isn't a present. It's more like a symbol that seals our vows. So let me have my wrapper and I'll go get it."

Frank lifted his hips and she pulled the gown free. When her arms were in the sleeves, she attempted to climb over him. He brought her down against his chest and kissed her soundly on the lips. "I don't want you going far."

"I'm not."

He released her and she left the bedroom, tying her wrapper as she walked. She went to her aunt Clara's room, opened the dusty, mirror-backed bureau, and sorted through the linens. When she found what she was looking for, she padded quietly back to her bedroom.

Frank rested his head on his folded arms, one long leg bent at the knee. He'd undone the bedclothes, the end of the bleached sheeting draped across his middle. She went to him, and he slid over enough for her to sit on the side of the narrow bed.

"I have something for you."

"What?"

She held out her closed fist. "Open your hand."

He did. His palm was wide and large, and she dropped her gift into it. He stared at the brass key, then up at her.

"It's a key to my house," she said proudly. "I have a key to your saloon. But now that we're married, both the house and the saloon are ours. Everything we have, we have together."

He closed his fingers around the key. "I guess that means you finally own that piano, huh?"

She bit her lip to downplay her grin of delight. "I hadn't thought of that."

"Am I going to find it missing one day and discover it in the parlor downstairs?"

"No. Things seem to be working out at the Moon Rock, so I think I'll keep it there until our other one comes."

"I appreciate that."

She smiled, so happy she was beside herself.

He smiled back and let the key drop out of his hand. It fell silently to the floor on his discarded shirt. "Come here."

She went into his arms, and he brought her back to his side. As they faced each other, he gave her a kiss on the tip of her nose. "You know, this bed isn't going to work out too well. My feet are hanging over the edge. I guess we'll just have to stay up all night so I don't have to figure out how I'm going to sleep in it."

"I don't want it to be morning yet either."

"You don't?"

"No. I don't want you to see me in the light of day. Not after . . . you know."

"You mean not after you saw Red Devils?" he teased.

Groaning, she buried her burning face against his chest, but he wouldn't let her hide. His fingers captured her chin, and he made her look into his eyes. "Don't, Amelia. Never feel like what we do is something you have to be embarrassed over. You're beautiful, and I intend to show you how much. Over and over."

Her arms went around him, and she pressed her cheek to his. "Do you know how happy you've made me? I never thought I'd get married. I never thought I'd have somebody like you."

"Me neither," he whispered in her hair.

For a while, they held each other in the drowsy warmth of the bed, both quiet and thinking.

"Amelia?"

"Yes?"

Several mindful seconds later he said, "My parents aren't dead. At least I don't think they are. I don't know. I haven't seen them in twenty years. Not since they dumped me in an orphanage when I was nine."

"Oh . . . darling," she sighed, her heart breaking. She wasn't really surprised to hear his confession echo in her thoughts. Having his parents abandon him would explain a lot. "Do you ever want to find them?"

"No."

She lifted her head, feeling such a love for him it almost troubled her. "Then I'll be your family, Frank. I don't have anybody else, either."

𝐹rank hadn't told Amelia he loved her.

His inability to utter those three words stemmed back to his childhood. He'd never had the endearment spoken to him, nor had he said them to anyone. Not even to Harry, who he had loved.

His brother had viewed the world through uncomplicated eyes and wouldn't have understood the emotional meaning behind the words. Their communication had been based on a simple level of language, mostly centering around the subject of water.

Ever since Harry could crawl, he'd been infatuated by the water in the Frisco harbor, by the ships that moored and sailed. Growing up, the sun-glistened bay had been the mainstay of their conversations and the site of many visits before they'd been disposed of at St. John's Orphanage. Once in the home, late at night in their cots, they'd whisper quietly about what they would do when they got out. Harry always said he'd walk straight to the ocean and stare at it.

In those unlit hours when the barracks were immersed in a black as dark as the nuns' habits, and when those inmates who were ruffians by day wept openly in their beds at night, Frank had vowed to see his brother through the misery of it all.

As a means of telling Harry how he'd felt about him, he'd shown him in ways Harry could grasp. By looking after him. By taking licks for him. By keeping him on his knees in the chapel during mass when the sisters were watching. By silently swearing to God during the long litanies in Latin to hate Jack and Charlotte, not for what they'd done to him—for he could have tolerated being abandoned—but for deserting Harry. For that, they deserved to be damned. Harry, who'd never cried, not even the day he was born, had been special and needed their love more than Frank ever had.

His little brother's boyish and blameless smile had been the only display of love Frank had ever been given. He'd grabbed onto it, like a dog starved for a bone, burying the gift deep inside of him. When the day came that he was released from the orphanage, without Harry's shadow trailing beside his, his most precious possession in the world had been hidden in his heart.

It went unsaid how they'd felt about each other. The need for words had never been there. And so he'd never learned to speak them. But he knew Amelia wanted to hear what he could not say.

His feelings for her were profound and unlike the unconditional bonds between brothers. Consciousness of being *in love* was different. He had no experience with that. There was no other passion that produced such contrary effects in so great a degree. He'd paid for love in the brothels, but he'd never had it given to him without a price. Never had the words been spoken to him from the cry of a soul, and Amelia's touched him deeply.

She loved him.

He hoped she would accept his silence, for he would show her how he felt, just as he had shown Harry.

The beat-up coffeepot behind Frank sputtered on the burner, pulling him from his thoughts. He turned away from the bar and poured an early afternoon cup to drink while he finished filling a box with his baseball equipment and fishing tackle. Right after the ceremony yesterday, he'd only taken the bare essentials to Amelia's house. Today he was moving in all his sporting gear. Tomorrow he'd tell Richard Hartshorn, the manager of the bank, his permanent address would be on Inspiration Lane with his wife.

His wife.

The dawn was barely discernible when they'd opened their eyes to each other early this morning. His stiff joints had felt the consequences of his cramped sleeping arrangements, but seeing Amelia first thing had made the kinks bearable. Half awake, he'd lifted her into the cradle of his arms, one palm on the soft cheek of her bottom—bare as a baby's.

He'd insisted she sleep without her nightgown.

She'd insisted she wouldn't be able to sleep without wearing it.

He'd insisted she leave her hair loose.

She'd insisted she always braided her hair for bed.

His argument had won on both counts—and in more ways than one—because she had fallen asleep naked with her head pillowed on his chest and her wealth of hair blanketing them both.

Amelia was the only woman he'd ever spent the night with without wanting to find his pants first thing in the morning and be on his way. He'd roused her with his kiss, touched her with a slow hand, made love to her until they fell into a pleasant exhaustion.

They'd drifted back to sleep to nearly noon. Stirring from the hot sun sloping through the window, Amelia had been frantic because she'd lazed in bed so late. She'd gone on about all the things she had to do, untangling herself from the sheets and scooping up her discarded underfrills while she walked toward the bathroom.

She'd looked damn good in the natural, forgetting about that fact while striding across the room. Her breasts were the perfect shapes to fill his hands, her stomach flat, and her legs were slender and long. Just thinking they'd been wrapped around his thighs not more than a few hours ago had made him want her again. He'd decided he better get up, too, and put his clothes on before he hauled her back to bed.

Amelia had called over her shoulder, "I wish I had time to visit Narcissa before going to the saloon. She's undoubtedly told the ladies about our wedding. I want to find out what they said."

Frank thought about Narcissa Dodge's caution. He had to face the facts. His one-night honeymoon was over, and he had to deal with what led him to his hasty marriage: the meddling crones. He could care less what was said about him. Amelia, though, didn't need her reputation raked through the coals. Even though they'd exchanged vows, there would still be talk. He had to prepare Amelia so they could handle things together.

Buttoning his shirt and slipping on his boots, Frank walked to the bathroom.

"Amelia, honey," he said through the door, but the slosh of running water drowned his voice.

He knocked, then turned the knob. Amelia stood by the sink in her robe washing her face. "Yes?"

"Amelia, there's something we need to—"

The front bell rang.

"Ah, hell," he cursed.

Amelia turned around. "I wonder who that could be? I wasn't expecting a soul. Maybe it's Narcissa."

Frank hoped so. He could use a little help in his corner. "I'll go see."

It turned out to be Cincinatus Dodge come to

inform him that during the night someone had knocked over and set the outhouse on fire behind the Moon Rock. It had gotten a little out of control in the alley, burning the porch post and part of the awning of his former living quarters. The mayor suspected the foul play was leftover Fourth of July antics and nothing more. But he needed Frank to check out the damage.

Frank had had to leave before talking with Amelia. Since she'd told him she'd be at the Moon Rock right after she finished dressing, he was waiting out her arrival by packing. As he put his possessions into boxes, he thought about hiring a carpenter to replace the charred wood on his porch. From the way the scene looked, he'd agreed with Dodge. A prank had gone awry, probably ignited by the older boys. At least the whole place hadn't gone up in smoke.

Taking a drink of his coffee, Frank thought of the other problem he still had to contend with: Pap O'Cleary. He would have to have a word with his friend. He hoped to hell things wouldn't come down to blows. Five minutes later, Frank found out.

Pap came through the saloon doors absently scratching the back of his bald head. He wore his black derby and a collarless shirt with deep wrist bands, but even that didn't discourage a beholder from staring at the nasty red welts peppered over his face and hands.

"Hey there, Pap," Frank greeted jovially, even though his stomach suddenly felt as if he were riding in the bed of a bumpy wagon after an all-night drunk. "How you feeling?"

"Better, but all this itching is becoming a pain in my ass."

"Well, you're not looking too bad anymore," Frank lied.

Pap trudged to the bar, an irritated gait to his stride. "I've been wondering where the hell you've been. I waited all yesterday for you to come over and tell me what happened at the picnic. If it weren't for Cobb, I wouldn't have found out a thing. Damn, I was going so nuts in that room, but I didn't dare show my face on the street. I still don't. I took the back way behind Gopher Road to get here." His fingers clawed the length of his shirtsleeve. "Anyway, desperate as I was, when I saw Cobb from the window coming out of the woods, I hollered for him to come up and keep me company for a spell."

Frank's mind spun. Cobb Weatherwax couldn't have known he and Amelia got married unless the mayor or the Rev told him. And those were two people who never crossed paths with Cobb.

Warming his coffee, Frank asked, "What did you find out?"

A sly grin lifted Pap's mouth, emphasizing the pock in the corner. "You old fox. Cobb told me you gave him twenty dollars to chase after Emmaline Shelby and leave Amelia alone. Now if that ain't smooth thinking. I owe you one, Frank."

Pap slid the box of sporting equipment down the counter a bit so he could stand directly across from Frank. Frank didn't say a word, waiting for Pap to make a comment as to why he'd packed up his prize possessions. "Pour me a cup of that mud, Frank, and tell me every little detail about the picnic. What did she wear? Did she smell like flowers? What did she make for her supper?" Grinning broadly, he quizzed, "Did she ask about *me?*"

Frank stalled for answers. He took a long minute to fill a cup and set it before Pap. As Pap slurped his hot coffee, he regarded the box over the cup's rim. "It's about time you cleaned up all that junk underneath the bar. Just because we're men doesn't mean we have to be slobs. I've told you before, an orderly run establishment will always get the most business." Blowing on the steam, he said, "I think Amelia will appreciate my neatness, don't you? And as soon as I'm looking more myself, I've decided to tell her my intentions. Hearts may be attracted, but affection's never known unless spoken. I've got it all planned out. You'll be my best man, of course, and I do believe Amelia favors Narcissa Dodge." He paused, only to muse aloud. "You don't suppose that preacher will refuse to marry us since I kind of offended him with my language, and I didn't get down on my prayer bones and taffy up to the Lord that one Sunday when he invited me to?"

Frank became more uncomfortable by the second. "Pap, there's something you need to know."

Pap only half listened. "I did offend him, didn't I? Well, hell, then I'll just take her down to Boise and we'll get hitched there. One church is as good as another when you ain't been in one since you got baptized."

"Pap."

Keeping his finger hooked through the handle of his cup, Pap declared, "Maybe we'll honeymoon in Boise while we're there. Don't worry, though, we won't be gone too long. I've got to keep my job. I'll be supporting a wife now, and I might even—"

"Pap." The force of Frank's voice was like an anvil ringing in the ensuing silence.

Pap shot him a piqued look. "What is it, Frank?"

"Amelia and I got married yesterday."

Amelia walked down Divine Street, her presence flushing the vibrant goldfinches from the magenta cosmos that grew alongside the road. Honeybees buzzed in the red-eyed phlox. Freshly cut alfalfa filled the summer afternoon with the smell of warm hay as the sun baked the cut green plants brown.

A lunch basket, packed with plenty of extra to be shared, dangled in the crook of her arm while she held her music bag in her other hand. She hummed a

happy tune, her eyes merry. She thought about last
night . . . about this morning . . . about Frank.

A giggle slipped past her lips.

He made noises in his sleep.

Not snores, but deep breathing sounds. Man
sounds.

The bulk of his shoulder had pinned her hair down,
and she'd been trapped in one position all night.
When she'd opened her eyes to the hues of a tawny
sunrise, she'd found his gaze on her. Waking with a
bona fide husband was far better than waking with the
plumpness of her pillow snuggled up to her chest.

She wished she could have made him a proper
breakfast, but they'd slept through that meal. She'd
been so rushed when they did wake up, that she'd
barely had time to pack a lunch for them. She
wondered which hooligan had set the outhouse on
fire, and hoped the damage to their saloon was
minimal. It felt funny to consider the Moon Rock as
partly hers, but it dawned on her they would be
merging their assets. She brought the house into the
marriage as well as a savings account on the brink of
emptiness. She didn't know how she was going to tell
him about that; she'd adamantly denied having financial trouble to him in the past. It wouldn't do to start
their union with the admission of a lie, so right now
she put the bank out of her mind.

It felt so good to be married! To make plans for the
coming seasons, knowing Frank would be there to
share them with her. In preparation for fall, they'd
stuff the woodshed to its roof, laying in a supply of
coal. Frank could put up the storm doors and windows, and clean the flues and chimneys. She'd stock
the cellar with enough food to last until the return of
spring.

And this Thanksgiving she'd stuff a turkey hen and
bake two kinds of pies, pumpkin and apple. They'd
share a cozy pallet in front of the blazing fireplace in

the coming crisp autumn nights. And when winter arrived, they'd watch the lacy flakes fall and make snowmen in the yard.

Her soft laugh rippled through the sweet smelling air. She was so in love, she couldn't keep her feelings inside.

"What you laughin' at, Miz Marshall?"

Amelia started and swung her head around. With her heartbeat thumping, she declared, "Why, Mr. Weatherwax, you gave me a fright."

"Didn't mean to, ma'am."

"Where did you come from?"

He pointed to the field of high weeds directly across from the laundry shop on Dodge Street.

"What were you doing there?"

"Watching for Miz Shelby."

"Oh." Her brows knit down. "Why?"

"Because I like watching her."

Amelia kept up her light pace, the composer busts in her bag jouncing together. "Does she know you like watching her?"

"I reckon." Resting the butt of his Kentucky rifle in the crook of his arm, Cobb tilted the moth-eaten brim of his hat to shield the sun from his eyes. "When I asked her if she could ever go after a man like me, she said yes. With a scissors."

She was momentarily speechless in her surprise. Cobb, for some impulsive reason, had taken a liking to the laundress. If there hadn't been the breach between her and Emmaline lately, Amelia would have been delighted and encouraged Cobb. He was a fine man, and despite his rustic way of life, he had a God-given talent for playing music from memory.

"I tried giving her a beaver skin, but she didn't want it."

His discouraged voice weighed upon her. "In matters of the heart, Mr. Weatherwax, one must pursue a partner without haste." Of course the advice didn't pertain to her and Frank. Some romances were just too passionate to be tamped down. "Are you sure you desire Miss Shelby's attentions?"

"As sure as I am about anything else."

"Then might I suggest, Miss Shelby must be won first and won romantically. A box of candy is preferable to a beaver skin during courtship."

Cobb's soft steps slowed as he pondered her recommendation. Amelia immersed herself in her own thoughts, wondering how Emmaline would take the news about her and Frank. She wouldn't offer her congratulations, that's for sure; she'd be downright envious. Biting her lip, Amelia also wondered how the other ladies in town had reacted when Narcissa told them. She hadn't planned on making any kind of formal announcement, leaving the matter up for public notice. The wedding ring on her finger said it all.

"What was it you was laughing at, Miz Marshall?"

Amelia glanced at Cobb, unable to contain her smile. "Why, I was laughing because I'm in love."

She would have told him she'd gotten married if it hadn't been for the fact they'd arrived at the Moon Rock. That in itself wasn't cause enough for her to refrain from telling him. But the argument Frank and Pap were having inside was. Their raised voices carried to the boardwalk, loud enough to make Amelia stop just shy of the bat-wing doors, reluctant to enter the saloon.

"You want to hit me," Frank asked, spacing the words evenly. "Go ahead. I guess I deserve it."

"I don't want to hit you, I want to kill you!" Pap shouted. "You damn sidewinder! You stole my girl! You went and married her right out from under me!"

"If I hadn't married her, her reputation in this town would have been shot to hell."

"I'm going to shoot you to hell, you son of a bitch!" Pap rallied. "I'm going to make you buzzard bait—if'n the buzzards could even stomach you!"

Amelia put her hand over her mouth and took a step forward.

"No, Miz Marshall," Cobb said, touching her arm. "I don't think you ought to go in there."

Frank explained, "I didn't plan on marrying her away from you, Pap. When I took Amelia to that picnic, something happened, and the boys saw what they thought was us in a compromising position—"

"Compromising position?!" Pap barked in a wail. A glass broke, the shards tinkling like icy slivers. "You snake in the grass bastard!"

"I didn't touch her in any untoward ways—"

"But you touched her!" Another glass flew and shattered.

"Yes, Pap. I did."

"You must have touched her in a way that made them boys think something was going on!"

"What those boys told their mothers got blown out of proportion. It looked real bad for Amelia and I . . . hell, I thought the best thing to do was to marry her. Save her reputation and her dignity. I would have . . ."

But Amelia didn't hear the rest; a sob of humiliation choked her.

"You've kissed her, haven't you?" Pap's question was wrapped in a painful groan.

"Yes, Pap, I have."

The saloon rocked with a heavy-handed sound—the smack of a fist connecting with a jaw. Another blow shook the wall. Then Frank staggered through the seam in the double doors rubbing his chin. Rather than going to him, Amelia jumped back. He didn't see her; his gaze was leveled on Pap as he backed into the street. Pap stood in the wide doorway, his eyes spitting nails. He may not have been as tall or as big as Frank, but he packed quite a wallop in his compact body.

"Give me your best hit, Pap." Frank put his hands up, giving Pap a direct target of his gut. "It'll make you feel better."

Pap took the challenge and charged like a locoweed-fed bull, headfirst, at Frank. Pap's derby fell off in his sprint, the crown wobbling in the dirt. As soon as he made contact with Frank's shirtfront, both men fell to the ground in a tangle of black trouser legs coated in dust. Frank made no real attempt to thwart Pap's jabs, taking his punches with hardly a grunt.

One-Eye Otis and several of his lunch customers from the Chuckwagon came out to see what was going on, crowding for a spot with the best view of the tussle.

It became apparent no one was going to put a stop to the pair rolling in the dirt. Amelia, despite her emotions being in turmoil, couldn't just stand there and let them fight.

She'd barely left the boardwalk, disregarding the pressure of Cobb's hand on her arm, when the blast of the stage horn broke her stride. A faded green coach with Wells Fargo emblazoned on its elegantly curved flank came rocketing down the street. The plume of airborne dirt behind its four big-dished wheels showered the water in the horse troughs and sent Hamlet squealing for cover.

The veteran reinsman perched on the box was eighty-two-year-old Casper Bean—a man known for his navigational mishaps. On more than one occasion, he'd cut the corner on Holy Road so tight, the side of the coach clipped the awning post off the roof to the office of the *Weeping Angel Gazette*.

Amelia quickly retreated, as did those around her. The only fools not scrambling to get away were the duo fighting in the middle of the street.

"It's Crazy Casper!" someone hollered over the thunderous hooves beating the ground. "Get on out of the way!"

Frank and Pap froze long enough to lift their heads and see the hulking rig descending on them with furor. They shot to their feet and ran for the boardwalk just as Casper flicked his long whip over the horses' ears. The tip cracked like lightning but didn't lay a scratch on the animals.

At the breakneck speed he was traveling, there was some doubt as to whether he'd make the turn at all; he was headed dead straight for the corner front door to Beamguard's Mercantile. In double-quick time, Casper's right foot stomped on the brake lever. Iron met with iron, and sparks flew off the rear metal-rimmed wheels like a host of disturbed fireflies.

A giant ball of grit clouded around the coach when it came to a standstill. Thoroughbraces wheezed and settled, the basswood panels choked and gasped. The arrival of the Wells Fargo had put an end to Frank and Pap's fight, but Amelia was still reeling from it. She was shaken to the core, her mind registering the significance of Frank's admission to Pap.

He hadn't married her for love.

She stared wordlessly at Frank, who stood at the curb of the saloon. Their eyes met and held. She sensed he knew she'd overheard him and Pap. Surely her hurt was written all over her face, and no sweetly phrased explanation he could offer could piece together her broken heart.

She would have turned and fled if the lacquered door to the stage hadn't been kicked open from the inside. It was the rare—and exceptional—traveler who rode up the mountain with Casper Bean in his Wells Fargo coach. Smart people waited for the Short Line to enter Weeping Angel, even though it ran only twice a month.

Through the chalky haze, diminutive coughs from the occupants inside could be heard but not seen since the leather curtains were drawn. The crowd on the street stared with mouths agape, waiting to see who the nitwits were.

A foot wearing a ladies' patent-leather shoe fastened at the side with innumerable lentil-sized buttons toed the folding step down. The owner had a shapely calf encased in all silk black hose. If there was a skirt to go with the leg, it had to be hiked up to her thigh. A slim hand whose wrist was encircled with a diamond bracelet materialized to grab hold of the door's edge. The demi-plumes of a decadent ostrich-tipped hat peeked through the opening, then the woman appeared. She stood, semi-stooped over in the squat aperture, but her dress didn't fall to her ankles. It stopped scandalously above her knees. She jumped down with a shake of her head.

"Honest to goodness! I've been pitched around in there like a loose mailbag." She two-fisted the low ruffled décolletage on her dark cardinal satin bodice and gave it a firm yank toward her chin. "My stamps are falling down."

"Hells bells, wasn't this one ass-bouncing ride?" stated a second female passenger, who was obscured in the dim interior. "It reminded me of—"

"Oh, you be quiet, Arnette," silenced a third lady. "I'm not in the mood for your idiotic man talk."

"I can always appreciate a story about fatuous men," piped in a fourth.

"Patricia, quit using big words nobody can understand without an encyclopedia and two dictionaries. Move out of the way, Jill. I've got to get out of this oven before I fall over in a dead faint."

After an exasperated sigh, Jill turned and offered her hand as assistance, since neither Casper nor any of the men milling around came to their aid. "Come on,

Sue. You'll be okay once you get something cold to drink."

After they'd all disembarked, the four women stood arm in arm examining the town's occupants as if they were the ones out of place instead of themselves. Each wore the same shocking style of costume, though they varied greatly in looks and mannerisms. Jill was the tallest and dressed the flashiest with her diamond jewelry. Arnette held a hand-rolled smoke clamped between her fingers while the palm of her other hand rested on her cocked hip. Patricia was the friendliest looking, but her smile was a tad too done up with lip rouge. Sue's complexion was flushed, and although the pencil on her brows was too heavy and running at the corners, she had nice brown eyes.

Jill seemed to be in charge of the motley group. "Howdy, folks." Her lips thinned when no one said a word of greeting back. "I guess you're all waiting for us to introduce ourselves. Well, fine. My name is Diamond Jill. That's Four-Ace Arnette, Society Patricia, and Sweet Sue. We're looking for Frank Brody."

Devastation swept anew over Amelia. Her mouth opened in dismay, but a suffocating sensation closed her throat.

A contingent of the male onlookers pointed at once. "That's Frank."

Frank's bruised face was set in stone, his mouth tight and grim.

Diamond Jill winked at him. "Well, here we are, sugar." She dug into the velvet reticule hanging off her elbow, took out a torn piece of newspaper and read, "Wanted: Waiter girls for the Moon Rock Saloon in Weeping Angel, Idaho. High wages, easy work, pay in cash promptly every week. Must appear in short clothes or no engagement." Looking up, she tucked the advertisement back into her drawstring purse. "Well, honey, when do we start?"

* * *

Amelia ran, tears streaming down her cheeks.

She wished she could undo everything. The Fourth of July picnic. Her marriage. Last night.

It had all been a mistake.

No wonder he hadn't said he loved her. He didn't. He never had. He'd gone and hired hussies. *Hussies!* Girls that wore face paint and swore and smoked. Girls that he intended to have work in his saloon. Girls like Silver Starlight.

He must have been planning their arrival all along, knowing as soon as they came, she wouldn't be able to give another lesson out of the Moon Rock. He'd finally have the piano to himself. No mother would ever allow their child to take instruction inside an establishment where dances—and Lord knew what else—were sold.

If Frank had intended to ruin her business, why then had he married her? She didn't understand. The only thing clear to her now was that the noise in the bushes hadn't just been a dog. General Custer hadn't been alone. How could she ever face a single one of those boys again, knowing they'd seen her with her bodice undone? How could she face anybody in Weeping Angel, knowing they were talking about her in their parlors? She'd been scandalized. Severely. For a second time.

The betrayal was happening all over. Her life was entangled in false hopes and lies. And if that weren't enough, it was as if Silver Starlight had come back. How could Frank do this to her? He knew what happened with Jonas Pray. Hiring four dancing girls was like rubbing salt into her wound. The stinging pain had the power to shed the love she felt for Frank. She could only endure so much hurt before turning numb.

Amelia fumbled to lift the latch on her gate, her fingers trembling.

"Amelia!"

Slipping through the opening, she dashed for the front door, her hand touching the knob and twisting when Frank caught her by her shoulders.

"Amelia. Wait."

The basket and music bag fell from her grasp. She turned and attempted to bat his hands off her. "Don't touch me!"

"You have to listen to me." His fingers pressed into flesh, unrelenting. "What you heard wasn't what you think. There's more to it."

"I don't want to hear anything you have to say. You *lied* to me! You made me think you . . ." She couldn't finish, loath to say the endearing words aloud. "I can't believe you'd let anyone force you into marrying me."

"I wouldn't have done it if I—"

"If you what?" she cut in, not giving him the opportunity to answer. "Don't you see? It's much worse now. Marrying me was like admitting we were guilty of something. I can't understand why you—*you* —who have always done as you please without a fig for what anyone thinks, would marry me just to save my reputation. It doesn't make sense."

Frank leaned her into the door and tilted her head up so she had to look into his eyes. "I married you because I didn't want you to have to go through what you went through with Jonas Pray. I didn't want you hiding in shame for something you didn't have to. I know we didn't do anything the day of the picnic, but I'll admit, I wanted to."

She licked the tears from her lips.

"I never made any false promises to you like Pray. But I wronged you just the same. I wanted you to be able to hold your head high and look them all in the eye, knowing you were my wife. That I cared enough to take you into the church." His fingers loosened their hold, but he didn't release her. "You may not think that's a lot, but a church isn't a place where I feel peace."

Her voice was as fragile as tissue paper. "Then you didn't mean the vows you took?"

"Hell, yes, I meant them. I wouldn't have repeated what the Rev said if I hadn't."

She felt bereft and desolate. Everything was hitting her at once. A cocoon of anguish wrapped around her. "When were you going to tell me about those girls?"

"I wasn't."

Her voice broke miserably. "It's not as if I wouldn't have noticed them."

"I meant, I just hadn't thought about it enough to tell you. I hadn't planned on getting married yesterday." He put his hand above her head, his hip close to hers. "When I put that ad in the paper, you weren't my wife. Things have changed. It wasn't my intention to hurt you, Amelia."

"You can send them away."

"No." The word was flat and unyielding. "I got them out here on the promise I'd give them work at the saloon. I'm not going to let them go."

Her breath came raggedly; her misery peaked, threatening to devour the last shreds of her self-esteem. "Then I don't think you should live here anymore."

His eyes narrowed and hardened. "I do live here, Amelia. I will come back. You're my wife. The Rev said for better, for worse." He pushed away from the door frame. "And hell, it can't get any worse than this."

*B*ut it could.

The scuttlebutt was, on good authority from Mrs. Dorothea Beamguard, that the newlyweds wore out their marriage bed the very first night.

"Disgraceful," was the sentiment echoed in the female huddle at the section of the mercantile where Oscar kept the leghorn poultry feed. "Shameful."

"If I hadn't been standing in the storeroom behind the drawn curtains," Dorothea stated, "I would have missed hearing the entire transaction." She pursed her lips. "Mr. Brody said to my husband, he wanted the biggest, *and sturdiest,* bed we could order. *And* to have it delivered to his *new* residence on Inspiration Lane."

Tsks of censure erupted.

"Gracious, the very idea of such a passionate wedding night," Dorothea said, "made me swallow a bonbon whole."

Esther Parks piped in, "What kind?"

"Yum Yum royal cream."

"I thought you promised Mr. Beamguard you were

going to refrain from sweets until you trimmed your waistline down," Viola Reed noted.

Dorothea waved off Viola's concern. "Bother any promises I make to Oscar. Why do you think I was hiding in the storeroom?"

Louella Spivey removed a speck of gray lint from her gloves. "I still can't believe Amelia married Frank Brody. I thought Narcissa had been fibbing to us yesterday."

"I still can't believe I didn't see a thing," Dorothea said. "Why, I'm always looking out from the porch to see what's going on. The church is in a blind spot, otherwise I would have been able to spy them coming out. Instead, I had to get secondhand information."

"I wonder why Amelia married him," Esther mused, adjusting her puff-bang wig. "You don't suppose they . . . that she's . . ."

"Esther!" Altana Applegate spoke up for the first time. "How could you even suggest such a thing? She obviously loves him."

"Loves him," the four peeped, as if that weren't possible.

Altana said, "Well, I for one feel responsible for Amelia getting married in such a hurry. If we hadn't jumped to conclusions, she might not have. Maybe there was an explanation for what our boys saw."

"Really, Altana," Dorothea chastised. "You're too kind."

"Well I'm not." Viola Reed squared her shoulders in military precision. "We must do something about those floozies he hired."

A round of agreement nods circulated through the clutch.

Louella asked, "What can we do?"

Dorothea spouted, "I think it's time the thunderbolts of heaven shiver the Moon Rock Saloon and its contents. We've been far too lenient."

"Yes." Esther nodded. "Lips that touch liquor shall not touch mine. Is that what you mean, dear?"

"Precisely." Dorothea put her hands on her full hips. "It's long past due Weeping Angel formed an anti-saloon league. Temperance, ladies. Complete extermination. The Moon Rock Saloon must be shut down."

Frank slept in the saloon the day he and Amelia argued, his old bed feeling cold and empty. When he woke up this morning, he was in a foul mood, made even worse when he faced the mess in the joint. Without Pap around, the place hadn't been cleaned up the night before. Butts of crushed smokes littered the floor, mixing with the sawdust that hadn't been swept out. The spittoons were unemptied. The chairs weren't on the tables. Water rings marred the walnut bar top.

Wearing only his underdrawers, Frank walked stiffly through the debris. He headed for the counter to brew some coffee strong enough to grow fur on the pot. He bent to open the icebox. There wasn't anything inside besides beer, so he closed the door. He wasn't hungry anyway; his stomach was recuperating from Pap's fist and One-Eye Otis's poor victuals. He'd taken the girls over to the Chuckwagon for supper last night after he'd made sure they got settled into the Oak Tree hotel. Eugene Thistlerod had been reluctant to allow the ladies to stay in his establishment, but Frank had convinced him otherwise by paying the first month's bill up front.

As Frank set the enamel pot on the burner, he put the flat of his hand on his belly. He felt sick. And it wasn't just from the food and Pap's pummeling. He felt sick in the heart.

He turned and put his arms on the bar, resting his head on the tops of his hands. "Amelia . . ."

He missed her.

He missed waking up in her bed . . . her hair draped over his chest. He missed her smile . . . her laugh. He already missed her coming into the saloon.

He could understand why she was upset. He'd wanted to tell her about the boys but hadn't been able to before she'd overheard him arguing with Pap. And right after that, the girls had arrived. If he'd known he was going to be married to Amelia, he never would have sent for the dancers. Now it was too late. In Amelia's mind, he'd betrayed her like Jonas Pray. Except Frank had no intentions of running off. If only he could convince Amelia. But she didn't want to talk to him. He should have explained things to her on their wedding night, but he hadn't wanted to spoil anything. His silence was costing him big now.

Lifting his head, he gazed at the New American upright. He was out a wife, and he was out a friend. And he'd lost them both in one day.

None of the new girls could play, so there was a big problem with dancing when there wasn't any music to step lively to. However, they had enticed enough curiosity seekers with their presence to make the Moon Rock do a prosperous business for a Tuesday evening. But what would happen when their newness wore off and Lloyd's organ lured customers over? He hated to think a stack of pipes that needed a tonic dropped down them could sway customers from socializing with four hurdy-gurdy girls. He didn't like the idea of leaving the dancers high and dry.

Frank straightened, rubbing his throbbing jaw. He had to think clearly, but his mind wasn't working. He had a headache so big, it wouldn't fit in a corral. Pap had knocked him ass over teakettle. "Dammit," he mumbled, "I should have hit him at least once."

He ran his fingers through his hair while he turned to grab a clean cup. Frank walked to a chair and sat down with his hot cup. He took a sip, the thick coffee potent enough to inoculate an ox. While he nursed the brew he thought. He could go to Amelia and try reasoning with her again. She'd had a night to think about everything. Maybe she'd be more forgiving. Maybe she wouldn't be. In any case, he could try.

"Frank?" Cobb peeked his face through the doors.

Frank dropped his chin to his chest. He wasn't in the mood for one of Cobb's beaver stories. Lifting his head, Frank said, "Yeah, Cobb. What is it?"

Cobb took Frank's greeting as a sign he could enter the saloon. He strode in on quiet moccasins, the fringe on his pants slapping against his outer thighs. His wild hair fell around his face, looking more bedraggled than ever. He plopped into a chair opposite Frank, his eyes wistful. "I've got a problem, Frank."

"Isn't it a little too early in the morning to be finagling free beers off me, Cobb?"

"It ain't that." Cobb combed his unruly beard with his fingers. "I did jist like you told me about the shirt."

"Shirt?"

"You know, the shirt you give me the dollar and twenty-five cents to buy."

"Yeah." Though at the moment, he was sketchy as to why he'd told Cobb to buy a shirt.

"I dirtied it up real good and brought it to Miz Shelby. She looked surprised as a dawg encountering its first porcupine when she see'd me in her laundry store. She wasn't one for talking much, so I saved her the trouble. Told her all about that beaver den I found up near Yeller Creek. She don't like beavers much," Cobb said with melancholy. "Anyway, she took the shirt to wash. When I got it after, it smelled purdy, jist like Miz Shelby herself. I kind of like the smell of soap, and—"

"Is there a point to this, Cobb?" Frank pinched the bridge of his nose.

"Yes, sir. Remember that dollar and ninety-five cents you let me borrow last night?"

Looking over the tops of his knuckles, Frank frowned. "I told you I didn't want to know what you needed that money for."

Cobb disregarded Frank's admonition. "I bought a thirty-pound pail of mixed candy from the merc."

Frank brought his hand down. "Thirty pounds?"

"Yes, sir. I gave the candy to Miz Shelby this morning." Cobb's expression grew forlorn. "She said she didn't have a sweet tooth. She weren't looking herself. Said she didn't sleep well last night, and for me not to bother her in her store no more."

Frank guessed Emmaline Shelby must have heard the news about him and Amelia getting married.

"I was wondering what you think I ought to do now, Frank?" Cobb asked. "I don't know what move to make. You see, the thing of it is, I 'spect I'm in love with Miz Shelby."

An edge of cynicism spilled into Frank's voice when he said, "Well, Cobb, I'm afraid you're asking the wrong person. You should be talking to someone who understands love. I sure as hell don't."

"Miz Brody—"

"Please, Mr. Weatherwax," Amelia broke in while standing on the threshold of her front door, "it isn't necessary to address me so formally."

His hat scrunched in his hands, Cobb replied, "But I can't call you Miz Marshall no more 'cause you ain't Miz Marshall. You're Miz Brody now."

"Just call me Amelia then."

His gaze grew contemplative. "Only if you call me Cobb."

"Very well."

Cobb said nothing further.

Amelia stared at him, waiting for him to state his business. The initial shock of discovering him on her doorstep after his unending ringing of her bell was wearing off. In its stead, curiosity was getting the best of her. Had Frank sent him over to speak with her? She shouldn't have concerned herself at all about Frank Brody. Thoughts of him should have been pushed to the back of her mind. Too bad she couldn't take her own advice.

She'd lain awake most of the night doing just what she was reprimanding herself for doing now. It would have been easy to shove Frank aside if she hadn't loved him. That was the hardest part. When Frank hadn't come home last night, she'd hated herself for worrying about him. She started watching for him from the bedroom window around two in the morning. By four, she knew he wasn't coming home.

What did she expect? She'd told him not to. But he'd said he would. A piece of her, that part of her heart that was still hanging on to her love for him, had hoped he would come home. That the whole horrible mess would go away and they would be happy again. Just as they'd been on their wedding night.

Amelia blinked back her tears, fighting not to cry again. She'd done enough of that, and she especially didn't want to in front of Cobb.

"Is there something you wanted?" she finally asked when he remained speechless.

"Ah, yes, Miz—I mean, Amelia, ma'am."

"What is it?"

"I was hoping . . . that is . . . I was wondering . . ."

Amelia could swear he blushed, but wasn't altogether sure because of the hair covering his cheeks. "Would you like to come in, Cobb, and have a cup of coffee?"

"Yes, ma'am."

Amelia let him in and showed him to the parlor. He stood in the middle of the room looking like an out-of-place bear amongst her delicate curios and finely upholstered furniture.

"Please sit down," Amelia offered. "I'll get the coffee."

"No need to, ma'am. I just had a cup with Frank."

She froze. "Oh." Her heartbeat picked up its pace. "Did he send you over here?"

Cobb's thick brows rose. "How did you know?"

Her knees weakened, and she lowered herself onto the edge of her pink tête-à-tête. "I . . . didn't. Not really. I . . . Forget I said anything."

Cobb didn't sit, despite the fact she had. "You see, t'other day when you said you were in love, it stuck in my craw."

"Well, things change."

"You mean, you ain't in love no more?"

Amelia sighed. "I'd rather not discuss my *affaire du coeur.*"

"Huh?"

"Never mind." Her fingertip traced the scroll-effect pattern on the divan. "I don't mean to be rude, but I have a . . . have a pie that I need to bake."

"I won't keep you, but I was hoping . . . that is . . . well, you see . . . the thing of it is . . . I been doing like you and Frank said. I got the shirt and I got the candy, but I ain't having no luck with Miz Shelby and I was hoping . . . wondering . . . if you could oblige me and tell me what I'm doing wrong."

Amelia thought a moment, not in the mood to play Cupid when her own love life needed a shot with an arrow. But seeing Cobb's hopeful expression made her think twice before refusing him. "Perhaps it's nothing that you're doing, Cobb. Perhaps it's your appearance that's putting her off. I know you for who you are. I find you . . . attractive because I know you. Reverend Thorpe says, 'Everything has its beauty, but not everyone sees it.' I'd quite agree in this instance."

"What do you think I should do?"

Amelia tried to think of something resourceful to say, but her ingenuity was sorely taxed by her own crisis. She had three weeks to come up with a mortgage payment, and she had no more income. She would never go to Frank and ask him for the money. She'd been half hoping the ring of the bell was her lady friends come to say they still believed in her and wanted their children to continue with their lessons on Dorothea's piano.

Early this morning, Amelia had had a heartfelt talk with Narcissa about the events of the past twenty-four hours. Narcissa had spoken in Frank's defense, which had surprised Amelia. Her friend related the conversation she'd had with Frank before the wedding, and Narcissa was fairly certain Frank cared very much for her. Be that as it may, their marriage was in a shambles, and Amelia had no bright ideas for the future. Narcissa had confirmed the ladies were not easily appeased by her new status as a missus. It didn't matter to them that she'd married Frank. They considered her a bad influence on their children and meant to keep them at arm's length.

Right now, Amelia was devastated by many things. But she'd always been able to count on the steadfastness of the Thursday Afternoon Fine Ladies Society. They'd deserted her, and she realized just how hypocritical they really were. With no one to turn to other than Narcissa, Amelia needed to focus on something besides Frank, the ladies, and her finances, or she would go crazy. Even if it was just for an hour, she had to look for the bright things in life.

She felt a spark of purpose flickering inside— slightly, then with more intensity. She considered Cobb Weatherwax a friend, and though Emmaline Shelby might not be a tried and true friend, there had been a time when they'd been civil to one another. There might come a day when Emmaline would thank her for sending Cobb her way.

"I think," Amelia said at length, "that you should start by cutting your hair."

Cobb's eyes went wide as supper plates. "Oh, no, ma'am. I couldn't do that."

"Oh, come now." Amelia was already on her feet. "I used to trim my aunt's hair, and I can trim my own. I'm certain I can cut yours, too."

Cobb started edging toward the door. "Well, thank you Miz Brody—ah, Amelia ma'am, for the advice. I don't think I'll be taking it none . . . ah, no offense."

She took him by the wrist. "Do you want to get Emmaline Shelby to notice you?"

"Yes, but—"

"Then a change is in order. While we're at it, you can shave your beard and mustache."

"No, no, no," he stuttered. "I don't think you understand the relationship a man has with his facial hair."

She disregarded his protest, beginning to get caught up in the idea. "I've never shaved a man before. But I can pare the skin off an apple in one long ribbon."

"I don't want my beard peeled off in one long ribbon, Miz Brody!"

"Then you'll have to do the shaving yourself while I get my scissors."

Before Cobb could object, she was hauling him up the stairs.

Frank let himself into the house without having to use his key. The foyer was bathed in patterns of color from the open transom window above the front door. Floorboards creaked under his weight as he entered the parlor. A breeze stirred the sheer curtains in the oriel, the glossy leaves on her spotted pink orchids flitting silently, gently. The clock on the mantel chimed the hour. One toll.

He went toward the kitchen. On the way, he deposited the box of baseball gear and fishing tackle he was carrying on top of the dining room table. The sound of his boot heels was muffled by the braided throw rug in front of the pantry.

The back door was open, and Amelia's voice drifted

through the screen mesh. "There really isn't much to trimming a man's hair."

Frank cut his steps, feeling like he'd just walked into a brick wall.

"You're being a good sport about this," she said with a trace of laughter. "Just wait until you see yourself."

Jealousy sliced him to the quick like the blunt edge of a knife sinking into his skin. He'd come home to settle things with Amelia. His lack of sleep last night had shortened his fuse, and the foremost question sizzling inside him was: Who the hell was his wife talking to?

Frank approached the screen door. He could see Amelia. Her back was to him, the fullness of her skirt blocking his view of whoever she was speaking to. All he could see were the arms of the green wicker lawn chair, not the occupant.

She held a comb and scissors; her hand was steady as she moved sideways to trim the brown locks from above an ear.

Frank put his nose close to the screen. He still couldn't see a face. He searched his mind, trying to place the shade of hair. Nothing matched up. Frank struggled with the uncertainty, swearing in his head.

"I'm almost finished," Amelia said. "When I'm done, I'll let you look in the mirror. Oh, don't nod. I don't want this side to be uneven." She clipped some more, brushing the flyaway strands off the man's broad shoulders with her fingertips.

Frank clamped his jaw together so tight, his teeth hurt. *Who the hell was he?* Jesus, she was touching him. *Touching him!* Resentment burned in his belly worse than One-Eye Otis's red bean pie.

The *snip-snip* of the scissors carved notches in Frank's pulse. He was just about to go outside when Amelia exclaimed, "There! I didn't do too bad." She leaned over to grab a mirror from the rattan table.

Holding her arm out, she let the man take the handle so he could view his face. "I can't believe it," she beamed with joy, clasping her hands together. "Why, you look so handsome, you take my breath away."

Frank's eyes narrowed to slits. "Amelia, *sweetheart,*" he ground between his teeth. "I'm home." He shoved the screen door open with both hands; the frame bounced off the back wall.

"Frank?" she gasped, turning abruptly.

Frank shot his gaze past Amelia, staring hard at the man who'd stood from the chair. He had eyes the color of a pond, and a complexion browned by the sun everywhere but the lower half of his face. He looked vaguely familiar, but he was outfitted in Cobb Weatherwax's buckskin pants. "Who are you? What the hell are you doing wearing Cobb's clothes?"

"I am Cobb."

The voice was Cobb's, but Frank was still doubtful. He took a hard look, sizing up the man's features, most notably the eyes and the wind-weathered crow's-feet at the corners. It was the craggy brows that betrayed him. "Jesus, Cobb. You don't look like you."

Cobb smiled, and for the first time, Frank could see the outline of his lips and all his front teeth. "No, I reckon I don't." He held the mirror up to his face. "I surely don't recognize myself."

"What are you doing here?" Frank asked.

"I took your advice."

"What advice?"

"To talk to someone who knew about love."

Frank darted his gaze to Amelia.

"I think," Amelia said, not acknowledging Frank, "Emmaline would be a fool not to encourage your company, Cobb. Why, you're a very smart man. You know more about beavers than anyone I've ever met." She lithely put her hand on Cobb's shoulder, a show Frank didn't need a ticket to see. "And," her voice went sugary sweet, "you're very handsome. If I weren't married, I would certainly be proud to have you as my escort to the Chuckwagon for supper."

"But you are married," Frank observed, his tone gritty.

"Yes, I suppose I am."

Cobb's fingers grazed his bald chin; he was oblivious to the dissension around him. "I'm liable to wake up tonight and wonder who the stranger is in my bedroll. I think I'm going to have to sleep with a beaver pelt so's I can feel like I still have hair."

Frank sent Amelia a private message that said he wanted to speak to her, but she didn't reply. The aloofness in her eyes told him everything she felt.

"Too bad you have to be leaving, Cobb," Frank said, nudging Cobb away from Amelia's hand. "You better go try out your new face on Em before she closes the laundry."

A faint thread of panic laced Cobb's voice. "Is it almost five?" Then he immediately cast his gaze toward the sun with a belated frown. "No, it ain't."

"Close enough," Frank insisted.

Cobb shrugged. "I'll just get my hat and be on my way."

"I'll show you to the door," Amelia offered.

Frank put his arm around her waist to prevent her from leaving. "Cobb knows what a door looks like. I think he can figure out how it works. Right, Cobb?"

"Ah . . . yes, sir."

"Good. See you around, Cobb. Stop on by the Moon Rock tonight and let me know how it all went."

Cobb put his hand on the screen handle. "Thank you, ma'am. I'll be beholden to you if this works. I guess if it don't . . . I can always grow everything back."

"I'm sure you'll make some progress, Cobb. You may keep me informed if you like."

Cobb nodded, then opened the door and let himself

into the house. As soon as he was gone, Amelia shrugged away from Frank.

"Really," she chided. "You might as well have given him a kick in the behind with your boot. You were as obvious as a newspaper headline." She moved to the table and began gathering her haircut implements.

Frank stood over her, feeling general resentment over Cobb's visit. "Do you like Cobb?"

"Of course I like him."

"How much?"

"A lot." She turned to face him, her brows furrowed. "Are you implying something?"

Frank gazed into her eyes, trying to read them; he couldn't make out a thing. "Pap told me Cobb thought of you as more than a friend. I didn't believe him. But now I'm not so sure. Maybe Cobb's trying to impress you instead of Emmaline."

Amelia had the gall to laugh at him. "Well, I like that! You are so wrong. I *was* helping him spruce himself up to catch the eye of another." Her gaze grew accusing. "Does it bother you he's interested in Emmaline Shelby?"

"No," he shot back. "I hope Emmaline finds someone. It's not her that I'm worried about. I saw the way you were around Cobb."

"The way I was?" she parroted.

"Yeah, real friendly like."

"I'm always friendly to Cobb. I like him. My goodness, Frank. You sound as if you're . . ." Her brown eyes widened, and she didn't finish her thought. Walking around him, she entered the kitchen.

He followed her, intent on making her see that their marriage was no sham on his part. But as soon as he saw her, he kept quiet. Her hands were gripping the edge of the sink counter, her profile pensive and fragile. "What did Pap mean when he accused you of marrying me right out from under him?" She looked at him, her expression somber.

"Pap thinks he's in love with you."

She didn't act surprised. "It dawned on me sometime around three o'clock in the morning that he felt that way. I don't know why I didn't see it before. You tried to tell me."

"Yeah. I guess I did."

She stared out the window. For a long moment, neither one said a word.

"How come you came back?" she asked softly.

"I couldn't stay away."

Turning her head, she gazed at him.

"I want things to be the way they were on our wedding night, Amelia. I want you in my arms again."

Her lashes cast shadows on her cheeks when she looked down. "Did you reconsider and send those girls away?"

Her question burned him at the stake. "No."

She raised her eyes. "Then how can we talk about anything?"

"We can, and we will." He moved toward her. "Right now."

Chapter

22

I wanted to talk the afternoon you proposed," Amelia said, "but you coaxed me into making a decision right then and there. Well I did. And you married me. Now I can't figure out the real reason why you did. There seem to be several possible ones, none of which I would have ever based a lifelong commitment on."

Frank stopped shy of the sink. "If I hadn't been sure I was the right man for you, I wouldn't have stood before the Rev and spoken those vows," he remarked in a low, composed tone. "I can't deny I was there in haste because of what the gossips were going to say. If I had told you about the boys spying on us and running to their mothers, would you have become my wife?"

She struck hard and immediately turned the tables on him. "If the boys hadn't found us, would *you* have made *me* your wife?"

"I wouldn't have rushed to get to the altar, no. But I wouldn't have ruled out the possibility in the future."

Amelia's eyes came up to study his face, but she said nothing.

Sighing, he said, "I care very deeply for you, Amelia. I thought I showed you on our wedding night and the morning after."

Her voice grew wistful. "I've told you I loved you, but you . . ." Her words trailed, but he knew what she was getting at.

"Saying three words can't express what's in my heart. It's not that easy."

"It's easy for me to say them."

A flat silence rang through the kitchen. Amelia stayed by the window, and Frank remained where he was. She bit her lip, then asked, "What were you thinking by bringing those girls to town?"

"All I wanted to do was improve my business."

"But what about my business?"

Frank's response held a note of disbelief. "I thought you'd have a piano in your house by the time they arrived. I didn't know your New American would be wrecked in a train pileup. Things have happened that I can't control. But we are married now, and I think that's the most important issue."

"Of course it is. I didn't take my vows lightly either." She fought the tears in her eyes and rapidly blinked. "So what do we do now?"

"You said yourself, we have each other. I'll take care of you, Amelia." He covered her hand with his. "Let me be your husband. You don't need to give lessons anymore, for fun or otherwise. I make a good living at the Moon Rock and with the addition of the—"

She slipped away from him, and met his eyes. "I thought you knew about Jonas Pray . . . about everything. You said Pap told you."

"Pap told me Pray ran off with Silver Starlight."

"Then you should understand," she said quietly.

"I fail to see the connection here. I'm not going to run off with anyone."

Anxiousness clouded her expression. "I didn't

think Jonas would run off either, but a spitfire dancing girl is a temptation obviously too strong for some men. Especially when their other choice is a prude like me."

"Oh, Christ, Amelia, don't talk about yourself that way."

"Well, it's obviously true, or else you wouldn't be surrounding yourself with four attractive women who are more footloose and fancy free than I." She pushed away from the counter. "I asked you to let them go."

"And I explained I can't do that."

"Then it would seem," her voice wavered, "this discussion has come to a stalemate, too."

Frank slept in the house that night.

Amelia heard him come in some time after two; the boudoir clock's hands were difficult to pinpoint in the gray shadows. Creaks on the stair treads as Frank climbed them had awoken her. She clutched the bedsheets to her breasts, her mind fluttering in mixed anxiety over which room he'd go to. By no accident, she'd chosen to retire in her aunt's apartment. Nothing had been resolved between them. The exchange they'd had in the kitchen had ended with him saying he'd return home after closing the Moon Rock Saloon.

Sounds and flickering candlelight flooded in from the hallway. A door squeaked open. Then silence. She imagined him standing in the doorway to her room, expecting to find her, but confronting an empty bed instead.

The clock on the cheval dresser by her head ticked off agonizing seconds. Finally, the door shut. Amelia closed her eyes, her fitful breathing echoing in her ears. Motionless, she listened for noises. The bedsprings grated. Boots hitting the floor landed with a thud. Minutes later, a still quiet enveloped the darkness.

Amelia tried to fall back asleep, but she couldn't. Once again, she played out their argument in her head looking for an obvious solution, but there was none. The complexity of the situation was like woolly twine, wrapping around them and seemingly ever-tightening. Always when she'd imagined having a husband, she'd wanted to marry for love. And she had. But she wasn't sure Frank had. Caring for someone deeply and being in love with them were two different things. The imbalance of mutual feelings fueled their dissension, making it impossible for the other to yield. She could see why a saloon owner would want hurdy girls to lure in customers in a city such as Boise, but Weeping Angel was a small town with house and hearth qualities. The scandal of such women entertaining at Frank's showplace would sweeten the tea of the citizens, and there would be no peace in their marriage until something was resolved. She'd already been a part of the brew, and it was a bitter drink to swallow.

A burning smell seeped under her door. She grew alarmed until she realized the odor was that of a cigar. Rolling onto her side, she tucked one hand beneath the pillow. Aunt Clara would have had a conniption if she apprehended someone smoking in the house. A part of Amelia wanted to side with her aunt, but she found a soothing comfort in the masculine scent.

She tried to block out thoughts other than dozing off. She would have gone to the kitchen and poured a glass of milk if Frank wouldn't hear. Unfortunately, the stairs were so sensitive, they could practically announce a spider's crawl.

For over an hour, Amelia tossed in the large bed directing her musings on subjects other than her husband. She had little or no luck. Somewhere around three-thirty, she finally drifted off. But there was no escape in her dreams. They were clouded by Frank's handsome face, the taste of his mouth, and the depth of his blue eyes.

The next morning, Amelia decided she wasn't going to let the Thursday Afternoon Fine Ladies Society run her life. Her slumber the night before had been deep and draining, and when she opened her eyes to the light of morning, a sharp headache resulted. She'd fit her arms in the wrapper draped over the end of the bed, then put on her lamb's-wool slippers. The bedroom door's lock clicked when she twisted the knob. It had sounded like a shooting gun ricocheting in the hall.

She'd paused, her gaze fixed on the door across from her. The tarnished brass knob hadn't budged. Letting out her breath, she'd gone to the water closet and mixed a dose of headache remedy. Contrary to her worry, Frank never woke while she dressed and went downstairs to fix a light breakfast. Afterward, she headed off to Narcissa's house so they could walk to Beamguard's Mercantile together.

"Are you sure you want to confront them so soon?" Narcissa asked as they approached the whitewashed steps to the Beamguard residence, which was attached to the rear of their store. "I wouldn't mind if just the two of us sat at my house. I don't want to associate with these women after the way they've treated you."

Amelia slipped her arm through Narcissa's. "I can't hide this time, Narcissa. I have to hold my head high. I've done nothing wrong."

She rang the bell and Dorothea answered, her lips falling from a greeting smile to an O of surprise. "Why, my dear . . ." she gasped, then called over her shoulder. "Ladies, Amelia is here."

Amelia could hear their whispers as she and Narcissa were ushered into the foyer, their gloves and hats taken from them. They followed Dorothea,

Amelia feeling the pressure in her stomach, but refusing to succumb to it.

The Beamguard parlor was filled with heavy furniture, lots of table shawls, and on the walls, numerous family portraits.

"You're looking well, Narcissa," Altana commented in a genuine voice. "Hello, Amelia."

"Hello." Amelia eyed the others sitting at the table. Esther Parks, Viola Reed, and Luella Spivey. They stared, their expressions pasted with surprise.

Dorothea came up behind her and Narcissa. "I'll get some extra chairs. We weren't sure if you were coming today."

"Why wouldn't we?" Amelia asked, keeping her tone calm and level. "It is Thursday."

No one made a comment.

Dorothea brought over two leather-cushioned dining chairs, and Narcissa and Amelia sat at the card table.

No one made a move.

Amelia's breath burned in her chest, but she forbid herself to be intimidated. "Which pairs are playing first?"

"I'll sit out this hand," Narcissa offered, resting her palms over the small swell of her abdomen.

The remainder of them paired up, Amelia with Dorothea as usual. Cards were dealt, but the tension surrounding the table was thick as frosting on a cake. Gazes seemed to keep slipping toward Amelia's hand, where her wedding ring shined like a beacon of light. She ignored their stares but was unable to concentrate on her canasta hand. As they played, the table conversation was governed by household hints for a time. Then it moved on to advice about men.

"An honest man is the noblest," Dorothea remarked.

Viola seconded with, "A Christian is the gentlest of men."

"I agree," Amelia added. "Isn't it nice we all have such husbands?"

Mouths dropped open and eyes widened.

"Take Frank, for example," Amelia went on, her heart pounding. "Why, he was a perfect gentleman while he was courting me. He even brought me cattails, just like he did Narcissa. It was extremely thoughtful of him. And then on our Fourth of July picnic, he picked some daisies for me. Isn't that a lovely gesture?"

The air fairly sizzled.

"My bridal bouquet was daisies also. I wish you could have been there, but things were so rushed. Frank wanted to marry me immediately. He said he couldn't wait another minute to make me his wife." She felt tears well in the backs of her eyes. "I don't suppose you'd know about the impetuousness of love. Sometimes it strikes, and a girl is helpless to do anything but give in to the moment."

"Yes," Dorothea said slowly. "We thought that's what it was."

All but Narcissa and Altana glared at her with censure, and Amelia suddenly realized they were referring to the picnic. There was no way around it, and perhaps it was a good thing it had come up in such a way. "It's unfortunate your sons misconstrued what they saw between Frank and myself. My corset string broke, and he was kind enough to fix it for me so I wouldn't be late to the recital. I'm sorry to disappoint your imaginations—since you seem determined to make more of it than there actually was—but I think it needs to be said, you were unfairly critical of me."

"Amelia." Esther sighed. "I've never heard you talk like this in all the time I've known you."

"And it's about time," Narcissa declared.

Amelia's hands were shaking so, she nearly dropped her cards. It seemed there was no stopping her once she got started. "I'd apologize to your children for the misunderstanding, but you would rather deny me the privilege by putting a stop to my piano lessons."

"That's not all we're putting a stop to," Dorothea sniped, just as she laid her cards faceup on the table; going out. "We're going to see to it that illicit den of flesh and drink is shut down. Frank Brody is nothing short of a felon for bringing in those abominable hussies."

Viola and Esther backed Dorothea's sentiments. Although Altana didn't speak her opposition, her expression spoke volumes; she didn't approve of the girls either.

It was one thing for Amelia to oppose Frank's business decision, but it was another matter entirely when anybody else took the matter into their own hands. She should have known they would go this far and prepared for their attack. Their temperance mission upset her greatly and made her realize she didn't want the Moon Rock Saloon boarded up. She didn't want Frank out of business; she just wanted the girls gone.

She found herself quickly defending her husband. "You can't insinuate yourselves in Frank's affairs."

"Of course we can," Esther clucked. "It's our obligation as God-fearing women to make sure this town is free of immorality."

Amelia tossed her cards and was on the verge of standing. "Why didn't you think of that before you voted the piano to go to the Moon Rock? All you wanted to gain from that vote was a chance to ogle the inside of Frank's saloon and see if he could slide beer mugs down the counter."

"Well, he never obliged," Dorothea said dryly.

Amelia countered, "And I'm glad he didn't." She took in a gulp of air, feeling Narcissa's hand reassuringly pressing on her arm. "You call yourselves Christians, but it's hypocrites that do the devil's drudgery, and that's what you're doing now that Frank has dancing girls. You want to run him out of business."

"You," Viola broke in, "should want those hussies run out of town more than any of us. Or have you forgotten about Silver Starlight?"

"No, I haven't. How could I? Every time we play canasta there's always a subtle hint, a vague reminder, a Bible brought out to quote scripture that was bought from Jonas Pray. I'll always remember."

"Then unite with us to close the Moon Rock down," Dorothea suggested.

"I will not!" she exploded. "I will not turn against my husband, no matter how much I disagree with what he's doing."

"Amelia!" Dorothea burst in disbelief. "You're not at all yourself."

"And I'm glad for it," she returned, her pulse hammering in her wrists. "You'd all do much better to channel your energies into figuring out a way to get rid of those girls. They're the problem, not Frank."

"What are you proposing we do with them?" Esther asked.

Amelia stared at the tops of her facedown cards, but they were a blue blur. She tried to collect herself as a rough idea formed in her mind. "Deter them from staying in Weeping Angel by making another town look better."

Viola rearranged her hand. "What shall we do, dear, summon them to tea so that we may discuss alternate options? I think not."

"I wasn't suggesting that. Surely there are other cities, bigger and more attractive for ladies with their calling. We could have Luella's husband place an article in the newspaper about the allure of . . ." She thought a moment, the only big—and faraway—city coming to mind was the one Frank and Pap talked about. "San Francisco."

"I forbid my Saybrook to print something so taste-less."

"It wouldn't be," Narcissa spoke up. "I think Amelia's idea has some merit."

"We could always employ them here," Viola blurted with a snide smile that garnered frowns around the table until Luella went along.

"Yes, of course. Dr. White could use an assistant to help him with his practice. I believe the one who wears diamonds would be perfect for the job."

"Do you suppose they're real?" Altana asked with soft curiosity.

"I wouldn't get close enough to check," Dorothea said. "But if they are, we all know how she earned them."

"You're forgetting One-Eye Otis, Luella," Viola tittered. "Oh, but drat, he doesn't permit anyone in his kitchen who has only two legs."

Esther chided with humor, "My dear, are you implying the Chuckwagon harbors roaches?"

"She most certainly is," Luella answered.

Altana called canasta amongst the chortles. Points were added, and before the cards were dealt for a new game, Amelia stood. "Listen to you. The truth is not exciting enough for those who depend on the characters and lives of their neighbors for all their amuse-ment." Her tone was tart. "The words out of your mouths are smoother than butter but are sharp as swords. I would rather find a more productive way to spend my Thursdays than to sit here."

Narcissa rose with Amelia, and the two of them left together. On the walk home, Amelia nearly broke down in tears but fought them off. With the exception perhaps of Altana, the ladies were conniving wretches, and she wanted nothing more to do with them.

She and Narcissa had parted, and Amelia went home after she assured Narcissa she would be all right. Closing the front door behind her, she situated her hat and gloves on the hall tree. The afternoon heat, and the steady buzz of ladies' high voices over the past several hours, had run her down faster than a two-dollar watch.

Amelia headed for the kitchen, desperately needing a cold glass of water for her parched throat. What had come over her? It was as if she'd changed into another person. One who put dignity before bigotry. Had she ever been as biased as her lady friends? She shuddered to believe she could have been so selfish.

Once she had her refreshment, she sat at the dining table to cool off. Frank had spread his fishing paraphernalia and fly-making accoutrements across the tabletop. There were dozens of feathers in piles correlated to their type: spotted feathers, brown feathers, white feathers, drab feathers.

Seeing his man things laying around the house felt strange. The bathroom was personalized with his Hood's tooth powder and toothbrush. He'd set his shampoo paste on the shelf in the tub. Her bureau now supported a glass containing coins, tokens, and an assortment of buttons. The hooks in her wardrobe held his linen collars and cuffs, a few neckties, and a pair of suspenders. She'd found black leather shoe polish in one of her bottom drawers, right next to a baseball, penknife, a box of lemon drops, and oddly, a can of corned beef.

Leaning forward, Amelia noticed an envelope on the tablecloth that she hadn't seen earlier. She picked it up and read the address. There was none. Just her name scrawled on the front in handwriting that was almost illegible. She recognized the slanted penmanship as Frank's. Intrigued, she opened the seal.

A bank draft fell out. Picking the narrow piece of paper off the table, she read the dollar amount. The size staggered her. Feeling more in the envelope, she produced a three-page document that, upon scanning the contents, she discovered was the deed to her house. Her gaze fell on the receipt once again and the bold signature at the bottom. Richard Hartshorn.

Amelia bit her lip to keep from gritting her teeth.

Frank knew! Somehow, he'd found out she'd fallen back on her mortgage payments, so he'd bought the house outright from the bank!

A mixture of shock, relief, and degradation collided, darting toward her fingertips. Her hand shook, and she dropped the papers.

Amelia rose from the chair, taking the envelope and its contents with her. On the heels of her patent-leather shoes, she took purposeful strides to the foyer. She haphazardly pinned her duck-wing hat over her hair and snatched her gloves.

In no time flat, she arrived at the Moon Rock thirty minutes prior to the saloon's opening. Huffing from her jaunt, she shoved the bat-wing doors inward.

Frank sat at one of the tables writing sums in a ledger. Upon her intrusion, he looked up. His brows raised while a hesitant smile played at the corner of his mouth. "Amelia?"

She walked to him, put the envelope down in front of him, and waited for him to explain.

His gaze lowered, then lifted. He didn't touch the flat paper containing the bank documents. "It's the deed to your house."

"I know what it is. I want to know why you did it."

Folding his arms over his chest and leaning back in the chair, he replied, "I paid off the house because Hartshorn said you were delinquent."

"How could you have gone behind my back and inquired about my personal accounting with the bank?"

"I did no such thing."

"Then how did you know?"

"I went to tell Hartshorn my residence had changed. While we were talking, he mentioned the late mortgage payment," Frank said matter-of-factly.

"Why did you lie to me about needing the money? I felt like an idiot in front of him when he said you'd slacked off the July payment with a drafty excuse. As your husband, I should have known about your financial problems."

"It wasn't at the top of our long list of problems."

"It should have been close."

She disregarded his admonishment. "I have a good mind to go over there and give Mr. Hartshorn what for and, while I'm at it, withdraw every last penny I have in that infernal bank. You shouldn't have to pay for my house."

Frank stood, the chair legs snagging the floorboards. "Why the hell not? You said it was our house. You gave me a key to it. I *am* your husband, and I should know when you're in trouble."

"I could have kept making the payments on my own."

"With what? You don't have any income now except for mine."

She was angry he had pointed out that detail. "Something creative would have hit me, and I'd have earned the money somehow."

"But you didn't have to. I had the funds in my bank account. And since I'm living in the house now, it seemed logical I pay for my share."

"From the size of that note, you've paid for way more than your share. I'd say my portion of the house is about the square footage of the water closet."

"Amelia," he said firmly, "stop being so damn unreasonable. I wrote out a check, for chrissake. It's not a capital offense."

"You just don't understand," she shot back. "I was earning my money honestly. You've gone and paid off the mortgage with money you're earning from those floozies."

His fingers raked his hair, tousling the inky locks over his brows. "You're not making any sense. I had the money long before I hired the girls. It wasn't much but enough to pay for your house."

"It would seem it's your house now."

Their argument came to a standstill, neither moving but standing barely a hand's width away from each other. She felt his body heat, the tenseness in his muscles. His deep voice was thoughtfully quiet when he asked, "Did you know the old bats want to shut me down?"

She gazed at him. "I just found out this afternoon. How did you know?"

"Dodge got wind of it and told me." Trying to shrug off the seriousness of the matter, Frank rubbed the shadow of beard on his jaw. "What do you think?"

She took a breath before replying in earnest, "I think you should be able to do what you want."

His sidelong glance was filled with wonder. "I'm surprised."

"Then you don't know me very well."

"But you still disapprove of the girls."

"Of course I do. I just don't think Dorothea and her clutch have the right to close your saloon—no matter how offensive they find your employees."

"I only have four. Pap is playing the organ over at Lloyd's place."

"I hadn't heard."

"Yeah, well, he's not speaking to me." Frank took a step closer, his thigh brushing her skirt. "As long as I don't have a piano player, I'm in jeopardy of losing business—most especially with the girls. They can't dance to air."

"Forgive me if I have no sympathy for your plight."

"I wasn't asking you for any, merely telling you how it is." His face went grim. "Those crones might as well nail my doors shut because without music, I don't have diddly. *We* don't have diddly."

"Are you asking me for my advice?"

"Do you have any?"

"None that you would like." When he said nothing to halt her, she continued. "If your conscience won't allow you to send those women packing, find other employment for them. Here if you have to. Then mend your differences with Pap. If you can't see your way clear with that, I can't help you, Frank."

Chapter

23

Closing his accounting ledger, Frank pondered Amelia's recommendation while she gazed expectantly at him. "Mending my differences with Pap is going to be a lot easier than finding other employment in Weeping Angel for the girls."

"You mean, you'd consider it?"

"I'm not promising anything, but I've been thinking. I can see that having the girls here is unfair to a wife, but that still doesn't mean they're bad women. The four of them are strictly dancers, and nothing else. I promised them jobs. I'm the reason they're here. I can't just fire them after one night—not without any plausible justification. They'd be nowhere with nothing. You know as well as I, the work in town for women is teaching, seamstressing, and laundry washing." Frank strode to the bar and chucked his accounting book underneath the counter. "And all those jobs are taken. We could use a decent restaurant, but that takes money to build. Not to mention, can any of the girls cook?"

"I wouldn't know."

Pausing, Frank folded his arms over his chest. "I wouldn't expect you to." Although he wanted his marriage to work, he wasn't going to make any ill-considered promises.

"But you're willing to think about an alternative?"

Frank glanced at her and replied, "I'll work on something." But no one that he knew would take the women on for a position in their establishment.

His brow furrowed. No one, that is, except Lloyd Fairplay.

Lloyd had been looking to put one over on him since the piano was voted to the Moon Rock. He'd be chomping at the bit to get girls over at the Palace. But would he treat them fairly? Iza Ogilvie didn't seem to have any complaints. She'd been there longer than gophers had been digging holes in Gopher Road.

The idea took root in Frank's brain, and if Lloyd hadn't gone on a trip to Nevada, Frank would have headed over to the Palace to feel him out on the subject. Frank had heard Lloyd went to Nevada to buy a seven-foot wheel of fortune game. He'd left Pap in charge of things during his absence.

Paper crinkling caught Frank's attention, and he gazed at Amelia. She'd folded and was putting the house title back into the envelope. He hadn't meant to undermine her when he'd bought it outright, but he'd wanted Amelia to be financially secure. The home was deeded in her name—with the addition of Brody after Marshall, and that would remain so. His cash on hand had gone down considerably after paying off the mortgage, and if he let the girls go, he wouldn't be making up the revenues as fast as he'd planned to.

"It's almost four," Amelia said. "I should be going home."

He wanted to make her feel better, but he wouldn't tell her about his decision to speak with Lloyd in case things didn't work out. Just the same, he needed to reassure her. "Amelia—" he started to say, but was interrupted by Dorothea Beamguard's voice booming from the street in front of the saloon.

"I stand for prohibition! The utter demolition! Of all this curse of misery and woe! Complete extermination! Entire annihilation! The saloon must go!"

He and Amelia exchanged glances, then went to the doors.

A demonstration of teetotalers, comprised of the Thursday Afternoon Fine Ladies Society, held posters with anti-saloon slogans painted on them.

Dorothea was at the front of the line, and when she saw them, she burst into another chorus. The others followed her example and began chanting the same motto until neighboring businesses emptied, patrons elbowing each other, to see what the ruckus was about.

Viola Reed shouted, "You are a rummy and a lawbreaker, Mr. Brody!"

"You should be behind prison bars instead of a saloon bar." Esther Reed waved her banner.

Luella shouted, "We intend to close this gin mill down and eradicate those filthy women from the premises."

Curses fell from Frank's mouth. If they hadn't been wearing corsets and skirts, he would have smacked every last one of them in the chops.

While his reaction was pure anger, embarrassment and resentment commanded Amelia's face. "Sweetheart, come away from the door."

Her fingers gripped the edge until her knuckles had turned white. "No." The tremor in her voice threatened to crack. "How could they go through with this?"

At that moment, Jill, Patricia, Arnette, and Sue appeared from the Oak Tree hotel. Attired in their low-necked clothes, and with their lace-up shoes freshly polished, they stood with their hands on hips. Before Dorothea could venture into another tirade, Jill called out, "What's all the fuss?"

The picketers turned to face off with the dance hall girls who were fast approaching the scene.

"Stay here," Frank told Amelia, then left the batwing doors to stand by the curb of the boardwalk.

"We demand you leave Weeping Angel," Dorothea pronounced in a haughty tone. "Your kind aren't wanted here."

Frank drawled, "That's not for you to decide."

Dorothea snapped her head in Frank's direction. "The matter has fallen into our hands since you've seen fit to ruin this town with your filthy saloon."

From behind Frank, Amelia gasped.

"It wasn't so filthy when you poked your nose into it to watch Daniel playing the piano."

"Don't you bring my son into this, Mr. Brody," she railed, "any more than you already have! When I noticed the opal wedding ring missing from the counter, I told Oscar we'd been robbed. I would have called in the sheriff if Daniel hadn't confessed you put him up to buying the ring and had him hide the money in our cash box. I won't allow him to keep that baseball bat you used to bribe him."

"Daniel did me a favor," Frank ground out, "and he got paid for his trouble with the bat. I won't take it back. He's a fine boy. It must be he gets his manners from his daddy, because he sure as hell never learned anything generous from you."

"I-I-I," she stuttered. "I'm appalled."

Frank didn't want the confrontation turning into slinging insults back and forth. Most especially, with Amelia a witness. He was saved from having to firmly escort her back into the Moon Rock when Mayor Dodge came out of the city offices to take charge of the situation.

"Mrs. Beamguard. Ladies," he greeted. "No doubt, they can hear you yelling in Boise City."

The Thursday Afternoon Fine Ladies Society rallied together and spoke all at once to the mayor in such a high-pitched confusion, Dodge threw his hands up in the air.

"Ladies! One at a time."

Luella Spivey spoke up. "We're demonstrating that this saloon be closed down."

The mayor frowned. "Do you have a permit?"

They gazed at one another. "No," Esther Parks replied.

"According to the town's bylaws, article three, section one, you've got to have a permit to conduct a public demonstration. And seeing as you don't have one, I have to officially disband this protest."

The ladies looked affronted.

"We have every right to keep our town pure and safe from sinful decay," Dorothea snipped.

"You don't have any rights when it's against the law." His hand rose to his collar to stretch the knot in his necktie. "So I suggest you break it up and do your grumbling in some other fashion."

They traded glances of resignation with each other, then walked off in a huff carrying their signs when Mayor Dodge cried, "Shoo!" The onlookers disbanded with them.

Frank looked at Cincinatus, who was gazing compassionately at Amelia. "There isn't any such article or section, Mr. Brody. I staved them off for now, but this problem isn't going to go away unless it walks away. Do you get my meaning?"

Nodding, he replied evenly, "I do."

"Good." Mayor Dodge tipped his hat to Amelia, then returned to his office.

Frank met Amelia's eyes. She was looking beyond him to the street. He turned and saw the four girls still standing smack in the middle of Divine Street studying Amelia with interest. He hadn't told them he was married—not that he was hiding anything. Introducing Amelia would satisfy their curiosity but put her in an awkward position receiving them.

Deciding to test fate and introduce her, he moved to face Amelia again, but she wasn't there. All he could see was her retreating figure as she crossed Dodge Street. He would have gone after her if he thought she'd be receptive toward him.

But in all probability, she wouldn't speak to him.

And the way he was feeling, he wasn't sure she'd be wrong.

The next afternoon when Amelia and Narcissa sat at the kitchen table sipping tea, the doorbell rang. They'd been discussing the four girls, trying to think of other places for them to work. So far, a cook to improve the menu at the Chuckwagon was about the only thing they'd come up with.

Amelia set her cup on the saucer. "Excuse me, Narcissa."

She walked out of the kitchen to see who was at the door. Frank had gone to the saloon an hour ago to give Cobb some practice time on the piano. She'd been surprised earlier in the day, just before he'd left for the Moon Rock, when he'd told her Cobb was playing the New American for him. Cobb had offered and, from what he'd retained in his head, had produced mixed-up tunes that were a combination of the classical composers she taught and the barroom ditties Pap pounded out.

As Amelia left the parlor, she smoothed her apron over her skirt feeling emotionally drained and not knowing how much longer she and Frank could go on the way they were. They'd spent the night apart; she in her Aunt Clara's room, he in hers. Because of his late hours, they had no time to talk in the evening. And in the morning, she was up long before he was. That only left lunchtime. They'd shared a noon meal, spent in near quiet, when he relayed the news about Cobb. He spoke nothing about the temperance scene yesterday nor did she. She was still trying to deal with hearing that Daniel Beamguard had picked out her wedding ring, not Frank.

The bell rang again. Swinging the door open, Amelia arrested her movement as soon as she saw them on the stoop.

The dancing girls were collectively on the porch, donned in their usual attire. Up this close, Amelia could see they used cosmetics, and she could smell their perfume—a mixture of four different types in variances of floral to woody.

There was no reason Amelia could think that they would come visit her. Surely they wanted to speak with the other occupant of the house. At length, she said, "Frank isn't home."

"We know that," Jill supplied.

Amelia had to tilt her head a bit to meet her eyes. Diamond Jill was taller than the others. Taller than Amelia herself.

Society Patricia wore a polite smile with her pearl choker. "We want to speak with you."

"There's something that we have to do." Sweet Sue fingered the button on her right glove.

Four-Ace Arnette inquired, "May we come in?"

Amelia was so taken aback, she could barely think. She shifted her stance, and they took it as a sign they could enter her home. Each one filed in on her right, filling the foyer and directing themselves into the parlor. Helpless, Amelia closed the front door.

They took over the demure room with their presence. Sue, Patricia, and Jill admired the furnishings. Arnette stood before the oriel, gazing at the multitude of plants.

"These are phalaenopsis orchids, aren't they?" she queried, taking Amelia by surprise with her knowledge.

Her reply was soft as the flower petals. "Yes, they are."

"I used to grow them myself." Arnette admired the foliage and pottery. "Ming pots. Very nice."

Amelia kept her hands at her waist, fidgeting with the band of her apron. She felt obligated to respond. "Thank you."

Narcissa entered the room, her expression just as marked with surprise as Amelia's had been. After exchanging glances with Amelia, she walked toward her and took up her side. "Um, this is Mrs. Dodge," Amelia finally said. The ladies all nodded courteously to her, and Narcissa, in turn, nodded back slightly.

Neither Amelia nor Narcissa sat. Amelia didn't want the four girls to settle in and stay, expecting her to offer them refreshments. She gathered her wits and asked, "What is it you wanted?"

"We've come to apologize," Jill said.

Astonished, Amelia's gaze darted to each of the women.

Arnette spoke as she stood next to Patricia. "We just wanted you to know, we don't want to cause any trouble."

"We didn't know you were Frank's wife," Sue chimed in.

"Frank never mentioned he was married," Jill admitted. "Not that he was hiding anything, mind you."

"Of course he wasn't," Patricia said.

Jill smoothed her skirt. "We won't take any more of your time, Mrs. Brody. We just wanted to set the story straight. Come on, girls. The saloon will be opening soon. Honest to goodness, I hope that grinning cowboy doesn't hit me up for another dance. He was way too cocky. I should have slapped him with my knee when I had the chance."

"You can say that again," Sue mumbled. "Give me a man who likes children and animals, and I'll show you a man I could love."

Patricia sighed. "That tall one who sports real fancy duds and wears his hair parted directly at the equator —he isn't too bad. In fact, he's pretty interesting to talk to. He told me he was building a house with a wraparound porch above some road named after a rodent. Do you know what his name is, Mrs. Brody?"

"Ah, Ed Vining. He's employed by the public works."

"Is he interested in monogamy?"

Sue cut in with, "Why in the hell would you want to marry him if he's married to someone else?"

Patricia gave Sue an exasperated stare. "That's bigamy you're thinking of. The practice of marrying only once is monogamy."

"Well, shit. I told you to quit using those big dictionary words. You mix me up."

"Is Mr. Vining available?" Patricia asked, brushing off Sue's reprimand.

"He's not married," Amelia answered.

Patricia's eyes grew thoughtful.

As the four girls made their way to the door, Amelia and Narcissa drawing up the rear, Arnette made the observation, "Since we're on the subject, any man can spark my interest. But most especially, ones that irritate me. Why, I don't know. Maybe it's because I want to show them a thing or two."

While the heels of her shoes tapped over the floor-board, Jill noted, "All I ask is that he's taller than me and can make me laugh. Humor is the harmony of the heart. Without it, our souls rust."

They stepped over the threshold and bid Amelia good-bye. She and Narcissa watched as they sashayed through her gate, their camaraderie continuing through their voices and giggles.

Closing the door, Amelia kept her hand on the knob, her subconscious thoughts surfacing. She looked at Narcissa, who might have been having the very same thought, judging by the sparkle in her eyes, but Amelia spoke first. "There is something the girls could do in Weeping Angel."

Narcissa nodded, and both of them said, "Be wives."

Two weeks later, the bed Frank ordered arrived.

If mattresses were hats, the Dream-Tide was the ten-gallon size. The bulk of the two pieces was more than Frank could handle, so he'd enlisted Cobb's help dragging the pair upstairs to Amelia's room after he'd assembled the birch frame.

Halfway up the flight, Cobb said, "I reckon I'll have to sleep in a bed soon myself."

"You trying to tell me something, Cobb?" Frank asked, easing his end over the top riser.

"Miz Shelby and me have been sparking. I can't understand it. One day she wouldn't look twice at me. And now that I shave the bristles off my face and cut my hair, she likes me just fine."

"Goes to show you how fickle women are."

"I reckon."

Walking backward, Frank guided Cobb to the room. "Turn right."

Cobb maneuvered the springy mattress around the corner and down the hall. "I'll be asking her to marry me, you know."

"I figured you would."

"I hope she's half as nice a wife as Miz Brody."

"You never can tell." Frank slid his corner onto the frame, butting the edge against the headboard. "The funny thing about rings—when they're on a woman's finger, it changes things."

The observation weighed on Frank. Things between him and Amelia should have been better, but the distance seemed to be growing. He'd been able to talk to Lloyd, and they'd worked out a deal that was acceptable to the girls, though the duration of their stay at the Palace was questionable—they all seemed destined for the altar.

Sweet Sue and Rupert Teats had been spending time together at the livery. He'd shown her the stockyard, let her feed the chickens, and given her a ride on his big palomino. Ed Vining had taken Society Patricia to see his house under construction, and they'd had a picnic on the second-story framework.

Four-Ace Arnette and One-Eye Otis squabbled in public more than anything. She called his restaurant a beanery and said if there was any other place in town to eat, he could bet she'd be picking up her fork there instead of dining off his sad menu every night. For all Arnette's grumbling, and Otis's snapping back, Frank had found the couple kissing behind the Chuckwagon yesterday afternoon.

That left only Diamond Jill without a prospective beau. But lately, she and Pap O'Cleary had been appreciating each other's humor.

Pap had come to the Moon Rock last week hauling Lloyd Fairplay's wheel of fortune game with him. Frank had traded Lloyd the girls for it. The batwing doors had squeaked open and Pap shoved the game inside, his stance hesitant. The black derby on his head put his eyes in a vague shadow. "Howdy, Frank."

"Pap." Frank had left the bar while Pap strode toward it, rolling the monstrous wheel on its rollers. The two met in the middle of the floor. "I'm glad you were the one to bring it over."

"Yeah . . . well, Lloyd asked me to."

An awkward silence passed between them.

Frank shifted his weight. "You like playing the organ at Lloyd's?"

"Do you like me there?"

"No, Pap, I don't. I liked it better when you were here."

Pap stuffed his hands in his pockets. "Me, too."

"You want to come back?"

"You asking?"

"Yes."

Pap gazed at his boot tips, then back at Frank. "I reckon I could."

"Start tonight?"

"I suppose."

"You know," Frank said, "you really beat the crap out of me."

Pap gave him a lopsided grin. "Never hit you in all the time I've known you."

"Hope to God you don't ever have to again."

Shrugging, Pap said, "I still feel a stirring in my heart for Amelia, but I know any chance for us is gone. Guess there never really was a chance for us to begin with. Just promise me you'll do right by her."

"I will, Pap. I swear."

So Pap had come back to the Moon Rock, bringing with him a new clientele—the gambler who liked to try his luck at the wheel. The girls were doing Lloyd's place a good turn; his business picked up, but the excitement sent the temperance league out in full force. Their mission had lasted all of fifteen minutes before their husbands disbanded them, threatening to cut off their expense accounts if they continued to publicly display themselves in such a fashion.

It seemed everyone had been able to sort through their affairs and put them in order. Everyone, that is, except Frank and Amelia. Though they lived in the same house, they were almost strangers. They saw each other only for lunch and a brief amount of time after. She'd thanked him for finding other employment for the girls, but that hadn't put the bloom back in their marriage. The late hour he closed up didn't help matters either. Amelia was already sleeping in her aunt's room when he came home. No more nights spent in each other's arms.

If he thought she was using sex against him, he wouldn't have allowed her to choose other quarters. But he sensed she was still hurt by the circumstances of their impetuous wedding and still having doubts about his feelings for her.

"You need me to help you bring this old one to the attic, Frank?" Cobb motioned to the narrow bed that used to be Amelia's before they were married.

"No. I can manage it myself."

"Awright. Then I'll be going now. Me and Miz Shelby are renting us a buggy for a ride. She don't know it yet, but I don't know how to drive a rig. Do you suppose she will? I'd hate to have to cancel a vittles picnic."

"I believe she does know how to handle reins, Cobb."

"Well, that's a load off'n my mind."

Showing himself out, Cobb left the bedroom, and Frank wrestled with the old mattress. He hoisted the edge on his shoulder and climbed up the third-floor stairs to the attic.

He'd only been in the room once—to store his box of sporting gear—and he'd been in too much of a hurry to take a good look at anything. The walls were stunted in the corners, and he had to duck his head if he didn't want to hit the top beam above the door as he entered.

A musty smell of old wood and the faint odor of spice invaded the space. He found several oranges with clove spikes stuck in them hanging from the rafters.

Navigating a path through the trunks and crates, as well as furniture relics such as mirrors, lamp stands, and an easy chair with the stuffing popping out, he headed for the northern wall. Halfway there, he almost killed himself by tripping over a crate that protruded from underneath a fire screen. He let out an oath and dropped the mattress where he stood.

Giving the crate a stiff kick, the lid jumped off under the aggression of his boot heel. An eddy of wood shavings flew over the sides onto the dusty floor.

Frank wouldn't have paid the books inside any attention if they hadn't looked expensive as sin. Bending down on one knee, he extracted a volume. It was bound in English red silk cloth and stamped with genuine gold lettering. Tilting the book toward the tiny window, he read the inscription on the cover: *The Legacy Collection.*

Thumbing through the marble-edged pages, he deduced the tome to be a large-printed edition of the Bible. With a glance at the crate, he estimated there were twenty-five blessed volumes.

Why had she kept a box of valuable books when she could have sold them and used the money toward her mortgage?

He didn't like the answer he came up with: She still felt an attachment toward Jonas Pray.

He couldn't understand her rationale and saw no logic, if that were the truth. The bastard had jilted her in public, and yet, she'd kept the goods as a memento.

The thought of her having any kind of lingering feelings for Pray ate at him.

Creaks on the stairs brought Frank out of his musings, and he looked up to see Amelia holding on to the oak banister. The olive-colored percale waist she wore enhanced her fair coloring, making her more lovely than ever. "I thought I heard noises. What are you doing up here?" she asked, walking toward him.

His voice was fraught with possessiveness when he asked, "Why did you keep these?"

Her gaze followed his hand to the crate of Bibles. "What was I supposed to do with them?"

"You could have gotten rid of them."

"How?"

"Sell them."

"To whom?"

Frank frowned. "I don't know. The mercantile."

"And have Dorothea Beamguard know I needed the money," she countered, frowning herself. "I would have rather starved."

"I'm sure you would have." He shoved the book back inside. "Were you keeping the Legacy Collection for sentimental reasons?"

"Yes."

Her answer cut him to the quick, the confirmation a buzz in his ears.

"For a long time, I did wish Jonas Pray would come back," she explained, "even though he humiliated me before he left. He was the first . . . and only . . . man who ever told me he loved me. I suppose I thought that was reason enough to keep the Bibles."

Rising to his feet, he hoisted the mattress and moved it where he'd originally intended. "It's not a good reason."

"But it's the only one I have."

He felt the tension in the attic thicken, threatening to collapse the shingled roof above them.

Amelia spoke softly. "We can't continue this way, Frank. I've got to know how you feel. We've never talked about the future. We've never made plans about what we want to do with our lives . . . about having children. I think we should if we want to start fresh in this marriage."

He took in a deep breath. "Kids are a big responsibility. I don't know if I can take the chance of failing one."

"Why would you say that? Parents make mistakes all the time, and they learn from them."

"But the wrong mistake can cost a life."

Amelia grew quiet a moment. "How did he drown, Frank? Why do you feel guilty about Harry's death?"

Bunching his hands into fists, Frank replied, "Because I should have been there, and I wasn't."

"What happened? Tell me."

Frank couldn't dismiss her gentle plea. "I was playing stickball in the yard on a hot day when Harry took off with a group of troublemakers I'd told him to stay away from. They snuck under the fence to find some water to swim in. The nuns were alerted, and I prayed to God to have them give me Harry's whipping when they caught him. But later that night, I was summoned to the office and told my brother had died that afternoon in a sand and gravel pit that had been filled with water. Harry didn't know how to swim, and he drowned with another boy who hadn't been able to climb up the embankment either." Frank went on, his voice a monotone of remembrance. "I couldn't believe my brother was dead until the next day when the nuns took us into the chapel and forced us to walk by the open coffins. Harry was laid out in a suit he'd never owned, made to be an example of what would happen if an inmate took it upon himself to leave the grounds."

Her tear-smothered whisper washed over him. "It was an accident."

"I shouldn't have been playing ball. I should have been with him." Frank dipped his head slightly. "I should have told him I loved him, but it was something we never said out loud. We just knew."

Amelia went to him and touched his cheek. Her palm was warm next to his skin, and he inhaled sharply from the contact. "It's not your fault," she said.

"It's taken me years to reconcile that, but the hurt still stays." His voice clogged with emotion, and he cleared his throat. "So, in regard to children, I'm afraid of what kind of father I'll be, Amelia. I never had one to look up to. And the father I was to Harry wasn't enough."

"You're the best man I know. You'd be fine as a father." She lowered her lashes. "I'm sorry I've made you feel that you wouldn't be because you've never told me you love me. I understand now." She held his gaze with hers. "You loved your brother, in the heart, where it counts. And he loved you. Just like I do."

Frank took her into his arms and rested his chin on her shoulder. Squeezing his eyes closed, he held her close. The sun waned through the tiny window and an orange dimness prevailed. He lifted his head, his large hands taking hold of her face. "I married you because I wanted to, Amelia. Don't ever doubt that again."

Tears shimmered in her eyes. "I won't."

He moved his mouth over hers. His kiss was slow and thorough. Amelia twined her arms around his neck and clung to him. Moving his hands over her back, he touched as much of her as he could. Their lips met, his tongue moving in and out of her mouth with deliberate leisure. He walked her across the room, all the while giving her slow, exploring kisses. With lips touching and legs entwined, he took her onto the mattress with him. He rolled with her until they were on their sides facing each other. Never leaving her mouth, he brought his hand to her modest collar. He fingered the tiny buttons and popped them free. Her shirtwaist separated, and he removed the garment with little effort. The rest of her clothing followed, and he shed his own.

"I've missed you, Amelia."

"I missed you, too."

Kissing her satiny skin, he found her breast. Her hands sank into his hair as his tongue teased her with infinite slowness. The heel of his palm slipped to that part of her he knew needed to be consumed with arousal. He rubbed with a light pressure and friction, refusing to relent his sweet torture even when she clutched his back, her fingers kneading into him. A cry passed over her lips, and he felt her body begin to pulse warmly. Only then did he thrust into her, filling her powerfully. Tightness enveloped him, hot and sleek.

His skin was damp with sweat, having fought to control his own desires. He wanted her to find release with him, so he orchestrated a rhythm as slow as one of the waltzes she played on the piano. He loved the feel of her, the hunger inside her when she arched to meet him. Repeatedly, he withdrew to nearly leaving, only to bury himself deeply. She writhed beneath him, her fingernails biting his flesh. Mindless, he responded to the grinding lift of her hips, moving faster and faster.

The heat of her climax closed around him, and her breathing filled his ears. His tempo escalated and grew unchecked as he sought his own pleasure. When it came, he felt his muscles burn, and he let go of everything he'd been holding back.

His mouth found hers, kissing her, worshiping her. In a hoarse and sated tone, he said, "I love being married to you. I love the flowers in the house. The tablecloths on the table. Your silly things in the bathroom. That crazy sponge you call a loofah. I love your scent on the bedcovers. The smell of the soap you use to wash my clothes. I love your smile and your gestures. I love when you say, 'Well, I like that,' but you really don't." He brushed a kiss over her lips, then nestled his face into the curve of her neck and whispered, "I love you, Amelia."

Epilogue

⤜⤝

December 1897
Christmas Eve

*T*he residents of Weeping Angel packed the Christ Redeemer to witness the baptism of Cincinatus Marion Dodge, Jr. who'd come into the world three weeks early. Mother and baby were doing fine, but the father had had to be treated with Dr. White's nerve remedy.

The mayor stood before the members now, his hands still a little jittery, but pride beaming so brightly on his face, his countenance could have put a flame to shame. Mrs. Dodge sat in the front pew next to the godparents, Mr. and Mrs. Frank Brody.

Baby Dodge, who was bundled in blankets the same color as the snow falling peacefully outside, began to fuss. Narcissa tried to soothe him with a pacifier, but the length of Reverend Thorpe's sermon and the water from the font had exhausted the baby's tolerance. His mouth opened wide, and a wail came out so loud, the congregation laughed.

"My boy's got the makings of a great orator," Mayor

Dodge said proudly from the pulpit. "He's got my lungs."

A new chorus of laughter erupted.

"But to get on with things since I know the Reverend wants to take back his services . . ." Dodge straightened his tie as the group settled down and the noise in the room died to only that of his son's cries. The mayor's brow arched, and he gave his wife a contemplative glance. She shook her head no, but he placed his right hand into the fold of his jacket and took on a Jeffersonian pose. "When in the course of human events, it becomes necessary for one people to dissolve the political bands which have connected them with another, and to . . ."

Amelia smiled as Cincinatus's words faded inside her mind. He went on, and not a soul stopped him. This was his day, and they all knew it.

She studied the scene surrounding her as if the display were a picture on a Christmas card. Friends were near, the smell of pine boughs and hot, spicy wax filling the air in the church. Her gaze passed over the town's piano teacher, Cobb Weatherwax, and his wife, Emmaline. Amelia had given him her New American as a wedding present when it had finally arrived. Cobb still couldn't read music, but he'd bought a gramophone and records so he could listen to the notes, then play the pieces on the piano in order to teach them.

The dancing girls didn't stay long at the Palace. Sweet Sue and Rupert Teats were expanding the livery, as well as their family. Their first child was due in April. The four new Columbus Canopy Top Park Wagon surreys for hire were due as soon as the snow melted.

Smiling fondly, Amelia viewed Arnette. She'd turned the Chuckwagon around with her talent for preparing French cuisine. No one minded the occasional cigarette ash dusting the top of their mouthwatering dinner, for One-Eye Otis's bean and vinegar pies were still too fresh in everyone's memory to complain. Not that Arnette would have allowed an unfavorable word to be spoken about her husband.

Patricia and Ed Vining had gotten hitched, and she'd taken on a small job writing articles for the *Weeping Angel Gazette.* She'd sit on her wraparound porch in the warm weather and write about the town, and people, and the happenings.

Amelia turned her head to see the newlyweds, Pap and Jill O'Cleary. Apparently love knew no height. After months of courtship, they'd finally given in to the differences in their statures and said I do.

Pap and Frank had continued on with their friendship as if there never had been a glitch in it. This morning, with rifles in hand, they'd gone traipsing off into the woods with a burlap sack filled with the lead-weight fruitcakes the town's women had brought on by the Moon Rock. Amelia thought it a waste they were going to shoot up perfectly good cakes, but Frank said it was either that or use them for paperweights because he wasn't a fruitcake-eating man.

There wouldn't have been any fruitcakes if Altana Applegate hadn't abandoned the Thursday Afternoon Fine Ladies Society and apologized to Amelia for her behavior. Soon after, the other ladies reflected on their conduct as well. This happened one Sunday when Reverend Thorpe had sermonized the loss of a true friend is the greatest loss of all. Amelia knew Dorothea, Luella, Viola, and Esther would continue to find fault in many things, but they seemed to regret their actions since the four girls had proven to be assets to the community.

Facing forward, Amelia vaguely heard Cincinatus as he persevered in his recitation. Baby Dodge's fussing had calmed down.

". . . for the support of this Declaration," Cincinatus went on, his fist raised for emphasis, "with a firm reliance on the Protection of Divine Providence, we mutually pledge to each other our Lives, our Fortunes, and our sacred Honor."

The church had gone deathly quiet, and when he looked into his audience to cherish his moment of triumph, having recited the entire declaration from start to finish, their sleeping faces were reflected in his eyes. Even baby Cincinatus had been lulled to slumber in his mother's arms.

"Ah, Reverend . . . ?" The mayor went over to the preacher and nudged him. "You can have the congregation back now."

Frank squeezed Amelia's gloved hand. "Dodge finally got his wish. Too bad we all had to sit through it. Or, rather, snore through it."

"Frank," she chastised with a smile. "Be nice."

"How can I be nice when I know there's a box under the Christmas tree with my name on it? It doesn't feel like there's anything inside. Give me one hint."

"Not yet."

"But I gave you your present already."

"Hmm." She lifted her hand to her collar and fingered the frog brooch that was embedded with tiny emeralds. "Yes, you did."

"So, you can give me one hint."

"No. I want you to experience a family Christmas morning, Frank, with the gifts Santa Claus brings and all the trimmings," she whispered. "So you're going to have to wait until tomorrow until you can open it."

Only he wasn't going to be able to see his present until July . . . right around the Fourth as far as she could tell.

**POCKET BOOKS
PROUDLY PRESENTS
Book Two in the
"Brides for All Seasons"
Series**

HOOKED

STEF ANN HOLM

**Coming Soon
from Pocket Books**

**The following is a preview of
Hooked. . . .**

"Margaret, why must you insist on displaying your petticoat?"

Meg Brooks stood at the side of the Brooks House Hotel's registration counter and gazed down at her feet. The insteps of her silk vesting top shoes barely showed because, indeed, lace flounce fell a half inch below her skirt hem. Raising her eyes, she replied to her grandmother, "I read in *Cosmopolitan* that a flirt of underskirt is considered vogue and can do wonders in catching the attention of the opposite sex."

Grandma Nettie didn't bat an eye. The word "sex" didn't suck the breath out of her as it would have done Meg's mother. "If it takes a peek of petticoat to catch a man these days, then you're better off without a husband." The elderly woman sitting in back of the desk laid her needlework in an open sewing basket. "I never remarried after Grandpa died, and I can honestly say I haven't missed a thing."

"I *want* to get married. I've tried to land a man all the usual ways, but none of them see my wit and charm. Which, I might add, has been much improved since attending Miss Huntington's—or rather, Mrs. Wolcott's—Finishing School." With a little sway, she moved her hips from side to side to view her efforts. This was her Sunday best petticoat, its bottom ruffle a fine quality tor-chon. "As a much needed new effort, I let down the waistbands of all my petticoats."

"You're going to trip on the hem."

"No I won't. I'll walk with my skirt lifted."

"You'll forget yourself and trip."

"I'll be careful."

"You'd best take every last waistband back up before your mother returns from her anniversary tour. You'll give her a conniption fit." Grandma Nettie rose from the plush tapestry chair. Spry for her age of seventy-two, she rearranged the two-foot-length of bicycle chain, with self-locking shackles and bronze metal lock, in a long spill across the front of the counter—smack next to the registry book. "Honestly, Margaret, I don't recall your being this rambunctious. Where do you get it from? Certainly not your father. My George is quite levelheaded. Now Iris, she's of a different cake. Don't get me wrong, I love your mother as if she were my own daughter, but she can be a tad . . . too delicate."

Meg threw her hands up in exasperation. "A tad? She's a good deal more than that. Mama calls a chicken breast a bosom because she won't say breast at the dinner table, or anyplace else for that matter. And she calls the leg the limb. She'll say to Papa, 'Papa, slice me the bosom.' Confound it all, it's just not . . ." Meg searched for the right word, the only one coming to mind her newly formed favorite, because it covered any topic of importance to her ". . . not vogue."

Grandma Nettie's parchmentlike fingers fussed and primped over the chain until its links were perfectly straight. Meg watched, her heart sinking. Even though her grandmother had told her she was going to put the bicycle lock on exhibit, Meg had wished feverishly she wouldn't. The humiliation of it left a suffocating sensation in Meg's throat, especially because Grandma told her she was going to tell every guest exactly what it was for. And she had done just that so far.

"Grandma . . . really. Do you *have* to set *that* out?" She'd done so for the past two weeks, and each time Meg's embarrassment returned tenfold.

Wizened smoky blue eyes lifted to view Meg over the

narrow lenses of her bifocals. "I most surely do. This chain represents the militant movement that I intend to personally bring to President McKinley's attention. That is, as soon as your parents get back from Niagara Falls."

Groaning, Meg lamented, "But do you *have* to chain yourself to the White House in order to make him notice you?"

"My fellow sisters and I plan to convene on the steps June the fourteenth at noon sharp. We have it on good authority that's the hour the President takes his lunch on the State Floor in the northwest dining room. Our intentions are to ruin his meal by locking ourselves to the ornamental iron fence along the north façade. Mrs. Gundy is even planning to swallow her key. I'm hiding mine down the front of my corset. Let it be said, that the man who dares to try and retrieve it will be sorry he ever laid a hand on my person. I know how to incapacitate a man with physical force. Have I told you how, Margaret?"

"Yes," she moaned.

"Good. Don't be afraid to do so if the need arises."

Meg's eyes closed for a moment, and she pretended her grandmother was a kindly old lady who smelled of sweet spices instead of printer's ink from the flyers that she made up to announce the time for women's freedom had come.

Slowly opening one eye first, Meg's illusions of her grandmother in gardening gloves, happily toiling over blue flags along the flower bed, instead of sewing a cloth flag with suffragettes climbing a mountain that resembled a man's head, were gone in an instant. Her other eye opened, and she couldn't dispel the image of rebellion. *Drat it anyway.*

Grandma Nettie's limber arm rose into a position much like the Statue of Liberty's. "We shall fight for equality and the right for all women to have the vote."

"I don't want to vote," Meg replied stubbornly.

"Margaret! Of course you want to vote."

"No, I don't."

"Why with your intelligence, you could be anything you wanted to be." With robust enthusiasm, she declared, "I think you'd make a fine first woman president."

Thoroughly mortified and feeling the heat of a blush work up her neck, Meg blurted out, "I don't want to be the first woman anything!"

"You have to aspire to something. What do you want to be?"

She thought for a moment, then corrected her posture and stared straight into her grandmother's waiting eyes. "I want to be irresistible to men."

Before Grandma Nettie could reply, the porter, Delbert Long, opened the hotel's double front doors and escorted a guest inside. Her grandmother walked from behind the desk to greet the new arrival.

In no mood to further battle wills with her grandmother, Meg turned to leave out the very same front doors. The thud of her shoes on the floorboards sounded childishly loud in her ears. She'd gotten no farther than five or so paces when she heard an ominous rip. Wide-eyed, she stopped dead in her tracks and slowly looked down. She could feel the damage before she could actually see it. A silky slippage of material passed her hips and thighs as the torn waistband began to make its descent. Her head awhirl with the consequences of walking home in such a state, she could barely think.

She felt through the fabric of her skirt, grabbed what she could, and sidled her way back to the counter. Reaching over the registry book, she fumbled for the room keys that were kept on individual hooks. She took the first one her fingers touched, then lifted herself on tiptoe to view the inside of Grandma Nettie's sewing basket. Spotting a safety pin, she stole that as well. With the loose gathers of her petticoat around her hips, and her skirt riding high above her calves, she shot up the stairs without a backward glance.

Knees knocking together, Meg half walked, half ran, across the runner of hall carpet. She glanced at the circular tag on the key ring. Room 32. In her haste, she hadn't noticed if two keys had been on the desk hook. One meant occupied and two meant vacant. The hotel would be full by this weekend when all the fly fishermen arrived in Harmony for the tournament. A few already had registered and were in residence now. Fortunately, none were in view.

Almost stumbling to keep her underskirt from falling below her knees, Meg started skimming the numbers on doors. Things like this didn't happen to Camille Kennison, the prettiest girl in town. And they didn't happen to Crescencia Stykem who was now Crescencia Dufresne. Although if they were to happen to somebody, Cressie was the likely candidate. Only she was married and underwear disasters didn't happen to married people.

Coming to the right door, she bunched her skirt in her left hand and inserted the key with her right. Before she turned the knob, she rapped twice on the door and waited to the count of fifteen. No answer. Letting her breath out, she slipped inside the room and shut the door behind her.

Meg made a cursory inspection of the furnishings. There wasn't a single piece of luggage or personal affect in sight. Spring sunshine spilled in through the window and made a cozy pattern on the floor that stretched to the closed bathroom door. *Thank goodness.* After tossing the key onto the bed, she relaxed and let her petticoat fall to her ankles. Opening the safety pin, she held it between her lips, then wadded her Manchester cloth skirt to her waist and bent to hoist the petticoat over her ankles and knees to her hips.

"This wouldn't have happened if Mama had a sewing machine," she muttered around the pin. "But no. She won't have one of those contraptions in her home." In a wiggle, Meg brought the torn waistband to its proper place.

Not the best seamstress, Meg realized after the fact that she had made her stitches too far apart. Tightness and neatness, Mama always said, when making a seam. Well, Meg was too impatient for that. She'd revamped all five of her petticoats in under a flat hour, and was rather proud of herself for her speed.

Just as she matched the raveled edges of the waistband and was about to take the pin from her lips, the bathroom door opened and Meg's head shot up. Shock flew through her as a man—half *naked*—stood in the doorway. The starched white muslin fell from her grasp, and the entire petticoat dropped in a pile around her feet. *Oh my goodness!*

He had a towel wrapped around his lean middle, and she couldn't help staring at his navel. A very light sprinkling of coarse brown hair swirled there, and against a belly so flat she could iron a shirtwaist on it and not have a single wrinkle. Upward . . . a chest like a washboard and shoulders wider than she'd ever noticed on a man.

He was tall and muscular, with wet hair that seemed more light brown than dark, a slight growth of beard, bushy brows tapered just enough to be utterly handsome, a set of eyes too dreamy a green to gaze into for longer than a few seconds . . . because she felt herself starting to swoon . . . and the nicest shaped mouth she'd ever had the pleasure of nearly fainting over.

"Where did you come from?" His voice, so manly and . . . deep, sent a delightful shiver through her body. Not to mention, his gaze ran over her hotter than her hair curler when she forgot about it on the lamp. She could almost feel the sizzle in the air, as he lowered his eyes to her legs—she, the big boob, not having had the foresight to have dropped her skirt. Now, all she could do was stand there, like a silly mouse, too stunned to do anything more than keep her lips together in an effort not to swallow the safety pin. So he really got his fill of her stockinged legs and drawers.

"Hello," she finally managed to mumble through the pin held in her teeth.

"Who are you?" Aside from his question and the furrow in his brow, the man seemed undaunted to find an uninvited female in his room. It must happen to him a lot, Meg concluded.

"I, ah . . . Mah-eg Bah-rooks." She spit the safety pin out, somehow managed to close it, and clutch the notion in her palm. "I'm Meg Brooks. My father owns the hotel."

He seemed to be in no self-conscious discomfort—being nearly nude in front of her, and all. She, on the other hand, felt the onset of dizziness. For all her talk about wanting a man to notice her, here she was face-to-face with one, and she had not a single worthwhile or intelligent thing to say.

His greenish-gold eyes narrowed . . . oh so very attractive with their blunt lashes. "What happened to you?"

Sighing as she struggled to keep a modicum of dignity, she feigned unconcern while dropping her skirt to cover herself. "Oh, I had an . . . accident. You see . . . my . . ." Her mother's stern warning came inside her head and she was told never to mention an article of clothing to a man—ever. Even if he was your husband. "I . . . that is my . . ." *Drat it.* Why couldn't she just say the word "petticoat" in front of him and explain what happened? Because she would be thoroughly flustered if pressed to do so.

Meg gazed at the layers of muslin that resembled ripples of untoasted meringue covering her shoes, then lifted her eyes. At length, she took the coward's way out and hoped he wouldn't notice she didn't give him a definitive answer. "Are you finding your accommodations here sufficient? Is there anything you require?"

He took a few steps, and she noted his stomach never flinched in the least. It stayed just as taut and hard when he moved. "Have you brought my bags?"

Guiltily flashing her gaze upward again, she said in a rush, "You have bags?" *Why hadn't he taken them up with him?*

"When I left the livery, I did. All I have with me are my saddlebags."

That explained it. A haphazard check-in. "Oh . . . then I'm certain Delbert will get them for you."

Think, Meg! She had to get out of here. If Grandma Nettie found her, Meg would be in hot water. Escape was the operative word here. But not until she could walk without tripping on her unmentionables. How did one make herself look a lot more at ease and calm pulling up her petticoat and pinning it while a man watched? She just couldn't . . .

Stepping out of her underskirt, she dipped down and bunched it in her fists. "I have to be going now." The stiff cloth pressed against her breasts as she cradled it with arms crossed over as much as she could to keep the petticoat snug and obscured. As if she could really hide the evidence!

"If you need anything . . . don't, ah, hesitate to ask the front desk." With a backward walk, she managed to get to the door and clutch the knob. Turning her body with what she hoped appeared to be a polished gracefulness, she opened the door. Checking first to see if the coast was clear, she didn't take a single step out of the room. *Gads!* Grandma Nettie was coming down the hallway escorting the new arrival to his room, while Delbert Long rolled the second-story bellman's cart right behind them *and* directly toward her!

Meg slammed the door and pressed her back against it, the petticoat still at her breast—only one-handed now. The other hand like a vise on the doorknob.

"Another accident?" the man queried. A single brow rose in a wry arch.

Panic welling in her throat, Meg couldn't reply.

The sharp reverberation against her shoulder blade as the wooden door panel was knocked on, made Meg jump away as if she'd been scorched.

More knocking. Then: "Porter, sir," came Delbert's announcement.

Standing in the middle of the room, looking helplessly from one end of its bed to the bureau and fireplace and bathroom door, she didn't know where to hide. And when the man proceeded toward her with that damp towel looking ready to fall off, she squeezed her eyes closed and took in a deep breath. Certainly no help for the situation, but if that towel unwrapped from his middle and exposed him, she didn't want to see. On the other hand, she could look through the fringe of her lashes, and he wouldn't be the wiser. It would satisfy her curiosity, even though the anatomy wouldn't be in clear focus.

Precariously close to her ear, and in a resonant-toned whisper so deliciously low and baritone it caused her to literally gasp, he bade, "Go into the bathroom and close the door."

Her bearings crashing in on her from the deepness of his voice, her eyes flew open. Through the repeated knock on the door, she said, "I can't hide in there. You don't know Delbert." Having no choice, she made a dash for the bed and scrambled down. She tucked herself beneath the mattress frame, making sure the full width of her skirt hem had been pulled in and hidden with her. Scooting into the middle, she roused the dust bunnies from the floor. The flying tufts of lint made her think she had to sneeze. She buried her nose in the wad of her petticoat and peered over the cloth.

She couldn't see the man's feet. He'd gone to the door. It opened and Delbert gave a hearty greeting.

"Good afternoon, sir. My apologies for the delay in fetching your luggage. As you can see, the matter has been rectified. I'll put them where you like."

The porter entered the room and came straight to the bed and stopped. She stared at his shoes. Lace-ups. Box calf bluchers. In need of polishing on the right heel.

"The bed will be fine," the man directed. She couldn't see him. He must have remained by the door.

Meg's nose itched. She rubbed it in the muslin.

Delbert walked away, then returned once more and set articles on the bed; it creaked some. The springs were slightly worn.

Two bare feet came close, then disappeared into the bathroom. He came back and stood by the bed once more. She studied the masculine toes. Nicely shaped. The nails clean with perfectly trimmed whites. Some dark hairs over the tops of his knuckles. Low arches. She thought they were very beautiful for being feet. Wait until she told her friends Ruth Elward and Hildegarde Plunkett.

"Thanks," the man said, as a jingle of coins exchanged hands.

She couldn't possibly be so lucky Delbert would leave without giving his full routine. Not him.

"Sir, allow me to show you the features of this room."

Meg's forehead lowered and bumped quietly on the floorboards. Nope. No luck for her.

"This is one of our better rooms. You'll notice the bed is quite comfortable, it being of the iron brass frame variety rather than solid oak, which can tend to warp and become creaky." Delbert walked on. His shoes were buffered by the large rug in front of the mantel. "We keep wood for the fireplace year round in case of a cold spell. With this being late March, one can never tell. The temperature drops quite considerably at night."

"I'll remember that. Thanks for telling me." Bare feet walked by the bed and toward the door once more. "If I need anything else, I'll call on the front desk."

"But I haven't shown you the bathroom features. Modern plumbing—just a year old. I can see you've tried out our shower bath. Was it acceptable?"

"Dandy."

Meg bit back a smile. He was being sarcastic and Delbert didn't realize it.

Thuds sounded as the porter walked to the bathroom, undaunted by the man's dismissal. Delbert Long was never put off. "This way, sir, and I'll demonstrate in case you overlooked anything."

The man must have sensed Delbert wouldn't leave until finished, so he went with him. Hot and cold water faucets turned on and off. Then the shower curtain slid on its hooks. The opening and closing of the cabinet. A flush from the toilet, or as her mother would say, the necessary.

At last, they exited the bathroom.

Meg turned her face to see if she could find a snippet of the porter's shoes. As she did so, she practically choked on a bouncing puff of linen fuzz. Her sneeze came through her nose before she could stop it.

"What was that?" Delbert asked.

"I didn't hear anything."

"It sounded like a sneeze."

"Somebody in the next room."

"Couldn't be. These walls are solid."

Meg held her breath as Delbert's shoes filled her view once more. She began inching her way farther back to the bed's headboard. As she did so, her pompadour caught on a coil and tugged. She bit her lip hard to keep from crying out as she got hung up, but a small squeak escaped her. Delbert would find her now. His hearing was impeccable.

"What's that I see on the floor?" the man demanded, his tone considerably irritable.

Delbert wasn't easily swayed. "I heard a noise again."

"There is no noise." Then angrily, "There's a safety pin on my floor."

"Indeed," Delbert conceded.

"The maid must have missed it." Before the porter could, the man crouched down on the balls of his feet and picked it up. His towel brushed the floor, his calf muscles straining for a moment while he moved. She gaped at the definition of his legs. "Here it is. I won't make a complaint about it. This kind of thing happens."

"Thank you for your understanding, sir."

"No problem." The man walked Delbert to the door and as Delbert wished him a pleasant stay, the door was closed midway through his oft-repeated sentence.

Meg did readily move. Her scalp throbbed where her hair had caught. If she could have, she would have lifted her arms to undo herself, but space didn't permit such a maneuver.

"You can come out now. He's gone."

"Ah . . . yes, I know. But I can't."

"What do you mean, you can't?"

"I've had a slight . . ." Dismal, she couldn't finish.

"Let me guess." He lowered again and stuck his head beneath the bed. She gave him her most bewitching smile, the one she practiced in the mirror after brushing her teeth. Unfortunately, it didn't have the affect on him she'd hoped. "You've had another accident."

Frowning her disappointment that he didn't find her divinely captivating, she mumbled, "Yes, I did. My hair is stuck and I can't get out. You have to get me free. My hands won't reach the springs."

She thought she heard him mutter an expletive as he stood. The towel fell on the floor in a clump, then more shuffling inside bags until a pair of worsted trousers came into sight and first one leg then the other slipped into the dark blue legs. He lowered onto his knees again, then laid on his belly and crawled in toward her.

This close to him, and in such a confining space, the scent of his bathing soap filled the air. *El Soudan*'s coconut oil. She'd know it anywhere. The traces smelled so good, she could . . . Meg swallowed . . . she could almost taste him. She got that fainthearted feeling again when he reached for her and his fingers tangled in her hair.

Explosions of tingles ran down her spine as he sifted through her hair and pulled out the pins in order to take down the high pile. Her gaze stayed fixed on the floor; she didn't dare risk looking at him. She didn't want him to know that she'd discovered paradise in his simple touch.

He was very gentle. A few more carefully orchestrated pulls that separated strands of hair, and she was free.

"All right, you can come out now." He backed away from her and extended his hand. It was big and square and inviting.

First a little hesitant, she relented and laid her fingers in his. He had a smooth palm with no callouses. His grip wasn't that of a loafer; she was acutely conscious of his impressive strength. She slid from under the bed, her petticoat still balled in her fist. He assisted her to her feet. As he did so, her hair tumbled into her eyes, around her shoulders, and down to her waist. She'd never liked the color. Copper. So . . . so vivid and . . . coppery. She'd stuck out like a sore thumb all through school. Well, maybe not only herself. Crescencia Stykem's hair was red-orange. Meg supposed copper was better, but not by much.

The man stared at the waves surrounding her as she pushed them aside so she could see him in return. He gave her a look over . . . but she couldn't tell what he thought of the copper color. Probably thought it was too . . . too much.

"Thank you . . . I have to go . . . but . . ." Now Meg had her hair to contend with as well as the petticoat. She couldn't face Grandma Nettie in the state she was in. She had to fix herself up before she left this room.

He reached for her and lifted her hand. At the base of her throat, she felt her pulse beat unevenly. Into her palm, he pressed her hairpins and the safety pin. Then in that husky voice of his told her to "Go into the bathroom and put yourself together."

If he hadn't nudged her with a light push of her shoulders, she doubted she could have moved. She'd been transfixed by the play of light from the window that reflected in his eyes.

Once she snapped out of her trance, she strode into

the bathroom and made short work out of repairing herself. In the process, she took in the items strewn on the floor. A pair of trail-dirty Levi's, a faded red shirt, a twist of white drawers, belt with holster . . . and gun. *My goodness.* And the avowed saddlebags. With a parting glance in the mirror, she poked the last hairpin home and told herself this would have to do.

Ready to face him once more, she threw herself into her most ladylike and gracious air of reserve as she stepped into the bedroom apartment once more.

The man had slipped into a shirt in her absence, although he hadn't buttoned it. A wedge of chest showed through the opening. That tantalizing glimpse of hair.

She paused at the bed, stared at the mound of luggage and fishing gear, then picked up the key she'd tossed. "My key," she explained. "It has to go back on the hook at the registration desk . . . or else . . . that is, my grandma. . . . It just has to go back."

His brows lifted slightly, but he said nothing.

"Well," she sighed, taking short steps to the door, "thank you for everything. I'm sorry for any inconvenience I might have caused you."

He made no comment.

She couldn't leave. Not yet. Not until she knew his name. She was halfway in love with him. She had to find out who he was.

"Well, thank you again . . . Mr. . . . ah . . . ?"

"Ga—" A heavy frown marked his forehead, as if he'd become quite annoyed about something. Then, "Wilberforce. Vernon Wilberforce."